THE
FINAL
RISING

BY A. E. WARREN

Tomorrow's Ancestors

Subject Twenty-One
The Hidden Base
The Fourth Species
The Final Rising

PRAISE FOR THE TOMORROW'S ANCESTORS SERIES

'A stonking good sci-fi & coming-of-age story all wrapped into one ... a book that tackles humanity, hardship, and classism at the deepest level.' *Magic Radio Book Club*

'An unputdownable exploration into the ethics of science.' *Buzz Magazine*

'Unbelievably compelling and readable.' *Ink and Plasma*

'Incredible ... without a doubt one of the best YA sci-fi books I've ever read.' *Out and About Books*

'Unique and engaging with full *Jurassic* vibes to boot.' *Fictional Maiden*

'Instantly engaging ... widens out from a tale of a girl trying to find her own identity to a broader story encompassing an entire population's burden of oppression, and the desire for freedom.'
Track of Words

'One of the rare debuts that are really five star reads ... grabbed me instantly and I couldn't put it down.'
Dom Reads

'Full of clever imaginings that make a thought provoking read.' *BookClubForMe*

'Absolutely fascinating! If you're a fan of *Jurassic Park*, Tahereh Mafi & Marie Lu's work, then this is the perfect book for you!' *A Bookish Star*

'Warren's ideas in this book are wonderful, playing on the current ambivalence about genetic engineering.'
The Idle Woman

'Incredibly well-written.' *Blam Books*

'This *Jurassic Park*-esque concept grabbed me immediately ... a fresh, gripping read with themes of suspense, trust, ethics and friendships.' *Book Phenomena*

'I absolutely devoured this book.' *Elle Reads Books*

THE FINAL RISING

A. E. WARREN

DEL REY

1 3 5 7 9 10 8 6 4 2

Del Rey
20 Vauxhall Bridge Road
London SW1V 2SA

Del Rey is part of the Penguin Random House group
of companies whose addresses can be found at
global.penguinrandomhouse.com.

Penguin
Random House
UK

Copyright © A. E. Warren 2023

A. E. Warren has asserted her right to be identified as the
author of this Work in accordance with the Copyright,
Designs and Patents Act 1988.

First published by Del Rey in 2023

www.penguin.co.uk

A CIP catalogue record for this book is available
from the British Library.

ISBN 9781529101379

Typeset in 10/14.5 pt ITC Galliard Std
by Integra Software Services Pvt. Ltd, Pondicherry

Printed and bound in Great Britain by Clays Ltd, Elcograf S.p.A.

The authorised representative in the EEA is Penguin Random House
Ireland, Morrison Chambers, 32 Nassau Street, Dublin D02 YH68.

Penguin Random House is committed to a sustainable future for
our business, our readers and our planet. This book is made from
Forest Stewardship Council® certified paper.

MIX
Paper from
responsible sources
FSC® C018179

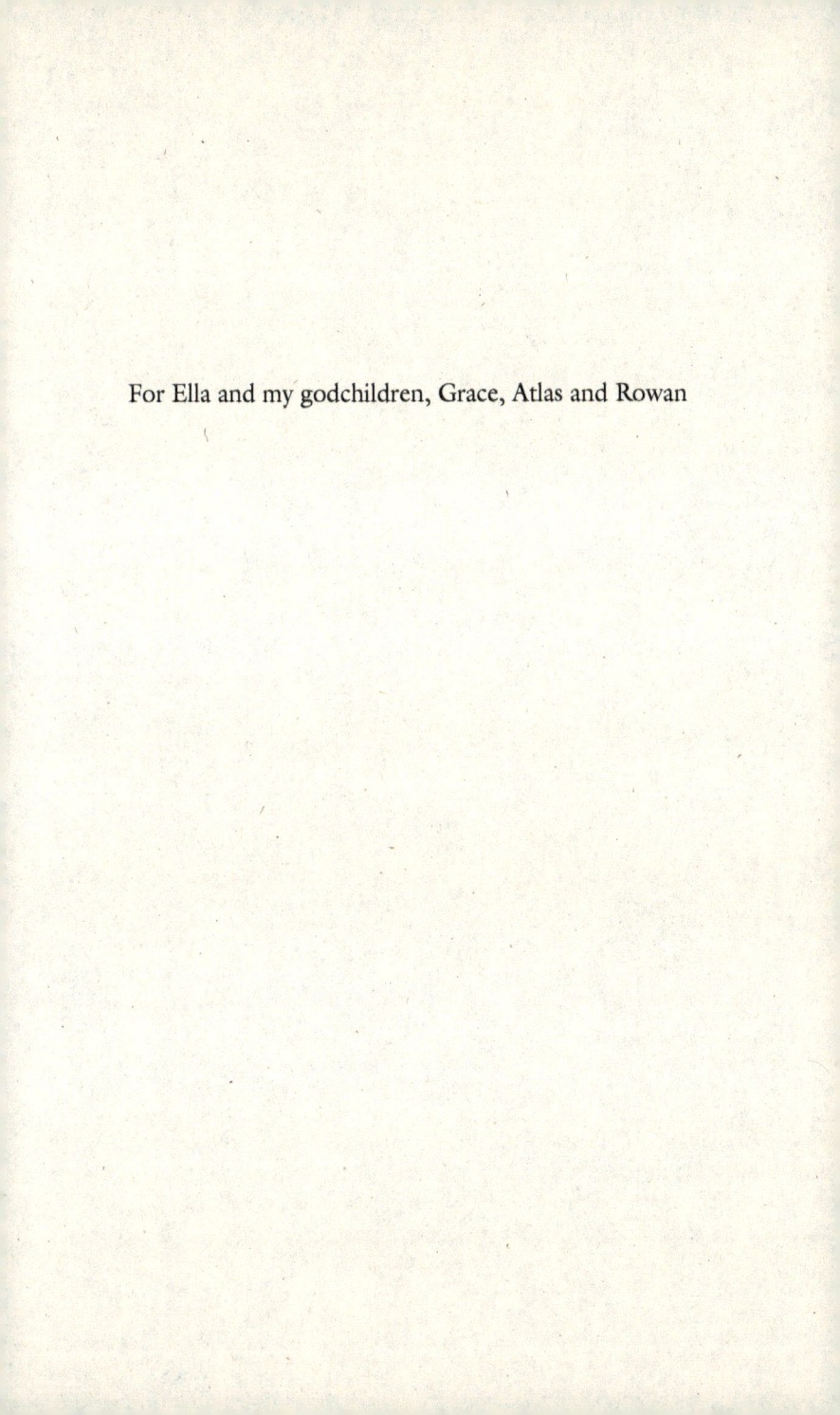

For Ella and my godchildren, Grace, Atlas and Rowan

'The end was contained in the beginning.'

George Orwell

CHAPTER 1

Elise

Elise wandered through the forest, towards a sheltered pool edged with mossy rocks and snowdrops. Desire for her own company had led her away from the low murmur of her companions and deeper into the forest, towards this quiet haven.

Pausing by its clear waters, tall reeds swaying protectively over the natural well, she crouched to fill her spare canteen, but froze when the morning calls of the birds above were abruptly silenced.

She glanced upwards; the natural inhabitants of the forest were always the first messengers of any change to her surroundings. Peering through the reeds, Elise wondered whether to retrace her steps back to camp or stay and see if there was a hunting opportunity for that evening's meal.

When she saw what had disturbed the forest's natural order, she realised that she had slipped from predator to prey.

A tall man with dark, coiled hair wandered into the clearing. A Potior – a thing so unexpected in this quiet glade that Elise couldn't trust what she was seeing.

His movements were fluid yet deliberate as he approached the other side of the pool. Short hair crowned the beauty of his sculpted features, and his skin glowed even in the soft light. Here, in nature's deepest hold, was a creature of pure design.

Suppressing her first instinct to scramble away from him, Elise carefully leant backwards towards the cover of the reeds. She silently prayed to the stars that he hadn't seen her – the element of surprise was her most important weapon. Elise was a fast and skilled fighter, but unenhanced. She was no match for a Potior up close; only her ranged weapons gave her an advantage, which would be obliterated if he noticed her.

Making herself as small as possible, she waited.

How do they know we're meeting at the spring equinox? Has someone betrayed us?

Her questions went unanswered. The Potiors were a step ahead of them again. Despite all their precautions to stay hidden over the winter months, the few remaining people of Uracil were at risk of being captured. Her anger flared – the Potiors really were intent on wiping them out.

The Potior stretched upwards, and a large goshawk baulked at the movement and flew over the pool to the safety of a higher branch. The bird's broad wings soared above the intruder's head, and he flinched at the closeness of its presence. The Potior glanced around and rubbed his face. He began to hum softly as he rocked on his feet, his muscled arms encircling his chest.

Still crouching, Elise took the opportunity to shuffle backwards, hoping the bird's warning calls would cover any sound she made.

She bent in on herself, her chin pressed into her knees. Her back ached at the unnatural position, but she held it to protect her companions, who had journeyed down from the northerly cave where her brother was still hidden.

The Potior stopped mid-rocking motion, arched onto his tiptoes and sniffed the air. Had one of her friends come to look for her? Was that what he had sensed? Elise resisted the urge to cry out her own warning. Her thighs ached in objection, but she didn't dare move again.

Still sniffing the air, the Potior began to circle the pool, searching his surroundings. Elise held her breath as she reached for the throwing knives strapped across her chest that she had been practising with all winter. In only a few more steps, he would see her.

She had to act now while the water was still between them.

Could he leap over it? She certainly couldn't clear its expanse, but a Potior might be able to. She would have to take the risk; the element of surprise was the only thing on her side.

In one smooth movement, she stood and drew the first of her knives. She hesitated for a split second. This would be her first time killing in cold blood.

In that moment of hesitation, she lost her advantage. The Potior whipped around and took a step forwards, ready to spring towards her. A warning snarl caught in his throat.

'Get *down*!' cried a voice behind Elise.

The Potior threw himself to the ground as Elise spun around to face the owner of the warning.

A body slammed into her side, knocking the knife from her fingers. She landed heavily. Groaning with the strain, she tried to push the weight of her attacker away with her elbows. She couldn't breathe.

She dug her elbow into the man's vulnerable throat, and his weight left her.

Seizing her chance as he gasped for air, Elise scrambled into a crouching position and rolled away. Without pausing, she stood and swung her leg around to deliver a powerful spinning hook kick, reaching for her push knives. She wouldn't hesitate again. This was her enemy.

But halfway round, she halted, her leg high in the air – her knives only inches from Samuel's chest.

'Stars, Elise. Is that what it is now? Throw knives and ask questions later?' He gingerly touched his throat. 'You could have killed him.'

She stared at the man she had not seen for almost two years. *He's come back.*

The shock of him being there left Elise without words. Unnoticed, the two small knives slipped from her hands.

Samuel walked away from her, and she followed his every move, not quite believing he was real. His skin was a deeper shade than before; he must have spent the past two years outside, no longer squirrelled away in a museum.

She had played out this moment in her head in the quiet hours of the night – mostly when she was trying to fall asleep on the cold floor of the cave. He would return to her, and she would allow him in. They could begin again and become what they always should have been.

In those empty midnight hours, she had found comfort in knowing that someone outside her family had once cared for her enough to put their own life at risk to preserve hers. He had loved her once.

'Are you hurt?' Samuel asked the other man, who was half a foot taller than him.

The Potior shook his head.

'Please don't run away like that again,' Samuel chided, his tone gentle. 'Elise,' he continued, holding on to the Potior's arm and guiding him towards her. 'I'd like you to meet my father, Vance.'

Samuel's face softened as he carefully walked Vance around the pool towards Elise.

'I'm glad you made it back safely,' Elise said to Vance.

He did not respond. Instead, he glanced at Samuel, a silent question passing between them.

Samuel shook his head. 'She's not a threat. She's ... she's a friend. Her name is Elise. She was only scared of you because she didn't know who you were.'

Vance nodded before turning from them and wandering back around to the other side of the pond. He arched onto his tiptoes again and began to survey the forest. Elise had clearly been dismissed from his thoughts. She frowned as her gaze followed his retreating figure. This was not what she had expected of the renegade leader who had founded Uracil. What had happened to him?

'I'm sorry I had to tackle you,' Samuel said. 'But I couldn't let one of your knives meet their mark.'

Elise nodded, brushing aside the apology. She would have welcomed the chance to do the same for her own dad.

'We've been trying to find you all for weeks,' he continued, glancing over at his father again.

The others. Soon it would no longer be just the two of them. She had to speak now, tell Samuel she had missed him more than she'd thought possible, before they became entangled with everyone else's concerns.

It was time to repair what she had broken.

Taking a deep breath, she began. 'I'm so sorry that I pushed—'

Samuel spoke at the same time. 'What happened to Uracil? Please—'

They both paused, the silence stretching, before something caught Samuel's attention and he turned from her.

'Neve's caught up with us,' he said quietly.

'Neve?'

'Neve! I've found him!' Samuel shouted, not answering Elise's question.

Elise frowned. 'Who's Neve?'

Samuel was still peering into the woods. 'Raul and Flynn's daughter. I tracked her down in Zone 5. She helped me locate my father.'

'Oh,' Elise said, unsure what to make of this news.

Samuel had mentioned Raul and Flynn's daughter to her before. She had been posted abroad for years, making trades and deals with the other Zones on behalf of Uracil. At one time, when Faye was still alive, the Tri-Council had wanted Samuel to join her in the other Zones, but he had refused.

At the sound of approaching footsteps, Elise turned to the woman.

Neve was tall, powerfully built, with thick hair pulled back in a tight ponytail. She strode confidently through the forest, which seemed almost to part for her.

Elise stared at her. Of course she was going to be tall and exceptionally beautiful. Elise ran her hand through her own hair. It was the shortest it had ever been and, for a moment, she was back to being a Sapien meeting a Medius for the first time.

'Neve!' Samuel called out, even though she was only a few steps away. 'I would like you to meet Elise, who is from Uracil. She might be able to tell us what happened there.'

'You don't know how good it is to see someone from back home,' Neve said, reaching an arm towards her.

Following the woman's lead, Elise accepted her brisk handshake, unused to this formal method of greeting.

'We went to Uracil first,' Neve continued. 'But ... it's gone. All gone. And then Samuel had the brilliant idea to come here – one of his many brilliant ideas – because he knew that the Infiltration Department always meets at the same place for the spring equinox.'

Elise remained rooted to the spot as Neve reached for Samuel's hand, her fingers lightly brushing his. He didn't pull away from her touch.

'Please tell us what happened to Uracil. We found a few graves, but not enough to account for the population as a whole. Did everyone relocate? We've been going out of our minds with the worry.'

Elise finally looked up at them, at Samuel. They didn't know of Uracil's losses. That so many, including her own mother, were still missing. How could they?

Both of Neve's parents were dead; Elise had buried Raul and Flynn herself. The two leaders had both selflessly stayed in the centre of Uracil, probably trying to evacuate as many residents as possible when the airplanes came. What should she say to a daughter who didn't know that both of her parents had died?

'The people I'm travelling with are farther back in the woods,' Elise responded, keeping her features still. 'Let me take you to them, and we'll explain everything.'

They both looked at Elise expectantly. The same height, the same beauty. Elise realised there had been little point to her imagined outcomes in the quiet hours of the cave. Elise had used them as a source of comfort, but they'd had an unknown price attached to them. One which she would now have to pay.

She turned away. 'I'll take you to the others.'

CHAPTER 2

Twenty-Two

Twenty-Two believed she had patiently waited while everyone repeated, yet again, what had happened to Uracil. Luca, who was sitting next to her, seemed to be the only one whose attention was also drifting.

'Why are you writing "field" over and over again in the ground?' he signed to her. 'It's making you look a bit weird.'

Twenty-Two squinted at her work in the dirt of the forest floor.

'It's not "field",' she responded, as Samuel went over to comfort Neve, who was crying again. 'It is "yield". A very old word that I have recently learnt. I was trying a different type of "y" this time. I thought an old word deserved an old "y".'

Luca peered down at her letters while the others continued to discuss the number of airplanes that had bombed Uracil.

'Still looks like "field" to me,' he signed.

Twenty-Two scrubbed out the words and started again. Perhaps her 'y's were too fancy for the forest floor.

Raising her head, she glanced over at the other side of the circle. The newcomer, Neve, was now crying in Samuel's arms, Septa sitting close on her other side. Twenty-Two could understand Neve's distress; she had just discovered that both of her parents had died. Her grief was fresh and raw, at odds with everyone else who'd had longer to process the news of Uracil's demise. The winter months they had spent in the northern cave had helped ease the immediacy of her own distress, and she could now view it with some distance. Collectively, they had lost a great deal. Still, she had begun to be accepted into a small community in those months and was even a member of the Infiltration Department.

Twenty-Two scratched out the new word she had learnt – it was definitely not 'field' – into the ground with a stick. She had practised her letters in a similar way with Dara in her abandoned pod back in Cytosine.

Since leaving there, she had learnt that everything came with a price. The price of having loving parents, like Neve had, was that one day they would be taken from you, or you from them. The price of Twenty-Two leaving Cytosine was that she often had to conform to what others expected of her. Duty tempered freedom. She had to learn to compromise, consent to others' wishes and work as a team. She did not like it. But she had to acknowledge that it was better than being left to starve in a steel cage.

Samuel had finally run out of questions, but the repeated explanations of Uracil's downfall had changed the atmosphere from one of anticipation to one of mourning. Twenty-Two realised that every time someone retold their individual story, layered with the others' perspectives, it took them right back to the event that had shattered their existence.

'Tell us about where you have been,' Luca finally asked Samuel.

Twenty-Two scrunched her eyes approvingly at Luca. Now she might finally hear about the other Zones and how he had found his father.

'Last time I saw you was nearly two summers ago,' Luca continued, glancing over at Vance. 'You were off to find your dad in Zone 5. It's taken a while, but looks like you succeeded.'

Vance was sitting farther away from them, cross-legged, his back perfectly straight. His gaze was fixed on a bird calling for his mate up in the trees.

'It took a while to find him, yes,' Samuel said, his arm still around Neve, whose eyes were closed.

Twenty-Two leant forwards. This was what she wanted to know. She, like the others, had suspected that Faye had killed her father to assume his place on the Tri-Council. She needed to understand how her assumptions had been incorrect.

'He was hard to locate, and he cannot remember much. He certainly doesn't remember any of us. I've tried to take him back to his last memories.' Samuel paused, glancing across at Vance, even though he was out of earshot. 'But he finds it so distressing it seems cruel. He doesn't remember Uracil; he remembers living as a Potior in Adenine and then, after that, nothing.'

'Has he laid down new memories?' Max asked, hardly raising his head.

Samuel smiled at this. 'Yes, he has. Thank the stars for that at least. They are patchy, but he remembers how I found him and that we journeyed back here together.'

'What happened to him?' Septa asked in a hushed tone. 'He was always so focused ... so centred and per—'

'So, he didn't just use to ignore everyone then?' Luca asked, casting a look towards Septa.

Septa bristled. 'Of course he didn't.'

'I've never met him before,' Luca responded. 'Thought it might be a snooty Potior thing.'

Max raised his head.

'Sorry, Max,' Luca said.

'Idiot,' Septa mumbled.

Luca grinned at Septa. 'Yet, you still stay.'

Septa frowned before smiling. 'My options are limited.'

Samuel ignored them both and lowered his voice. 'As far as I can work out, he had to take his memory blocker. I don't know why. If he did take it, he has lost around fifty years of memories.'

Twenty-Two tried to hide her disappointment that they might never find out what happened to him.

Raynor let out a low whistle. 'No one's lost that amount of time before. If I remember rightly, when another member of the Infiltration Department took his, back when he was nearly captured in Thymine, he lost maybe ten years. And he was a bit sparked afterwards. They put him to work in the Foraging Department after that.'

'So, it's not too good for the brain cells then?' Luca asked, glancing towards Elise, who had volunteered to patrol the area. 'If you take the pills?'

Kit, who was sitting next to Twenty-Two, stared at Luca. 'Does that need confirming?'

Twenty-Two had stopped practising her words. She glanced over at Elise's distant figure. Elise had lost three months of memories when she had been captured in Cytosine. For the first time, Twenty-Two wondered if Elise's lost memories meant that she had come back with a fraction less of herself. If individual experiences made a person, was Elise not quite complete?

'Well, it's not the best for the old noggin,' Raynor said hurriedly. 'But the shorter the memory loss, the better.'

'I had two weeks of memories knocked out of me,' Septa said, systematically cracking the bones in each of her fingers. 'Maya shoved a pill down my throat back when ...' She stared at Elise's retreating figure. 'Anyway, I woke up and thought I still had to get Elise out of the containment centre. Nearly got myself captured going in there again. But I didn't feel any different afterwards.

'They recorded Elise,' Septa continued, re-crossing her legs beneath her, 'in the containment centre after she came around from her blocker. Maya told me. She scratched her arm, where her tattoo was, until it bled. Elise was mumbling, "Thymine, not Cytosine," on repeat. Maya said that she had no idea that three months had passed. She completely lost the plot. I thought of all people Elise would have been able to keep it together. Seems her controlled exterior might only be surface deep.'

Everyone fell silent for a moment.

Samuel coughed. 'When I found my father in Zone 5, he was working on a remote farm and treated no better than an ox. They even made him sleep in one of the barns. They don't idolise Potiors over there as they know they are just Sapiens with enhancements.' He paused as he pulled his coat tighter around Neve. 'If you are allowed access to the truth, the veneer that coated it chips away over time.

'For nearly two months, Neve and I would slip into the barn at night, talk to him, try to remind him who he was and where he had come from. It took seven weeks to persuade him to leave with us. He still doesn't really understand who I am, even though I spent the entire eight-month journey trying to remind him.'

Raynor stood and approached Vance. He glanced up at her before patting the space next to him. Together they stared up at the lonely hawfinch in the tree.

The following morning, Twenty-Two settled down amongst the lines of operatives. She waited patiently for Maya to finish addressing the newcomers, ensuring they were up to date about what had happened to Uracil. Not everyone had been aware of the bombing; they had just realised something wasn't right when the messages and drop-offs had ended. Twenty-Two didn't envy Maya the task of informing them that several members of the Infiltration Department, along with many of Uracil's residents, had died or been captured when the Potiors had sent airplanes to bomb Uracil.

Maya had been one of the first to arrive the previous evening. She had slipped into the camp in the middle of the night and had been crouching over the operatives when they woke. Luca had been on watch and had hurt his toe kicking a tree trunk upon discovering how ineffective his patrol had been. After that, he had been taken off watch duty. Twenty-Two could tell that the demotion stung.

After she had finished relating their losses, Maya looked at her silent audience. 'I told myself that it would be a miracle from the stars if thirty of our operatives realised that this was the best place for us to regroup. And here are thirty-seven of you. It shows that the stars still watch over Uracil.'

Twenty-Two scrunched her eyes at the thought of having witnessed her second miracle from the stars, the first being when they had returned Kit to her when Uracil was bombed. At the time, she had promised that, in return for his life, she would do everything in her power to help the other Neanderthals. But she had been unable to act on this yet. 'Compromise' was a word she was beginning to dislike, and it seemed unlikely that something as powerful as the stars would value it.

'So,' Maya continued, 'our first concern is locating the missing people of Uracil. We believe they were taken to an unknown location in the airplanes. Why were they taken? We don't know, but we can guess. Most likely as a form of punishment and to ensure that Uracil is not established again.' She paused. 'Does everyone agree that they should be our priority?'

There was mumbled assent. Twenty-Two stared at Kit, who was sitting next to Elise. He looked like he'd been going to say something but then thought better of it.

'Have we got any more leads on where everyone was taken?' one of the newcomers asked.

'I have a good idea of where they *weren't* taken,' Maya said. 'I don't think they were flown to one of the other Zones, as the Potiors would be breaking all sorts of treaties by offloading their unwanted "cargo" there. I believe they were taken somewhere in Zone 3.

'When I realised Uracil had been destroyed, I spent the next few months scouting Zone 3, trying to see what the Potiors were up to. I haven't seen any large transports other than the usual biannual deliveries of goods. We'll have to visit the parts of the mainland I haven't covered and the surrounding islands. See if they were taken to any of them. We'll split into teams. And on that note, I have a few new members of the Infiltration Department to introduce you to.'

Twenty-Two's head snapped up.

'Would Kit, Twenty-Two and Luca join me so we can welcome them properly to the Infiltration Department?'

Twenty-Two's cheeks burnt with pride as a round of applause accompanied her advance to the front, where she took her place between Kit and Luca.

When the applause died down, Max held up his hand to speak. 'I understand why you want to make the lost residents our first priority, but even if we find them, we have nowhere to take them. It's not safe near Uracil, and we need an established infrastructure so we can feed everyone and remain hidden. We cannot forage enough to feed them all.'

Twenty-Two was disappointed that he had not spoken about the new recruits, but she had to admit that his point was a valid one. Before Maya could answer, another voice, one Twenty-Two didn't recognise, interrupted.

'I might be able to help you with your relocation problem,' said a tall woman with blonde hair from the edge of the glade. 'If there's room for an old undercover agent.'

Twenty-Two turned to stare at the woman. She had never seen her before, and concluded that she must have just arrived for the spring equinox. Twenty-Two glanced over at Luca, who seemed to have brightened, perhaps at the realisation that Samuel's patrol had been equally ineffective.

The newcomer dropped her bag to the ground. 'I've been camping at what could be a suitable settlement for the past few weeks.'

'Beth,' Maya exclaimed, striding towards the tall woman. 'By the stars ... you made it out of Adenine.'

The two women embraced, petite Maya reaching well below the other woman's shoulders. Twenty-Two scrunched her eyes as she witnessed the warmth that spread across both of their features.

The tall woman smiled. 'It's Genevieve now. I've had over twenty-five years with that name. I don't think I can return to the old one again.'

Maya gave a broad grin, showing the gap between her teeth. 'It doesn't matter to me. I'd happily call you Ladle if it was what you wanted.'

Genevieve turned to address the group, her arm still around Maya. She spoke with ease, and a touch of humour played at the corners of her lips. 'I'm sorry I'm late to the equinox. It's been a while since I left Adenine, and to be frank, I got a little lost. I appreciate that you have the problem of where to take everyone, and I want to let you all know that my journeying took me to a possible location for Uracil.'

'Where is it?' someone called out.

'About a hundred and sixty miles north of Guanine.'

'Near the lakes?' Raynor asked.

'That's the one. It's sheltered by the edge of a forest near one of the smaller lakes. Plenty of wildlife and cover. But not as far north as the old Uracil and on the opposite side of Zone 3.'

Everyone who knew of the rough location began speaking at once. Twenty-Two looked around at them – they were interested.

Genevieve turned to Maya. 'Perhaps I could take you all to see it?'

Before Maya had a chance to respond, Samuel rushed across the clearing, knocking bowls and cups over before abruptly stopping in front of Genevieve. Twenty-Two watched with interest while Samuel teetered on the edge of embracing the woman before scooping her into his arms.

Silent tears slid down Genevieve's high cheekbones as she clung to Samuel.

Eventually, Samuel pulled away. 'Mortimer?'

The woman shook her head. Samuel gathered her up again, and she rested her head on his shoulder.

It was at that moment that Twenty-Two placed Genevieve as Samuel's mother. Her heart sank.

That also made Genevieve the mother of Faye. The mother of the woman Twenty-Two had pushed to her death back in Uracil.

CHAPTER 3

Elise

Elise didn't care about the positioning of logs for the meeting area at the new site for Uracil or which streams they would use for bathing and drinking water. She had not given a second thought to which of the mighty branches would hold her tree house – without her mum and brother by her side, it was all inconsequential. And yet, the other residents had been engrossed in spending the previous day marking tree trunks for felling with lengths of rope and dithering over the position of the sun in relation to the mirrors they planned on installing high up in the leafiest of branches.

By her second morning at the site, Elise was silently infuriated by their lack of action. Her brother was still in the cave they had spent winter in, probably imagining her finding their mum every second of every day. And all she was doing was watching people argue over intangible partitions. Her gaze swept the undulating landscape dotted with scree slopes and hidden caves that everyone could escape to if there were another attack. Yes, it was the perfect location with its nearby streams and abundant game to hunt, but all of this was futile if most of Uracil's residents remained missing.

Leaving her bag on the ground, Elise picked her way through the edge of the dense oak forest that would soon be their new home. It had taken a week to walk there and, in Elise's opinion, it was time they could ill afford to lose. After asking around, she was told that Maya had last been seen heading over to the west side of the future Uracil. Elise hurried to find her, walking west until she could hear voices up ahead.

Elise halted when she recognised Genevieve's calm voice drifting over to her. 'I am so pleased that we are all back together again. My only wish is that Faye and Mortimer were with us.'

Elise stopped and peered into the distance; she didn't think they had seen her. She was about to keep walking then decided to wait so she could listen to their conversation.

'I still can't believe they didn't question you,' Maya said.

'They must have decided I wasn't important after all,' Genevieve said. 'I was left in my cell for four days and was just lucky a guard grew sloppy delivering my food on the final morning. Thanks to the stars, I was able to overpower him and take his pass.'

'Well, only a few of us could escape the Protection Department, and I always said that you were one of them,' Maya responded.

Elise leant her head against the rough bark of a tree. She hadn't realised that Genevieve had been arrested and escaped from the Protection Department. She had never heard of anyone doing that before. How had Genevieve managed it? And why hadn't she been questioned? Elise had been interviewed for hours when she had been arrested in Cytosine. Why would the Protection Department detain a high-end Medius and not get around to questioning her? It didn't make much sense, and she wondered why Maya wasn't pressing Genevieve for a more detailed explanation.

'Anyway,' Genevieve said, 'enough of that. We keep on repeating the same stories over and over again. Just like the old people used to do when we were young. And besides, I think we have company.'

Elise's head snapped up. Genevieve had been aware of her approach. She gingerly stepped away from her hiding place and walked past the last few trees.

She held her head high as she passed Samuel and Neve sitting together, leaning against the same tree trunk. Vance was a few feet away, silent as always, but with an air of power that circled him, stubbornly refusing to leave its master. Even sitting on a fallen tree trunk, Genevieve had a similar presence, but she was far more alert to her surroundings. As Elise approached the group, Genevieve looked her up and down. She seemed to absorb everything she needed to know in only a few seconds.

Elise kept her gaze fixed on Maya as she approached her. 'I need to speak with you about Uracil's plans.'

'If this is about the positioning of the meeting area,' Maya responded, 'I've said before that it needs to be in a natural clearing. That way the trees have had time to grow over and conceal us from above. We cannot fell the trees to make the meeting area as no amount of mirrors would reflect the foliage cover we require.'

Elise felt her anger begin to surface, and she struggled to contain it. 'With the greatest respect, I don't give two middle fingers where the meeting area is. They can put it at the bottom of the lake for all I care. I want to find my mum.'

Standing up, Genevieve glanced over at Samuel. 'I'd better take Vance back to the main settlement. This is clearly the business of the Infiltration Department. We also need to start work on building our first tree houses. I think Vance might enjoy having a project to assist on.'

Maya turned to address Genevieve. 'No, please stay. This isn't anything private; there's no point in trying to pretend that we haven't all been discussing it.' Her gaze slid back to Elise. 'I was going to announce it at tonight's meeting anyway, but there's no harm in telling you now. We are far enough along with our relocation that I'm sending out the Infiltration and Undercover Departments in teams of two tomorrow. We have a lot of ground to cover.'

'Tomorrow?' Elise was taken aback. 'We'll leave tomorrow?'

Maya nodded. 'We've delayed long enough – we all have loved ones who are missing.'

A coil that had been tightly wound inside Elise for months began to loosen. She felt as if she could breathe deeply again. The guilt she carried for pushing Uracil to turn their sights outwards and its consequences began to ease slightly. Perhaps there was still a chance of finding her mum and the others they had lost.

'I think I'll go back to the settlement anyway, Maya,' Genevieve said. 'Are you coming, Neve? Samuel?'

'Yes, I think so,' Samuel said, standing and holding out his hand to help Neve up.

Elise ignored them. It had not escaped her notice that Samuel could touch Neve with ease, when previously that was something he had only ever done with Elise. She tried not to think about the gesture and its implications.

Instead, she fixed her attention on Genevieve, whose upturned mouth made it seem like she was always half-smiling – a useful thing, as Elise knew her own mouth naturally turned down at the corners, giving her an unintentionally sullen air. Lines were beginning to creep onto Genevieve's face but not enough for her years; she had clearly been using Dermadew in the past even if she no longer had access to it. While Genevieve waited for the others to gather their belongings, her demeanour reminded Elise of the unshakeable confidence that she was used to seeing in the high-end Medius back in Thymine, but there was none of the aloofness that usually accompanied it. Her hands were soft, and Elise guessed she was not used to living outside, yet Elise had not heard her once complain about it – she clearly had self-control.

Elise tried to guess what Genevieve's reaction to her would have been if they'd met a few years ago and Samuel had introduced her as his partner, but she found it hard to picture. The woman was incredibly difficult to read – something that Elise admired. She had worked hard to be the same since she was a child. It was one of the first things her mum had taught her.

Would Samuel's parents have thought Elise was beneath them, or would they have welcomed her? She shook the thought away. Why even consider these notions when Samuel had barely left Neve's side in the last week, and Elise had done everything she could to pretend he wasn't there?

As if she knew she was being watched, Genevieve smiled over at Elise, who straightened up and fixed her features so they would not reveal her thoughts. From the corner of her eye, she could see that Samuel was now trying to persuade Vance to stand up and leave with them.

'I've seen you before,' Genevieve said, staring at Elise.

Elise desperately searched her memories for Genevieve, but they were empty. She wondered if she had met her in the three months of memories she had lost. Had Samuel taken her to meet his mother? She was at her most vulnerable when her lost memories came into play.

'You have?'

'Yes, but I don't believe you saw me. You collected my note by the bridge in Adenine. You bent to tie your shoelaces, and there was some light fingerwork that I couldn't follow.'

Elise smiled at the compliment. 'You were the woman in the long coat on the bridge. I wondered if you were an agent for Uracil but thought it was best to stay away from you.'

Genevieve nodded.

'I hope you make some progress with the tree houses,' Elise said, trying to fill the silence that had descended.

'We'll see,' Genevieve responded. 'I don't think I will be very useful as I haven't done a day's manual labour in over twenty-five years. But that is no excuse. I shall begin with a tent; I've spent so long indoors that I cannot acclimatise to facing the elements every night. I'll begin with that this morning.'

Vance finally stood, and Genevieve took his arm with a smile. They looked more like brother and sister to Elise than husband and wife. When Genevieve led him away, Samuel and Neve followed closely behind them. An altered but reunited family. Elise could only hope for the same.

'You said we're going out in teams of two,' she said to Maya. 'Who are you going to put me with?'

'I was thinking you could go with Kit, show him how we operate,' Maya responded. 'We were just discussing where the residents could be, and Genevieve had a few good suggestions.'

Elise smiled at the thought of being put with Kit, but it quickly faded when another question came to her. 'What about Twenty-Two? Who will she be with? She's Kit's shadow.'

Maya frowned. 'I'm still working on that. But don't worry, I have an idea.'

The tone in Maya's voice clearly indicated that Elise shouldn't pry into the missions assigned to the others.

Quickly changing the subject, she nodded in the direction Genevieve had taken. 'Is it good to see her again? Samuel once told me that you were best friends.'

Leaning down to pick up her canvas bag, Maya straightened before she spoke. 'We were both just saying how much we have changed. But then who doesn't in that amount of time?'

They made their way back to where the main settlement would be, falling into a leisurely pace.

'People alter over the years,' Maya continued. 'Every experience has an impact. I honestly don't believe anyone is the finished product before they die.' She turned to Elise and smiled. 'You probably won't believe it, but I was a bit of a wallflower when I first got to know Beth – I mean Genevieve. I was a year younger than her, back when a year mattered. We were both born in Uracil but didn't spend much time together until she was thirteen and I was twelve. She had presence, even back then, and I was happy to be part of that, even if it meant taking my place behind her.'

'What changed?' Elise asked, watching the leader of the Infiltration Department.

Maya rarely discussed her past, especially not as long ago as her childhood.

'She left to work undercover in Adenine. I was still in the Guard Department in Uracil, a role I'd been destined for all my life, since my mother and father founded it when Uracil was first formed. It's where I learnt to fight. For a while, I was lost without Genevieve. I became disillusioned. I didn't want to patrol the borders of Uracil; I wanted to see what was beyond those borders. And a few years later, I decided to leave.'

Elise slowed her pace. They were close to the main settlement, and she wanted to hear more.

'I went farther than anyone expected,' Maya continued, slowing her pace to match. 'I travelled to the other Zones. On my journey back to Zone 3, there was a storm. We were close to the shoreline, so I was lucky in that regard. I washed up on the coast, and that was when the Protection Department picked me up. With no tattoo, I was slung into one of their containment centres. It took me three years to break out of there.'

Elise stopped. 'What happened then?'

'When I escaped, I was in a bad way. So I had no choice but to go back to Uracil with my tail between my legs.'

Maya shrugged before beginning to walk again.

'Luckily, things had progressed in the time I'd been away. I wasn't forced to become a guard again. Instead, I was able to choose my role. I worked in the Agricultural Department for a year, kept my head down, embraced the monotony of the work as a way to heal, and that's when I started spending time with Fiona. With Genevieve gone, she became one of my closest friends. Of course, Fiona wasn't Head of the Infiltration Department back then, but she was a member of it. I started training with her, and a couple of years later I was accepted into the department.'

They reached the main settlement. The noise and clatter of nearly fifty people trying to build a base sprang up around them. Maya looked around and blinked as if she had to remember where she was before her gaze settled on Genevieve and Vance.

'Yes, if you could put them over there, it would be appreciated,' Genevieve said to a taller man carrying four sturdy branches.

He smiled up at her in response before carefully laying the stripped wood at her feet.

'Is there anything I can do to help Vance?' the man asked.

Genevieve cocked an eyebrow towards her former partner. 'I'm sure he could use some assistance.' She raised her voice to bring those nearby into their conversation. 'I think we could all use some help. Perhaps we should build one tent and tree house at a time. Our work will be quicker then.'

'I think that's a very good idea,' the man responded. 'And we should start with yours and Vance's.'

Elise watched as Genevieve shook her head. 'Oh, no, we should draw lots for it.'

'I agree,' Vance said.

They were the first words Elise had heard him utter.

'Not a chance,' the tall man said, while others around him nodded. 'To have you two unsettled would bring bad luck for the new Uracil. Vance founded it along with Raul and Flynn. We can't have him without a place to sleep.'

Vance turned from them and lifted the four branches placed at Genevieve's feet. She quickly glanced at him, but he didn't respond.

'If you insist,' she eventually said, 'and please know that we do appreciate it.'

A flurry of activity swelled around Genevieve and Vance. Elise turned away from them. She saw little of Samuel in their actions, only Faye.

That evening, Elise sought out Kit's company to tell him they were being put in a team together. At a time when she wanted to escape her day-to-day life, she couldn't have been given a better partner. Elise could sit with him for hours, and he wouldn't demand anything of her. She didn't have to try and be witty or engaging; in fact, Elise suspected that he preferred it when she didn't.

She found him sitting alone by a small fire.

'You've cut your hair!' she exclaimed, forgetting to sign.

Kit patted the top of his head, where his inch-long, dark brown hair now messily stood up. Gone was the long ponytail he had always tied at the base of his neck.

'My head feels lighter,' he signed. 'And colder.'

'It suits you,' Elise responded, sitting beside him. 'What made you decide to cut it off?'

'I was training with Maya and Samuel today; they are teaching me how to throw my spear and use it as a long-range weapon. I asked Maya about her braided hair as I like it. She told me she does it so when she is fighting, no one can grab hold of her hair and use it against her. We did not have time for her to teach me, so we decided to cut it off instead.'

Elise tried not to stare, but she had only ever known Kit with long hair. His new haircut made him look a bit younger, and she had to remind herself that he had just turned eighteen, even though she had always thought of him as much older. Maybe his time alone in the pod had aged him. Or perhaps even if he had grown up with a family like Elise's, he would have appeared older than his true years. Elise tried to imagine him as a child. All she could see was a solemn little boy, the weight of his situation pushing down on him as he constantly struggled to keep upright and bear its load.

She raised her head at the sound of laughter from the group sitting on the other side of the clearing. A few operatives who had worked for Uracil for years had gathered and were recounting stories to one another. Maya and Genevieve were sitting on the ground next to each other, clearly enjoying the tales that were getting louder as the night wore on. Elise dropped her head and poked at the fire again with a long twig.

'Where did Twenty-Two go?' she eventually signed with one hand, turning herself away from the other scattered groups so no one could see her.

Kit's expression did not change. 'She said that she wanted to get some rest tonight and has taken her sleeping roll over to those trees.'

Elise raised her eyebrows at him in query.

'She tells me only what she wants me to know,' was his simple response.

Elise frowned. 'That's not like her. She normally stays so close to you.'

'She will have her reasons.'

'Is she cross that she's not been put in a team with you?'

'Maybe. I have not seen her since she was assigned her own mission. She would not tell me anything about it, not even who she is with. Something is bothering her.'

The group with Maya and Genevieve burst into laughter again, and Elise glanced over at them.

Kit patted her knee to get her attention before signing. 'What is it that is worrying you?'

Elise gave a half-smile. 'Is it that obvious?'

'To me, it is. Maybe not the others.'

Elise knew she should give him something, so she told him half of what she was thinking and left out her uneasiness about the new coterie that was forming. 'I'm worried about my mum. I want to find her, take her to Nathan and make sure they are both safe. I've been waiting and waiting to be allowed to go and find the others, forcing myself not to think of what might have happened to them. And now that we can finally leave, I'm growing even more anxious. Do you think me worrying more is a sign that something has happened to her?'

Kit glanced up at the sky again. 'I do not believe the stars work in that way. Twenty-Two does. But I think they have a different role to play.'

'Yes, I suppose you're right. I'm sure she's fine. She has to be. I won't think about it again.' Elise stared at the flames. 'What will I tell Nathan if something has happened to her?'

Kit leant over and put his arm around Elise. It was such a rare event that, at first, she found it difficult to lean into him as they had always kept to their very clearly defined parameters. His jacket smelt of woodsmoke, which she found comforting, and she began to relax. They stayed like that for a moment before Kit straightened.

'What will you do once you have found your mother?'

'I don't know. I haven't allowed myself to think that far ahead. I suppose firstly keep her and Nathan safe, whatever that takes.'

Kit glanced up at the sky again. It was cloudy, and the stars were not watching over them tonight.

'What do you want to do, Kit?' she asked after a few minutes.

He took a moment before answering. 'Something meaningful.'

Elise waited, but he did not elaborate.

Knowing that he was usually hungry, as it took many calories to sustain his muscled frame, she looked over at the communal cooking area and offered to get them something to eat.

It was darker over by the food station, but she could still see that most of the offerings had already been taken. As she pondered whether Kit would prefer some baked eggs or the rest of the venison, she heard someone approach the table.

'You're late to eat. That's not like you,' Samuel said.

Elise's heart dropped as she turned around. Caught off guard, she didn't know what to say to him.

'Uh, I didn't mean you eat a lot,' Samuel stuttered when she finally faced him. 'You have a healthy appetite, average, in fact. Absolutely average. That should be your new name.'

Elise eyed him. He was clearly as uncomfortable as she was; he only rambled when he was uneasy. She would have to clear the air.

She pulled herself up. 'Samuel, I just want you to know that if you're happy, that is good enough for me. That's all I want for you.'

The candlelight cast a glow over him, and she wondered, not for the first time, at the beauty of him.

'Happy?' Samuel said, raising an eyebrow quizzically. 'Of course I'm happy. I have every reason to be. My family is back together. For the first time in my life, everyone I love is in one place.' He paused. 'Although what happened to Uracil makes it feel wrong to be so.'

Elise felt physical pain at his words. She'd been right – he was happy with Neve, and she would have to live with that.

Wanting to hide her reaction, she grabbed the nearest plate and said, 'I have to get back to Kit,' before hurrying away.

Startled, Samuel called out to her. 'Elise! I wanted to say how sorry I am ... about your dad and your mum ...'

She didn't look back.

The following morning, Maya stood in front of fifteen teams of two operatives. 'Okay, now we're beginning to settle into our new location, it's time to find our missing friends, family and loved ones. Each of you has been set a destination where they might be, based on my and Genevieve's scouting of the countryside during the winter. At the same time, we'll send a separate team back to the caves near Uracil to bring those residents to us.'

Elise shifted her weight between her feet. Her brother would be in that group, Georgina as well. She would feel better when they were all reunited; they would be safer then.

'Everyone will meet back here in six weeks and report on their findings. If a team doesn't return, it will be assumed that they have either found the captured residents of Uracil or been captured themselves. A scout team will then be sent out to check on them. Now, on to your memory blockers ...'

Now that the Potiors knew of the existence of Uracil, the memory blockers found in the wreckage had been reduced to only cover the last few weeks to prevent anyone from revealing Uracil's new location. People like Maya and Genevieve wouldn't lose a lifetime of memories any more.

'Remember, take it if you are close to being captured,' Maya concluded. 'Uracil is at its weakest right now, but we will continue rebuilding it while you are gone. The most important thing is not to lead the Potiors to our doors. We do this for Uracil.'

There was a general murmur of agreement and a few shouts of 'For Uracil' amongst the Infiltration Department and the former undercover agents. One by one, they loaded their new pill into the storage compartment inside the semi-precious stone set into each of their bracelets.

Elise scanned the group. Luca was paired with Raynor, and she couldn't decide whether it would be the most riotously fun partnership or they would end up killing each other mid-journey. Eli, the undercover operative in the crematorium in Cytosine, whom Elise had refused to allow to return to Uracil, was paired with another woman Elise hadn't met before. He caught her eye and gave her a small nod of recognition; perhaps he was grateful for her decision now.

Her gaze slid over to Samuel and Neve, who were standing close to each other, having been put in a team together. Samuel touched Neve's arm to get her attention. The small gesture sent a pang to her core, but Elise was careful not to react openly. She had folded away his grey jumper last night and would not wear it again.

Elise consoled herself that at least her pride was still intact, and no one knew her secret – she would never let anyone know how she felt about him.

She turned around and caught Kit staring at her.

She sighed, then signed, 'Don't say it. Forget you saw it.'

'It has passed already.'

Elise nodded while adjusting her expectations to never letting anyone other than Kit know how she felt about Samuel. And possibly Twenty-Two.

She scanned the group for the other Neanderthal, whom she hadn't seen all morning.

Lifting her backpack, Elise turned to Kit. 'Did you get to speak to Twenty-Two this morning?'

'No, she had already left when I woke.'

Elise frowned. 'Should we—'

Kit shook his head. 'She is an adult. If we treat her like a child, she will remain that way.'

'We should go, then,' Elise said, turning towards the slowly rising sun. 'I just hope she is okay.'

CHAPTER 4

Twenty-Two

Twenty-Two had spent the morning of her first full day in the new Uracil trying to decide where to build her tree house. It was a monumental decision as she had never really had her own home before, and its location seemed very important. Should it face east or west? The edge of the forest or the centre? High above the others or close to the ground? With each of these options came variables and more compromises than she was willing to accept.

Mid-morning, she took a break to stroll through the main settlement, where several people were busily building two tents. In the centre was Vance, who was holding three sturdy branches together while someone else knotted rope around them.

'Here, take this if you want to help,' said a tall man, holding some folded canvas out to her while she loitered nearby.

Twenty-Two cocked her head at him in an open question.

'We're all pitching in to help build a home for each other. You're stronger than most. You'd be a good addition to the group.'

Twenty-Two scrunched her eyes at the praise.

'It's a collective. You help us, and we'll help you.'

She reached for the canvas, but another hand got there first.

'I don't think we'll be needing any more help.'

Twenty-Two stared up at the owner of the voice. It was Genevieve.

'We have enough already.'

Twenty-Two looked between them, knowing that neither of them would understand her if she tried to speak to them. Genevieve steadily returned Twenty-Two's gaze and a flash of anger crossed the older woman's features before they settled into curated stillness. Twenty-Two had carefully avoided Genevieve so far, but she'd known she would have to face her at some point.

'Sometimes, if these arrangements become too big,' Genevieve continued saying to the taller man, 'they become unmanageable.'

Genevieve didn't even look at Twenty-Two as she spoke. It was as if she didn't exist.

Twenty-Two reached for the canvas again to try and show she could still help without needing anything in return. Without looking at her, the taller man nudged it away. It was an intentional act, and its meaning was clear. Her invisibility was spreading.

That afternoon, after shaking her canteen, Twenty-Two realised she was almost out of water. Deciding she would like a walk to clear her head after her run-in with Genevieve, she made her way to the stream that ran along the perimeter of their new home. While she walked, she considered whether Kit would want to share a tree house with her, or possibly Ezra; they were family, after all. Perhaps all three of them could even share a home. Above the blustering gale came the sharp call of a green woodpecker. The winds were wild, and her hair, which she had allowed to grow over the winter, streamed out behind her.

After filling her water bottle, she straightened and saw she was no longer alone. Maya and Samuel were hurriedly approaching across the long grass.

Samuel kept checking behind him that they weren't being followed.

'What's wrong?' Twenty-Two signed to them, finding her gaze also pulled into the empty distance.

'We need to talk to you,' Samuel signed, before speaking the words so that Maya could understand him. Samuel glanced behind him again. 'My mother, Genevieve, knows what happened with Faye.'

Twenty-Two nodded. She had suspected as much following their encounter that morning. She had hoped that Genevieve would understand Twenty-Two's actions, or be pacified by hearing she had served her punishment for her supposed crime, but it appeared not.

Twenty-Two held her hair back from blowing onto her face with one hand and signed with the other. 'Did you explain to her why I did it? That her daughter was corrupt. That she had sent Septa to kill Elise.'

Samuel dutifully spoke her exact words. He and Elise were the only people Twenty-Two knew who always interpreted her words accurately and did not bend them for their audience. For this simple fact, she had grown to like him, respect him even.

Maya stepped forwards. 'We have explained those things to her, but a parent can't always be expected to see these things rationally.'

Twenty-Two considered this. She had read about a parent's love being one of the strongest kinds and that the death of a child was the rawest of losses. She could not imagine what it would be like to have someone care for you that much – that they lost all rationality and perspective when it came to your life.

'But she hadn't seen Faye for over twenty-five years—' Twenty-Two began while Samuel interpreted for her.

'It doesn't matter how long they were apart,' Maya said, her body rigid against the wind.

Twenty-Two took a step back. 'I only meant that she didn't have the chance to see what Faye had become.'

Samuel glanced at Maya after translating Twenty-Two's words. 'Twenty-Two did not mean it like that.'

'I thought she did. She has a different way of viewing things,' Maya responded. 'Which brings me to why we are here. Genevieve has always felt guilty for leaving Faye as a child. Then that child she loves is killed, and she has to face the person who did that every day. She finds it impossible to be around you. She has told me so.'

Twenty-Two blinked. 'What are you saying? You want me to leave Uracil?'

Samuel straightened. 'We need you to leave Uracil for a short while. All the operatives are leaving tomorrow, and you will join them, but you should avoid Genevieve this evening. You might not be able to return between missions either, but I hope it won't come to that. I just need some time to explain over the coming weeks that her daughter was not the innocent five-year-old girl she left in Uracil. She still sees her that way.'

Twenty-Two stared at the people she had called friends.

'Where do you want me to go? Back to Ezra and the others in the cave?'

'No,' Maya said, glancing at Samuel. 'We are sending out a party to bring them back here. And anyway, you are a member of the Infiltration Department now, and we should be using your many talents.'

Samuel frowned. 'We also have another problem. It is a very obvious one when you stop to think about it, but it doesn't seem that many here want to consider it. Maybe they find it too unsettling.'

'Is it about who told the Potiors of Uracil's location?' Twenty-Two signed.

Maya sighed. 'It is not a prospect I want to consider, but it is very likely that we have someone on the inside working for the Potiors. We don't know how long they have been compromised. We don't even know if they have returned to us or remain in one of the bases.'

Twenty-Two had thought that no one had raised this point about Uracil's betrayal because it was so plain, not because it was too uncomfortable to consider. How else would the Potiors have known where to send the airplanes? Once again, she marvelled at people's ability to ignore what was blindingly obvious if you dared to look at it properly.

'We know it cannot be you who betrayed us,' Samuel continued. 'Because you've had no contact with the outside world the entire time you've been in Uracil. We also know that Michael highly rated your moral perspective. I think "righteous" was the term he used to describe you to Maya.'

Righteous. Twenty-Two had always liked the word and it was agreeable to have it linked with her name.

'It's best you're out in the field at the moment. We know we can trust you,' Maya said. 'But you're inexperienced as you are new to the Infiltration Department, and you have a lot of catching up to do, so we want to send you out before dawn with two other operatives. Two of our best.'

Samuel shifted his feet and glanced up at the sky.

'You are not comfortable with this idea, are you?' Twenty-Two signed.

'To be frank,' Samuel responded, while avoiding looking at Maya, 'no, I am not. I worry that it's too soon for you to be sent out on such a long mission without a set time for you to return—'

'It is for the benefit of Uracil,' Maya interjected. 'Although I would never say this publicly, Uracil is on its knees right now. We have lost our home, our people and, for the first time in fifty years, the Potiors know of our existence. For many people, Vance and Genevieve are a beacon of hope that we can rebuild around. But if Genevieve is visibly upset every day, it will unsettle everyone else. And maybe turn them against you.'

'You don't have to agree to leave,' Samuel signed, giving Twenty-Two a half-smile. 'We can find another way.'

Twenty-Two looked at them both. What were her alternatives? To leave, or to watch her invisibility spread through the entirety of the camp. She knew what she had to do.

That evening, Twenty-Two slept away from the others. In the process of collecting her belongings, she saw Genevieve and Vance at the other side of the clearing. They were sitting together on a spread-out blanket, and Genevieve was talking in hushed tones to another older man, an undercover operative who had returned to Uracil.

Crouched down, Twenty-Two peered at the face of the woman whose daughter she had killed. She could read nothing of her thoughts. Years of working undercover had helped Genevieve hide them from her audience. It frustrated Twenty-Two that she couldn't scratch the surface, so unused was she to being denied access to another's true meaning.

Before they could see her, Twenty-Two slipped off, farther into the woods, where she settled for the night. As she lay curled up against the cold, waiting for sleep to come, she thought back to her time in her pod when she had been alone at night – all those years with no one to talk to in the dark.

She did not want to be alone any more.

Her thoughts turned to the other Neanderthals trapped behind steel, her brothers and sisters, whom she had made no effort to help. What would the stars say to that?

It was still night-time, her thoughts stubbornly refusing to let her sleep, when she heard someone approaching through the undergrowth. Sitting up, she peered into the distance, but there was no moonlight to guide her. The owner's steps were light and Maya soon crouched by her side.

'It's time to wake up,' Maya said. 'You're with Septa and Max for the next few weeks. I want you to head southeast to the old Pre-Pandemic capital and see if our residents were taken there. Come and find me when you return, and I'll find another mission for you.'

Twenty-Two nodded. It was time for her to learn her new role.

CHAPTER 5

Elise

As they walked the last part of their journey before they reached the coast, Kit was transfixed by the sea. For an hour, he stood and watched it, no words forming on his hands. Instead, he pulled at the bracelet around his wrist. It wouldn't be long until they could check the neighbouring islands for the residents of Uracil. Maya had told them that some of the islanders might be willing to provide information.

'Don't worry,' Elise signed. 'It's unlikely you'll have to take the blocker. I think I was just unlucky.'

Kit let go of the bracelet. 'It is not that. It is just that I have never worn jewellery before. It feels strange.'

Elise turned away from him so he couldn't read her expression. She still forgot that the first fourteen years of Kit's life had been very different to her own.

'Although,' Kit continued, 'Samuel told me that he found some Pre-Pandemic studies, back when he was in the museum, that showed my ancestors might have made jewellery. Not metal, like this bracelet. Sapiens did not learn to make metal jewellery until thousands of years later.' He turned to Elise and scrunched his eyes. 'But my ancestors might have made jewellery out of animal teeth, feathers and shells.'

Elise smiled. 'I'm sure my ancestors were doing the same across the other side of the valley.'

'I like that idea.' Kit paused. 'But I do not like the idea of getting on a boat.'

'Me neither,' Elise signed. 'When I went on a boat with Maya last year, I was sick for two days straight. I'd never felt so ill.'

Kit paled.

'Don't worry,' Elise quickly added. 'The journey won't be anywhere near as long as that one. Maya said it would only be a couple of hours. Apparently, on a clear day, you can see the outline of the small island we are heading to from the coast. I'm going to try and find the cove Maya told us about. Wait here, and I'll be back within an hour.'

Kit only nodded.

As she trudged down the pebbled shoreline, the wind pushing against her body and her hair dancing in protest, she decided that if she ever had the option, she wouldn't live by the sea. Not on this coastline anyway. Every step was twice the effort as she leant towards the wind. She thought that if she ever did get to choose where she lived, it would be somewhere as effortless as possible. Not that she expected to live long enough to have that option; she knew that with the risks she took each day, her life was likely to be a short one. She had come to terms with that years ago.

The shoreline was narrow, and when it eventually swept her around one of its contours, she spotted a cove up ahead. She quickened her pace and pushed forwards even though nature was trying to turn her around.

When she stumbled into the adjacent cavern, the wind dropped. Stillness descended. Dripping water echoed farther down in the gloomy cave. Elise tried to use her other senses to assess her situation. The space appeared empty, but *appearing* a certain way wasn't enough for her. She knew she would have to walk into its depths to check that she had the right place and that Uracil's people operated it.

The darkness pressed in on her.

'Hello?' Elise called out. 'I've been told you can help us.'

She jumped as a figure peeled itself away from the wall and stepped in front of her.

'Who sent you?' the man said, standing as still as stone.

Elise couldn't quite make him out in the gloom, but he wasn't a Potior and seemed unlikely to be a member of the Protection Department.

'Maya said you could help us.'

'Well, why didn't you say so earlier? Another two steps, and I would have clubbed you round the back of the head with Skulker!'

Elise peered at the figure and, as her eyes adjusted, his features emerged. A wiry older man was standing in front of her. He looked as if he was approaching his final years, but there was an energetic alertness in the way he talked that suggested he would disagree with her presumption.

'Skulker?' Elise enquired.

He held up a mallet and waggled it at her. 'Skulker.'

Elise tried not to imagine the damage Skulker would have done to her. There was no doubt in her mind that he would have been true to his word.

'I'm glad I didn't take those two extra steps,' she responded. 'I need to get to the small island northwest of here. Can you help me?'

'Of course I can. It's my job, after all. Let me get Diana up and ready and we can be off in two hours.'

'Diana? I thought you lived alone here.'

He frowned at Elise. 'Diana's my boat. Who else would it be?'

While the man began to gather his belongings, Elise made her way back along the shoreline to collect Kit, who was now sitting cross-legged, facing the cresting waves. She waved at him, and he reluctantly got to his feet. Picking up his spear, which Samuel had recently helped him make, he jogged towards her.

'I've found the right cove,' Elise signed to him. 'We're leaving in two hours, so let's eat quickly when we get back there. There's a man—'

Elise stopped when she realised that she knew the name of the man's mallet and his boat, but not his own name.

Not having time to cook, Elise and Kit sat outside the cave and ate some of their reserve supplies from their backpacks. Both were silent while they listened to the noises of the sprightly older man preparing Diana. Half an hour later, they both got to their feet in response to a huffing sound coming from inside.

They followed the noise into the cave's depths and found it was coming from behind the boat. The man's back was pressed up against her as he strained to push Diana along the rollers underneath.

'The first bit is always the hardest,' he said, between each panting breath. 'Then when she takes off, it's much easier.'

Without asking if he could help, Kit stepped around the man and put his broad shoulder to the back of the boat. With a grunt, he pushed against Diana. She juddered in protest to begin with before realising it was a lost battle and sweeping along the tracks. The man landed lightly on the ground after the sudden removal of the boat's weight. He looked up at Kit in shock and then shrugged.

'Strong one, your friend. Isn't he?'

Elise held out her arm and helped him to his feet. They both turned to look at Kit's progress, but he was already out of sight.

At the beginning of their journey to the island, Kit clung to the edges of the boat, his eyes squeezed tightly shut. The sea was gentle that day and, bit by bit, his grip loosened until he was staring all around, his eyes wider with every passing minute.

'It is so big,' Kit signed with one hand, the other still lightly holding on to the boat's rim. 'It is strange to think that it never ends, that you could sail forever around the continents if you wanted to.'

Elise had never thought of it that way.

As the island crept closer, she couldn't take her eyes from the singular vast hill in its centre.

'Do you know much about the island?' Elise asked their skipper.

She was seated on a worn bench, screwed to the boat's hull, which had seen better days.

'Not much,' the man said, his gaze fixed ahead. 'The people who live there call it Synthium. I don't think they leave very often.'

'What are they like?' Elise asked, sitting up.

Even Kit leant forwards so he could hear more clearly.

'Same as the rest of them, really. There's people on a few of these islands,' the old man continued. 'I don't see many boats leave them. They might visit another Zone once or twice a year for any supplies they can't make or hunt. But mostly they keep themselves to themselves.'

Two hours later, Kit and Elise stood over six figures sprawled on the ground in a meadow at the base of the hill. All of them were fast asleep. They looked entirely at peace in the afternoon sunshine. A few had flowers tucked behind their ears or chains of daisies around their wrists or ankles. They each wore baggy pantaloons that nipped in at the ankles and straight tunics that reached midway down their thighs. From afar they had looked like colourful flags laid to rest on the grass.

Kit glanced over at Elise as he signed to her. 'What do we do?'

Elise shrugged. 'Give them a poke with your spear?'

Kit shook his head. 'That might be considered aggressive.'

Elise sighed. This was not what she had anticipated on their journey to the hill in the island's centre. The only experience she'd had of people outside of Zone 3 was David and the fenced mud encampment that Maya had taken her to last year. These people seemed to live in a different way.

Elise loudly cleared her throat, and Kit thumped his spear into the ground.

The man closest to them opened one eye and stared lazily up at them.

'Well, hello there,' he said as he pulled himself up. 'You're new around here. Are you visiting or come to join us?'

He stretched his arms above his head but stopped halfway, focusing on Kit.

Kit stared back at him.

The man hastily scrambled to his feet, the peace clearly broken. The others, hearing the commotion, began to stretch and rouse themselves.

'No weapons,' the man said, staring at Kit and backing away. 'We have a rule that says no weapons on this island.'

He couldn't pull his gaze from Kit, who stared back at him in return.

Elise stepped backwards, holding her hands up, having already tucked her sling into her pocket. 'We didn't mean to surprise you. We've only come to ask for some information. My friend here will leave his spear back on the beach, and we should be gone in a couple of hours.'

Kit gave her a look that said he certainly wouldn't be leaving his spear on the beach, and she rolled her eyes at him.

The man glanced between them, his soft hair falling over his face. His friends had stood up and were now quietly talking amongst themselves, throwing furtive glances at Kit at the end of every sentence. They were all dressed in the same baggy linen pants, taking their colour inspirations from all that nature had to offer. Elise stared down at her heavy boots as she pulled her hood away from her face. She imagined what she and Kit must look like to them in their dark, robust clothing, worn for a practical life of journeying and surviving outside. She guessed that their clothing reflected that they were never at ease, and that was not a first impression that anyone would feel comfortable around.

Elise tried to smile at them and use her gentlest of tones. Her features did not respond to her commands to soften as she was not used to acting this way. The life she'd led over the last few years had been one alert to dangers, with Elise always prepared to fight her way out of a corner if needed. Her ability to relax the mask that shielded her thoughts was one that required practice when underused.

'We only need to ask a few questions, and then we will be on our way. We didn't mean to alarm you.'

The islanders looked at each other.

'You'd better come with us,' the man said. 'The Elders will want to speak with you.'

Elise and Kit shared a glance, and Kit tucked his spear between his back and rucksack so that it was securely held.

'Could you not take it back to the beach?' Elise signed, while they followed the strangers to the west side of the island.

'No. I do not trust them,' Kit responded. 'There are layers to them.'

Elise was about to reply when one of them turned around. He frowned and Elise dropped her hands; she did not dare sign to Kit again. Nervous now, she checked her back pocket for her sling, a habit of hers, and calculated how long it would take them to run back to the beach and the old boatman waiting for them.

Half an hour later, after passing along the trampled pathways that ran around the outskirts of the fields of corn and other crops, Elise realised that this settlement made no attempt to hide its presence on the island. The inhabitants either did not know of the Potiors or did not fear them. Bemused, she looked around, wondering how they had come to live here.

Up ahead was a field with white linen tents of various sizes pitched across it. In the centre was an open tent that only had a covering on three sides to shade it from the spring sun.

'Doesn't living out here in the winter get cold?' Elise asked the man who was walking a few steps ahead of her.

'We manage just fine,' the man responded, looking round and smiling at her. 'We only use this field for half the year and rotate it with others to let each one recover from our presence. In the wintertime, we move our main campsite to the woodland, where we borrow the strength of the trees to support our seasonal enclosures.'

He pointed into the distance. Squinting, Elise could make out the dark green line of a forest.

The early afternoon appeared to be set aside for rest as all the islanders, both inside and outside the tents, were lounging in the sun. Some were fast asleep, and others were lying on their sides and quietly talking with one another. A few children were curled up on a large blanket made from cloth squares. Tied to some of their backs were wings fashioned from a shimmering, opaque material – a mound of brightly coloured but snoozy butterflies. A few people drifted between groups, tentatively smiling at Elise and Kit as they passed. Elise made an effort to return their smiles as she tried to remember the last time she had seen so many people at ease.

'Please take off your shoes,' the man said, slipping off his leather sandals outside the main tent.

Kit and Elise stared at each other. It was a request they had never heard before but, not wishing to offend, Elise bent down and untied the laces of the sturdy boots that had seen her through so many years. Kit followed her lead, and Elise tried to ignore the hole in her sock. She felt at a disadvantage, uncovered, exposed.

The man they had followed through Synthium indicated that they should walk to the end of the tent where five bent, white-haired figures with clothes to match were seated. They were surrounded by a circle of plump, brightly coloured cushions. From a distance, they could have been a line of infants with a protective mother keen to prevent any bumps.

'Leave that with me, please,' the man said, indicating Kit's spear.

Elise nodded at him, and slowly Kit pulled it out from where it was secured on his back. He did not hand it to the man but instead placed it on the ground near the entrance of the tent.

'And your knives too,' the man said, indicating the two push knives strapped to Elise's thighs.

Elise placed these next to Kit's spear and, in a show of candour, unzipped her jacket and plucked each of her throwing knives from the diagonal strap across her chest. She kept her sling in her back pocket. She didn't have to give away all her secrets.

As they walked into the tent's centre, Elise's attention was drawn to a man a few years older than her who was sitting to the side behind the Elders. Unlike the others, he was dressed in darker, more robust clothing. He stood out amongst the other islanders, his shaved head in stark contrast to their loose hair, making him conspicuous. He stared at Elise and Kit but gave no indication of the thoughts behind his hooded eyelids. Elise guessed that he had been trained to fight. He wasn't particularly tall but appeared strong and muscled, unlike the other islanders, who were lean from days spent tending the fields. Sitting down, Elise decided he was the one to monitor – he would be the first into a brawl.

She approached the cushioned Elders and bent down to greet them. Kit was close behind her but remained standing. His attention was fixed on the man at the edge of the tent.

Not having much experience in diplomatic matters, Elise decided to address all five of the Elders, her gaze constantly shifting between them.

'Thank you for agreeing to see us,' she began.

She sat cross-legged in front of them and quickly adjusted her sock so the hole was no longer visible.

'Synthium is always open to visitors,' the oldest of the women said, her bright eyes alert and darting over the two newcomers. 'Particularly young ones who might stay a while. We need youth and vitality on this island. The future is younger than the five of us.'

Elise smiled. 'We appreciate your ... hospitality. We come from the mainland and are trying to find some of our people.'

'The mainlanders always bring their problems with them,' the man farthest to the right of the line muttered. 'Always the problem, never the solution.'

'I don't want to bring my problems with me. I just want to know if you have seen any large creatures in the sky ...' Elise realised how absurd this must sound but pressed on. 'Very large creatures. You may even know them as airplanes.'

She found herself gesturing with her arms out wide in the shape of airplane wings.

Behind the Elders, the younger man raised his head. He began to parody her arm movements, amusement lighting up his features, and Elise immediately dropped her arms to her sides.

The woman in the middle snorted. 'Say what you mean, girl. I might have passed to the other side by the time you've stopped stumbling around the truth.'

Elise pulled herself up and stared into the older woman's clear grey eyes. 'People from our base were captured. Perhaps transported in Pre-Pandemic airplanes. We are trying to locate them.'

'Better, much better,' the older woman said while eyeing her. 'Arlo, could you come over here, please?'

In one smooth motion, the man in the corner stood and made his way towards the cushioned seating area. Elise tried not to stare at him but couldn't pull her gaze away. Now that he was closer, she could see that he had large brown eyes with flecks of hazel running through them. He possessed a certain easy confidence that she found intriguing.

Arlo stopped at the edge of the circle across from Kit. The two men eyed each other before Arlo turned to the Elder.

'Have you had any reports of any things flying around that could have been Pre-Pandemic airplanes?' the older woman said, not bothering to turn to him.

'A few months ago, some of the children said they saw a large beast which landed on the island to the north.'

As he spoke, his gaze flicked over to Elise, and she felt a jolt of something deep in her stomach. She stared back at him.

'There is your answer then,' the Elder said. 'Try the island to the north.'

'I will take one of our boats and show you the way,' Arlo interjected.

'That is very good of you,' the Elder said. 'But mind you come back.'

CHAPTER 6

Twenty-Two

At first light, having been woken by Maya, Twenty-Two joined Max and Septa. The newly formed team walked three abreast around the dark shapes of the gorse. As the world unveiled itself, Twenty-Two dropped behind Max and Septa. The terrain was too rough and uneven for all three to lead the way. Septa, the most experienced navigator in Zone 3, strode ahead.

With every step, Twenty-Two felt more alone as they took her farther from the new Uracil. Uracil was the only place she'd ever called home; it was where all her friends had lived. It was unjust that she had lost the chance of finally settling somewhere because of Genevieve. Faye had been corrupt, and Twenty-Two had served a term of imprisonment anyway. The scales had been reset, but that wasn't enough for Genevieve.

Up ahead, Septa motioned at her to hurry up. Twenty-Two had not spent much time with Septa or Max before. Neither of them had learnt sign language, so any interactions she'd had with them in the past had been limited. Still, Maya had said they were two of the best in the Infiltration Department, and she wanted to learn by watching them.

She had studied them from afar before, as she did everyone, while she'd waited for winter to pass in the cave. Her impression of Septa was that she radiated an anger that was misdirected on many occasions. It was only Luca whom she ever softened for. Septa's aggression did not blind Twenty-Two to the brittleness beneath. Twenty-Two had observed that the loudest, most aggressive people were often not the strongest.

Max held more interest for Twenty-Two, and she realised that it was because he resembled Fintorian, the Potior who had been the director of her museum back in Cytosine. Max's bold good looks were not cultivated in the same way as Fintorian's, but they still shared many features – their height, a strong but lean frame, glowing skin and alertness. Max was not as sure of himself as Fintorian, but Twenty-Two knew that this was probably because he felt like an outsider, just as she did again. Not everyone relaxed in Max's company, and she suspected he must be aware of it.

Four hours later, they stopped by the side of a hill to eat. It offered little protection from the racing winds, and Twenty-Two buried her head deeper into her coat. She still found 'weather' an anomaly that she was having to get used to after spending her first fourteen years in a near-silent pod and then eighteen months as a prisoner in an even quieter cabin.

'Have you ever visited the old capital?' Max asked Twenty-Two, as he unwrapped some dried meat that was to be his lunch.

Twenty-Two shook her head. She liked that he had still asked her the question, even though the answer was obvious. It was nice of him to think she could be more worldly than she appeared.

'You are in for some true delights then,' Max continued, popping bits of meat into his mouth between sentences. 'Before the pandemic, the largest Sapien city was located in the south. Then, around a hundred years ago, the Potiors sent out Sapien workforces to tear down all the remnants of the infrastructure and homes that remained in Zone 3. They said it was to "return the land to nature". But Uracil suspects that the Potiors didn't want pathways linking up the settlements or alternative homes for people to live in.'

Twenty-Two nodded her encouragement – she knew that the other two wouldn't understand her if she signed, and she wanted him to continue. After briefly studying her face, Max went on.

'The Pre-Pandemic Sapiens had a material called tarmac, which was made up of ground-up stone and tar, that they laid in strips all over Zone 3. They called them "roads". They were enormous pathways, sometimes as wide as twelve people lying down. They also constructed buildings as high as you could see into the sky. All of that was pulled down or dug up and either sold to the other Zones or shipped off to an island in the southern sea.'

'They left some of the capital,' Septa said, tearing meat into strips with her teeth. 'Only a small bit, the worst of it. It was called an industry area.'

'Industrial park,' Max corrected. 'It was where everything was manufactured, a sort of Thymine, I suppose. Not that much industry existed in the capital before the pandemic. The land in the capital was too valuable for that and was sold for homes. The factories that formed parts of the industrial parks were relocated to other cities and towns or even to the middle of the countryside—'

'Anyway,' Septa interjected, 'the Potiors tore down most of the capital apart from a few buildings and a handful of these tarmac roads. They probably had nowhere else to ship things. The Isle of Grey is towered high with the stuff, a wasteland now. Bloody eyesore to sail past.'

'When I was in school,' Max continued, 'I asked why they had left some of the old capital in place, and I was told that the Potiors wanted to preserve part of the past for when they needed it.' Max shrugged. 'They wouldn't tell me any more. Maybe they were going to film it to show the Sapien schoolchildren what their ancestors had produced.' Max popped some food into his mouth. 'They always enjoy showing the Sapien children the failures of their dynasty.'

Twenty-Two grabbed a stick, cleaved a few words into the muddy pathway and then stared at Max.

'Why did I leave?' Max repeated, reading what she had written.

It began to rain, and as the drops hit his face, his features hardened.

'Yeah, Max,' Septa said, staring unblinkingly at him. 'You've never told us why you really left your place as a princely Potior.'

'I wasn't a *prince*,' Max spat.

Septa's eyes widened in delight. 'Touchy subject is it, Mr Prince?'

'I wasn't a prince,' Max repeated, having controlled his tone. 'There is no monarchy amongst the Potiors.'

'I don't care whether you were a prince or not. I want to know why you left.'

'I told Maya, and it was enough for her,' Max responded.

'Sounds to me like you have a shady past. Something to hide,' Septa said, looking directly at him.

'I have a past that I don't like to talk about. I'd rather forget it.'

Twenty-Two leant back on her hands and watched them both. She had not meant for it to develop in this way, but she was happy to let events unfold.

'Doesn't work like that,' Septa said. 'There's no secrets in Uracil now.'

'Bollocks,' Max retorted. 'Of course there are secrets in Uracil. More than ever. And if you don't realise that, you're even more naive than I first thought.'

Septa leapt to her feet. 'Who are you calling naive? Just because I didn't get the chance to get some fancy Potior education doesn't make me stupid.'

Max stared up at her. 'No, it doesn't. But you're being pretty naive if you think Uracil is an open screen now. Because it's not.'

A glint in Septa's eye made Twenty-Two feel uneasy; she rarely glimpsed flashes of pure hatred in others, and she couldn't be sure why Septa had begun to direct it towards Max.

'Perhaps they just keep the secrets from you,' Septa said. 'Because they don't trust you. Because you'll always be one of *them* in their eyes.'

Max flinched. Septa's words had hit their mark.

Twenty-Two closed her bag. It was time to go.

They spent the next ten days walking, stopping only to eat and sleep. They took it in turns to hunt, and Max showed Twenty-Two how to build a snare to catch rabbits. In exchange, Twenty-Two began teaching Max sign language, and she was impressed at how quickly he learnt the basics.

On their twelfth day of travelling, approaching from the north, Twenty-Two caught her first glimpse of what had been the Pre-Pandemic capital – off in the far distance was a patch of grey. She felt drawn to it. She wanted to know its secrets.

'The buildings and tarmac roads would have stretched all the way out to here and beyond,' Max said, noticing her interest in what lay ahead.

'Have you been here before?' Twenty-Two signed carefully, before fingerspelling the words for him as well.

Max frowned as he followed her movements. 'Once, when I was much younger. But when my parents found out about it, they banned me from returning. I came again a couple of years ago when I had time between missions. I like it here. It's a doorway into the past that the Potiors have allowed to remain, which is a rarity indeed.' He pulled a face. 'It's not pretty. But sometimes I think that the requirement for beauty is unnecessary, irrelevant even.'

Twenty-Two signed again.

'What happened here?' Max said aloud, repeating her question.

'What happened here made the stars turn away from us,' Septa said, coming up behind them after stopping to empty her boot of a stone.

She gestured for them to keep walking.

Twenty-Two pushed her hair from her eyes as all three of them trudged in a line, descending the hill that had taken them an hour to climb. The morning held the promise of being the first true spring day, and the land here was less rough, less wild. The grass reached their knees but was easier to walk through than the thick, woody stems of the bracken farther north that constantly threatened to trip them.

'When the pandemic hit,' Septa continued, 'and everyone in the cities knew there was no one left to save them, it quickly turned into each person for themselves. Those who didn't die from the initial wave of the virus streamed out to try and find food. A few stayed, scavenging whatever supplies they could find. They eventually left or died when the food ran out.'

Septa stared straight ahead. 'Millions died here. Their bones have all decayed, and the dust of the dead has been washed away. It's for the best. I wouldn't have wanted to come back here in the first years. Would have been an open graveyard.'

Twenty-Two tried not to think about what it would have looked like in those early years. She had read enough Pre-Pandemic books to be able to imagine the worst things in life.

An hour later, Septa stopped them by a triangle of three trees. 'Right, I'm in charge of this mission. We're doing a quick recon of the area to check the buildings to see that no one from Uracil is being kept here. If it takes longer than a day, we camp outside the city. No splitting up. If we do get separated, we meet at this point. Understood?'

Max and Twenty-Two both nodded. Max looked over Septa's head, never meeting her eye.

Twenty-Two thought of all the people who used to reside here and gestured to Max to interpret for her. 'What do we do if we meet anyone who still lives here?'

Septa stared at her. 'Run.'

Twenty-Two flinched before realising that she was not telling the truth.

Septa snorted. 'I'm just ruffling you. As far as we know, no one is living in the capital. Not that I've seen anyway.' She laughed again. 'You should have seen the look on your face! Oh, it was worth it!'

Twenty-Two thought about tackling Septa to the ground and changing the look on her face, but the idea was only fleeting. She knew that her own weakness lay in knowing very little of the world. And that needed to change.

CHAPTER 7

Caitlyn

As can so often be the case, Caitlyn Guider was unaware of the moment when she was pulled from one path and set down on another. It wasn't a tangible event as such. Instead, it was a simple thought.

That year, spring had been late to reach Guanine. Caitlyn had pulled her winter coat tighter around her as she trudged up the steps leading to the university. Staring at its majestic presence, all the knowledge it contained only available to the few, she had begun to wonder if it was better to burn brightly, briefly absorbing all that life could offer, than to exist merely as embers.

This was the first time she had considered such a notion. Before that day, she had rarely thought about her choices, or lack of them. She had been given a place in the world and had never questioned it. There was no point; she was a Sapien. Nothing would ever change for her. Acceptance of this had been drilled into her and her peers since they could first form words and understand their meaning. This belief led to a lifetime of atonement that united her with the other Sapiens and made her indistinguishable from the rest.

Her enthusiasm for her staid life had begun to ebb in recent weeks, ever since she had begun to work under a new professor at one of the universities in Guanine. She had tried to please him, but nothing she did was right. She knew she was highly regarded amongst the academic staff, for a Sapien at least. There had even been a minor tussle over who would inherit her as an assistant when her former professor had retired. She was quick, diligent and responsible. But this wasn't enough for Professor Gudd, whose mind raced along the curve of paranoia.

At some point, Caitlyn had begun to consider whether the problem lay with him, and not her. The thought went against everything that had been instilled in her. As a Sapien, she was responsible for the legacy of her ancestors, and without the Potiors and Medius to guide them, their world would be one of chaos and destruction fuelled by greed. But once this new thought had broken through, it lingered, unwilling to return to the recesses of her mind. Even more alarming, a sort of mitosis had surfaced, and the ideas had begun to split, duplicate and evolve.

The door to the room she shared with the other administrative assistants slammed open, and Professor Gudd's frame took up all its space. As she stared over at him, she tried to remind herself that this was the price to pay for the prestige of working for one of the most senior professors in the university.

'Caitlyn!' he shouted, rather unnecessarily, as he was already advancing down the rows of desks towards hers.

Caitlyn looked to her colleagues for support, but they had busied themselves with whatever was in front of them, eager not to pull him off course.

'These papers are the work of an ignoble ignoramus,' Professor Gudd said, slamming his screen down on her desk. 'The apostrophes are incorrectly placed in two sections, you have used the wrong type of dash throughout, and I counted six, yes, *six*, mistakes of the spelling variety.'

Caitlyn blinked, unsure what to say. She had stayed until nine the previous night re-reading the five-thousand-word study on lithic knapping, a method of shaping stone into tools in the early Pleistocene era. It was a subject Caitlyn now knew well, even though she'd never heard the term before joining the university as an administrative assistant.

As a Sapien whose job it was to help with the administrative work of the professors, including writing up research papers from their notes, she had access to more educational information than most Sapiens could ever imagine. She knew about the intricacies of stone tools, ancient weaponry and the rolling ice ages that came and went. What she didn't know was what had led ancient humans from their first upright steps to living in four bases on an island. She only ever saw a few pieces of the puzzle, with no completed image to work from.

The Medius professors did not mind the assistants accessing more educational material than most. It had no bearing on their current lives, and most of the professors doubted the Sapiens would understand it anyway. But Caitlyn understood it. Caitlyn absorbed it all at an impressive rate, but this had to be hidden, from both her colleagues and her superiors.

It had not been easy, as nothing was ever explained in simple terms here. Instead, knowledge was shrouded in complexities to ward off those deemed unworthy. Dead languages were raised, and ancient terms were slid into place to bar entry. But that didn't stop her active mind, which naturally craved stimulation. She thanked the stars every day that she had not been shunted off to work in the recycling centre when she had turned fourteen.

She had done a good job with the paper and knew it was for another administrator to conduct the final proofread of the document at a later stage. When her previous supervisor, Professor Guare, a jovial woman of later years, would read a paper before it was proofread, she would just circle the required amendments and provide the correct spellings in her neat handwriting. Sometimes, Professor Guare would even include an explanation if she believed that Caitlyn would benefit from it. She would then quietly send the revisions to Caitlyn's screen. No fuss or bother ensued.

Professor Gudd instead tipped his portly figure in Caitlyn's direction, his belly hovering over the edge of her desk. It looked as if it would like to rest there for a moment.

'It is just slapdash,' the professor said, clearly warming to his theme. 'Sloppy and ... mortifying. To think I nearly submitted this to the museums.'

'But it hasn't got to the final proofreading stage—'

'No, no. I'm not ready to hear your implausible excuses,' he said, holding up his hands. 'Especially after that time, not even a month ago now, with the Anglo-Saxon mouldboard ploughs.' Caitlyn dropped her head to avoid the accusation shining in Professor Gudd's eyes. 'There is no hyphen between mould and board. I am astounded that you didn't try to hyphenate plough as well! If I'm not mistaken, it is the beginning of a pattern forming. And it's bordering on *sabotage*.'

Caitlyn stared up at him. Another unannounced thought popped into her head.

He's belittling me to make himself feel better.

A fiery response licked her insides, always suppressed, never allowed to be uncovered to scorch an adversary. Instead, she did the only thing a Sapien in her position could do: she hung her head and waited for him to run out of steam. On he went, threatening this and that, spittle catching in his moustache before he lurched onto the topic of Professor Cylett's new paper, which he was keeping very close to his chest. Caitlyn knew then that this was the root of the matter. He couldn't lash out at an 'esteemed colleague', so he'd have to settle for Caitlyn.

She had seen it in some of the university professors before. What often occupied their thoughts was not their own research topic but what their peers were researching. The risk was always alarmingly close that other papers might be released first, and then their own work would slide into oblivion. Like many Medius professions, there was a giddy scrabble to the top and an inevitable burying of those below.

Professor Gudd paused for a moment and pinched the skin between his eyebrows.

With a loud exhale, he released the puckered skin and sighed. 'Right, stay late. Fix it, and we will move forwards. Always onwards.'

'Yes, sir. I'll fix it now. It will be done by nine.'

She put her head down and wondered if Guanine's National Library would take her as a trainee indexer. It was fewer tickets, but it might be a price worth paying.

*

It was late when Caitlyn made her way through Guanine's lanes to her Sapien home at the base of the second mountain. She was one of the last to leave the university, and as she crossed its gardens, she saw a young woman waiting underneath a pear tree. The woman looked away, and Caitlyn wondered whom she was waiting for.

Caitlyn lived in a settlement of staircases, either chiselled into the rock or laid as jagged pathways of jutting stone slabs. Halfway around the rough mountain steps was an open plateau where the university had been built from the same stone as the mountain, so they blended perfectly. If she followed the second set of circling staircases down and round again, she would arrive at another plateau that housed the office buildings and Guanine's Museum of Evolution.

Instead, Caitlyn's journey took her down the main staircase, across the lowest of the three rope bridges that connected the twin mountains, past the Medius schools and houses on the open expanse below, and down to the Sapien homes that were burrowed into the sides of the mountain. These draughty, undesirable dwellings were accessed by stone slabs bolted onto the mountain. A rope circling the stone slabs was the only barrier between the residents and in places a fall of hundreds of feet.

Caitlyn walked down the steps with the same ease as someone from another base would cross a flat meadow – she had never known any different. The children of Guanine were taught early on that they couldn't play on these chiselled, treacherous walkways. Every mountain circle had a tale of someone who had slipped and fallen to their death. The steps were treated with respect but, as thousands of uneventful journeys were taken each week, never with fear.

Coming up the stairs was a young father with a toddler strapped to his back, the way all children were carried until they could understand the dangers involved. As custom dictated, the man holding the young girl stopped on the side closest to the rock while Caitlyn took the added risk of picking her way past on the outside. He nodded his thanks.

She crossed the lowest plateau on the mountain where she lived, which acted as a playing field where the residents and their children could stretch their legs or relax. As part of their Reparations as Sapiens, they were not supposed to step off the mountainside – they weren't to spread across the landscape as they had before. Not that any of them were inclined to try to do so. They were safe here, and the views they saw were of a land alien to them in many ways. They had been born into the base of 'Education and Enlightenment', and this was where they would stay. Even if they wanted to leave, they didn't have the water or supplies to make the perilous journey.

Taking the steps leading to her arc of Sapien dwellings, Caitlyn looked out over the small mountain range she had always called home and breathed in the crisp air. She avoided the sight of the river that ran close to the base of the mountain and joined the sea through an estuary miles away but still visible on a clear day. From her vantage point, her view was of a flat land of hidden viruses and concealed disease. The threat of another pandemic following the one that had nearly wiped out her species always lurked at the edge of the residents' minds.

Outside the wooden door to her family's home, she stamped her boot-clad feet to remove any dirt or dust from them and smiled to herself as she heard the chaos within. Eight family members, spanning four generations, shared these hollowed-out rooms, and it was never quiet.

Stepping inside, she blinked at the bright electric bulbs strung along the wall. She pulled off her thick winter coat, which she soon wouldn't need once the seasons settled into summer. With a thump, two small figures catapulted into her legs and proceeded to tug at her jumper and ask her a thousand questions.

She leant down to her youngest brother and sister and pulled them in for a hug.

'Yes, we can make some pastry for a pie if you want,' she responded to their eager questioning. 'But only if Gran says we have enough eggs.'

'Good,' said Frankie, the second youngest of the clan. 'Because Pops ate nearly everything at breakfast and the school lunch was tiny and I'm starving!'

'You're late!' Pops announced from his chair, turning to peer at Caitlyn. 'Gran needs your help, so quick to it.'

Caitlyn glanced over at Pops, her wrinkled great-grandfather, who was sitting on his usual chair with a rug over his knees, holding his walking stick in his right hand. He liked to think of himself as the head of the family and consequently took more than his fair share of their tightly controlled rations. But everyone knew that his daughter, Caitlyn's grandmother, kept everything and everyone in order.

'I'm on my way there now,' Caitlyn responded, not bothering to warm her tone for him. 'If anything, your chiding has delayed me.'

'What?' Pops said, cupping his ear. 'You're giving me cheek now, are you?'

'I'll go to the kitchen,' Caitlyn said, a little louder, but refusing to look at him again.

She had openly argued with him enough times in the past, and all it succeeded in doing was upsetting her younger siblings. Caitlyn and Pops both had the same fiery temper, and the same desire to steer their family unit in their decisions. But, unlike Pops, Caitlyn was aware of the impact their clashes had on the younger members of the family. Pops didn't seem to care. He always wanted to make the final point and would then look around an empty room for applause.

Peeling her two younger siblings from her legs, Caitlyn made her way across the rugs, their patterns worn away in the middle, through the living area, to the kitchen, where she could smell Gran's cooking. Her stomach rumbled at the aroma and she tried to ignore it – they were all hungry at this time of day.

'Are Mum and Dad not back yet, Gran?' Caitlyn asked, as she pulled open the lid of the pan that was bubbling on the stove.

The pot seemed to consist mainly of vegetables, although she spied some barley grains simmering at the bottom.

'Not yet,' Gran responded, smiling over at her. 'Frankie, Owen, go and set the table and be quick about it.'

'I thought we were having pie?' Owen, the youngest of Caitlyn's siblings, said.

He was clutching his stomach in an exaggerated swoon.

'Not today,' Gran responded. 'Maybe on Friday if I can get the eggs.'

Owen's mouth turned down. Gran and Caitlyn exchanged a glance as it began to wobble.

'I'll dig deep in the stew pan when I serve you both, more barley down there,' Gran said with a smile.

Placated, the two youngest began to diligently choose which items of cutlery to use to lay the table. They tried to remember everyone's favourite spoon and tussled over which of them would get the special one with the pine cone stamped into its handle.

'Where did I put that wooden spoon?' Gran muttered, wiping her hands on her apron.

Caitlyn looked over at her grandmother. The spoon was right in front of her on the wooden chest that served as a work surface.

'It's right there, Gran,' Caitlyn said, pointing to it.

'Could you just pass it to me, dear?'

Caitlyn picked up the spoon and pressed the handle into Gran's right hand.

'Your cataracts have come back again, haven't they?' Caitlyn whispered, not wanting the others in the living area to hear. 'Why didn't you tell anyone?'

They both paused as Pops began chiding the two younger children.

Her grandmother turned to her and, in the bright light from the bare bulb above, Caitlyn thought she could already see the film beginning to form over her weathered eyes.

'No point worrying anyone,' Gran said, taking the lid off the pan and stirring the contents with the wooden spoon. 'Not enough Medi-stamps to fix both my eyes and Pops' at the moment. And he's next in the queue; he's had them longer than I have.'

Caitlyn's shoulders slumped. Yet again, they'd have to accept that they didn't have the Medi-stamps to help multiple family members at once, despite saving up their tickets.

'But he doesn't even try and be nice to us,' Caitlyn hissed. 'Even if he had his eyes fixed, he'd still just sit in that chair and boss us around.'

In a flash, Gran turned on Caitlyn. 'We don't jump the queue in this family. Never have. We take the Medi-stamps in turns unless it's an emergency. Always have done for six generations, ever since I was a girl. It's what keeps us together. And I've seen the alternative rip many a family apart.'

'But—'

'You're old enough now to start looking around you with clearer vision. Pops isn't the problem. He is family.' Caitlyn wasn't sure what Gran was suggesting. 'I'll not hear any more of it. Pops is next. I'll just have to wait my turn.'

Caitlyn thought about continuing to argue the point, but she knew that when Gran made up her mind, her stance turned to stone.

As Caitlyn carried the pan of vegetable and barley stew out to the table, she pushed aside her hopes of transferring to one of the libraries. Her family needed all the tickets they could get, and if she wanted to help Gran, she would have to find more.

CHAPTER 8

Elise

Elise, Kit and Arlo silently retraced their steps back to Synthium's shoreline. Elise was very aware of Arlo's presence, and she tried not to glance over at him.

'You don't have to come with us, you know,' she said to him. 'If you have other things to do ...'

'There's not much to do on an island like this,' Arlo responded, giving her a half-smile. 'The two of you turning up will probably be discussed for weeks.'

Elise's curiosity eventually won, and she decided diplomacy was overrated. 'Don't you worry about the Potiors finding you?'

Arlo raised both his eyebrows; his face was often animated, and Elise enjoyed the fact that he spoke with candour. 'The Potiors already know that we are here. If they decided to come for us, they could. But they don't. We've lived out here for nearly two hundred years, since our ancestors split off from the mainland. Some of the other islands are similarly occupied.'

Elise stopped dead, and Kit bumped into the back of her. 'The Potiors know of your existence?'

Arlo also stopped and eyed them both. 'Of course they do. They know of all the islanders out here. There is an unspoken agreement that we keep to ourselves and they leave us be.'

It was a very different way of life from all the precautions that Uracil had been forced to take over the years.

'The sailboat I will take is over there,' Arlo said, pointing farther along the shore. 'Go out to sea and wait until I come out from the cove. Then follow me.'

Half an hour later, Elise's boat sailed out behind Arlo's, the old man at the helm. The going was slow as the wind was not in their favour, but the sea was gentle with them. As she watched the small sailboat up ahead slice its way across the water, she thought, for the first time, that she could actually enjoy sailing.

Kit nudged her.

'Do you think our missing people will be on the island?' he signed.

'No, not really,' Elise responded. 'As much as I'd like them to be. It was Genevieve who suggested we search this island, but she hasn't left Adenine for years. She's hardly abreast of what's happening in the outlying islands. But we've got to check.'

An hour later, Elise and Kit helped their skipper pull the boat onto the pebbled shore. Arlo was farther along, and once he had secured his from the tide, he jogged over to them.

'I suppose you'll be leaving now,' Elise said, stepping forwards. 'Thank you for showing us to the island.'

'I could help you search it if you want,' Arlo responded. 'It's been a few years since I've been here, but I know the general layout. There's a freshwater stream in the middle. There's no one living here, but if anyone was they'd need access to that.'

Elise nodded, secretly pleased that their time together would be extended. 'Take me to it.'

They began to scout the east side of the island. A few hours later, the three of them jogged through the low grass, up the side of a small hill. For a moment, Elise's mind took her back to the museum in Thymine, where she had crested a similar hill and looked down at two men trying to contain a sabre-tooth tiger.

How much my life has changed since then.

When they reached the top, Elise stopped and took in the scene below. In the distance were rough shelters, and people.

'Are you sure that no one normally lives here?' she stammered to Arlo.

'Very sure.'

Forgetting about the other two, forgetting about her own safety, she sprinted down the hillside.

She could hear the thump of the men behind her, and she pushed on. Approaching the edge of the settlement, she began to draw the islanders' attention. They backed away from her. Realising she was frightening them, she slowed her pace and peered desperately at their faces, trying to recognise someone, anyone. They were all painfully thin, their clothes torn and filthy. Elise clenched her fists as she searched each of their faces.

A man pushed through the huddled people.

'Is that really you?' he asked.

Elise frowned as she studied his face. It took a while to place him.

'Michael?'

Elise stared at the leader of Uracil. Could one person really alter so much in only a few months? His natural strength had left him, abandoned him on this island. Instead, one of the broadest men had become a brittle figure who seemed years older, so withered was his frame.

'Stars! What has happened to you all?' Elise asked, taking a step forwards.

'We were dropped here by the Potiors,' Michael responded. 'And then they just left us here with no food, no tools, nothing.'

Elise blinked back her tears as she surveyed the crowd in torn and bedraggled clothing that was now gathering around her. A few reached out to touch her arm as if not believing she was real. For this many people to live off the natural produce of a small island was impossible. And they couldn't even have swum to the surrounding islands or mainland to get help. It was too far. Without proper tools to help them, it was a slow death sentence.

'We've stripped the island of nearly all there is to forage,' Michael continued. 'We planted crops, but they will take months to grow. We set traps, but to feed so many ... The animals started to die out before they had time to reproduce. We turned to the sea, have been trying to net hauls of fish, but we mostly get by on one meal a day, two if we're lucky.'

Elise looked around her and slowly began to recognise the others. Excitement bubbled up as she searched the sea of faces for her mother's familiar features. She sent a silent message to Nathan that it wouldn't be long now.

'Can you take me to my mum?' she asked Michael, eager to embrace the woman she had thought about every day since returning to find Uracil in ruins.

Michael's face collapsed. 'Elise, I'm so sorry, but Sofi died two months ago.'

His words did not register. She could not process them.

'No. She can't be dead,' Elise stuttered. 'I haven't told her about my dad yet.' Her voice rose. 'I need to tell her about my dad!'

Michael tried to pull her into him, but she resisted. 'I'm so sorry, Elise. She caught pneumonia. There was nothing we could do to help except make her comfortable.'

Michael continued talking, but she struggled to absorb what he was saying. Her vision blurred, and she sank to the ground.

'*Elise!* Wake up!'

Elise turned her head to the woman who called her name, but she was not there.

'*Elise!* You have to wake up!'

She blinked open her eyes and stared at the figure peering down at her. There were hands on her shoulders. A man and woman she couldn't quite place were crouched next to her, and above them the soft green leaves of a silver birch covered most of the sky. She turned her head to the side. In the distance was a crowd of people, and she recognised Kit's broad frame. She tried to sit, but her head swam, and she slumped back down again.

'I thought ...' the woman said, tears welling in her eyes.

'Tilla,' Elise said, trying to lean on her arm and reach for her friend's matted hair. 'Georgina has been out of her mind with worry.'

Tears poured down Tilla's face, and she gave the widest smile at the mention of Georgina's name.

Elise tried to sit up again, but darkness blurred the corners of her vision. She touched her hand to her head, where she felt a lump already forming.

'You hit it when you passed out,' the man said, his brow creasing in concern. 'I'm so sorry I didn't catch you in time.'

Arlo. That was his name. He must have carried her over to the shade of the silver birch.

How did she know him?

And then a fog of memories came back to her reluctant mind. Michael hesitantly explaining that her mum had died along with nearly a third of Uracil's residents during their time on this stars-forsaken island. How they had battled to keep everyone alive but the odds had been so against them, the winter months cruel even in the island's southernly position. Tales of people trying to swim the miles to the neighbouring islands but never seen again. Her mother passing on a cold January morning, too weak to fight the pneumonia that had seized her lungs.

Elise turned her head to the side, and her grief rolled along with her, almost tangible in its weight. 'I never got to apologise for taking them out of Thymine. They'd have been safe, still alive, if I'd left them there.'

Tilla stroked Elise's hair, just like her mother used to do. 'They were never safe in Thymine, Elise. None of you were.'

Tears pricked Elise's eyes. In the distance, she could see the uniform mounds of earth, some so small they could only hold children. She pulled her head, so heavy, back around to Arlo as her fingers clasped at his sleeve.

He leant in closer. She did not blink, her gaze never faltering.

'Will you help us again?

CHAPTER 9

Twenty-Two

Twenty-Two had never seen anything so old that the stars had not created. She stared at the squat building, unable to believe something had stood for three hundred years. Was it even possible? The settlement she had grown up in was less than half that age.

'It's rather ugly, isn't it?' Max said, as he looked up at the pebbledash front. 'They pulled all the beautiful ones down. The twisting spires, Corinthian columns, stained glass ... all gone.'

He sighed.

Twenty-Two's gaze swept across the building, trying to take it all in. Perhaps it was not obviously attractive, with its sandy colouring and the cracks that had become home to shoots of green, but she thought it was beautiful. It represented a point in history that she could not imagine, and she loved it for having existed before her and everything else she knew. If she could only stretch farther back in time, she would see the places her own ancestors had lived.

'And what is this under our feet?' she asked, fingerspelling the words for him.

She slid her boots over the tiny stones that covered most of what she could see. If she spun around in a circle, all she would see were looming grey buildings and tiny grey stones.

'It looks similar to something they called gravel,' Max responded. 'Gravel was a quick, cheap way for them to prevent plants from growing.'

That seemed nonsensical to Twenty-Two. 'Why would you want to prevent plants from growing? They bring life.'

Max watched her signs carefully, but he couldn't follow them, so she resorted to fingerspelling them for him again.

'I suppose they wanted to control where the plants grew. They liked to contain a lot of things. Their farms were often monocultures where they only grew one type of crop.'

'What was that place used for?' Twenty-Two signed, pointing towards a building several storeys high, with no glass in its openings and curving slopes running up through the middle.

Max smiled. 'That would have been a municipal car park. A particularly fine example of an unseemly lump taking up a prime piece of city space so that people could abandon their polluting automobiles until they needed them again.'

Twenty-Two didn't understand half of what Max had said. She could only assume that the Sapiens had travelled in smoky land vehicles so impractically big that they couldn't take them everywhere.

Anyway, she had other, more pressing questions to ask. 'If the other buildings were more beautiful, why did they pull them down and leave these ones?'

'Because that's how the Potiors think,' Septa said, after Max had repeated Twenty-Two's words. She scuffed her boot against the loose stones. 'They couldn't leave anything good that the

Pre-Pandemic Sapiens did as that would cause too many questions. So they just left the crappy ones to reinforce the idea that the Pre-Pandemic Sapiens were all a bunch of delusional, uncultured, destructive imbeciles. And that we are lucky to have the Potiors to right everything for us.'

Twenty-Two stared at Max.

'It's true,' he said. 'I wish I could have seen it as it was before. At school, I had access to vast ranges of Pre-Pandemic books in the Potior libraries. We were allowed to study them because we were Potiors and had to know our enemies.'

Twenty-Two looked up at him enquiringly. 'Enemies?'

Max gave her a half-smile. 'They have many enemies. The past, present and future being the most pressing ones. But I was too interested in the past for my elders' comfort. I wanted to be an architect, build what had existed before, and continue in the footsteps of the greats preceding me. But no. It would not do. Two-storey office buildings were the extent of the freedom I would ever get. And then only when the present ones had deteriorated enough to require rebuilding.'

Septa snorted and ran her hands through her spiky hair. They had moved on to a large hangar and she was trying – unsuccessfully – to jimmy the lock. The hangar was so enormous that it could easily house several other buildings.

'So, that's why you left?' she said. 'Poor little Potior didn't get to be the architect he wanted to be ...'

Twenty-Two watched Max. There was another reason that he was not telling them.

'Why are you so awful?' Max said, turning to Septa.

Septa curled her lip. 'Because it's better than being a whiny, heart-on-his-sleeve Sap who's actually a Potior.'

Twenty-Two looked between them both before signing, 'Because she is angry with her past.'

Max raised an eyebrow. 'Perhaps.'

'What did she say?' Septa said.

'She just said we should go and look at that building over there.'

Twenty-Two hated it when people didn't interpret for her correctly and decided to mask her meaning. It happened more often than she liked, but she had observed that it rarely ever happened to Kit. She made a note to speak to Max about it later.

'Come on then,' Septa said, nudging her chin towards the building that Max was pointing at. It lay across a tarmac pathway with weeds bursting out of it. Septa had clearly grown bored of trying to break into the corrugated-iron hangar. 'Let's look at the last few, and then we can get going.'

They traipsed over to the two-storey building with metal grilles over all the windows. Just approaching it made Twenty-Two shiver. It looked like nothing good had ever happened within its walls. The wind picked up, and Twenty-Two closed her eyelids to the fine dust that wanted to settle in her eyes, up her nose and down in her lungs. She tried to push away the images of skeletons disintegrating over the years, slowly piling up outside the building's doors. She didn't want to breathe in the dead and have them inside her.

She followed Septa, peering into the grimy windows and trying some of the doors whose rusting handles felt rough in her grip.

The wind picked up and moaned as it flew through the narrow cavities of the buildings.

'It's empty,' Septa said.

From the corner of her eye, Twenty-Two thought she saw a fleeting movement at the window above. She spun around and pointed to where it had been, but there was nothing now.

'Did you see something?' Max asked.

'I think so. I'm not sure,' Twenty-Two responded.

'We should go inside. I think I can break down this side door.'

'No,' Septa snapped. Her skin had paled and beads of sweat were gathering along her hairline. 'It's my mission, I'm leading it, and I want to return to Uracil.'

'But there might be someone in there,' Max retorted.

'Are you questioning an order from a team leader? I'd have to report that back to Maya.' She turned to Twenty-Two. 'I'll report both of you, and it won't look too good for your first mission. Now can we just go?'

Twenty-Two glared at Septa. Being in the Infiltration Department was the last thing securing her place in Uracil, and she couldn't afford to lose it. She stared up at the window where she thought she had seen movement. Why would someone decide to live in this fallen city of bone dust and gravel? Perhaps freedom came with this particular price that some were willing to pay.

She zoned out as the other two continued to argue about whether they should return to Uracil or investigate the building in front of them. It had become a direct threat to Septa's authority now, and Twenty-Two knew she would never back down. Seeing the lone movement up in the window of the building made her think of the other Neanderthals and where they were. Were they mistreated like she had been, or were they still alive and waiting?

Without warning, Septa ran around the corner of the building. Retching noises could be heard, and Twenty-Two cocked her eyebrow towards Max, now understanding why Septa had been desperate to leave. It was not uncommon for one of them to become sick while travelling because of the poor quality of their provisions.

She turned to Max. 'I'm sorry, but I think we should go. Septa is sick and there are more important things in this world at the moment.'

The journey back to Uracil took almost two weeks, and they arrived exhausted in the early evening after not stopping to rest all day. Still with their backpacks on, they made their way towards the unmistakable sounds of a meeting. Slipping into the last row, Twenty-Two listened as Maya spoke. Once Maya was finished, Twenty-Two would then report in and leave for her next mission.

'So, on to the main news of the day,' Maya said, smiling. 'None of the returned teams has managed to locate Uracil's lost residents so far. But we have sent for those residents who stayed in the caves close to Uracil. There are also still a couple of teams out looking for the other residents, and we believe they should be back any day now. Hopefully, with some good news.'

Everyone began talking at once. Twenty-Two scrunched her eyes at the thought of Ezra being back with them soon.

'They should all be with us shortly, so we need to finish our preparations to accommodate them immediately.'

'What if they haven't found the missing residents?' someone shouted from the back.

'Then, after a few days' rest, we shall send the teams out again. And again. Until we find the people who belong with us!'

There was a cheer from the crowd. When the spontaneous applause died down, Genevieve stood up from the felled log she had been sitting on and made her way to Maya.

'I've asked that Genevieve say a few words,' Maya continued. 'From her time living in Adenine, she has learnt what the Potiors are planning next, and I think it's something we all need to hear.'

Genevieve clasped her hands in front of her and smiled around at her audience.

Twenty-Two stared at the woman who couldn't bear to be near her. It was strange to know that someone disliked her so much that arrangements had been made to keep them apart. Yes, back in Cytosine, Twenty-Two had been neglected, teased and starved, but that had been out of petty maliciousness. Genevieve was different. She earnestly believed that Twenty-Two had wronged her. And there was nothing Twenty-Two could think of that would change her mind. Genevieve had been presented with the facts of the matter and had chosen to ignore them.

Did this make them enemies? Twenty-Two had read of such things in Pre-Pandemic books but wasn't sure that she would want to classify this woman as such. She thought there was still hope for reconciliation if she waited long enough. She comforted herself that this was one thing she was skilled at – the passage of time could easily be ignored.

'Thank you, Maya,' Genevieve said, clasping her friend's shoulder. 'The Potiors' interests have moved on in recent years. And, therefore, so must we. They have new projects, and we must keep abreast of what they are doing. While working for the Department of Disclosure in Adenine, I was privy to some alarming changes.'

Genevieve paused and slid her gaze to stare directly at Twenty-Two.

'At one time, the Potiors were obsessed with reversing the order of extinction as a way of highlighting the supposed "wrongs" of the Sapiens. However, this came to a sticking point with the Neanderthals. They have let me know, in no uncertain terms, that the Neanderthals have proved to be a *disappointing* outcome, and they have decided to channel their resources into something quite different. Apparently, the catalyst for these changes was the death of a Neanderthal during childbirth and the subsequent escape of another. They have now abandoned the project, for one reason or another, and moved on to other things.'

Twenty-Two felt sick. Abandoned the Neanderthal Project? Abandoned her brothers and sisters? She had hoped it was just Cytosine's museum director who had done this. She hadn't realised that it was now a wider policy.

She noticed that those around her, apart from Max, were shifting uncomfortably. A few glanced back at her. She searched the clearing for Kit, whom she drew strength from, but he was not there. He would never miss a public meeting like this, and she concluded that he must still be out on his assigned mission. She tried not to let her shoulders sag when she realised she would have to face this alone.

Genevieve's voice pulled Twenty-Two back into the present.

'... we don't know how long it will be until the Potiors announce this new supposed "species" of human, but we know that it won't be long. Genetically altering the Sapien offspring in this way as a widespread policy is something that we always feared.' She glanced over at Maya before continuing. 'In my opinion, we must take this opportunity of relative quiet to ensure the safety of Uracil.'

This was the exact opposite of what Twenty-Two thought they should be doing. They had tried hiding from the Potiors before, and it hadn't worked.

Genevieve's voice grew in strength. 'We should lock down Uracil's borders. No one in or out once the other residents from the north return to us.'

Twenty-Two stared up at Genevieve. Locking down Uracil would restrict everyone's movement and make Uracil isolated.

Maya looked as though she was about to speak, but Genevieve placated her by placing a hand on her shoulder.

'And we should remain this way for several years to come. We need to make sure we are safe.'

The previously mumbled agreements from the crowd grew louder. Genevieve was clearly masterful at galvanising people to adopt her viewpoint.

Twenty-Two jumped to her feet and walked away from the group, back to her belongings, which she kept next to Kit's.

From behind, she could hear Genevieve's soaring voice. 'We need to protect our future generations, our children. And the only way we can do that is by securing the safety of Uracil. Never again can we have a situation where we open ourselves up to attack! *For Uracil!*'

Twenty-Two winced as the enthusiastic shouts of '*For Uracil!*' rang out from the clearing.

Why should she care about Uracil when they did not care about the Neanderthals? They were deserting them just as the Potiors had done. She wished Kit were with her, but she knew that wishing wouldn't change anything. Let Uracil fall – she had to act.

She began to sort through her belongings, swapping her dirty clothes for clean ones and gathering food supplies.

It was only when the footsteps were a few paces behind her that she heard another person's approach.

'Going somewhere, missy?'

Twenty-Two swung around to face the owner of the voice.

She stared at Raynor, the last person she'd expected to see.

'I don't think I am welcome here,' Twenty-Two signed.

Raynor followed the movement of Twenty-Two's hands. 'I think I got most of that.'

Twenty-Two was surprised. 'Where did you learn sign language?'

'That boy, Nathan, began to teach me back in the cave. I would practise with him for hours every day as there was little else to do while we waited for the snows to pass.' She stared down at Twenty-Two's half-packed bag. 'So, where will you be heading?'

Twenty-Two decided that she would stick with the truth. 'I'm going to Guanine to rescue Twenty-Four and the other Neanderthals there. And then I'm going to Adenine to get the last ones.'

The silence that greeted her made Twenty-Two uncomfortable. Perhaps she had made a mistake in confiding in Raynor.

'Are you going to stop me? Or tell the others?' Twenty-Two signed.

She had already decided that she could outrun the older woman if it came to it. Time had not been kind to Raynor; she had broadened with age and didn't look like she had taken care of herself for years.

'I'm going to do better than that,' Raynor said, her eyes creasing at the corners. 'I'm going to come with you.'

CHAPTER 10

Elise

'It is out of the question,' the old woman with the clear grey eyes said from her pillow kingdom.

'But, Minerva, think what will happen if we do not allow them onto our island,' Arlo responded, his legs crossed and back straight, a position he had not moved from for the past hour.

Elise stood behind him, watching the Elders' reaction as Arlo pleaded their case. It had only been a matter of hours since she'd found the lost residents, but time had fractured for her. Sometimes her discovery was fresh and raw, as though it were only seconds ago. At other times it was as if the news had cloaked her in grief for months.

'It does not have anything to do with us,' said an older man, whose chin had recently drooped with sleep – she'd had to hold herself back from shaking him awake. 'And if the Potiors left them there, it is not for us to interfere. What if they turned their sights on us? We are a peaceful community, not one built for war.' He raised his gaze to Elise in her dark clothing. 'Not that being built for war has helped them much.'

Elise tried not to clench her fists. In her mind, she was upending their tent, raging at their selfishness and desire for self-preservation above everything else. Her grief was an open wound that she could not even bear to look at, but it fuelled her, drove her on.

The older woman stared up at Elise. 'You are very quiet for a change. Do you not have anything to say?'

Elise stared down at her, not allowing even a glimpse of her thoughts to show. 'I am quiet because I have just found out that my mother died on that island.' The older woman flinched, and Elise knew she had her attention. If she couldn't shake them with her actions, she would upend them with her words. 'Uracil was, and is, a peaceful community that also lived quietly, until we were betrayed to the Potiors. In times like these, we all need allies, and Uracil promises to be yours whenever we are needed.'

The older woman's disquiet was brief. 'If you believe that the Potiors didn't know of such a large community, especially on their own island, then I have overestimated you.' She leant in farther. '*Nothing* passes by them. They will have known of Uracil for years, if not from the very beginning. You must have done something to provoke them. Did you change something about the way you were living in recent times?'

Elise kept her face still as the woman spoke, but her heart raced at the words. Was it possible that the Potiors had known about Uracil all along? The change of policy fitted too. It was the change that Elise had pushed for, for years, to turn their attention outwards.

'With the greatest respect,' Elise began, 'the minutes and hours are ticking by, and my people are still starving on an island just north of here. Hundreds of lives are in your hands. So please could you reconsider your answer.'

'No,' the grey-eyed woman said. 'Our answer is no. We will not put our lives at risk for the foolish ones from Uracil who believe everything they are told.'

Elise blinked as she scrambled for what to do next. None of the residents was strong enough to walk back to Uracil, even if they lasted the weeks it would take to ferry them off the island with only a single boat. How many would die while in her care?

Arlo uncrossed his legs and stood. 'Then I shall have to leave. I thought Synthium stood for peace and prosperity without harming our neighbours. I have taken a different path to protect you all. I do not get to enjoy the leisure of our community. But I was willing to forgo that as I thought the home you had created was something worth protecting. But to leave all those people to die? I cannot have any part in it.'

'Arlo, no!' the old woman said, a slight tremor in her hand as she reached for him. 'You cannot leave us. I forbid it!'

Arlo crouched down in front of her and took her hand between his. 'You cannot forbid what is outside of your control. No one here can stop me from leaving. But to save those lives is within your power. Exercise it wisely.'

The older woman stared up at him. 'Go. Bring those people to us. Our reserves will support them for two months, but no more. But you must return and never talk of leaving again. If it brings the Potiors to our shores, then you must be here to defend us.'

Arlo lightly held the aged hand in his own. 'For your actions, I am grateful.'

*

Over the following week, they worked tirelessly to ship all Uracil's residents to Synthium, who had agreed to lend what boats they could spare. From dawn until dusk Elise helped supervise the transport of her people to safety. Each hand she held as they clambered over a boat's hull, each person she lifted if they were too weak to stand, enforced her decision not to let this atrocity go unpunished. During that time, Elise had shut down all thoughts of the past. What fed and fuelled her was planning her revenge and how she would bring it to the Potiors' door. She fantasised about it and often found her hands straying to the knives strapped across her chest.

It was late afternoon when Elise stood on the beach where they had first landed on Synthium. Within an hour, she would be leaving the island, crossing the sea once more, but this time to the mainland. The sun was bright and, for once, the wind had dropped to a gentle breeze. She had positioned herself so that she was facing the island of graves; each one now held a flower she had placed upon it.

The sound of spraying sand behind her brought her attention to the approach of Michael and Arlo.

'I just wanted to come and see you off,' Michael said. 'If you and Kit hadn't found us ...'

Elise dropped her head. What she and Kit had done wasn't enough. There were still hundreds who had died.

'I had a lot of respect for your mum,' Michael continued, as if reading her thoughts. 'I want you to know that she held us together in an impossible situation, all the time knowing that she had lost your dad. She helped me when I was much younger as well, back in Thymine.'

At the mention of her mum and dad, Elise had to force herself to remain looking at him. 'She knew Dad had died?'

'Yes, she was there when it happened, before we were herded onto the airplanes.'

Elise's grief was only a week old and consequently untested. The only way she had found of coping was to force all thoughts of it away. She quickly changed the subject.

'Mum told me about what happened to your mum and siblings back in Thymine.' She held his gaze. 'I was sorry to hear about it. We've all lost so many of the people we love over the years.'

'My loss was a long time ago,' Michael responded. 'It never leaves you, but it does settle into a size you can carry. Your mum was a good woman. Back in Thymine, she was one of the ones who gave me a ticket for the antibiotics that saved my life when I was fourteen. She had nothing to spare, but she still passed it on.' Michael squinted in the bright sunlight. 'And then I found Uracil.'

'How did you find Uracil?' Elise asked, trying to steer the conversation away from her parents.

Michael stared out to sea. 'I'd heard talk in Thymine about a base to the north, a fairy tale really. But with nowhere else to go, it was my only option. I walked north, and then I walked north some more until I saw people tending what I later realised were crops. I didn't know whether they were friendly or not, so I hid and watched them for days. Every morning, as soon as the sun rose, I'd pick everything I could see for them and lay it out in a line, there for them to collect – a fourteen-year-old's attempt at a peace offering. I did that for a couple of weeks. It wasn't until I actually got up the nerve to speak to one of them that I realised I'd been scaring the life out of everyone the entire time. Most of Uracil had been put into lockdown.' He smiled at the memory. 'They thought it was the Protection Department playing games with them.'

Elise found herself smiling for the first time in days at the thought of the residents' reaction to the fruit and vegetables laid out for them.

'Michael,' she asked, her features suddenly still. 'Do you think there's any chance that the Potiors knew about Uracil for years before the bombing?'

Michael opened his mouth to respond and then closed it quickly. 'No. It couldn't be. We were so careful.'

Elise watched his reaction closely. His confusion at the possibility seemed genuine.

'Anyway,' Michael said wearily. 'I should be getting back to the others now.'

He pulled her into an embrace, and she put her arms around him. She felt his shoulder blades jut through the cloth of his shirt.

Elise watched as he picked his way across the beach to the dunes leading into the island's centre. Perhaps his belief in Uracil's concealment was honestly held.

'I thought I would come and say goodbye as well,' Arlo said.

He had remained silent and still during her conversation with Michael.

Elise stared up at him, and he steadily returned her gaze.

'I don't know how to thank you for everything you've done for us,' she said.

'There is no need. It is only what I should have done.'

'Will you look after them until I can send others to help bring them back?'

Arlo frowned. 'Will you not be coming back yourself?'

Elise held her hand to her face to shield it from the sun. 'I don't think so. There are other things I have to do.'

He gently laid his hand on her arm. 'This really is goodbye then.'

Over Arlo's shoulder, Elise could see Kit striding down a sandbank with Tilla's arm looped through his. Gone was Tilla's long crimson skirt, torn in places and dirty beyond repair; in its place were the travelling clothes that Elise had loaned her.

'Are you sure you can do this?' Elise shouted up to Tilla, frowning at her friend.

Tilla had insisted that she would accompany them back to Uracil. She had fared better than most of the residents, but she was a shadow of the joyous, flitting woman she used to be.

'I am coming with you whether you let me or not,' Tilla shouted back. 'So, either you walk with me at your side, or you walk with me three paces behind you. It's your choice.'

Elise shrugged and smiled up at Arlo, who was watching her intently.

'I'm sorry,' she said. 'Were you saying something?'

He gave her a half-smile that she couldn't help but return. 'Nothing that you were ready to hear.'

The rain battered down on them from every side. At the start of the storm, the forest canopy had tried to shield them, but after only a few minutes, it had had to part under the storm's force. Wet to her bones, Elise had not been able to sleep and was waiting for first light so they could continue the second leg of their journey.

As she pulled her hood over her face, she checked on Tilla, curled up with Elise's waterproof jacket draped over her.

Night was the hardest time to keep the thoughts of her mother from coming to her. Elise found herself imagining her last hours, how it must have felt to grow weaker each day, not knowing if she would see her family again. Had anyone been holding her hand when she'd finally slipped away?

Elise knew that when she arrived in Uracil, she would have to tell countless others that they had also lost loved ones, and this kept her awake at night. With a few words, she would share her grief, but never lighten it.

When the sun rose, the rain passed with it. Stretching her legs, Elise was glad that Kit was already packed and ready to leave.

He dug around in his pocket and pulled something out. 'Here, I made this for you.'

Elise took the necklace from him and held it in her hands. It was made from small shells, each with a tiny hole bored into it so cord could be threaded through. As with everything Kit made, it had been crafted with care. Each of the holes was at the same height, the shells chosen for their similar sizes.

'It's beautiful, Kit. But when did you get the time to make it?'

Elise tried on the necklace. It sat high up, around the base of her neck.

'I made it in the mornings before you woke up. It is to remember our ancestors by, both the recent ones and those that stretch back to the dawn of our time.'

As he spoke, Kit pulled down his shirt to show he had a similar necklace, although it was slightly longer.

'It is also to say thank you,' Kit continued. 'For taking a risk and helping me escape the museum. I never properly thanked you for helping me. And I should have done.'

Elise touched her hand to the necklace and thought of those who had gone before her.

'Not everyone would have done what you did,' Kit signed, when she did not respond. 'In fact, I think very few would have taken that risk. You changed the course of my life, and the lives of so many of my people. Firstly, by being brave enough to leave your family and become my Companion. And secondly, by realising that being a Companion wasn't enough, and what I really needed was a friend.'

Elise turned away, unsure what to say. She couldn't accept his kind words because a thought nagged at her. How many other lives had she changed by pushing to bring the Potiors down? Had she tipped the scales away from her, cancelled out all the good she had previously done?

He stared at her. 'Do not blame yourself. I did not make this so that you could carry your losses. Instead, I want you to remember how many people you can help if you only take the chance to do so and do not hide away.'

CHAPTER 11

Caitlyn

It was midnight, two weeks after her altercation with Professor Gudd, when a national release silently downloaded onto Caitlyn's family screen. She was asleep at the time, touching on hidden possibilities in her dreams, and it wasn't until she woke at six the next morning that she saw the flashing light indicating that there was something new to watch. Padding across to the other side of the bedroom, she sucked in her breath at the cold. Grabbing the screen, she took it back to the warmth of the bed that she shared with her middle sister, Heather.

Watching the opening scenes, Caitlyn guessed that the release had been planned for a long time. The production quality was much higher than the usual local releases updating the residents on rations increasing or decreasing, shift changes, and the seasonal adjustment to the opening hours of the Emporium. This latest release was a story in itself with a selection of hovering shots of Guanine.

The lilting voice of the presenter wove its way over the images. 'A change is coming for every base in Zone 3 …'

Caitlyn knew that the same release would be watched at the other three bases, just with differing opening shots. She imagined another young woman in a different base, tucked up in her bed for warmth, watching a near-identical release. It comforted her.

Caitlyn tried not to wake her sister as she shifted on the wooden crates that formed the base of their bed. Images kept rolling of the Sapiens, their workplaces in Guanine, shots of the recycling centre ...

'And that is where it comes down to you,' the faceless presenter continued in reassuring tones. 'We believe that a change is needed to meet the future head-on. After much careful consideration, we have concluded that some Sapiens may deserve the chance of genetic modifications for their future children. This system, this science we hold in our hands, has to be expanded and utilised.'

Caitlyn sat up. They were changing the rules. For the first time in her nineteen years, she felt that something momentous was happening. She was on the cusp of something life-changing and would always remember this moment, down to the colour of her socks when the news broke.

'We have more announcements to come. But for the moment, please know that you will be the first to be informed once we have finalised our decision. A further announcement is scheduled in exactly one week.'

That morning at work, the canteen was abuzz with news of the change to the genetic modification system. Caitlyn, her parents, Gran and even Pops had no living memory of anything as significant as this, of any chance beyond the monthly lottery to change their circumstances. It had simply never been an option.

The Medius had always been able to select three genetic modifications, depending on how many tickets they had saved, and these were tiered according to importance. Caitlyn had heard rumours that the Potiors had ten modifications and, as everyone knew, the Sapiens had none. This was what made them a separate species. This was what defined them. Apart from the monthly lottery, the Sapiens had never dreamt of having the power to select traits for their children.

Caitlyn ate her breakfast at a busy table filled with Sapiens talking loudly about what genes they would select for their children. Height, strength, intelligence, metabolism, hearing, eyesight and stamina were all thrown around loudly for everyone to hear.

Caitlyn didn't join in the discussion. She looked around and caught the eye of one of the canteen workers, who blushed and quickly looked away. Caitlyn glanced at the other tables in the canteen where the Medius were sitting separately from them. They had their heads low and were talking amongst themselves. The odd one would glare over at the Sapiens when another modification was shouted out.

The status quo had been altered, and with that came hope for the Sapiens and disquiet for the Medius. There was usually an uneasy truce between the two, and the gulf was widening. She could see that trouble was coming.

A week later, Caitlyn, like every other inhabitant of the Lower Ring, stayed up with the rest of her family until midnight, waiting for the next release. Her two youngest siblings, determined to stake their claim in this historical event, had fallen asleep on their parents' laps by ten. Pops had also dozed off in his chair in the corner, and the family spoke quietly so as not to wake them.

Her parents were mild, gentle people. They had been drawn together by a young love that had lasted over twenty years. As Caitlyn sat watching her parents cradle their youngest, her mum stroking her brother's hair, she felt a burst of love for them. Their excitement was palpable. All they had ever wanted was the best for their children. And this announcement meant their children would have more choices, and their grandchildren could be anything they wanted.

As the minutes slowly ticked by, Caitlyn found herself checking the family screen every thirty seconds in the hope that the announcement had been released early. Everyone fell silent as the final two minutes before midnight crept by. Never had time seemed to move so slowly. Caitlyn crossed to the other side of the living room, holding the screen out in front of her, careful not to trip, and sat between her parents. Heather leant in closer as they all peered at the screen's black surface.

Finally, a flashing light notified them that there was something to watch. In her haste, Caitlyn tapped the wrong button. Sighing, Heather snatched the screen from her hands and smoothly navigated to the latest release.

Soaring music played over the black screen before an aerial shot of Guanine taken by a drone camera panned out in front of their eyes: lofty peaks tipped with snow, fog hugging the tree-lined base of the twin mountains.

The same presenter's voice broke over the crescendo of the stirring strings. 'Thank you for your patience. As we explained last week, a change is needed. There is much more work to be done before we can erase the wrongs of the Sapiens. Everything we do is based on this one core fact. It is what guides us at all times.'

Caitlyn felt uneasy. *The wrongs of the Sapiens.* Would she ever escape that phrase?

'Genetic modification is the cornerstone of an advanced society, and to this end a new lottery will be put in place.'

Gran leant in closer, and Heather quickly turned the sound higher. The youngest two stirred in their parents' laps but did not fully wake.

'Starting from the first day of the next calendar year, half of all future Sapien pregnancies will be modified.'

Caitlyn's dad gasped, and she turned to him. Tears were forming in his eyes. She couldn't remember the last time she had seen him cry, let alone in happiness.

The presenter paused. A second shot of workers in the libraries and the archiving basements of the universities flitted across the screen.

'It's finally over,' her mum whispered. 'We're being allowed to move on.'

'Shhh ...' whispered Gran. 'She hasn't finished yet.'

'The modifications will consist of a new selection, separate from the ones for the Medius. There will still be a distinction between species. But it is time that a new species is formed.'

Caitlyn frowned.

The music grew louder, as did the presenter's voice. 'Now is the time to embrace change! Seize opportunity! And welcome the new species, Homo vitalis, into our world!'

The music cut out, and there was silence in the room.

It was Gran who spoke first. 'Don't get too excited. We need to see the list first. Then we'll know what this is about.'

*

Reassuring releases continued to drop onto Guanine's screens over the coming weeks, which buoyed most of the Sapiens' spirits. Caitlyn did not share the general optimism. Her gran's words had stayed with her. Where were the details?

She felt alone in her lack of enthusiasm, even amongst her family. She had become an outsider once she'd begun working at the university and had to hide what she learnt from the other Sapiens. They were always quick to tell her if she was 'acting like a Medius'. Her reaction to the screen release compounded her isolation. Her gran had remained tight-lipped on the subject and wouldn't discuss her thoughts even when Caitlyn pleaded, but her parents had been swept up in the younger children's games of becoming mighty warriors or quick-thinking professors. Caitlyn knew that the family needed to have aspirations, but she wondered what the long-term price would be.

Late to leave the university once again at the end of a long day, Caitlyn passed a woman standing by one of the gates. The gardens that circled the university, with their blossoming pear trees, were deserted apart from this one woman with her woolly hat pulled low over her forehead. Caitlyn had seen her there before and always assumed she was just waiting for someone. But that evening, the woman caught her attention as it was so late, and Caitlyn was sure she was the last to leave.

As she took the left stairway down to the lower rings of the mountain, she heard footsteps behind her on the deserted pathway. The heavy evening fog had made it difficult to see the woman's face when she had passed her, but the sound of these footsteps didn't slow or turn off towards any of the other stairways.

Caitlyn stopped dead in her tracks and swivelled around. 'Why are you following me?'

The woman, who sounded younger than Caitlyn, stammered out her words from afar. 'I'm not ... not ... following you.'

Caitlyn peered into the mist, unable to see more than an outline.

'You are. I've seen you hanging around the gates before,' she said accusingly.

'No, not following you,' the soft voice came back, before the woman darted off down one of the side stairways.

Caitlyn watched the figure disappear. A split-second decision and she was following the woman – her temper had flared and she wanted to know more about her. Caitlyn would turn the tables on her and find out where she lived.

Down the steps the two women went, coiling around the outside of the mountain, Caitlyn making sure that she slipped silently through the night. The mist had clung to the top of the mountain, refusing to descend with them, and Caitlyn had to be more careful that she wasn't seen when she got to the lower rings. The cold stung her face, and she pulled her coat tighter around her. With each step, she became more confident. No one would chase her through Guanine and make her cower. Instead, she would take control of the situation.

Up ahead, the woman stumbled across the bridge, both hands clinging to the side ropes to prevent a fall. Caitlyn hung back in the shadows until the woman had crossed. Once she had turned the corner of the twinned mountain, Caitlyn ran across the swinging rope bridge, her step quick and light.

When she got to the other side, she turned the same corner and saw the figure dart into a distant entranceway. Caitlyn counted along the openings; it was the eighth one along. She crept forwards, familiar sounds coming from within the Sapien homes. Arriving at the edge of the eighth dwelling, she scanned the deserted stone steps bolted into the sides of the mountain. The wind picked up, and she touched her hand to the rope boundary between her and the foothills below. No one was coming in either direction. She pressed her ear against the door.

The woman's faint voice came from inside. 'It's not my fault. It just didn't go very well this time.'

'We'll have to try another way,' an older woman responded.

A gruff man spoke next. 'Perhaps I'll try.'

Caitlyn re-checked the walkway – still empty – then pressed her ear back against the door.

'You?' the older woman snorted. 'You'd scare her off before we even had a chance to explain what we need.'

'How about I try?' a younger man said.

There was a pause. 'And how do you think you'd go about doing that?'

'Like ... this!' the young man said dramatically.

The door was flung open from the inside and Caitlyn toppled into the room. She only just managed to stop herself from falling, and the young man grabbed onto her arm to steady her. Despite his lean figure, his grip was strong.

Snatching her arm from him, she spun to leave, but he had already closed the door behind her, barring the way.

'Don't be frightened,' he said, smiling at her. His silky, dark hair shone in the bright electric light. 'You can leave as soon as you've heard us out.'

Caitlyn stared up at him, her heart still drumming in her chest. 'What do you want? Why were you following me?'

'Well, we wanted to speak to you in private. But it seems you have come to us,' the man said.

He had the straightest, whitest teeth she had ever seen on a Sapien, and she began to wonder if he was a Medius. He certainly talked like one.

'What's your name? What do you want?' she asked, backing away towards the wall.

The residence was sparsely furnished with only a sleeping crate and a small table, so Caitlyn was able put some distance between herself and the others. They all stared at her but didn't approach. They were each clasping a steaming mug of tea. They didn't seem that threatening, but she couldn't be sure – she'd never been followed or ambushed before. She didn't believe the type of people to do those sorts of things would have a tea cosy with an image of a hamster knitted into it.

Caitlyn turned to the older woman, who appeared to be in charge. She was wearing mittens with the fingers cut off and a woolly hat that was slipping off her head.

'Do you normally go following people around late at night?' Caitlyn asked.

'Not unless it's necessary,' the woman responded. 'Tiro is right. We didn't want to alarm you.'

She nodded to the man who had opened the door on Caitlyn. His two-syllable name meant that he was a Sapien after all.

'We've been watching you for a while,' the older man said. Caitlyn found his bushy white eyebrows distracting as they had a life of their own when he spoke. 'You don't seem as enthused about the recent announcements as the others.'

Caitlyn's heart began to beat faster. He seemed an unlikely choice for the Protection Department. But then, what did she know?

'If you'd watched me harder, you would've seen that I don't get excited about much. It's not my way,' she responded, hoping her explanation would be believed.

The woman who had followed Caitlyn took a step closer. Caitlyn recognised her from somewhere but couldn't quite place her. The thought nagged as she scrambled to remember where she had seen her before. It was difficult to see her clearly as she was still wearing a thick bobble hat pulled down to her eyelids, and her head was bent low. From what Caitlyn could see, this woman had one of the most nondescript faces she'd come across – she was mousy personified.

'We're clearly Sapiens,' the younger woman said. 'We're not from the Protection Department. You don't need to worry about that.'

Caitlyn decided not to respond. Instead, she took the time to assess her ambushers in turn. They each looked tired, their shoulders hunched. The younger man, Tiro, was the only one with any real life force to him.

'We are a group of inquisitive scholars,' Tiro began, 'who call ourselves the Excluded Erudites. We happen to have been born Sapien and therefore don't have the access we require to develop our studies.'

He moved around Caitlyn and flung his arm over the older man. 'This is Stephen. He has a particular interest in taxonomy and all offshoots of that particular discipline. He works at one of the council offices as a cleaner.'

The older man shrugged off Tiro's arm and stepped around him.

'Sylvie,' Tiro continued, 'is our founding member and resident chemist. She likes to make things go "boom". However, she was a bit, umm ... uncensored in her youth and was shipped off to the recycling centre.'

'I wasn't "uncensored",' Sylvie said, still clasping her mug. 'That isn't even a word. I was pissed off with all of this. And I didn't have the sense to hide it.'

'That is what happens when the sense is removed from censored,' Tiro continued.

'Sylvie is interested in theoretical chemistry,' the younger woman added hastily. 'She doesn't have access to a lab or actually blow anything up.'

Tiro nodded. 'And what a pity that is. Anyway, over here is Alice.' He nodded to the younger woman who was half bobble hat. 'She is drawn to all things to do with genetics. She works in the canteen at the university, which is where you first caught her eye.'

Caitlyn stared at the woman's dipped nose and chin. That was where she had seen her, the canteen. It had been difficult to place her without the hairnet.

'And you?' Caitlyn asked.

'Well, I am Tiro. As Sylvie said before.'

'And your particular interests?'

'I enjoy learning about palaeoanthropology. A vast subject, as I'm sure you know, and one that keeps me fully occupied outside my hours working as a landscape gardener.'

'Pfff,' Sylvie said. 'Closest he gets to landscape gardening is weeding. He's an outdoor odd-job man for the council offices.'

Tiro's eyes glistened. 'One can but dream, Sylvie. One can but dream ...'

Despite her annoyance, Caitlyn found herself smiling. 'So, how do I fit into all of this? Have you opened up your membership to become a secret Sapien scholar? Or is there something more specific that you want my help with?'

'We need access to some more materials,' Tiro explained. 'But you have probably already guessed that. You are the perfect candidate.'

'No,' Caitlyn said firmly. 'I am not. I could lose my job, or worse.'

'We understand the risk you would be taking,' Sylvie responded. 'And that's why we'd pay. We'd give you some spare tickets we have. We all live quiet lives and save what we can.'

'We only want to read what they've written,' Alice said, while Caitlyn strained to hear her. 'We don't want to steal it; we just want to see what they are researching and form our own theories. Discuss them amongst ourselves. We won't share it with anyone else.'

'Yes,' Sylvie said. 'Just copy it onto your screen; let us read it and take brief notes. Then you can delete it. That's all you have to do.'

'How many tickets are we talking about?' Caitlyn asked casually, while her brain whirred, working out how many she would need for Gran's cataract operation.

Sylvie handed over her screen. 'This many.'

Caitlyn's eyes widened as she thought of how quickly she could save them for her grandmother and turn them into Medi-stamps.

'How do I know this isn't a set-up?' she asked. 'And that you're not Midder-loving Saps who like to catch other Sapiens out? How do I know you won't go straight to the Protection Department with this?'

'Because of these,' Sylvie said, walking over to the crates that formed the base of her bed.

She lifted them up and her sleeping roll slid to the floor. Caitlyn stared at the ordinary crates, not sure what she was supposed to be looking at. Sylvie tapped the panel, which made a hollow noise. She carried on tapping until it responded with a dull thud. She pushed down hard on the board and it sprang open, revealing something that Caitlyn hadn't even seen at the university – Pre-Pandemic books.

'Where did you get those?' Caitlyn stammered.

'We have our ways,' was Sylvie's simple response. 'You know the risk that comes with hiding these supposed "Infactualities". It would be expulsion before we could even open our mouths to protest.' She paused. 'Now do you believe that we just want information and won't turn you over to the Protection Department?'

Caitlyn did. A Midder-lover would never have such items. It suggested that Pre-Pandemic Sapiens had possessed knowledge that was worth learning. It went against everything that the Reparations stood for.

'And you won't publish it anywhere or make copies?' she asked.

She was slightly in awe of the steps these people would take just to satisfy their intellectual cravings. She had never met Sapiens who took such risks.

'We promise,' Alice said, barely raising her head. 'We just want access to the academics' findings. We want to learn, and because we're Sapiens, it isn't permitted.'

Caitlyn thought for a moment. Why shouldn't they have the same access to material as she did? The only thing that separated her from them was their employment. Didn't they have as much right to read what she worked on?

Copying the university's research papers wasn't something she was particularly comfortable with, but not because she thought it was morally wrong. She had a small part in their production, after all. Instead, it was because she feared getting caught. But she was also reassured by the fact that Alice worked in the canteen at the university. She, and the rest of the group, had just as much to lose as Caitlyn did. They would not turn on her. Whether she could get the papers out without getting caught was the real issue.

It was time for Caitlyn to burn a little brighter.

'I want half the tickets up front and the other half on delivery. Agreed?' she finally said.

Tiro broke into a big grin. 'Agreed.'

Caitlyn shook his hand. 'So, what is it that you want?'

CHAPTER 12

Elise

When Elise arrived in the new Uracil, she handed over the list of the living and the dead. One by one, the residents lined up to confirm if those they loved were still alive on the island to the west or if they were now with the stars.

Turning from them, Elise spotted a huddled group of people who had recently arrived – the residents of the caves, with whom she had shared the winter months. Rushing towards them, she sought only one face. Nathan. She spotted his tall frame and, as if sensing her presence, he turned. For once, Elise did not still her features, and a message passed between them. Without waiting for her, he fled into the surrounding forest. She hesitated but did not follow.

Elise was still waiting for his return when Genevieve approached her, worry etched across her features.

'Is it as bad as they say?' Genevieve asked, her eyes searching Elise's face.

Elise nodded. 'Hundreds died on the island.'

Without warning, Genevieve burst into tears, and Elise found herself pulling the older woman into her embrace. The two women held each other for a few minutes before Genevieve drew back.

'I honestly didn't think it could get any worse after I found out my daughter was killed,' Genevieve said. 'But I was very wrong. Stars, look at me! Crying like a small child who hasn't experienced suffering before.'

Elise touched her sleeve. 'Everyone will feel our losses. There will be many tears tonight.'

Genevieve looked at Elise with sadness in her eyes. 'Some of us might have forfeited the right to cry.'

Before Elise could ask her what she meant, Genevieve turned and headed for her tent.

An hour later, Nathan returned to Elise and quickly signed that he did not want to talk about it. She had prepared for this moment but had not anticipated this request. What could she do other than follow his lead? She sat next to him and they quietly watched the queue of people waiting to check the names on Elise's list.

'I'm so sorry about Mum,' she eventually signed to him.

She reached for Nathan's hand and held it tightly while they waited for their tea to boil. She had not left his side since he had emerged back into the clearing. She had noticed this at all the hearths – family, friends, even strangers, with their arms around shoulders and hands on knees. Always united by touch, as if at any moment they could also be torn from each other. It was a collective, communal grief. And in only a day, they would be separated again. Tomorrow, a party would return to Synthium to bring back whoever was strong enough to make the journey.

Nathan shrugged and looked away from her. She knew he was crying but sensed that he didn't want her to draw attention to it. Elise hadn't cried since she had left Synthium; she had tried to draw a line between what had happened on the island and the present. She had to be strong for Nathan; he was all that mattered now. He was all she had left.

With his head turned from her, Elise took the time to study her brother, who seemed to have grown half a foot in the three months they had been apart. He was taller than her now. But it wasn't just his height that had changed. His time in the cave as the oldest of the children had pushed him more towards adulthood. She had watched with pride over the winter months while he had cared for the others, helped Ezra teach their lessons and settled their arguments. In turn, they had looked up to him. He wasn't quite old enough to be unapproachable but still firmly held on to the gravitas of being more muscular and a better fighter than many of Uracil's adults.

'What can I do to help you?' she signed, when he finally turned back to her, his eyes red but free from tears. 'I don't know how to make it bearable.'

Nathan rubbed his face. 'I don't want you to start trying to be my mum and dad again like you did back in the cave. They're gone, and you can't replace them.'

Elise nodded.

'I want to do something practical to help, go on a mission with you.' Elise was about to interrupt when the glare he gave her told her to let him finish. 'Back when we lived in Thymine, we used to talk about visiting the other bases all the time. Why can't I do that with you?'

'It's too dangerous.'

His face reddened. 'Do you not remember what it was like at my age, when you were just waiting for your life to *start*?'

'Of course I do. It was agony being told I was too young, weak and inexperienced.'

'Then why are you doing it to me?'

Elise felt her frustration surge. 'Because it's not a *game*, Nathan. This is it. This is the only life we get, and I want to make sure that yours is as long as I can make it. Let me do the fighting for you.'

Nathan jumped to his feet. 'I'm fourteen next year! Stop treating me like some child that can't be trusted to look after himself. Do you not remember what it was like at school back in Thymine for me? How I was picked on?'

'Nath—'

'And when you left Thymine, do you think that got any easier for me? Do you think they would let it go when they thought my dad wasn't really my father? And I couldn't say *anything* to set them right, or it would put all of us in danger.'

Elise began to cry silently. He had never told her any of this before.

'But I survived,' Nathan signed. 'I got through all of it because I knew something better was waiting for me. I always knew I would leave Thymine. I always told you that I'd visit the other bases. And now that it's finally come, you can't see that *this* is what I was meant to do all along.'

Before Elise could scramble to her feet, he was gone, back into the woods that closed around him.

Elise stared at where he had been. Should she follow?

'I wouldn't go after him if I were you,' Samuel said behind her.

Elise quickly wiped her tears away before turning to him. She noticed a few other residents peering at them from their hearths.

'Stars, was everyone watching us argue?'

He smiled at her, and her heart broke a little more.

'All they saw was two people signing to each other. Perhaps quite forcefully, but I think I was the only one who could understand what you were saying.'

'At least he left his bag,' Elise said, gesturing to it on the grass. 'He won't have gone far.'

Samuel nodded. 'May I sit?'

She paused for a second before answering. 'Of course.'

Elise drew her knees up to her chest. She found the position comforting and she rested her chin on her legs, gazing over at Samuel. She longed to sit closer, let her hand rest on his knee, lean into him, let him take some of the burden from her for just an evening, but she knew it wasn't possible. She laced her hands around her legs so they couldn't betray her.

'You look well,' she said.

'Thank you,' he replied, absent-mindedly pushing his hair from his face. 'Look, I know it's none of my business, but perhaps you shouldn't push Nathan back into the role of a child. He's experienced too much to go willingly.'

Elise stared over at him. She missed him, but not enough to endure a misplaced lecture.

She let go of her knees and switched to signing so only he could understand. 'You're right; it is none of your business. I'm trying to give him his childhood while he can still have one.'

'His childhood has gone,' Samuel responded, also now signing. 'Your mother and father gave him as long as they could. He's strong and capable. Don't push him back into a box he's already outgrown.'

'He's still too young,' Elise signed forcefully.

'He's much older than I was back in Adenine when I was first told that I was living a double life and that Mortimer wasn't my real grandfather. Once someone knows the truth, you can't tell them to cast it from their mind and return to the trivialities of life. Nathan knows the realities of this world. And he can't be asked to ignore them.'

Elise dug the heel of her boot into the grass and spoke quietly. 'What if he got captured, or worse? It would be my fault.'

Samuel gave her a half-smile, and he suddenly looked very weary. 'I think with the way things are panning out, we all risk capture or death wherever we are.' He paused, clearly trying to read her reaction. 'In my opinion, he would be better served by you training him. So, if anything does happen to you, he will know more about the world and can live independently for a time if he needs to. Perhaps start with the geography of Zone 3 and basic survival techniques.'

Elise hugged her legs closer as she thought about what he was suggesting.

She was about to ask him to stay for dinner at their hearth when Samuel glanced over her shoulder and moved to stand. 'I've got to go. Neve's waving me over. But please think about what I've said.' He paused. 'And I'm so very sorry about your mother, Elise. I truly am.'

Crouching next to her, he leant over and touched her hand. It was a small gesture for anyone else, but she knew what it meant coming from Samuel, even if he could touch Neve all the time now.

Elise raised her chin, but at the last moment, she held back her invitation for him to stay. Samuel always wanted to be with Neve. Anyone could see that.

When he was safely out of view, she looked down at her hands, now holding torn blades of grass. She hadn't even known that she had pulled them from the earth.

She opened her palms and let the breeze take them. She would have to let him go.

A day later, Elise stood by the bank of the bathing stream. She had decided to direct her energy elsewhere, needing something to distract her from the pain of the past few weeks.

'Do we have any undercover agents in Guanine's university who didn't return to us?' she asked.

'Elise! I am trying to wash,' Maya responded, knee-deep at the stream's edge. 'Could this not wait?'

Elise had purposefully chosen this very moment to confront Maya as it was the only time she was guaranteed to be alone. Maya had taught Elise well.

'It has to be now,' Elise responded, as Maya reached for her towel. 'So, do we have any undercover agents at the university?'

'Why?' Maya responded. 'We really shouldn't be talking about this. I keep all of the agents' whereabouts secret. You know that.'

'Because I need to access some information.'

Maya frowned. 'What information? You can't just go trundling into the university at a time like this. Uracil needs us more than ever.'

'This is for Uracil.'

Maya concentrated as she waded through the reeds to the dry shore. 'I set the missions around here.'

Elise straightened. 'I'm going whether I have your permission or not.'

'If it's so important, why can't you tell me what it is?' Maya said calmly, holding her hand out for her clothes.

Elise bent to pick them up, all the time tensed in case Maya decided to apprehend her. She couldn't believe it had come to this – that she had to be wary of Maya and take steps to protect herself from her.

'I can't tell you what I plan on doing because there is someone in Uracil who has been betraying us for years.' Maya's face dropped at Elise's words. 'You know it's true, but you don't know who it is. I need to do something – which won't jeopardise Uracil – but I don't want anyone to find out about it.'

'You think it's been going on for years?' Maya said quietly.

'Yes.' Elise stepped back so that she was more than three arms' lengths from Maya. 'The people on that island, Synthium, the Potiors know of them. They said we are fools to think that the Potiors weren't aware of Uracil long before they bombed it.'

Maya rubbed her forehead. 'Have you told anyone else this?'

'No, but Kit was there with me when it was said.'

Maya quickly got dressed, and Elise waited for her considered response.

'We know that there is likely a traitor in Uracil,' Maya said, pulling her light jacket over her T-shirt. 'We do not know who it is or how long they have been operating.'

Elise dared to take a step forwards. 'Did you really think that the Potiors didn't know of you? I look back at it now, and they must have noticed that people had gone missing from the bases.' She held out her arm to show her tattooed wrist. 'They kept track of us all.'

Maya sighed. 'Honestly, it's not something I like to think about. It changes everything. To know that the Potiors tolerated us means we were useful to them in some way and not a threat. I don't like to be thought of as weak.'

Elise softened her tone. 'Please. Just tell me if there is someone in the university I can approach. I need some information. I've been working on gathering as much as I can ... I think it might help.'

Maya looked at her appraisingly, and Elise tried to stand up to the scrutiny.

'There is one person,' Maya said eventually. 'But whether they will co-operate with you is out of my control. The undercover agents may not be as hardy as us when it comes to living between bases, but mentally they are stronger than you could imagine, having coped with living double lives for so long. Some agents who stayed in the bases must have intentionally decided not to return to Uracil. They have deliberately chosen another path for themselves.'

Later that evening, Nathan returned to their hearth. He would not look at Elise but he sat down and solemnly accepted the fish she had caught and pan-fried for them both.

Elise watched while he hurriedly ate, clearly wanting to escape back to whomever he had spent the day with. She had noticed that he spent all his time with a small group of friends from the caves. Even from afar, she could tell by the way they circled around him that he was their leader.

'I'm going to Guanine tomorrow,' Elise signed.

Nathan put his plate down and wiped his mouth on the back of his sleeve. 'I'll be shipped off to Georgina's hearth then?'

'No, not this time. I've thought about what you said, and you can come with me. If you want to.'

Nathan's eyes widened. 'I can come on a mission with you?'

'You can come on the journey to a mission with me, but not the actual mission itself,' Elise responded, holding his gaze. 'And there are going to be a few rules.'

Nathan nodded eagerly.

'You can come on a few select journeys with me as I think it's time you learnt the routes between the bases and how to live outdoors.' Elise watched as a wide grin spread over Nathan's features. 'But you won't participate in any of the missions inside the bases until you are well past fourteen, have been tested multiple times, and I know that you are both completely capable and well trained.' Nathan lifted his hands to interrupt, but Elise stopped him. 'Those are my terms. You take them all or none.'

Nathan didn't even wait a moment to think about it. 'I'll take them all.'

'Good.'

Elise stood up and waved Max over from the hearth three down from hers. He raised his eyebrows at the unexpected request but then pushed himself to his feet to join them.

'That's exactly what I needed,' Max said, accepting a mug of tea from Elise after he had settled at their fire. 'For most of today, I've been predominantly used as some sort of ox to move felled trees from one part of the forest to another.' He shrugged. 'At least they didn't harness me to a cart.'

Nathan smiled at the image when Elise interpreted it for him.

'I've been talking with Maya,' Elise responded, setting down the mug that she had been clasping close to her chest. It had been warm during the day, but the temperature had dropped by the early evening. 'I want to find an undercover agent in

Guanine. I'm taking Nathan with me, and I wondered if you would come with us.'

'Me?' Max said, staring at them both for an answer.

'I didn't know about this either,' Nathan signed, with Elise interpreting for him. 'It's the first I've heard of it.'

Elise turned to Nathan. 'It's safer with three of us, and you didn't think I was going to leave you outside of Guanine by yourself, did you?'

Nathan sighed, and Elise chose to ignore it.

'Well, if it's between days of manual labour and babysitting, I'll think I'll take the babysitting,' Max said, grinning at Nathan as Elise interpreted for him.

'I don't need a babysitter,' Nathan cut in.

'No, you don't,' Elise responded. 'But I'd feel better if you had one of Uracil's best fighters with you.' Max smiled at the compliment. 'And think about it this way. Who better to begin your training with?'

CHAPTER 13

Twenty-Two

'As long as you keep your head down and your hood up, we'll be fine walking through the Emporium in the daytime,' Raynor said, stopping yet again on the steps leading up to Guanine. 'People like me don't get noticed by anyone. That's where our strength lies. We're background noise, not the main show. And with a few small adjustments, you can be that too.'

Twenty-Two tried not to react to the older woman's words. She'd had plenty of time in Cytosine's Museum of Evolution to realise that she was too inconsequential to be cared about, but she didn't think she blended in as well as Raynor believed. On their first morning after leaving Uracil, Raynor had cut Twenty-Two's hair so that she had a long fringe again that covered the top half of her face and, most importantly, her brow ridge. But would that be enough?

'Are you sure that I should go into a public place?' Twenty-Two signed, stopping beside Raynor.

'Don't you want to see a bit of the world?' Raynor said. 'See what really goes on in the bases? I've been following that Companion for two of her afternoons off now, and I think I've got the gist of her. I even spoke to her on one of the days. Pretended

I was a Neanderfan, and she spent an hour telling me everything about the older Neanderthals she used to look after.' Raynor frowned. 'But she wouldn't talk about the current ones.'

Twenty-Two tried to feel reassured. She did want to see what the bases were like; she just didn't think she should be doing it in daylight with only a hood and a fringe for cover. She sighed to herself. It wasn't as if Raynor would purposefully put her in danger – she had been in the Infiltration Department for years and, despite a few near-misses, had never been caught by the Protection Department. She was obviously very good at her job.

Twenty-Two felt ready to carry on up the steps to Guanine and stretched her arms above her head. Dawn was breaking, and they had risen early to ensure they were the first ones in the Emporium. Turning to the older woman, she noticed the flushed colour of her cheeks and her short, panting breaths. Raynor was clearly not ready to continue. Twenty-Two stared up at the sky. She had found that in the alpine hills and mountains surrounding Guanine, her attention was always pulled upwards. There was always higher to go.

'We'd better get a shifty on,' Raynor said, following her gaze. 'Come on, Tutu. Let's get going.'

Twenty-Two scrunched her eyes at the nickname; she'd never had one before and it made her feel as though she belonged. In the past few weeks, the two of them had been given plenty of time to get to know each other. Raynor's time learning sign language with Nathan meant she could understand a lot of what Twenty-Two signed and she used fingerspelling to clarify the rest. It was one of the many reasons that Twenty-Two liked her. Raynor, this woman of middling years who blew her nose loudly and snored, was as free as any of the animals they passed during their long walk, and Twenty-Two respected that. Consequently, Twenty-Two had opened up about her past and told Raynor about the time she had tried to say her name to the Collections Assistant back in Cytosine and its consequences. The nickname of 'Tutu' had stuck.

Up they plodded, Raynor leading the way and setting the pace. Twenty-Two found herself staring at her own booted feet, each stone step similar to the last, the moss-lined cracks pulling her attention, a diversion from the monotony of the climb.

When they finally reached the last step, Twenty-Two took a peek at what lay ahead. They had arrived on a large grassy plateau on the middle level of the left mountain. Stallholders who worked at the Emporium set out their wares in the early morning light, next to the larger, official Emporium storage lockers where the smaller goods were kept. Raynor made a beeline for one of the vacant tables, which held everyday cleaning supplies of so little consequence that they were clearly viewed as unlikely to be stolen. With her hood pulled low over her face, Twenty-Two followed and inspected the rows of neatly folded cloths and scrubbing brushes. She had once possessed such an item when she'd had a tree house back in Uracil. She wondered if she would ever be the proud owner of a scrubbing brush again. The likelihood of Uracil allowing her to stay and have a tree house when she brought back more Neanderthals with her seemed slim.

From the corner of her eye, Twenty-Two noticed a woman heading directly towards her. A lightweight scarf held her wild auburn hair from her face. Twenty-Two turned away from her, tugging on Raynor's sleeve.

'We have to go,' Twenty-Two signed, keeping her hands close to her chest. 'Someone is walking directly towards us—'

Before she could continue, there was a tap on her shoulder.

'Excuse me for bothering you,' the owner of the tapping finger said. 'But I just had to ask—'

'Ah, lovely to see you again,' Raynor said, stepping in front of Twenty-Two's turned back. 'I thought you'd be at work today.'

Twenty-Two tried to make herself smaller and disappear behind Raynor's not inconsequential frame.

'Oh, it's you again,' the woman with the frizzy hair said. 'I had to pick up some supplies for my ... friends, so I came to the Emporium early. We're allowed to leave the museum sometimes, you know.'

'And rightly so,' Raynor said, the smile evident in her voice. 'You're pretty much on call twenty-four hours a day up at the museum. Sleep there as well. You need more than an afternoon's break.'

There was a pause, and Twenty-Two tried to edge farther away from the two women, her back turned the entire time.

'I came over because I wanted to have a word with your friend,' the woman said.

'Who, her?' Raynor responded, jerking her thumb backwards at the retreating Twenty-Two. 'You don't want to be having a word with her.' She lowered her voice. 'Nasty temper, that one. She bit someone last time they interrupted her morning routine. Stickler for her morning routine.'

Twenty-Two made a break for it and began to purposefully stride towards the steps leading down to the Sapien homes and the mountain's base. She remembered from her time in the museum that the worst thing she could do was run.

She heard Raynor call behind her. 'We'd better be off. Time for her morning constitutional. It's like clockwork!'

Heart beating faster with every stride, Twenty-Two didn't stop until she had counted fifty of the steps on the way down. When she had passed a bend and was out of sight of any entranceways to the Sapien dwellings, she paused to let Raynor catch up with her.

'That was a close one,' Raynor said, puffing behind her. 'But what is life without a little bit of excitement, heh?'

'You could have got me caught. She could have been the Protection Department.'

'What, her?' Raynor said, pointing behind her. 'No, she wasn't Protection Department. She's Lynette, that Companion I was telling you ab—'

They both froze when Lynette appeared from around the bend.

'If you don't mind,' Lynette signed. 'I'll be having a word with your friend. It's not often I see a Neanderthal outside of the museums.'

'Now, look here,' Raynor said, swinging into action and jutting out her chin. 'You'd better bugger off if you don't want to see the bottom of that cliff.'

The woman held firm. 'I'm not going to report you or stop you about your business. But I need your help. The other Neanderthals need your help.'

Twenty-Two raised her head for the first time that morning.

'You'd better come with us,' she signed.

'I've been at my wits' end with what to do,' Lynette signed.

The three of them sat hunched together underneath the shelter of a rowan tree near the last pathway at the bottom of the mountain. Lynette had steadfastly refused to step off the mountainside, so they had settled where no one was likely to see them.

'When I saw your chest – no offence – I knew something odd was going on. I made a guess and it paid off.'

Twenty-Two stared down at her torso. It was true that it was more rounded than a Sapien's, but it was only the eagle eye of a desperate Companion that would take the leap that she might actually be a Neanderthal roaming free outside the museums.

'The other two Companions left months ago,' Lynette continued. 'The museum said one Companion was enough for three Neanderthals. Can you imagine? I've been darting between all three pods for months, trying to keep their spirits up. The youngest, Thirty-One, is only five years old. I take her with me at night to the other pods. I can't leave her alone next to a stream.'

Lynette shivered at the thought.

'You've been breaking the rules then?' Twenty-Two signed.

Lynette looked sideways and patted down her crown of fluffy hair, which was unwilling to follow her guidance. 'Well, yes, quite a few of them. But only recently, mind. I must keep them going, and if that means explaining a bit of the world to them, then that's what I'll do. They're everything to me. And I can't look after them properly if I have to leave a five-year-old by herself overnight. It's not right.'

Twenty-Two nodded. 'I had to break the rules too. I wouldn't be alive if I had stayed in Cytosine.'

'We do what we have to,' Raynor said quietly.

'I thought there were five Neanderthals in Guanine?' Twenty-Two signed, remembering what Kit had told her. 'Where are the other two?'

'Oh, my love,' Lynette responded. 'The other two, Twelve and Fifteen, died a year or so ago. They were older, hadn't always had a Companion. I'm sure you've heard of it happening before. They both got ill, and all fight left them.'

Twenty-Two nodded. It was a tale that plagued her species.

'What happened to the Denisovans?' Raynor asked.

Lynette froze. 'How do you know about them? No one knows about them outside of Guanine's Neanderthal Project.'

'We have our ways,' Raynor responded. 'They weren't doing too well from what we heard.'

Lynette glanced around, and when she looked back, there were tears in her eyes. 'They both passed on before they were two years old. It broke my heart. The Companions thought something must have gone wrong when they brought them back. Something slipped out of place, and no matter how hard we tried, we couldn't get through to them. They just didn't develop as they should. It was as if we weren't there.'

Raynor stared up at the sky but didn't say any more.

'But I've got Thirty-One and Twenty-Four with me,' Lynette continued. 'And Nineteen has been a great help.'

'Nineteen?' Twenty-Two signed.

She had not heard of a living Neanderthal older than Kit.

'Yes, Nineteen. He's an older male, twenty years of age. Been star-sent for the other two. I was never his full-time Companion, but I'd spent some time with him. Years ago, after my first charge left for Thymine, I was given Twenty-Four to take care of.' Lynette's voice swelled with pride. 'She's as bright as a button, just turned eleven.'

Twenty-Two scrunched her eyes at the thought of how lucky Twenty-Four was to have Lynette.

'Nineteen was fortunate to have a good Companion too,' Lynette continued. 'An older man who didn't give up his job without a fight. When he was forced out, I promised him I'd also look after Nineteen. Thirty-One didn't have the most enthusiastic of Companions, but I've been looking after her these last few months, and I think it's turned things around for her to have the older ones to look up to.'

Twenty-Two wondered at there being a twenty-year-old Neanderthal. It gave her hope that some of the older ones in Adenine might have survived too.

'I just don't know why they've lost interest in them,' Lynette said, glancing at them both. 'I knew something was up when they were taken off the curriculum for the university students.'

Twenty-Two thought about this for a moment as she admired the clusters of white blossoms that punctuated the green leaves of the rowan tree. While listening to Lynette, she had decided that it was her favourite of trees.

'They have other interests now,' Twenty-Two signed. 'I nearly starved in Cytosine, and I think Ten actually did. I left with Twenty-Seven. He is safe now.'

Lynette leant forwards. 'But where can I hide them in Guanine? My family won't accept them; it's too dangerous. And we're not on the best terms anyway. I don't have anywhere else to take them.'

'You will bring them to us,' Twenty-Two signed. 'We will take care of them. We have somewhere we can take them outside of Guanine.'

Lynette sat up. 'Outside of Guanine?' She was silent for a moment, and it looked like she was tussling with a decision in her mind. 'Then I'm coming with you. Thirty-One needs me. Twenty-Four too.'

Twenty-Two caught the slight shake of Raynor's head over Lynette's shoulder but decided to ignore it. Uracil would just have to accept another stray if it would help the other Neanderthals adjust.

'You can come with us,' Twenty-Two signed, meeting Raynor's stare. 'I will take full responsibility for you.'

Twenty-Two didn't know if she could take the strain for much longer. She had been left pacing at their base camp outside Guanine for six hours, and there was still no sign of Raynor's return. It was four in the morning, and Twenty-Two knew it wouldn't be long until Guanine would wake up for the day. The nighttime rustlings began to play games with her senses – a furry coat brushing up against a leaf could mean their approach, and then for the hundredth time, she was left disappointed.

Raynor had agreed to help the Neanderthals and Lynette leave the museum on the condition that Twenty-Two stayed behind at their base camp. Twenty-Two had stood her ground and argued that she would be needed to help convince them to come with her. At that point, Raynor had put her hands on her hips and squared up to Twenty-Two, explaining in no uncertain terms that the last thing she needed was to go back to Uracil and tell them that Twenty-Two had been captured on her watch. It would fall to Lynette to explain the plan to the Neanderthals, and Raynor reassured Twenty-Two that they trusted her. They would follow.

Two days later, Raynor had left the base camp at ten in the evening, having slept for most of the day. She'd already stolen a key card from an unsuspecting museum employee the day before and had agreed to meet Lynette in the corridor outside the pods at one in the morning. The plan was that the Neanderthals would already have changed into some Sapien clothes and would be waiting for Lynette to open their pod doors. They had two hours to lead the Neanderthals out of the museum and to the outskirts of Guanine. The timings were crucial.

As Twenty-Two gathered some more fallen twigs to feed the small fire she had built to signal her position, she thought she heard a larger rustle to the northwest. She slipped behind a tree and faced away from the flames to let her eyes adjust to the forest's darkness.

Yes. There was something coming. Twenty-Two was entirely still while she waited.

Several sets of footsteps approached, but she didn't dare peek out from her hiding place until the agreed signal was given.

'Come out, Tutu,' Raynor called. 'I can't remember the agreed signal, something about herons. Or maybe penguins. It was definitely a fish-eating bird of some sort. But anyway, it's me and a few extras for you to meet.'

Twenty-Two suddenly understood that she was on the cusp of a defining point in her life. She wanted to savour the sweet anticipation before tipping into it. She held herself there for a moment before peeping around the tree. Nervous excitement enveloped her, and she didn't know how to contain it. She felt as though she would make a fool of herself by spontaneously clapping her hands, stamping her feet and shaking her hips in the way Tilla had tried to show her.

Safely behind the tree, she observed Raynor making her way to the fire, followed by Lynette, who was holding the hand of a young girl.

Twenty-Four?

The girl's wide eyes never stopped searching her surroundings. Eventually they locked on to Twenty-Two.

Realising she could no longer delay, Twenty-Two stepped out from behind the tree and slowly approached the girl. She bent down until they were the same height and cocked her head to the side, studying her. The girl had been fed at least; she was not the worn-out shell that Twenty-Two had been.

The girl took a step forwards. 'Hello. Is this where you live?'

Twenty-Two scrunched her eyes at her. 'No, this is just where I was waiting for you.'

'Good,' the girl signed. 'Because it's far too cold and whooshy. It's always blowing.'

A man, whom Twenty-Two purposefully avoided making eye contact with, stepped around from behind Lynette. In his arms, he was carrying a sleeping child. She was the youngest of the three Neanderthals, and her head was nuzzled into his chest, her arm hanging loosely by her side.

'Twenty-Four,' he signed with one hand, addressing the older girl. 'Remember when we talked about not saying everything that you think? Some thoughts are not meant to be shared.'

He stared at the fire the entire time he was signing.

Twenty-Two quickly straightened. She did not want to bend before him.

Instead, she followed his gaze to the fire. 'It is pretty, I know. But don't touch it as it's very hot and will burn your skin.'

Nineteen nodded, still unable to pull his gaze away. His long, dark brown hair was tied back by a thin leather band at the base of his neck, just like Kit's. She wondered if all the male Neanderthals were encouraged to have the same hairstyle.

'Don't worry,' Twenty-Two signed to the girl. 'It took me a long time to get used to the wind. It will get better, the cold too.'

'Right,' Raynor said, kicking dirt over the fire. 'We need to get as far from here as possible. Three missing Neanderthals and a Companion is not going to go unnoticed.'

'But I'm tired,' Twenty-Four signed, tugging on Lynette's layered skirts.

'Have you ever had a piggyback?' Twenty-Two signed to the girl.

She shook her head.

'Well, you're in for a special treat then,' Twenty-Two responded, switching the straps around, so her bag hung from her front.

Three hours later, Twenty-Two's arms began to ache. Twenty-Four hadn't made the journey's beginning very easy by excitedly kicking her legs around. The sun had risen as they'd cleared the forest's expanse, and they were now hurrying through gently rolling green meadows swaying with early-summer flowers. The overwhelming sight of how vast their world really was had quickly quietened the older child's excited jiggles. Twenty-Two tried to see it from her eyes – the sheer scale of it compared to their pods was quite unbelievable.

Twenty-Two took a peek back at Nineteen to see how he was coping. He was still carrying Thirty-One but kept his gaze firmly down. She wondered at the size of him, even with his head bent. He was a couple of inches taller than Kit, but the width of his chest was the most impressive thing. He made

Twenty-Two look petite. She scrunched her eyes at the thought; she would have to start practising her exercises with Kit if she wanted to be one of the strongest Neanderthals again.

They carried on walking for the next five hours, sometimes with Twenty-Four holding one of the women's hands and trotting alongside them, sometimes with Twenty-Two carrying her. Whenever Twenty-Two glanced over at Nineteen, his eyes never shifted upwards, even when he let Thirty-One down so she could walk and stretch her legs.

Raynor struck off towards a small grove when the sun was hanging low over the horizon. Slinging her bag to the ground, she sat down heavily and peeled off her shoes.

'Bloody hell,' she said, staring up at the others. 'If that doesn't put enough distance between us, then I don't know what will.'

Twenty-Two began to collect firewood but stopped when Raynor told her there would be no fire that evening. They couldn't risk it in case Guanine had sent someone out to search for them. So, instead, she began sharing out her food and water rations with them. They all eyed the water hesitantly, despite Raynor and Twenty-Two reassuring them that it was safe to drink for the tenth time. Twenty-Two realised that a lot needed explaining, but she also didn't want to overwhelm them. She could remember what it was like when she had first left Cytosine; she flinched when she recalled that naive girl who'd thought that twelve sandwiches would sustain her group on the walk to Thymine. For the first time, she appreciated how patient Kit had been with her, and she quickly sent her thanks up to the stars for placing him in her path.

After they had eaten, Twenty-Two sat next to Nineteen while Lynette tucked blankets around the two girls.

'How did you find the walk today?' she signed to him, the setting sun providing just enough light for him to read the movement of her hands.

Nineteen glanced over at the two girls before responding. 'I have never walked that far before. I didn't even know there was that far to walk.'

'It took me a long time to get used to the size of it too, but you will. I barely notice it now,' Twenty-Two responded.

'I have to get better,' Nineteen signed. 'For the other two. I have to show them everything will be fine, and we made the right decision by leaving with Lynette.' Nineteen stared over at the girls again. 'They are the future. I must deliver them safely. Lynette said there are other Neanderthals where you come from. That they will have friends.'

Twenty-Two was taken aback by how earnest he was in his expressions; she was so used to Kit, whom she struggled to read. In comparison, Nineteen was as clear as a bright screen.

'There are two younger ones where I am taking you,' she signed. 'Bay and Twenty-Seven. Twenty-Seven was in Cytosine with me and had been abandoned by his Companion. He didn't sign at all when I first met him and used to kick everyone. Now he's at school and plays with the other Sapien children. He still has outbursts, but he is doing much better. I think he'll look up to Twenty-Four and, in turn, try to help her adjust. Bay has just turned four and left the museum in Thymine when she was only a few months old. She has an adopted mother and doesn't know anything other than growing up outside of the museums. She will help Thirty-One.'

Nineteen nodded, and his body seemed to relax slightly. 'I must sleep. I will help carry Twenty-Four tomorrow. We will take it in turns.'

Twenty-Two wasn't feeling tired yet, as it was still early in the evening, so she went and sat with Raynor, who was leaning against a tree trunk, massaging her feet.

'How are they doing?' Raynor signed.

'Better than I expected, although Nineteen seems overwhelmed by it all. I think it must be harder the older you are when you leave. And he is six years older than both me and Kit were when we first stepped out of the museums. But at least Lynette explained to him what the outside world is like before they left. And the museum was still giving him food and water. It wasn't like Cytosine.'

A look of concern passed across Raynor's features, and Twenty-Two realised she'd divulged too much about her treatment back in the museum. She needed to change the conversation.

'I wanted to ask you something,' Twenty-Two signed.

Raynor's eyes scrunched up in amusement, and the lines deepened around their corners. 'You can ask, but that doesn't mean I will answer.'

That was good enough for Twenty-Two.

'Why did you leave Uracil to come with me?' Twenty-Two signed, carefully watching Raynor's response.

'If I have to be honest with you, which I do,' Raynor said, still amused, 'I don't like Genevieve. She's a stuck-up, snub-nosed goodie-two-shoes who hasn't known a day's hard toil in her life. She just seems to glide from one easy life to another, and you wouldn't ever guess I was younger than her! And seeing her swan back into Uracil makes me shudder. I don't think Faye fell too far from the tree, if I'm perfectly honest.'

Twenty-Two stared at her. She didn't know what it meant to fall away from the tree, but she could see that it wasn't a good thing in Raynor's opinion.

'Do you think she will take over Uracil?' Twenty-Two signed.

'I think she'll get onto the Tri-Council,' Raynor responded, sucking the air between her teeth. 'And then, who knows? They don't seem to learn their lessons well these days ...'

Twenty-Two's face dropped. It was happening again. It was just like Faye all over.

Her gaze was drawn to the sleeping Neanderthals. Was she putting them in danger by taking them back to Uracil? But where else could they go?

Raynor leant towards Twenty-Two and, as if reading her mind, said quietly, 'It's the only place you can take them for the moment. They will be safe there. Kit and Georgina will look after them.'

Twenty-Two stared at the older woman. Raynor was clearly able to read some body language too.

'How about we take them back to Uracil,' Raynor said, 'and then I'll head straight to Adenine while you try and get them settled? That way, you'll be able to check that they're welcome, but you won't lose any time finding out what the situation is in Adenine with the last of the Neanderthals.'

Twenty-Two scrunched her eyes at Raynor in thanks. 'And you promise you'll try to help the Neanderthals in Adenine?'

Raynor gave her a broad smile, and Twenty-Two noticed that some of her back teeth were missing. 'Of course I will. Anything that will pish Genevieve off is a good thing in my book.'

Lynette came and sat with the two women. 'They're all asleep, and I'll be that way soon.' She paused. 'I just want to say how grateful I am to you both for bringing them out of that place. I feel like a pressure that I've been struggling with for months has lifted from me. For the first time in a while, I will sleep well and look forward to what tomorrow brings.'

'Well, anything to help Twenty-Two here,' Raynor said, giving her a smile.

'And to help a fellow Guanine,' Twenty-Two interjected, remembering Raynor had been raised there.

Lynette began digging through her bag. 'I didn't realise you were born and raised in Guanine. That makes me feel even more at peace.'

Twenty-Two settled back, and half watched the women while they discussed the different Sapien rings where they had grown up. All the time she thought about the other Neanderthals, just happy to be near them.

CHAPTER 14

Caitlyn

As promised, half of the tickets had arrived in Caitlyn's family account the following morning. She had explained them away to Gran as an additional payment for some administrative work she would take on weekends for one of the professors. Gran had raised an eyebrow at her explanation but hadn't probed any further.

Caitlyn now had to be patient and wait for the right time to begin her work for the Excluded Erudites.

Two weeks later, an opportunity arose for her to follow through with her commission. It was late in the afternoon when Professor Gudd called her to his office, his eyes wild from too much caffeine and the sweet high of potential discoveries.

'I've found something that might just change the course of what we know about lithic knapping,' he spluttered, as Caitlyn stood at the other side of his desk – he never invited her to take a seat. 'If this lines up ... well. It would put Professor Cylett's paper to shame. As sure as my name is Algernon.'

Caitlyn nodded; her input was not needed. She was merely a receptacle for his words.

'I want you to go to the archives and pull up a study that came out...' Professor Gudd paused as he shuffled through his notes, 'in 2269, on discoid techniques, and make a generalised search on a few keywords as well. It will turn up a lot of papers, but you can spend the rest of the day sifting through them.'

Caitlyn noted what he was requesting on her screen and, once he was done, she took the stairs down into the archives.

The corridor to the archives was akin to a bunker; it had a low ceiling and dark grey walls framing metal doors that Caitlyn had never entered. They contained the Pre-Pandemic research that she, as a Sapien, was never allowed to access. Only the professors could enter those rooms. She continued down the corridor where one of the electric lights announced its final hours by flickering on and off. The air hummed from the vast cooling system that protected the delicate pages of the Pre-Pandemic papers and the servers that contained the more modern research. She knocked on the door at the end of the corridor.

'You again,' Dahlia said, peering over the top of her glasses as she stayed seated at her desk. 'What has he demanded of you today?'

'A paper and a few keyword searches,' Caitlyn said, as she wandered over to the access station in the corner of the ordered office and plugged in her screen. 'He thinks he's onto something.'

Dahlia's keen eyes followed Caitlyn, clearly hoping for more information. Caitlyn allowed the quiet to hang there as she tapped away at her screen, searching for the right article. She felt no need to respond to the expectant silence that radiated from Dahlia. Caitlyn went down to the archives most days to pull up whichever paper Professor Gudd wanted, often to be discarded by him after a cursory glance. It was more unusual for him to ask her to do a keyword search.

'He thinks he's onto something, does he?' Dahlia said, now absent-mindedly sucking on the temple of her glasses. 'Professor Cylett will be interested.'

Caitlyn didn't understand why Dahlia involved herself in the minutiae of the university gossip mill when she didn't have to. Perhaps, shut away in the basement all day, it gave her a connection to the thrumming life above.

'Is there anything else you want to divulge?' Dahlia asked.

Caitlyn stared down at the screen as she selected the relevant articles. Searching through the results, her eyes flicking over the lines of text at high speed, she alighted on the three articles that would satisfy Tiro's request for the latest research about the Upper Palaeolithic period. All she had to do was slip one extra keyword in there. If they ever bothered to check her requests, she could explain it away as an error. It was so closely linked to Professor Gudd's searches, after all.

Tapping the downloads onto her screen, she turned and smiled at Dahlia. 'He doesn't tell me anything of importance. You know how it is. And I barely understand half of what he's talking about.'

Dahlia looked Caitlyn up and down and pushed her glasses back up her nose. 'Now, we both know that isn't true.'

That evening, in the safety of her bed, Caitlyn read through the articles that Tiro had requested. She wanted to check what they contained before sharing them with him. There was still time to return the tickets and pull out of the agreement if the research articles seemed too important. Long-winded and rambling was her conclusion after she read them. Still, they were harmless enough and centred on the growing evidence that Neanderthals used throwing spears similar to the ones that Sapiens had used.

She tucked her work screen under her pillow and fell into a deep sleep, her conscience clear.

The next day, after finishing her shift at the university, she made her way back to the eighth Sapien home along the lowest ring of the twin mountain. After checking the walkway was empty, she knocked on the door.

Tiro pulled it open with some force, a homemade scarf looped around his neck. She did not tumble inside this time. Instead, she closed the door behind her and took off her heavy coat.

'I've only got a few hours, so I think you'll want to start reading,' she said, settling down on one of the two chairs by the tea-stained table.

Tiro gave her a broad grin and the other three scholars crowded around him – four crows huddled around the pickings. While they read from Caitlyn's work screen, Sylvie and Tiro made notes on their screens. Tiro's expression constantly shifted from frowning concern to wide-eyed wonder to a knowing smile in only a few minutes. Caitlyn enjoyed covertly watching him. He was utterly absorbed, his features shifting to show his unconscious reactions. He had the sort of face that was a pleasure to observe – taut and smooth with high cheekbones. He had not yet turned to ageing and still held firm against the harsh elements of Guanine that eventually weathered all of the residents' features.

After an hour and some audible sighs from Stephen, the group moved to sit down on the crates that served as Sylvie's bed, where they continued to read. Satisfied with their change in setting, Stephen ceased his sighing. Their fixed concentration immediately returned and took them away to a bygone era when men and women hunted with spears and were not always top of the food chain. Caitlyn shifted uncomfortably on her chair and began folding a small tissue she had found in her pocket before abandoning it on the table. For the following hour, she circled the small room, pleased to be stretching her legs for a while. Hours of sitting at her desk at work meant that in the evenings she liked to pace to restore some life to her muscles.

'Fascinating,' Tiro concluded when he had finished. He looked at his three associates and smiled around at all of them. 'The acknowledgement of different types of spears sheds new light on the Neanderthals and can only shift our previous perceptions. If they used throwing spears nearly as much as the Sapiens, and came to this knowledge independently of them, then it further narrows the capability and innovation gaps between the species. It has given me plenty to think about.'

Caitlyn reached over and took back her work screen. Within two taps, she had permanently deleted the articles that the Erudites had just read.

Alice walked over to Sylvie and whispered something in her ear. While Sylvie listened, her eyes widened.

She approached Caitlyn. 'Alice has a request. And she's willing to add a lot of her personal tickets for it.'

Caitlyn nodded. 'What would you like this time?'

After Caitlyn had accepted her next commission and received both the second payment for the last one and the new fee, she began gathering her belongings to go home. The work she had been given was turning into quite a profitable source of income, and she wondered how she would explain away the additional tickets to Gran. The sums weren't large enough to worry about the authorities noticing them, but still, she might need to pause the work once she had enough tickets for Gran's operation.

'I'll walk you partway to your home,' Tiro said, holding Caitlyn's coat out for her. 'It's on my way.'

She took the coat from him and wrapped it tightly around her torso to protect herself from the forceful winds.

They walked in silence for a while before Caitlyn asked a question that had been bothering her. 'If you're all so interested in academia, why didn't you apply for jobs as assistants at the university?'

Tiro stuffed his hands farther into the pockets of his thin jacket. No one would choose to wear such a thing on the mountainside at this time of year, and she realised that he had been unable to afford a winter coat. She wondered how long he'd had his last one before it had perished beyond repair.

'There are not enough jobs at the university to take everyone,' he responded, not looking at her. 'And the rest of Guanine has to be run by someone. They can't have all the Saps in the university when there's recycling still to be done.'

Caitlyn flinched at the term; it wasn't often she heard a Sapien refer to themselves as a Sap. It usually came out of the mouths of the Medius.

'But why would someone like you not push to work at the university – or even the museum?'

'Because I didn't get to leave school at sixteen like you. I had to leave at fourteen. There are five children in my family, and my mum died giving birth to the fifth. As the second oldest, my family needed me to be out and working as quickly as possible.'

Caitlyn's cheeks reddened. Of course, why hadn't she realised? Tiro, like so many Sapiens, couldn't afford to stay in school until he was sixteen, and there was no chance of a job as an assistant to a professor without that extra two years of formal education.

'And it's not like I can go back to school now that my younger siblings are older and in work themselves,' Tiro continued, staring at his shoes; the sole was coming away from the right one. 'Once you've left, there's no returning. Nor can I swan into the university and tell them I've educated myself. They'd want to know how and where. And then they'd probably launch me into the containment centre and throw away the pass.'

'What about the others in the group?' Caitlyn asked.

'As I said, Sylvie was barred when she'd only turned fourteen. She was seen as a troublemaker at school by the Medius teachers. As for Stephen, he never really knew of the assistant jobs to the professors until it was too late, and he'd worked as a cleaner for a couple of years. We both know they wouldn't want an ex-cleaner as an assistant.' Tiro sighed. 'Alice didn't have any choice in the matter. Her parents wanted her to work in the canteen as it's what they'd done, her older sisters too. So they pulled her out of her school at fourteen. They thought she should stick to the family trade. Bloody shame – she's only seventeen, but she has an exceptional mind. Her parents thought she should put that to the inner workings of the canteen. And the irony is that she's a terrible cook.'

'It's wrong, isn't it?' Caitlyn said. 'That you get stuck in one place for a lifetime. Especially when you are all so intelligent.'

Tiro looked at her for the first time.

He shrugged. 'It depends on what you believe intelligence is, really. I often think that word is used to categorise people and limit their options. I believe there are many different types of intelligence, and they should sit alongside each other rather than exist as a hierarchy. There's academic intelligence, which can be split into various groups, such as mathematics, linguistics or even the retention and recall of information. I believe there's also social intelligence, artistic intelligence and perhaps even the intelligence of preservation, cunning or happiness. It can't all be neatly divided, and often people overlap. But to say that academic intelligence is the only one of note is probably championed by those who wish to preserve their supposed uniqueness.'

'This coming from a group calling themselves the Excluded Erudites?' Caitlyn said, raising her eyebrows. 'It's a pretentious name for a group preaching the equality of different forms of intelligence.'

Tiro snorted. 'I suppose it is. Sylvie always says that the first rule of being intelligent is knowing that there's always someone more intelligent than you. And that probably includes a lot of people. I have often observed that to be true. It is usually the most arrogant of people who believe they are the cleverest. Their arrogance is not confirmation of their intellect, just their over-inflated opinion of themselves.'

'I can agree with that,' Caitlyn said, thinking of several people she had met in her working life.

'Anyway,' Tiro said, with a sigh, 'this is where I turn off to the other side of the mountain. I wish you luck in obtaining our next commission.'

He nodded to her before walking away, shoulders hunched against the cold.

Caitlyn stood for a moment, watching him. She recalled that the last time she'd seen him he'd actually had a winter coat. He must have traded it for the tickets to pay her. Staring after him, she felt the tug of another path to take, another life to explore.

She wished that she could follow.

CHAPTER 15

Elise

'Guanine,' Max said, looking up at the alpine forests. 'The land of steps.'

And information, Elise thought. She had been careful not to tell Max and Nathan why she was here, other than trying to contact an undercover agent who hadn't returned to Uracil. Elise trusted Nathan with her life, but the less he knew, the safer he would be. She thought she could trust Max but didn't want to test it with her brother in her care.

'The steps shouldn't be any problem for you,' Elise responded, taking two at a time. 'You're built for relentless uphill exercise, aren't you?'

'I am,' Max responded, his long legs taking three of the steps at once. 'But that doesn't mean I won't find it tedious.'

Nathan bounded up behind them after bending to tie his bootlace. 'You wouldn't even know Guanine was here from a few miles away.'

'All the bases are like that,' Elise signed. She stopped concentrating on climbing the steps. They had both been helping Max with his sign language, and Elise would act as an interpreter for

Nathan when needed. 'That's why I wanted to take you to them. You'd never find them by yourself.'

Nathan smiled. 'You've told me about the people in the other bases, but what about the islanders you met over the last couple of years?'

Elise said the words aloud for Max while she gave herself a moment to think. 'They were strange to me, but maybe I was strange to them.'

'Probably,' her brother signed. 'You're not half pensive since you left Thymine. You might as well have a long coat that swishes around your ankles like some of the Medius do.'

Elise punched her brother lightly on the arm. It was the first time since their mum had died that he had teased her, and she was pleased that the sadness that had enveloped him over the last few weeks was beginning to loosen its hold.

'At least I don't carry my sling around with me all day,' Elise signed, 'in case one of the children asks for a demonstration and that pretty fourteen-year-old Jessica happens to be around.'

Nathan punched Elise back on the arm. His face turned bright red, and Elise was pleased that her suspicions of a crush forming had been confirmed.

'What's this you ask, small child?' Elise signed, pretending to be Nathan holding up his sling. 'Oh, it's just my deadly sling. I carry it everywhere for protection and killing things.'

Nathan's eyes glinted with amusement. 'It's better than, "Swish, swish, here is my long coat. I brood in it because the *entire* fate of the world rests upon these shoulders. What's that? No, I can't possibly have a normal life because it is the fate of a hero to deny themself even the simplest of pleasures. Apart from an ankle-length coat, of course."'

Elise grinned at him. Her brother was starting to come back to her, bit by bit.

They carried on climbing while Elise buzzed with pleasure. She had finally made a correct decision by bringing Nathan with her.

'I'm glad Thymine didn't have all these steps,' Nathan signed to Max after a while. 'It just had one giant hill that circled the valley, but you could weave your way up it slowly if you wanted.'

'Do you ever miss Thymine?' Max asked them both.

'Not at all,' Nathan signed.

'Occasionally,' Elise signed at the same time.

Nathan raised his eyebrow at her reproachfully and she felt she should explain herself. 'I don't miss the person I was there or how I was made to feel. I had no real friends until I met Georgina, Luca, Kit ...' Elise stopped for a moment; she didn't think Holly, who she had spent most days with, should be added to that list or if she should include Samuel any more either. She couldn't imagine a time when she could sit easily and watch him and Neve together without thinking it should be her next to him. 'But I suppose it was a more secure way of life. Before I began working at the museum, I always knew I was likely to reach old age.' She shrugged. 'Doing this type of work, day in, day out, makes you wonder if you'll see the next one.'

She watched Nathan from the corner of her eye to see if he was absorbing her meaning. She had ensured their journey hadn't been the easiest, with twelve-hour hikes followed by collecting firewood, hunting and locating water. But Nathan's energy was rarely depleted, and he did everything she directed him to without complaint. She had hoped the monotonous, and at times exhausting, reality of life travelling between bases would change his mind, but he had taken to everything with gusto.

Max nodded. 'This life certainly makes you appreciate every sunrise that you witness.'

They all looked down as they continued trudging up the seemingly endless steps circling the mountain.

'Do you know what I miss from my old life?' Max continued, Elise interpreting his words for Nathan. 'Sometimes I miss that sense of belonging. I don't miss having servants. They're more trouble than they're worth as you have to constantly watch what you are saying. I don't miss having the best food or the power or even the medical surety. I miss knowing my place in the world. And how I fit into it. These last few weeks in Uracil ...'

Elise glanced over at him; she had never heard Max speak so candidly. 'Are you feeling pushed to the outside?'

He nodded. 'The way they stare, after what happened to Uracil ... as if I wasn't followed, spied on and vetted for years before they accepted me. All that doesn't matter in the wake of great tragedy. They rightfully need someone to blame, and I look too much like a Potior for them to direct it elsewhere.' For a moment, he squeezed his eyes shut. 'That's why I came with you. I needed a few weeks of respite. I think some of them were gaining giddy thrills treating me like an animal and ordering me to lug things around for them.'

'Well, if it makes you feel any better,' Elise said, after signing Max's words for Nathan, 'it seems that unless you were born in Uracil or have lived there for a minimum of twenty years, they will always look at you like a newcomer.'

She didn't mention how difficult it had been to be around someone who looked like a Potior after losing her mum. Sometimes, she would catch a glimpse of either Max or Vance from the corner of her eye and her whole body would ratchet up into panic, readying to flee or fight for her life.

'Well, I'm not just a newcomer. I'm a Potior newcomer,' Max said, his head down.

Elise took a chance. 'I know it's none of anybody's business. And I know in a perfect world you shouldn't have to tell anyone about yourself. But I think it might help if you spoke more openly about your past.' She glanced across at Max to see what effect her words were having, but his head was still firmly down. 'So that people have something to grasp and can form a different opinion of you. Maybe then they would find it easier to understand how you are different to the other Potiors.'

'Is that what you think of me?' Max asked, still not looking up. 'That I'm just another Potior?'

Elise stopped dead and grabbed onto his sleeve to stop him from striding ahead. 'No, of course not. I know you're not a Potior. I know that a Potior is not another species of human. It's actually a choice that people make to remain a Potior. To place themselves above all others, to control, to rule.'

Nathan had been watching them intently while Elise interpreted and he lifted his hands to sign, 'I agree. It is a choice to be a Potior, and you're not all that handsome, really. Not like the other ones I've seen on the screen releases.'

Max gave him a grin. 'That actually makes me feel better.'

Watching Max made Elise think of the Potiors she had seen on her screen over the years, each of them designed to replicate perfection, overwhelm others and influence. His softly curled hair shone in the late-afternoon light, and she admired the contrast of its closely shaved underside – he'd recently had it cut. She had to disagree with Nathan. Max really was a thing of beauty.

Max dipped his head. 'You two are among the few people who aren't either incredibly suspicious of me or weirdly pandering, as if I'm special. Neither makes me feel comfortable, and the latter group is rapidly diminishing.'

'You've tried not telling people about your past,' Elise signed, 'and it hasn't worked very well. So, why don't you try telling people about it? Surely it can't hurt?'

'I don't want to divulge more about myself as I wasn't just *another* Potior. Only Maya knows this about me. And the members of the Tri-Council, both past and present.'

'Not just another Potior?' Elise said, her smile freezing. 'Then ... ?'

'Do you promise that this is just between us three?'

'On my brother's life,' Elise signed.

'On my sister's life,' Nathan signed simultaneously.

'I'm not just any Potior. I'm technically the nephew of the Premier.'

'You're *what*?' Elise signed, glancing around wildly at Nathan.

'You're Potior *royalty*!' Nathan signed, ignoring Elise. 'They'd have been miffed when you left.'

Max groaned. 'I *knew* this would happen if I told you!' He rapped his knuckles repeatedly against his forehead and said quietly, 'Idiot brain telling me it would be fine.'

'And what do you mean, technically?'

'Well, I was the child of his sister. I suppose I still am. Although they all think I died. So, I am, technically, his nephew. But I don't think of myself that way.'

'Bloody hell,' Elise signed. 'No wonder you don't want to tell anyone about yourself.' The pained look on Max's features made her gather herself. 'I'm just saying that it's understandable. Not that you're high Potior scum.'

Max turned to carry on up the stairs, and Elise reached to stop him. 'Look, it's fine with me. We can't choose who we are born to. It's just a bit of a shock.' She stared up at him. 'You're going to have to tell us more once we get out of Guanine.'

Max nodded and took the next three steps without looking back.

'Are you sure that's her?' Elise signed to Max a few hours later.

All three of them were staring at a woman crossing the Emporium who was possibly an undercover agent for Uracil. Nathan's eyes were wide at the sight of the bustling marketplace perched upon the mountain ledge, his first view of one of the three other bases. People were calling out the tickets required for purchases, and grandparents perused the wares on the tabletops with the youngest children strapped to their backs and the older ones' hands held tightly. Even from their position in the shrubbery at the edge of the mountainside, Elise knew it was an exciting scene for Nathan to witness.

'Well,' Max signed slowly, with Elise correcting him along the way, 'she matches the description Maya gave us, and she came from the right dwelling. Odds are she's the right person.'

'"Odds are" isn't really good enough for me,' Elise responded.

It was almost dark, and she wanted to ensure they hadn't made a mistake. Contacting the undercover agents in the bases without getting caught was difficult enough. Throw in a case of mistaken identity, and they were asking for trouble.

'I'm going to follow her,' Elise signed, stepping out from the foliage they had been sheltering behind.

She had already changed into her Sapien clothes, which were less conspicuous than her travel wear.

'I should come with you,' Max signed, straightening.

'You know you can't,' Elise responded, as gently as she could. 'You stand out more than anyone. And what would a Potior and a Sapien be doing walking down a pathway together? It so rarely happens we'd draw more attention than it's worth. Also, someone needs to look after Nathan.'

'I could come too,' Nathan chipped in.

Elise gave him a look that conveyed everything she thought about that suggestion.

Max sighed. 'Fine, but don't try and make contact unless you're certain she's the right person. And be prepared to run. She might have refused to come back to Uracil for a reason. She could have turned.'

Elise knew that these were the risks they now took.

'I'll be back in a few hours,' she signed. 'Wait by where we camped last night.' She stared up at Max. 'And please, look after Nathan.'

Elise kept her head down while she followed the woman up the twisting stairways, careful that she was always far enough behind to ensure she wouldn't be spotted. Up and up they went until Elise had to pull her jacket tighter around her as they entered the fog cloaking the highest peak. Once they reached the final ledge, it was clear that the woman was returning to the university, even though she must have spent the day there already.

The sun had set when Elise pressed her stolen key card against the university side door. Head down, she followed the woman through the hallways that circled the administrative areas and the functional back rooms, tucked away from the students so they didn't intrude on their learning experience.

It had been a year since Elise had last visited the university on another mission, but she still remembered its general layout from the maps she had studied at the time. She raised an eyebrow as the woman made her way down the stairwell to the archives.

Elise glanced around before following her.

CHAPTER 16

Caitlyn

'And you're sure it's all above board?' Gran asked, as she examined the family screen again. 'It's a lot of tickets you're bringing in and everything has become so unsettled with the talk of the new species.'

Speculation about what the new species would mean for the Sapiens and Medius had been flying around Guanine the past few weeks. With little to go on, people had been forced to fill in the blanks with conjecture. Their musings rolled late into the night, and the knowing, tight-lipped smiles of the professors did little to ease the tensions during the day.

'It's all above board, Gran. Just some extra work for one of the professors.'

Caitlyn peeled carrots while they spoke, the two women standing next to each other by the stove. From the other room threaded the muffled conversations of the rest of the family. Gran had clearly decided to broach the topic outside the earshot of her daughter and son-in-law.

'I worked out that in a couple of months, we should have enough Medi-stamps to fix your eyes too,' Caitlyn said.

Gran wiped her hands against her apron. 'Well, that would be good.' She lowered her voice. 'I don't want to upset your mum, but they are getting worse.'

Caitlyn glanced at the family screen. 'I have to head back to the university. It's easier to do the extra work there.'

'But you've only been back an hour.'

'It's quieter.'

'Caitlyn,' Gran said, clasping her hand. 'I want to say how grateful I am for you taking on this additional work. For trying to make my sight better. I don't know what we'd do without you.'

Caitlyn squeezed her grandmother's hand gently. 'We'd be lost without you, Gran. You're the one that makes everything run around here. And that's why we need you fit and healthy.'

Gran chuckled. 'They're good people, your mum and dad, but after a long day cleaning the libraries, they've got little capacity for anything else.'

Two small figures slammed into Caitlyn's legs. 'If you're going out, can we have your share of the stew?'

Caitlyn bent down, so she was level with two sets of brown eyes. 'If Gran agrees, you can. I can get something to eat at the canteen.'

The excited hugs made the loss of a hearty meal worth it. A sandwich from the canteen would fill her up for a few hours at least.

'I'll be back soon,' Caitlyn said, as she grabbed her work satchel and waved goodbye to Gran. 'Love you.'

What Caitlyn had told her grandmother was true. She did have a lot of work to catch up on. Firstly, she had to finish up the mountain of tasks that Professor Gudd had set her, including a search for more articles. Secondly, she wanted to go down to the basement to retrieve the documents that Alice had requested. An added bonus was that her trip to the university proved to Gran that she was actually doing extra work, which would explain the influx of tickets into the family account.

It was still light as Caitlyn made her way along the pathways to the university. It was finally beginning to warm up, and she didn't need to pull her coat as tight as she had done for the past eight months. Soon she might even leave it at home. Her thoughts turned to Tiro and his lack of coat, but she pushed them away. If he wanted to exchange his jacket for her services, that was his business.

The office was empty; all the other assistants had gone home for the day. She enjoyed the quiet, although it did not stop her mind from wandering. Try as she might, her thoughts settled on the most curious thing that she had encountered in years – a group of Sapiens whose desire for knowledge was so strong that they'd take such risks to quench it. Who would have thought it possible? Caitlyn wondered what Tiro was doing at that very moment. His alert brown eyes flashed into her mind. She shook her head and tried to focus on her screen again; she had work to do.

What was his family like? Did they crave knowledge too, or were they a different type of person? Caitlyn had never met anyone like him. Everyone at school had been intimidated by her interest in learning. It had been an anomaly that had made them uncomfortable around her. Tiro was different. He aroused a desire in her to tell him every thought she had ever possessed and hear his opinion on them.

Sighing at her inability to control her wandering mind, she glanced at the counter on her screen. It was almost 8 p.m. She should go down to the basement and try to retrieve the next lot of information.

The corridor down to the archives was even more oppressive late at night. Caitlyn was not one to scare easily, but even she had to admit that the university at night was not for the fainthearted. The hum of electric lights as they flicked on did little to cover the voices coming from the archiving room. Caitlyn dithered partway down the steps. Should she continue if there were others in the room? She stood for a moment, undecided, entirely unaware of the two paths that stretched before her.

Perhaps it would be better if there were other people in the room; everyone would then pay less attention to what she was doing. She didn't want Dahlia peering over her shoulder.

Caitlyn tapped on the door, and the two people inside stopped speaking. She pushed it open. On the other side of the desk was Dahlia, her hands folded under her chin, face expressionless. In the corner of the room was a woman a few years older than Caitlyn, a Sapien with short brown hair. Caitlyn didn't recognise her, but then she didn't know all the Sapiens who worked in the university by sight.

'Ah, it's you again,' Dahlia said, staring up at her. 'You're working late this evening.'

'You know how it is with Professor Gudd,' Caitlyn said, glancing towards the woman in the corner, who openly returned Caitlyn's stare.

Not a trace of her thoughts passed across her features and Caitlyn was unnerved by her still expression.

'I wouldn't want to keep you,' Dahlia said to the woman with short brown hair. 'I know you have other places you need to be.'

Perhaps she wasn't a Sapien after all. Dahlia would never speak so deferentially to one. No Medius would. Caitlyn bowed her head and tried to avoid looking at either of them. She turned away and began her keyword search, the one that Alice had requested.

'If that is what you want, I'll be on my way,' the woman responded, stepping towards Caitlyn. She stopped abruptly. 'I won't come back again.'

'I know.'

The woman stared at Dahlia for a moment. 'Before I go, there is still that thing I need from—'

Caitlyn's head jerked up at the sound of several sets of heavy footsteps coming down the stairs. The short-haired woman tensed and stared at the door. Unsure how to react to this development, Caitlyn continued her keyword search, while trying to hide her face from them. She was only halfway through processing it and had to complete it before anyone came over to check on what she was doing. What if it was the Protection Department? What if they had found out she was selling university documents?

Finally, the studies finished downloading and she unplugged her screen – she would come back another time for the rest. She told herself to stay calm, but she still jumped when the door to the office slammed open and ricocheted off the wall.

'Which one is she?' came a voice from outside the room.

Caitlyn's mouth dropped open at the sight of four university guards crowding the doorway.

They know what I've done.

One of them raised his hand. His taser was pointed towards the short-haired woman, who had begun to make her way around the desk.

Instinctively, Caitlyn stepped in front of her. 'No, you've got the wrong—'

Her chest exploded with pain as her screen shot out of her hand. It felt as if her muscles were tearing away from the bone, and she dropped to her knees. The lick of fire spread through her veins, gathering pace as her body crumpled beneath her.

The others froze, and the only sound was that of Caitlyn's limbs juddering against the floor. Her skin sparked with the force of the electricity.

As quickly as it came, it was gone. Leaving her open-mouthed and panting on the cold stone floor.

When her body came to a rest, everyone else sprang into action. Chaos ensued. Caitlyn felt a rush of air as the younger woman leapt over the desk.

Gradually, the commotion melted into the background as she retreated into the sensations of her own body: her cheek pressed against the hard floor, her little finger still tapping involuntarily as her nerves struggled to regain control, her chest growing tighter.

Another burst of pain shot down her arm, taking her breath with it. Her eyes rolled upwards in response, and stars appeared across her vision.

She felt the soft beat of her eyelashes flicker against her cheek. Never had she been more aware of the sensations within her body, this casing that was solely hers. She knew she would never dismiss it again or glare at its supposed failings. It was hers, and it was precious.

Caitlyn wished her gran were here. It was the ones she loved who filled her thoughts now, as her finger involuntarily beat the rhythm that her heart could barely sustain. She could even feel the pressure of their touch. Her time had been too short. It hadn't been enough.

It isn't en—

She breathed out. She had burnt brightly, but not for long enough.

CHAPTER 17

Elise

As the young woman lay juddering on the floor, Elise leapt over the desk and snatched the taser from the guard's hand.

'Stop it!' Dahlia screamed at the guards. 'She wasn't the one I warned you about.'

Everyone froze and Elise took a step back. Had Dahlia really called the guards on her?

Dahlia stood up from her seat behind the desk. 'You incompetent fools, wait until the university board hears about this.' She jerked her head towards the young woman on the floor, whose eyes were rolling up into her head. 'Leave now, and we'll say no more of it. I'll take care of her. I am sure she will be fine after a cup of sugared tea.'

The guards stared at each other, appearing unsure what to do. This sort of event had clearly not been covered in their training, and the mention of the university board had halted them. One of them reached to take the taser from Elise's hand, and she let him. Maya had always instilled in her that violence was the last resort. Not because it was morally wrong but because it produced too many variables.

Elise leant down to check on the young woman on the floor, whose face was contorted in pain. She was still a girl, really. She might have been given the label of adult, but she should've had more of the in-between years granted to her before being swept up in work and worry. Elise touched a hand to the young woman's face and considered how she could help her – perhaps something sweet before taking her home to sleep.

The girl's fingers stretched towards the door, and Elise wished the guards would just leave so she could concentrate on her. Another spasm of pain passed across the girl's features, and she twisted in on herself. The effects of the taser should have worn off, and Elise wondered if there was something else at work.

Elise returned her hand to the woman's cheek as her eyelashes fluttered. She left it there while she stared up at the guards, waiting for their next move. The girl had stepped in front of Elise and protected her. Now she was Elise's responsibility.

The curled-up woman breathed out slowly. Elise waited for the next breath in, but it did not come.

Elise turned and peered closely at her. Blank eyes stared back. They were no longer of any use. The pain was smoothed from the young woman's features; they had come to rest in their final pose.

'Stars, she's dead,' Elise whispered, unable to process what had just happened. She stood, her voice growing louder as she searched each of their faces. 'You *killed* her.'

'Now, hold on a minute there,' one of the guards said, stepping forwards. 'She was an intruder. We were called to deal with an intruder, and we dealt with her.'

'But she wasn't an intruder, was she?' Dahlia spat. 'She was an assistant to Professor Gudd and has worked here for over three years.'

The guard baulked, and all four of them looked at each other.

'It was a mistake,' another guard said. 'In the rush of the moment ...'

'She must have had a weak heart,' the shorter guard said. 'It's not supposed to happen that way.'

Dahlia glared at him. 'Well, cardiac arrest is a known risk when you shoot them *directly in the chest*. You're supposed to go for the limbs!'

The guards were silent.

'I can understand your discomfort,' Dahlia continued, softening. 'And we don't need to make more of this than it was.'

Elise was about to speak when Dahlia cut her off and pointed at the woman on the floor. 'Take her away. She had an unfortunate heart attack. No tasers were used. Go and report it now to your superiors. I'm sure none of you wants an investigation into all of this.'

Dahlia stared at each of the guards in turn. Without a word, two of them walked over to the lifeless body of the woman on the ground and picked her up. Elise moved out of the way, her eyes never leaving the nameless woman. As she stared down at her, she saw herself in her place. If the young woman hadn't stepped in front of the taser, it could have been Elise lying there.

'*Gently*,' Dahlia barked at the guards. 'You've already taken her life. There's no need to take her dignity as well.'

The guards left the room, and Elise waited a few minutes until their steps faded into the distance.

She couldn't even look at the older woman as she spoke to her. 'What was her name?'

'Caitlyn. You should leave.'

'You think you can stay after this?'

'I had better stay after this. If I left now, the whole of the Protection Department would follow.'

'You called the guards on me.'

'I was being followed. You would have done the same.'

'No,' Elise said. 'I wouldn't. And for that, you'll give me everything I asked for.'

An hour later, Elise left the museum and returned to the base camp where Nathan and Max were waiting. Every step she took through Guanine felt as though it did not belong to her. Another person's split-second decision had given her a second life.

Elise reasoned that, as the intended target, the shot might not have landed on her chest but caught her arm or leg as it should have done. Then she might have lived. But she would still have been incapacitated, turned over to the Protection Department. And then, either way, she would have died at their hands or rotted away in a containment centre again.

It was not the first time Elise's life had been saved, but it was the first time a person had forfeited their own in return. Was that fair? No, of course not. Did Elise deserve to live longer than Caitlyn? Most likely not. She had not known Caitlyn, but she could not pretend that her own life was more valid or worthy. Perhaps this was the price Elise would now have to pay, always knowing that each step was stolen, each breath borrowed.

She thought about what this meant as she made her way through the still evening forest. She had always assumed that her life would be shorter than most, having taken so many risks over the past four years. She had accepted that their accumulation would catch up with her soon. If it had been her life taken, would she have achieved what she had set out to? Would she have been able to meet the stars with little regret? She did not think so.

Max was alert to Elise's presence long before she was to his. She drifted through the forest, unaware of her surroundings, her mind elsewhere. Stolen steps and borrowed breaths. When she found the meeting place, the light from the small fire did not provide the expected comfort, but she sat down next to it anyway.

'What happened?' Max asked, all traces of lightness gone from his voice.

'You look like death,' Nathan signed.

Elise flinched at his words. 'You were right. I shouldn't have gone after her.'

Nathan stared at Elise. 'Was she not who we thought she was?'

Elise blinked, trying to focus on them, but her vision would not clear. 'She was. I followed her down into the archives. She had an office there. She knew I was from Uracil when I closed the door behind me without asking. A Sapien would never act in that way.'

Elise barely felt the mug of hot tea that Max had slipped into her hands. She held it for a while before placing it at her feet.

'I told her we were pulling all undercover recruits out of their roles, but first, she had to supply some information. She wanted to know what had happened to Uracil, and I gave her only the barest details, wouldn't say where the new Uracil would be. She asked if there was an option to remain in Guanine, and I confirmed that there was. The last thing we need in Uracil is reluctant returners. That was settled then, she said. She would remain. She liked her life, had grown used to the comforts, was too old to start again. As I was about to leave ...'

For the first time, Elise looked directly at them both. 'A young woman came in. Nineteen at the most. Sapien. Some guards came. Dahlia had called them. She had noticed that she was being followed but didn't know by who. The guards were going to arrest me. The young woman, Caitlyn, stepped in front of me. They shot her with a taser, right in the chest. It was meant for me. I didn't realise she was having a heart attack. I just thought it was the electricity that had knocked her to the ground. She died, right there on the floor in front of me. And even though I didn't know her, I wish it had been me. She didn't deserve to get caught up in all the risks we take.'

Nathan put his arm around Elise, and she leant into him.

'When I was a boy,' Max said after a few minutes, with Elise signing his words for Nathan, 'my parents thought that I was a bit slower than the rest of our kind. They desperately tried to cover it up, terrified that I would be taken from them if the Potiors didn't think my enhancements had worked. Because that's what they do to the Potior children whose enhancements don't quite take. They thought I grieved too much for the few who died in my childhood. Now that I'm older, I understand that it just made me human. And it is our ability to grieve and reflect that makes us so. You must register the loss of this woman, even though you did not know her. But it is equally important that you reflect on what this means and why the stars chose to grant you a longer life than perhaps you believe you deserve.'

Nathan held Elise tighter, and she relaxed into him. She was so tired, so weary of the life she had chosen for herself.

Max watched them both, and Elise realised he had no one he could turn to. She and Nathan had lost many people, but they still had each other.

'Have you ever heard about the size of the cities in Zone 2?' Max signed, staring at the fire.

Elise shook her head, grateful to be discussing something that didn't make her think of Caitlyn's lifeless face looking up at her.

'They only have a few settlements, like we do, but they contain thousands and thousands of people. More than a mind is capable of imagining ...'

Elise settled back and watched him, relieved to be taken over the oceans and to another world.

The following morning started slowly. Elise was tired to her bones, and it took an hour of sipping hot tea before she could contemplate moving. She used the time to consider her situation. Max and Nathan sat quietly next to her, sensing her need for solitude.

'Where are we going next?' Max asked an hour later as they ate the watery porridge Nathan had prepared from his supplies. 'We can't return to Guanine for months. It isn't safe. Stars know if Dahlia has been picked up by now.'

'She'll be all right,' Elise signed, before spooning the tasteless oats into her mouth. 'She's a survivor. She'll have at least eight back-up plans.'

'I'm sorry you didn't get what you needed,' Nathan signed after finishing his food. 'Perhaps we could visit one of the other bases before returning to Guanine?'

Elise glanced over at him. 'I got what I needed; we don't need to return to Guanine.'

Nathan gave a broad grin. 'So, our first mission was successful!'

Elise didn't respond. She had gotten what she'd set out to, but the price paid by someone else wasn't worth its procurement.

They ate in silence for a moment.

'Do you think we should travel down to Cytosine?' Max asked, washing his bowl and spoon with the water in his canteen. 'We could show Nathan the way. I always think there is a quiet grandeur to Cytosine. It really is the most underrated of bases.'

'We should go back to Uracil,' Elise signed before unscrewing her water container.

'Uracil?' Nathan signed, his eyebrows shooting upwards. 'But we only left three weeks ago.'

The basis of a plan had begun to form in Elise's mind. If she were honest, it had been sitting there quietly for months, if not years. Long before her journey to Guanine, she had taken steps to gather the information she required. But it was Caitlyn's death that had solidified it in her mind. Only one of them had lived, and Elise had to use the time she had left wisely.

'We need to get back. We can't carry on like this.'

'What do you mean?' Nathan signed.

Elise leant forwards and briefly placed her hand on his knee. 'There will be more journeys, I promise. But there is something I have to do first.' Nathan lifted his hands to sign, but she continued. 'And I can't tell you what it is either.' Her gaze flicked over to Max, who was sitting slightly behind her. 'It's something I'm going to have to do alone.'

Nathan shifted slightly and glanced over at Max. He had understood her meaning.

'If you say so,' Nathan signed. 'If we pack up now, we might make it in ten days.'

'Good, I need to speak to my friends.' Elise turned to Max. 'Can you do something for me? It's quite a big favour, and I would owe you one in return.'

'Of course,' Max said, leaning in.

'Thank you,' Elise responded. 'It's going to be a bit of a journey, and you might need your running shoes if you're going to make it in time.'

CHAPTER 18

Twenty-Two

It was with some trepidation that Twenty-Two approached the outskirts of Uracil. She knew she had broken several rules by bringing back three Neanderthals and a stray Sapien. She had heard of the lengths Elise had taken to secure her own family's residency in Uracil, which hadn't ended very well in Twenty-Two's opinion – Elise had been captured, her father was dead and her mother was still missing. Perhaps abiding by the rules didn't always produce the best result.

Standing at the top of the hill, Twenty-Two could see the sweeping curves of the forest that hid its occupants. From her position, it could have been as uninhabited as any other part of Zone 3. The sun beat down on her back, and beads of sweat clung to her hairline. She brushed them away as she waited for the others to catch up. She had to conceal her fears from them; the Neanderthals needed to believe that they would be welcome in their new home.

'That's as far as I'll be going, Tutu,' Raynor shouted, wobbling her way up the hill. 'I'm striking off for Adenine now.'

'Are you sure you can't come with us?' Twenty-Two pleaded. 'Just for a day even. It would help with settling them in.'

Raynor shook her head. 'We've been over this. If they see how many we've brought with us, they might stop me from leaving again. And then we won't be able to check on the Neanderthals in Adenine. You know what Genevieve is like. So bent on stopping Uracil being discovered, she'll squash anyone who gets in her way.'

Twenty-Two nodded, conscious that the others would be with them in a moment. She usually had the evenings to talk with Raynor alone as the others would fall straight asleep as soon as their bags hit the ground, so unused were they to the long daily treks.

Farther down, Nineteen was struggling to crest the hill.

'I should go and help them,' Twenty-Two signed. 'I hope your journey is successful.' She turned back for a moment. 'And please do everything you can to help my brothers and sisters in Adenine. You know how much this means to me. I need as many as possible if we are to ensure our survival in the future.'

Raynor held her hand up to her eyes to shield herself from the sun. 'I promise. I once knew what it was like to have people to love.'

Satisfied at the sincerity of the promise, Twenty-Two hurried down the hill to help the other Neanderthals.

It was in a sombre mood, brought on by the exhaustion of the journey, that they entered the outskirts of Uracil. Even Twenty-Four's hands were still. There were no questions left in them. Twenty-Two led them around the forest's edge before striking inwards to find the settlement. She held her head high when she spotted the clearing, determined not to show any weakness.

She noted the stares from the few residents scattered around the newly sawdusted meeting place. But, as they had not yet built their treetop homes, their inquisitive looks did not penetrate down from the lofty heights of the branches above. None of them approached her, and she was happy to ignore them in return.

As Twenty-Two navigated the indirect route through the encampment, littered with felled trees, she held firmly on to Twenty-Four's hand. She tried to shield the girl from the worst of the stares. Thankfully, Nineteen had his head down as usual, and Thirty-One was fast asleep in his strong arms. All the time, she feared Genevieve's statuesque figure would appear, but she was nowhere to be seen.

'They don't look pleased to see us,' Lynette whispered, as Twenty-Two tried to circle outside the main meeting area, rather than walk through the middle of it.

'It is probably me that they are not happy to see,' Twenty-Two signed with one hand.

She knew this wasn't the entire truth, but she wanted the Neanderthals settled before facing the full force of Uracil's disapproval.

Before long, she spied the person she wanted. Georgina was sitting cross-legged, head bent, with her striking red hair hanging loosely over her face. Frowning in concentration, Bay and Twenty-Seven sat on either side of her, helping prepare vegetables for their evening meal. Georgina would understand. She would fight with both strongly enamelled tooth and neatly filed nail for the Neanderthals to remain.

A streak of movement made Twenty-Two flinch. She swung around to face it, letting go of Twenty-Four's hand and pushing her behind. She had known the residents would disapprove of what she had done, but she hadn't imagined them so outraged as to confront her so directly.

The muscles in her face relaxed as she recognised Kit pounding towards them. But it was not Twenty-Two whom he was rushing to greet. His gaze was firmly fixed on someone behind her.

'Oh, my boy!' Lynette cried out, tears trickling down her cheeks as Kit skidded to a halt in front of her. 'How you have grown! Let me see all of you.' She turned Kit this way and that while making approving noises. 'A man now, aren't you? And you've cut your hair. It suits you very well!'

Kit stepped forwards and hugged Lynette to him.

Twenty-Two was so taken aback by this show of emotion from the normally reticent Kit that she stared around at the other Neanderthals, hoping they would be able to explain what was going on. None of them would meet her gaze, and she realised they were overwhelmed by so many people staring at them. In a flash, she was taken back to being curled in a ball with all Uracil's residents staring from the treetops. She had wanted to shrink herself out of existence at that moment.

'I did not think I would ever see you again,' Kit signed, after pulling away from Lynette and running his hand over his short hair.

Nineteen raised his head for the first time. 'How do you know each other?'

'I was Kit's Companion years ago,' Lynette signed. 'Back when he was a boy in Guanine, before he left for Thymine.'

'The carving of the woman with the headscarf?' Twenty-Two signed to Kit, referring to the carvings he had made of the people most important to him.

'Yes, she was my first attempt.'

Nineteen stared at Kit. 'He left for Thymine? And at the same time, I was left in Guanine?'

Nineteen's deeply set eyes flicked between them for answers.

'Yes, dear,' Lynette responded. 'But we can talk more about that in a bit. Let's—'

'Twenty-Two.' Maya's voice rang out from the other side of the clearing. 'Come over here. I need to speak with you.'

Twenty-Two turned to Kit. 'Take them to Georgina. Quickly. And find Samuel if he is here.'

Kit nodded and began ushering the Neanderthals towards Georgina's hearth. Twenty-Two managed to untangle Twenty-Four's hand from hers with some difficulty, so firm was her grasp. The young Neanderthal's eyes never left the woman who was glaring at Twenty-Two.

'It will be fine,' Twenty-Two signed quickly to her. 'Now go and find Bay and Twenty-Seven. They will be so excited to meet you.'

'Twenty-Two!' Maya shouted.

Not looking convinced, Twenty-Four transferred her hand to Lynette's, and Twenty-Two hurried over to Maya, hoping she would stop calling her name.

Maya's face was like steel. Not a flicker of emotion passed across it as Twenty-Two joined her.

'Your actions will bring the Potiors to our doors,' Maya said, lifting her chin. 'You will bring death to everyone you love and care for.'

Twenty-Two took a step back at the force of Maya's words. She had never witnessed her react this way to anything, let alone something Twenty-Two had done.

'They were going to die in there,' she signed, hoping that Maya would understand her. 'I had to free them.'

Maya frowned in frustration. 'I cannot follow your meaning.' She drew out her screen and unfolded it. 'Write it down.'

Twenty-Two did as she was told.

Before she had finished, Maya's head snapped upwards. 'And they will die here, too, if the Potiors come looking for them. All you have done is transfer the location of where it will happen and included others in it.'

Twenty-Two pulled herself up and wrote her next message. 'The Potiors have better things to do than look for a few strays they wanted to get rid of anyway.'

Maya's eyes flashed. 'Do not presume to know what the Potiors care about. They also have their pride, and they won't appreciate you making fools of them.' She gestured around her. 'Have you not heard of Uracil's losses?'

Twenty-Two shook her head, struggling to understand.

'We found the lost residents. What was left of them.' Maya's dark eyes blazed. 'A third of our people have died. Starved to death or succumbed to sickness. And you! You are trundling around Zone 3 as if only your people matter. Uracil is on her knees, and we need all members of the Infiltration Department here following orders, not disobeying them. And you were ordered to return to me after your mission with Max and Septa for a further one.'

The sudden news of Uracil's losses threatened to knock Twenty-Two's legs from beneath her. She steadied herself, determined not to stumble in front of Maya as she was sure this was the effect she wanted. Twenty-Two's mind flitted back to her time in Cytosine – clawing hunger, slowness of thought that deteriorated with each passing day, the sense of hopelessness that threatened to consume her, debilitate her. She had nearly starved to death back there, and she wouldn't wish it on anyone.

'What the stars is going on?' Samuel shouted, running across the meeting area towards them. 'There are three new Neanderthals with Georgina. *Three!*'

'I think you understand what has happened here,' Maya responded, folding her arms.

Samuel stared between them. 'No, I really don't.'

'Twenty-Two has gone against everything we have asked of her and brought back those Neanderthals. And her actions may bring the Potiors to our doors.'

'But the chances—'

'The chances are high enough for us to warrant a full lockdown for the next week. Which will delay all our plans,' Maya said, her voice rising again.

'But they are only children. We cannot blame them.'

'I don't. This lies with Twenty-Two. She should never have broken into a museum and brought them with her, and she knows it. She knew we would refuse permission for her to do such a thing, with no thought for the lives of the people in Uracil.'

Samuel's voice began to rise. 'Twenty-Two brought children with her, who deserve our compassion and welcome. Haven't we lost enough children already?'

Maya held up her hand to silence him. 'I won't hear any more.' She turned to Twenty-Two and pointed her finger at her chest. 'You are no longer a member of the Infiltration Department. If you cannot take the simplest of orders, then you cannot be trusted to protect Uracil.'

Twenty-Two's face fell. The only thing that had made her feel accepted in Uracil, valued even, had been taken from her. And this decision had come from Maya, whom she had always admired.

Samuel watched Maya's retreating figure. 'That didn't go very well.'

Twenty-Two's mind went blank. Her losses had barely begun to register.

'Perhaps you could take me over to meet them,' Samuel signed, peering at Twenty-Two's face.

They walked over to greet the huddled group.

Samuel's pace quickened as they drew closer. 'Lynette? Is that really you?'

The older woman blushed. 'I didn't know if you would recognise me, so many years have passed.'

'Of course I do. You haven't changed a bit.' He looked around him, where quite a crowd had gathered. 'Wait until—'

'I have already seen her,' Kit signed, scrunching his eyes up at Samuel. 'I now have two of my previous Companions living with me.'

It was an evening like no other Twenty-Two had experienced. Celebration mixed with loss, laughter with sudden sadness when someone who was no longer with them was mentioned. But for Twenty-Two at least, one outweighed the other. She watched with pleasure as Bay confidently introduced herself to Thirty-One, who shyly accepted her offer of a warm jumper that Georgina had knitted over the winter. This was what Twenty-Two had hoped for, and it pained her that they might have to separate themselves again if the Neanderthals were not allowed to remain in Uracil.

As everyone began to get to know each other, Twenty-Two stood to greet someone she had not seen for months.

'You've returned!' Ezra signed, bobbing up and down on his feet in excitement. 'I didn't know when I'd next see you!'

His wide grin took over his features in the way it had always done, and she noticed that he had begun to fill out a little.

He looked around in amazement. 'Three new Neanderthals as well! That is a thing to celebrate.'

Without waiting for introductions, he sat down in front of each one to greet them, signing his welcome and sharing his amazement as they told him about their journey.

Twenty-Two scrunched her eyes. Ezra watched in awe as Twenty-Four described the length of their journey, which in her mind had taken months. Twenty-Two knew that Ezra would make the newcomers feel both wanted and valued. She had missed her closest friend and, with him by her side, she believed she could face whatever would arise over the next few days.

The evening crept into night, and Samuel never left their camp.

'I think they are all asleep,' Lynette signed, returning to the fire after checking on the three exhausted newcomers.

'We should all be getting some sleep,' Georgina signed, stifling a yawn with the back of her hand. 'It's been an eventful day.'

Tilla leant towards Georgina and rested her head on her shoulder. Next to them were Luca and Septa, whose hands were intertwined.

'Would you mind if I brought my sleeping roll over and stayed here tonight?' Samuel asked.

Twenty-Two watched as a silent message passed between him and Georgina.

'I think the more the merrier,' Georgina signed. 'But I hope you're not bringing that giant tent with you. It will take up most of the hearth.'

Samuel gave her a half-smile. 'It was my mother's idea that we each make one. After twenty-five years under a roof, I think she struggles with staring at the stars at night.'

Twenty-Two wondered at this. Around the Neanderthal hearths, they all slept facing the stars, nothing between them and their makers.

In only ten minutes, Samuel was back again, with Neve, his sleeping roll and a few blankets.

'I'm sorry about Maya,' Samuel signed, sitting between Twenty-Two and Neve. 'Since my mother has been out of action, Maya seems to have taken over her campaign to shelter Uracil. A bit too enthusiastically, if you ask me. I think she's doing it for Genevieve. And for the people who died. She knew nearly every one of them.'

'What has happened to Genevieve?' Twenty-Two asked. 'I haven't seen her since my return.'

Samuel cleared his throat. 'Since the news of Uracil's losses reached us, she hasn't left her tent.' He rubbed his face with both hands. 'She just sits there. Eats, of course, and washes. But won't say a word to me or anybody else.'

Neve leant forwards and helped herself to more rosehip tea. 'It has affected everyone differently. Thank the stars that Vance cannot remember the people we have lost. At least he has been saved from this misery.'

Twenty-Two studied the newcomer to their group. She spoke with honesty, and Twenty-Two had begun to like her.

Neve smiled across at Samuel, and Twenty-Two recognised a longing in her eyes. A few years ago, Samuel had looked at Elise that way. But what did Twenty-Two know of such things? She had never felt romantic love and had no desire to. Along with the joy it brought, there was, in her opinion, a heavy price to pay. As well as the possibility of heartbreak, it clouded judgement and shaved away a person's core to make room for another. Twenty-Two could love her friends without losing part of herself, and she wanted nothing more.

Her thoughts darkened as she considered what Maya's response might mean for the future of the Neanderthals. How could she ensure there would be another generation if there were so few of them?

Lynette stretched her arms above her head before signing goodnight and making her way to her sleeping roll. Thirty-One was already fast asleep, the new green jumper that she had refused to take off peeping above her blanket.

Twenty-Two waited until Lynette was out of sight and the others were talking before signing to Kit, who was sitting across from her. 'I made a mistake in bringing them here. Uracil will not accept them.'

'You have to give them time,' Kit responded, his face still. 'They will come around to the idea eventually.'

'And what if they don't? Genevieve has made it clear that I am not welcome. What if she has decided that she can't be around any Neanderthal, and it's not just me? Will she punish them as well?'

'She hasn't punished me,' Kit responded. 'Well, not when I last saw her anyway. Not that I've seen her for weeks. Perhaps she isn't the threat that you fear her to be.'

Twenty-Two stared across at Kit. She was beginning to wonder whether he was naive. But then he hadn't seen the way Genevieve had reacted to her.

The others had begun to drift away to their own hearths for the night. Even though she was exhausted from her journey and the worry about the others, Twenty-Two waited until everyone fell asleep before creeping away. There was something she had to do that evening that she should have done a long time ago.

Moving as quietly as possible, Twenty-Two pushed aside the fold of canvas and entered the darkened tent.

'I've been waiting for you,' Genevieve said from the darkness. 'Samuel dropped by when he collected his sleeping roll to let me know you have returned.'

Twenty-Two froze, crouched near the entrance.

'Honestly, I thought you would have come earlier; I must have miscalculated somewhere.' There was a sigh as Genevieve sat up. 'It has happened a few times recently.'

A match was struck, and the small flame touched the wick of several round candles in a glass bowl. The light cast an amber glow under Genevieve's face. Lit from below, she looked older, her brow bridge more prominent, her intention unclear.

'There,' Genevieve said, blowing out the flame. 'I can see you now. Tell me, have you come to kill me and remove a corrupt leader from a position of power as you did with my daughter? Or something else?'

Twenty-Two frowned then lifted her hands to sign. 'Something else.'

She moved farther into the tent. Not too close – she still needed to quickly leave when she had finished with Genevieve.

Genevieve held out her screen. 'Perhaps you could write your response out on this.'

Twenty-Two obliged. 'I came to ask you to welcome the Neanderthals I have brought with me from Guanine. They have done nothing wrong and deserve your compassion, not your disdain. I understand the weight of the power you hold over Uracil, and I am asking that you use it wisely.'

Genevieve leant forwards, the soft light from the candles dropping away from her. 'That is a serious request indeed, and I have something to ask of you in return. But first, do you know why Uracil was named as it is?'

Twenty-Two shook her head.

'The four bases in Zone 3, Thymine, Adenine, Guanine and Cytosine, are named after the four bases in DNA. But to pass on its instructions, DNA needs to copy itself and, when it does, it becomes RNA.'

Twenty-Two stared at Genevieve, wondering where this was leading.

Genevieve raised an eyebrow. 'RNA still has three of the bases, Adenine, Guanine and Cytosine. But for the fourth base, Thymine is switched for another called Uracil.'

'So, it is named after the lesser-known base, Uracil?' Twenty-Two stated, thinking that she was beginning to understand.

'Precisely. But there is more. For a long time, people believed that RNA was just a messenger. But it plays an important role in gene expression and what that cell can do. It literally affects the outcome.'

Twenty-Two nodded. 'So, Uracil is not just a messenger. It is also a guide.'

'Yes. And I had forgotten why Vance gave it that name nearly fifty years ago. He can no longer guide us as he once did. But he did not build Uracil just to hide us. He built us to lead as well.'

'Do you think the others will welcome the Neanderthals if I help? Do the others in power, such as Maya, know that you wanted to discuss this with me?'

'They do, and they don't.'

Twenty-Two grabbed Genevieve's arm, pulling the woman closer. She squeezed Genevieve's wrist, wanting her to know that she was not weak or easily played with. Genevieve's eyes widened at the strength of Twenty-Two's grasp.

'Are you threatening me?' Genevieve said.

Twenty-Two wrote her response with her free hand. 'No. I do not make threats. They are used by weak people who are unsure of their actions. If I decide to do something, I do not warn people about it and give them a chance to prepare. I just do it. I grabbed your arm to bring you closer so I can read you. I want to know what you are hiding from me.'

'Enough to keep us all alive,' Genevieve said, slowly circling Twenty-Two's hand with her own and prising her fingers away.

She, too, was built with strength coursing through her. Twenty-Two realised that sometimes the stars were generous with their gifts – wisdom, aesthetics and strength. What had one person done to deserve all of this? And then she remembered that the stars were not the only ones who had handed out Genevieve's gifts.

'I can't tell you what I want you to do until we are safely out of Uracil. Our plans cannot be discussed here,' Genevieve said quietly.

'If things must be hidden, why would you ever confide in me about them? Of all the people in this base, why would you want help from someone you hate for killing your daughter?'

'I do hate you for taking my daughter from me. But I am not blinded by it. You cannot alter your perception of reality based on an emotional response. I was taught that on the first day of my training to become an undercover operative.' Genevieve rubbed the wrist that Twenty-Two had been holding. 'I choose you for three reasons. Firstly, because I know for certain that you are not a spy for the Potiors, which I can only say about a handful of people now. I can't even guarantee my own son's stance. Secondly, because you have the conviction to carry out your actions, which is an unusual quality even amongst the bravest. So many dither and second-guess themselves. Thirdly, because you can read the truth of a situation, so you will know whether I and the others you encounter are speaking honestly.'

Twenty-Two studied Genevieve. 'There is one more reason that you haven't shared with me.'

Genevieve gave a tight-lipped smile. 'There is. My fourth reason is that if you decide to betray me to Uracil, tell them I am keeping things from them, no one will believe you. You have no weight or wealth here. You cannot raise an army against me.'

'Why did you not choose Kit if you hate me so much? He can read others just as well as I can.'

'He does not have your same conviction to act. He is more of an observer of this world, less of a participant.' Genevieve stared directly at Twenty-Two. 'And he garners more respect than you do amongst the people of Uracil. Many of them like him. But they do *not* like you.'

Twenty-Two blinked. The truth in Genevieve's words pierced through her thickened skin, and she felt very alone. The older woman's eyes shone, and Twenty-Two knew then that she was enjoying her discomfort.

Twenty-Two pulled herself up. 'Why would I do anything for someone who enjoys seeing me suffer and won't even tell me what they want me to do?'

'Because six months ago I made a bad bargain, a very bad bargain,' Genevieve said quietly. 'I must begin my atonement, but I need some help with that. It will mean a long journey for us.'

'Your inability to bargain well does not affect me,' Twenty-Two wrote, her conviction clear in her body language. 'I will not assist someone who does not respect my people or me.'

'I know,' Genevieve responded. 'But I need your help and so I have spent quite some time considering what is within my power to offer you. If you assist me, I will help welcome your Neanderthals as you have requested, but I'll also offer you something else that is far more valuable. In one of the bases is all the genetic information that the Potiors have stored over the years. Including that of the Neanderthals. If we are successful, you can bring back as many Neanderthals as you wish.'

Twenty-Two squeezed her eyes shut.

'I am glad you have already given some thought to how you will ensure the continuation of the Neanderthals,' Genevieve said. 'But without access to the genetic material and equipment that allows you to bring them back in a controlled way, you leave the task of repopulation to a group of ... how many are there of you? Seven? It would be a difficult decision to make. Wait and hope for romantic love to blossom between at least two couples and risk your extinction? Or enforce pregnancy and increase your chances? It is not much of a future for the younger ones to look forward to.'

Twenty-Two had thought about it in recent weeks. She had never discussed it with Kit or any of the others. It loomed over her like a darkened sky threatening a storm. She could turn from it, but it remained there, hanging heavily, waiting for its time to rain down impossible decisions on them all.

'There are still the Neanderthals in Adenine,' Twenty-Two wrote. 'Our number may not be that small.'

Genevieve smiled sadly. 'There are no Neanderthals in Adenine any more. The Potiors have moved on to other matters.'

Twenty-Two's breath caught in her throat. 'That can't be right.'

'I'm sorry, but it is.'

Twenty-Two felt sick, and her head swam. She couldn't gather her thoughts; they were beyond order.

'But we could work together,' Genevieve said, her tone suddenly neutral. 'You assist me, help me atone, and in return, I help you retrieve the means to make more of your kind.'

'I will do it,' Twenty-Two wrote.

'Excellent,' Genevieve said. 'We must leave tonight before the others wake. I will instruct Maya that the Neanderthals are to remain in Uracil until I return.' She stared up at Twenty-Two. 'And I'll leave alternative instructions for if I do not.'

CHAPTER 19

Elise

'Would someone please explain why I am sitting in the middle of a field at seven in the morning?' Luca said, peering around at the group. 'The sun is already strong, I forgot my hat, my head is going to burn, and I don't see what can be so urgent that it can't be said in the main camp, preferably with a bowl of stew clasped between my hands.'

Elise looked around at her original companions, whom she had asked to meet with her as soon as she'd returned to Uracil. None of them seemed that impressed by her urgent request for a meeting, especially as she had banned them from bringing anyone else with them. These were the people Elise trusted more than anyone else. Not just in the usual sense of the word; she also trusted them to be brave when it was most needed.

'I have to agree with Luca,' signed Samuel, who seemed unable to look directly at Elise.

Luca gave him a broad grin. 'Thanks, Samuel.'

Samuel tapped his forehead. 'We're not in the museum any more. We can't creep off together like this. People will get ideas.'

Elise tried not to think about whom Samuel was referring to.

'That's what I want to talk about,' she signed. 'Back when we were in the museum and decided to leave together, did we really imagine that this would be the end result? That we would be hiding away with a group of people who are getting picked off by the Potiors?'

Glancing at each other, they all shifted uncomfortably. Elise had a sudden suspicion that they had been discussing her while she was away.

'We're all so sorry about your mum, Elise,' Georgina signed. 'But we have to concentrate on keeping everyone who's left safe.'

Elise was not disheartened. She had been expecting this.

'There's a spy in Uracil and we all know it. So, we might as well be open about it. While they exist, Uracil will never be safe.'

Samuel's face fell. 'I didn't think that was common knowledge.'

'It is when you've got half a brain,' Georgina signed, after dropping the blades of grass she had been rolling between her thumb and fingers. 'What I can't stop thinking about is how those airplanes knew where we were. There weren't any ground troops that came close to us. Our scouts would have seen them. Instead, the planes just flew directly for us.'

'I think the Potiors have known about Uracil for years,' Elise signed. 'They know about all the islanders around here. So why wouldn't they know about Uracil too?'

Luca's eyes widened. 'But why wait? If they'd known about us for ages, why didn't they come for us before?'

Elise had known this question would be raised, and she had to tell them her suspicions if she was going to convince them to go along with her plan.

'I think it's because Uracil set its sights outwards. It had a policy change to take proactive action against the Potiors, which must have gotten back to them.'

Kit stared at her. 'If that is the case, I would never mention it again outside this circle. People have long memories. The Infiltration Department was behind that change in policy, and their members will recall that you campaigned for it for over a year.'

Elise drew herself up. 'I did. And you could believe I am partly to blame for what has happened to us all. I certainly do.'

Georgina leant over and rested her hand on Elise's knee. 'But I've thought about it for a long time, especially since my mum died, and I'm not going to lessen the actions of the Potiors by shouldering their blame. It lies at their doors. They bombed us and left the residents to starve on an island that didn't have enough supplies.'

'Certainly it lies at their doors,' Samuel signed. 'Everything always has. Uracil would not have been needed if the Potiors were benevolent leaders.'

Kit nodded.

Georgina dropped her head into her hands, her fingers lacing their way through her red hair. 'Bay and Twenty-Seven are never going to be safe, are they? Whatever I do. However well I try to hide them, the Potiors could come and find us in mere hours and finish what they started.'

'You know I will do everything I can to stop them,' Kit signed.

They were all silent for a moment, and Elise waited for the full force of what they had been discussing to settle on them.

Luca lifted his head. 'So, we've all agreed that the Potiors are still scum. Was that the only point of this meeting? Can I get back to my breakfast now?'

Elise swatted him with her arm when he tried to stand.

'There's another reason for this meeting,' she signed. 'And if your empty stomach and pink head will allow, I'll continue.'

'Have it your way, Thanton.'

Elise ignored him. 'I needed to check first that you are all in agreement that those we love will never be safe here.'

'If it's a full-scale attack you're thinking of,' Samuel signed, 'it would never work. Even if we called in every person from Uracil who was strong enough to hold a weapon, we would lose within minutes. There are too many of them. A thousand Potiors, plus all the Protection Department and all the misguided Medius and Sapiens who would side with them. It would be a suicide mission.'

Elise shook her head. 'I was thinking of something else.'

Luca's keen gaze whipped around to Elise. 'You're bloody mental. You're going to try and assassinate the Premier?'

Elise shook her head again. 'No. Another Potior would quickly take his place, and nothing would change. They'd probably try and hush it up and say he died of natural causes, just like they hushed up Fintorian dying at the museum in Thymine. They don't want anyone to know that a Potior bleeds like the rest of us.

'I've thought about it for a long time. Years, in fact. And that's what they would expect us to do. That's what everyone expects one single person or a tiny group like us to do. Perhaps that's why no one has done anything about this before. They've just been waiting for some fantastical hero to come along and save the day. But we all know that's not real life.'

Georgina nodded. 'I never thought I'd say this, but my brother used to talk about something similar, and it was the only bit of sense he spoke. He said that from what he was able to study, the most significant events in history are a collection of smaller ones brought about by individuals who didn't even know each other. But all their small impacts led to another, and then another. A chain of events that would take years to piece together.'

'Exactly!' Elise signed, excited that Georgina understood what she was saying. 'It's what I realised when that young woman stepped out in front of me at the university. Each life affects the outcome of countless others. There is no single hero who will save us all. They may save a few, but no one can be expected to save the future of thousands of people. It is up to us to help save ourselves.'

'So, if no one is going to be hero-ing around the place,' Luca signed, 'then what's the point of this discussion?'

A look of understanding passed across Samuel's features.

'Oh, stars,' he signed, glancing up at the sky. 'You're going to get us all killed.'

'What?' Luca said, staring at him. 'What does she want us to do?'

Samuel's gaze settled on Elise. 'She wants to tell them the truth.'

'And that means we'll have to go to Adenine,' Elise said. 'And figure out a way to send a screen release.'

They were all silent on the walk back to Uracil, the enormity of what they had decided to do weighing heavily on them. Elise glanced around at each of her friends. Had she asked too much of them?

'I've thought about it,' Georgina announced, stopping on a sheer scree slope, 'and I'm coming to Adenine with you.'

Four heads swung around to face her.

'You don't have to,' Elise signed.

'What about Bay and Twenty-Seven?' Kit signed at the same time.

'With the greatest respect, you're not a fighter—' Samuel began.

Georgina held up her hands, and they all dropped theirs. The sun beat down on the five lone figures in a near-deserted landscape that stretched for miles.

'I know I'm not a fighter. But that doesn't mean I can't be of use.' She tapped her head. 'I have a brilliant memory, which you might need. And you may have forgotten, but I managed to take on a Potior back in Thymine and saved Elise's life in the process. I'll stay behind you all when we're in the depths of it and I'll make sure I have a few tricks up my sleeve.'

She gave a wide grin that showed her perfect white teeth.

'But your children ...' Kit signed.

Elise glanced over at him; it was the first time she had heard Kit refer to them in that way.

'... will be safe with Tilla,' Georgina signed back to him, 'for the moment. But they won't be safe with anyone in the long run. I'm doing this for them.'

Luca frowned. 'We could get someone else to help.'

'We can't trust anyone,' Georgina signed firmly. 'We all know that. None of us is the spy, as we only learnt of Uracil recently. I'm afraid we will have to treat everyone with suspicion from now on. So, we need to leave quietly and with minimum fuss. I won't even be telling Tilla the details. She has a habit of letting things slip.'

'It's your decision whether to come,' Elise signed. 'No one can make it for you.'

She held Georgina's gaze while silently sending a prayer to the stars to watch over her if she did come with them. If anything happened to Georgina, she knew she would never forgive herself for putting her best friend in danger.

Luca groaned. 'Septa's going to kill me.'

'She can't know about it,' Samuel signed. 'Whatever your instincts might tell you.'

Luca shot him a look.

'I'm sorry,' Samuel continued. 'But she does seem to have you wrapped around her little finger. Sometimes, when I see you together, I want to ask if you are all right and that you should blink twice for yes.'

'It's not that bad! And you're one to talk with the way you run around after Neve!'

Samuel held his hands up before signing, 'Well, I certainly won't be telling Neve about this, and you should do the same with Septa. We all have to be incredibly careful. The spy has managed to assimilate themselves within our group for several years.'

'I know,' Luca signed reproachfully. 'It's not that. It's, well, there's something I haven't told you all. I'm going to be a dad.'

All of their mouths fell open in unison, even Kit's.

'I know,' Luca signed, blushing, before rubbing the back of his shaven head. 'Poor kid, eh? Having me for a dad.'

'Oh, no, we didn't mean it like that!' Elise cried, stepping forwards to hug him. 'It's just so unexpected.'

'He'll be the luckiest kid in Zone 3 to have you as a father,' Georgina signed with the widest of smiles, joining in to hug Luca on his other side.

'This is excellent news,' Kit signed enthusiastically. 'The next generation is on its way!'

Kit also wrapped his arms around the huddled group of three.

'I am so very happy for you and Septa,' Samuel said, stepping towards the group and then stepping back. 'But I don't think I can join in with the hug. I can cope with one person now, but four ...'

Luca glanced up at him from the mound of arms around him. 'That's okay, Samuel. Theoretical hug accepted.'

Samuel grinned back at him as they slowly unlaced their arms and began walking again.

Partway down the hill, Samuel smiled to himself. 'But Septa is going to kill you.'

Luca punched him on the arm. 'It's nice that I can do that now.'

'If you're going to be a father, don't you think you should consider not coming as well?' Samuel signed after rubbing his arm.

'I know,' Luca signed. 'It puts me in the same boat as Georgina. But like her, I want to do this for my child. Maybe even my children in the future, if it all works out.' He paused for a moment. 'And I want to do it for Seventeen as well. We can't let that happen again. She should be here with us, with Bay.'

'Seventeen, whom we shall never forget ...' Samuel said quietly to himself.

They all fell silent. Elise thought of the losses they had all suffered over the past four years, and she suspected her friends were doing the same. Her mind stretched back farther, through her first adult years and childhood, to the grandparents and Sapien friends who had died too young, not having the Medistamps for treatment. Her family's losses had begun before she was even born, when her only aunt and uncle had been taken from them.

Elise stopped when they neared the outskirts of Uracil but were still in low grassland, so she knew no one could hide and watch them. 'So, we all know what we've got to do?'

'Kit is going to wait for Max to return,' Georgina said, ticking off the points on her fingers. 'Samuel will speak to Maya and make sure that Uracil has protection plans. Luca is going to see if he can find any more of the gloves Uracil's guards have. I'll collect medical supplies.'

'I'm still not sure bringing Max in on this is the best idea,' Luca signed. 'He is a Potior, after all. Prime candidate for the spy.'

'I know it's risky,' Elise signed. 'But we need someone with insider knowledge. And it might be better to have Max with us. At least we can keep an eye on him then. It will make it a bit more difficult for him to send any warning messages.'

She looked around at the others, but she could tell they weren't comfortable with the idea.

'I've spent quite a bit of time with him, and I'm pretty certain he's genuine,' she continued. 'And I'm hoping when we get back, he'll have returned from doing what I asked of him. Then we'll have another safety measure with us.'

Sure enough, as they walked back into Uracil, Elise spied Max's tall figure at the edge of the meeting area, standing alongside a shorter one.

She barely registered Samuel's face souring before breaking into a run.

Hearing her approach, the two men turned, and Arlo's face broke into a broad grin.

Elise skidded to a halt in front of him. 'Thank you so much for coming.' She turned to Max. 'And thank you so much for bringing him to me.'

Max nodded. 'It took quite of bit of persuading for the Elders to let him go.'

Arlo sized Elise up. 'I think we'd better go for a walk, and you can explain exactly why you've brought me here.'

They were silent until they reached the outskirts of Uracil.

'It is not until you leave Synthium that you remember how small it is,' Arlo said with an appreciative gaze. 'Of course, I've been to the mainland before. Quite a few times when I was younger and wanted to test the few boundaries I had been set. But it always makes me a little sad when I am reminded that I grew up in a chicken coop.'

Elise smiled over at him. 'Thank you for coming. I didn't know who else I could trust.'

'Thank you for trusting me,' he said, his mouth curling into a smile.

'Do you mind if I ask you a few questions first before I begin?'

Arlo shrugged. 'If it helps.'

'What do you think of the Potiors?'

Arlo burst out laughing. 'Stars, you don't begin with the light ones, do you? Favourite colour or food to eat?'

Elise glanced over at him as she led them towards the base of the highest hill. It was a hot summer's day, and she tried to let the heat tease the knots out of her muscles.

The amusement stayed with Arlo; he had clearly relaxed despite the topic they were discussing. 'I think that the Potiors are dangerous, merciless and unpredictable.'

'Is that what the Elders of Synthium think too?'

The change in Arlo was instantaneous. 'I agreed to come here to provide my assistance to a friend. Minerva was distraught when I told her I would be gone for weeks.' Elise turned to him, drawn by the sharpness in his tone. 'If you think I'll be telling you everything about my people, then you are dearly mistaken.'

'No, no. I didn't mean it like that.' Elise touched his arm. 'I'm sorry, that was clumsy. I didn't mean it to come across that way. I understand that you must protect your people and I don't need to know what the Elders think. It's you I'm interested in.'

Arlo stared at her for a moment. 'What is this about?'

'There's something my friends and I want to do,' Elise said. 'And I need another fighter on board, one that I know isn't involved in all the underhandedness that surrounds Uracil at the moment. We have to bring Max, and I need someone to watch him quietly. I have to focus on the task, and I can't be checking my back all the time to see if he's about to stab it.'

'I can do that,' Arlo said. 'I don't think I would fare well up against a Potior one-on-one, but I could slow him down enough to warn you.'

Elise ran her hands through her short hair and stared at the sky. 'There's something else.'

Arlo raised an eyebrow in enquiry.

'It's highly dangerous, and we might not come back.'

'But ... ?'

'If it works, it could change ... everything.'

The following morning, the five companions met again on the same hillside to report back. This time Elise brought a bowl of stew for Luca, which he happily accepted.

'I'll go first then,' Elise signed. 'I've spoken with Arlo, and he's agreed to come with us to Adenine to try and find a way to let people know the truth about the Potiors. He understands the dangers, but I think he is itching to do something. He's tired of living on that small island. I think he wants to see a bit of the world, maybe have an adventure.'

Samuel sat down heavily, and the others joined him. 'Pfff ... what we are about to do is hardly having "an adventure". But I suppose that's what happens to your perspective when you grow up in an elfin camp.'

Elise glanced over at him, unsure why Samuel was so grouchy that morning. 'I only meant that he's keen to do something a bit riskier than he has encountered before.'

'And you're sure we can trust him?' Georgina signed, biting her lip. 'None of us knows him.'

Elise thought about it for a moment. Was this the right thing to do? There were so many variables.

'I haven't known him that long, but I have to trust my gut on this,' she signed slowly, measuring her words. 'And I'm certain he's not in league with the Potiors as he persuaded Synthium to save the other residents. He's lived on that island all his life. And he can fight. He might not be a match for Max, but he'll be able to slow him down and warn the rest of us if it's needed.'

'I don't want to sound arrogant,' Samuel signed, dipping his head. 'But we do have someone already. Me. I could be a match for Ma—'

'It's true,' Luca interrupted. 'Samuel's practically a Potior, just not as pretty. Or as clever. But he is strong.'

'I know,' Elise signed, ignoring Samuel's frown. 'But there will be times Samuel will have to act separately to Max, and we need someone who can watch Max all the time.'

Georgina nodded before changing the subject. 'I've spent the day collecting the medical supplies we might need. I've also explained to Lynette, Nineteen and the rest of the Neanderthals that we are going away for a while. Tilla will look after them, but she's not very happy with me.' Georgina wouldn't meet any of their gazes. After a moment, she continued signing. 'But I couldn't find Twenty-Two. Does anyone know where she's gone?'

'She left me a note saying she would be gone for a few weeks,' Kit signed. 'She did not say where or who with.'

'I know a little more,' Samuel signed. 'She left before dawn yesterday morning. With my mother.'

Kit's head flew up.

'All I know is what my mother put in a note to me. It was encrypted. Rather too well, actually. I couldn't decipher what they were doing, but she took Twenty-Two with her. I don't know where or for how long.'

'Is she safe with her?' Kit signed to Samuel.

For once, the concern was evident in his body language.

'Honestly,' Samuel signed, 'I don't know. Genevieve still mourns Faye, and what happened to the residents on the island hit her hard. Harder than I would have anticipated.'

'But you must know whether your mother is capable of harming Twenty-Two,' Kit signed quickly.

Samuel reached over and touched Kit lightly on the shoulder before signing. 'I'm sorry, but I cannot promise it. My mother has spent most of her life working undercover; she is challenging to read and tells me only what she wants me to know.'

Georgina threw her hands up in the air. 'Why would Twenty-Two agree to go anywhere with Genevieve? It's insane. I thought she wasn't that naive child any more!'

Kit returned to his usual self-control. 'She isn't. Genevieve must have promised her something she could not refuse or threatened her with something she could not ignore.' He glanced up at the sky. 'Her fate is with the stars now. May they watch over her.'

The others were all still for a while.

Eventually, Elise asked quietly, 'How did you get on, Luca?'

He sat up. 'I couldn't get five pairs of the gloves, but I did get three, including my own.'

Elise smiled. 'I didn't think you'd get any, so that's brilliant.'

'Who should I give them to?' Luca asked, pulling them out of his pocket.

Elise stared at the innocuous-looking gloves that amplified the kinetic energy of a punch and knocked a person several metres away. At one time, all the guards in Uracil had had them.

'You keep one pair and give the others to Samuel and Georgina.'

Georgina leant backwards, away from the gloves. 'Surely Kit would be the better option, or yourself?'

Elise shook her head. 'I'm a long-range fighter. So is Kit, now that he's got his new throwing spear.' Kit's eyes scrunched up at the corners. 'Samuel needs one set if we meet a Potior or have to take down Max. Samuel's strong but needs everything we've got to try and equalise with them. You are our other close-range fighter, Luca, so you should have a set. And Georgina, you need something if someone takes you by surprise. I need to know that you have a chance of escape. On the walk to Adenine, I'll teach you how to punch without doing more of an injury to yourself than the other person.'

Georgina nodded and held her hands open for the gloves. Samuel took his own set from Luca and tucked them into his pocket.

'How did you get on today?' Elise asked Samuel, trying to keep her tone light.

His task had been the most difficult.

Samuel ran his hands through his hair before lifting his head to sign. 'I've spoken with Maya. She's agreed to temporarily move everyone to the nearby network of caves. They will train in evacuation processes and completely lock down Uracil. Those who want to will be allowed to travel and join the others on Synthium.'

Elise's eyes widened; it was more than she had dared hope for.

Luca clapped Samuel on the back. 'How did you get her to agree to all of that?'

Samuel looked uncomfortable. 'I may have told her that we are close to finding out who the spy in Uracil is. And that we are doing this to root them out. She had already placed Uracil in lockdown because Twenty-Two brought back the other Neanderthals; I just had to convince her to move Uracil temporarily.'

'Stars, Samuel,' Luca signed, his eyebrows high. 'Have you bent the truth for our own gain?'

'I prefer to think of it as going undercover.' He sighed. 'But I do not feel good about it. She trusts me. And I have lied to her. Repeatedly.'

'I used to have to lie a lot,' Georgina signed, re-crossing her legs. 'Back in the museum in Thymine, as I'm sure you'll all remember. It doesn't feel good at all, but your intention behind the lie is the most important thing.'

Samuel nodded. 'In a strange way, I think it helped that my mother has left. Before she went, she instructed Maya on what should happen if she didn't return and also said that if I or any of my friends should try to leave, she should let us. She said, "The final times have come." Even though I hadn't spoken to her about any of this, she is, as always, one step ahead.'

'I really wouldn't want to get on the wrong side of your mum,' Luca signed.

'So, we leave in the morning,' Georgina signed. 'It's nearly time to say our goodbyes.'

'And Max?' Luca signed to Kit. 'What do you think?'

'I have spent the day with him,' Kit responded, 'and he appears to be genuine. Max rarely lies and only to save other people's feelings. If he weren't a Potior, I would not have any more concerns about him than anyone else. As far as I can tell, he is speaking the truth. But I would not swear to it on Bay's life.'

Elise nodded. 'But would you swear to it on your own?'

'There's something I have to do,' Elise signed to Nathan when they were far enough into the woods. 'And I'm going to have to leave for a while.'

Waiting for his response, she bent to pull up some grey-scaled medusa mushrooms and placed them in her basket. Foraging duty was always a good way of having a private conversation away from the prying eyes of Uracil.

'So, it's back to Georgina's hearth for me, then?' Nathan signed, his own empty basket hanging from his forearm.

'No, she's coming with me,' Elise responded, still crouching.

Nathan's eyes widened. 'So, who will I stay with?'

'Stick close to Tilla. She knows you'll be joining her hearth for the next few weeks. But I need you to do something for me.' Elise straightened. 'I've noticed how you are with all the younger people here. They look up to you. If something happens ...'

'What sort of something?'

Elise knew she had to be honest with him. What she asked of him carried a burden of responsibility that demanded the truth. However unpleasant it might be.

'If the Potiors come again, I need you to take them all back to Jerome's cave. The Neanderthals, Tilla and Lynette too. Keep them safe up there with you. Teach them how to hunt, fight, forage.' Elise paused. She knew it was a lot to ask of him. 'Do you think you can do that?'

Nathan straightened. 'I can. I'll look after them.'

'I'm sorry to have to ask this of you, Nathan,' she signed, taking a step closer to him. 'You know if there was another way ...'

Nathan smiled. 'I've been waiting years for you to trust me with something. Anything. I'm not a child any more.'

Elise stared up at her brother, and for a moment, she saw a glimpse of the man he would soon become. 'I just wish I could have given you longer.'

'But that's what you can't see. It was never yours to give.'

CHAPTER 20

Twenty-Two

Genevieve and Twenty-Two's speed quickened as the soft summer light began to illuminate the moors. Twenty-Two had taken this route with Septa and Max and knew the way; she could guide herself by the sun's position in the sky and a few familiar landmarks.

A few hours earlier, Twenty-Two had slipped quietly out of Genevieve's tent and packed up her belongings, careful not to disturb the others. She knew she had to leave in the night so that questions were not asked, persuasion not used and decisions not reversed. She had, therefore, decided to leave a note in Kit's bag telling him that she would be back in a few weeks and the Neanderthals would be safe in Uracil while she was gone. That was all she had dared say.

The half-moon's light had allowed her to walk through the scrub without falling, but her progress had been slow. She had agreed to meet Genevieve two miles outside Uracil. Every step had to be considered, and she had frozen on more than one occasion, sure that the darkened shapes up ahead were moving. Her eyes had played tricks, and her mind had followed their lead.

When she had approached the boulders, which had been positioned against each other by some unknown ancient civilisation, she had tried to pick out Genevieve's shape amongst them. The first light of dawn had begun to break, and her shoulders had relaxed. She hadn't realised they had been hunched in worry, curling in to protect her from unseen and over-imagined dangers.

But as the skies had become clearer and wisps of low cloud could be seen, Genevieve had stood up from the rock she had been perched upon and Twenty-Two had realised she wasn't alone. Vance had also stood, and Twenty-Two's heart had begun to flutter.

Faye's parents turned to her.

Twenty-Two drew out her screen and typed a message before holding it up for them to read. 'We didn't discuss bringing Vance with you.'

She didn't dare go any closer.

'I couldn't leave him,' Genevieve responded. She was wearing practical clothes for travelling, with her backpack sitting by her feet. Two sheathed knives hung from a belt around her waist. She was dressed for war. 'I believe Samuel might be leaving soon, and then who would look after him?'

Twenty-Two eyed Vance suspiciously, but his thoughts were elsewhere.

'I don't feel comfortable with him coming,' Twenty-Two typed out.

'Then we go back,' Genevieve said. 'And you leave the future of the Neanderthals up to fate.'

Twenty-Two jutted her chin out. 'If either of you tries anything, I won't hold back to protect myself.'

'Is that a threat?' Genevieve said, amusement in her tone. 'I thought you didn't make them?'

'It's not a threat, just a statement.'

'Well, with that in mind,' Genevieve said, 'shall we go?'

Twenty-Two had been walking a few steps behind Genevieve and Vance for hours, not because she couldn't keep up with them, but because she wanted to watch them. Their countenances told her little. Vance was buried deep inside his mind, only momentarily jolted out of his thoughts by a bird flying overhead or a fox scurrying away in the undergrowth. Genevieve walked steadily, never slowing, even if she wanted something from her bag. They did not speak or turn around to check on Twenty-Two, even when she occasionally stopped to stare behind her. She could have slipped away, and neither would have noticed.

When it was close to midday and Twenty-Two's brow was beaded with sweat, Genevieve halted abruptly in the shade of an elm tree and suggested they eat. Twenty-Two nodded her agreement but sat slightly farther away, out of grabbing distance.

She surveyed the haunch of cooked venison that she had taken from Uracil's communal supplies earlier that morning. She had been taught to start the journey eating her fresh food, saving her dried supplies for when she could not forage or hunt.

She glanced across at Vance, who was peeling an apple he had found earlier on the walk with a small knife. He wouldn't meet her eye.

'We are going to the old capital?' she wrote on her screen before holding it out.

'Yes, that's right,' Genevieve responded conversationally. 'But do you know why?'

Twenty-Two shook her head as she slowly chewed the meat.

Genevieve leant forwards. 'We need to weaken the Potiors by removing their means of destroying Uracil again. Once that is done, the Potiors will be vulnerable to having their position of power removed. Once they are removed from power, we can access the genetic information you need.'

'You want to destroy the airplanes?'

'Yes, the airplanes.'

Twenty-Two studied Genevieve. 'You know where they are.'

'I do,' Genevieve said, leaning against the tree trunk. 'I spent my time after leaving Adenine searching for them. You actually visited their location. When I suggested to Maya that one of the teams travel to the old capital, I was hoping you would discover them. But you did not. Unfortunately, as I understand it, Septa decided to exercise her authority and cut short your explorations. Another example of what can happen when an incorrect calculation is made.' Genevieve sighed. 'It would have been much easier for me if they had been naturally unearthed.'

Twenty-Two eyed Genevieve. 'I thought you believed that Uracil should remain hidden. Surely if we succeed in destroying the airplanes, we will make ourselves known, and they will come again.'

Genevieve's eyes widened slightly, but she quickly recovered. It was the smallest of movements, but Twenty-Two had seen it; she knew that Genevieve was in conflict about the future policies of Uracil.

'I think the time for bending to the Potiors' will has ended. Right when they left those people on the island to starve. They are making their own rules, and that is not something we can engage or bargain with.'

'Your bad bargain, it was with the Potiors.'

Genevieve did not answer.

As Twenty-Two bit into her apple, she strained to hear the person who had been trailing them, wondering if they would show themselves. She had earlier caught a glimpse of a distant figure before it launched itself to the ground. She had already decided to wait for them to approach rather than alert Genevieve and Vance to their presence.

She did not have to wait long.

'Now, before you think of sending me back,' shouted Ezra as he made his way down the last hillock, 'I've got as much right to be here as you do.' He strode towards them. 'You can't stop people exercising their right to walk around Zone 3 if they want. That's what a Potior would do.'

He glanced over at Vance, who was silently watching him.

'I had hoped it was you,' Twenty-Two signed, scrunching her eyes at him. 'I couldn't be sure as you kept your distance. At least I will get to say goodbye to you properly. But it's not safe where I'm going. You will have to return.'

Genevieve stared up at Ezra.

Ezra bobbed up and down on his feet, his smile forewarning Twenty-Two that he thought he had her beat. 'You can't send me back as I don't remember the way. I could walk in circles and be lost out there forever. I'd go feral and be found years later counting berries like they were Medi-stamps. You can't have that on your conscience. And you can't afford to risk escorting me back as they might not let you out again.'

Twenty-Two cocked her head towards him. 'We have walked in an almost direct line southeast.' She pointed her finger over his shoulder. 'If you walk in that direction, you will make it back to our forest before nightfall.'

Ezra stopped bouncing. 'I'm not going, and that's that. You can't make me.'

Twenty-Two patted the grass next to her, and he sat down. 'No, I can't, but I can ask you to as your best friend. It's not safe. If you come with me, it might make it harder as I will have to look after you.'

Ezra stiffened. 'I'm not completely useless, you know. And I'm also very good at hiding. How do you think I got through my childhood at the orphanage?'

Twenty-Two eyed him as she bit into her apple again.

'Any sign of trouble, you do whatever it is you do, and I'll slip behind a curtain,' Ezra proclaimed with an air of finality.

'I don't think there will be any curtains where we are going.'

'All right. I'll slip behind a bush. I'm adaptable like that.'

Twenty-Two scrunched her eyes at him. She knew she was going to be selfish and allow him to stay. She wanted company, *his* company, in what might be her last days.

'You can walk with me, but I'm going to leave you on the outskirts of where we're going.'

Ezra nodded vigorously. 'That's settled then. We walk. You infiltrate. I hide behind a bush.'

With that agreed, Ezra stared at Genevieve and Vance before signing, 'Twenty-Two, can I have a word with you? In private.'

*

'What in stars' name are you doing going for a walkabout with the parents of the woman you killed?' Ezra signed furiously, once they were safely away from the others.

'I am going to help them destroy the airplanes in the old capital, and in return, they are going to help me. They know of something I need and will help me get it.'

Ezra raised an eyebrow, and Twenty-Two knew it required more explanation.

'The genetic information for the Neanderthals. Genevieve knows where it is, and if I help her, she will show me once the Potiors have been pulled out of power.'

'Well, that's a crap bargain if ever I've heard of one,' Ezra signed.

Twenty-Two bristled. 'You do not think that bringing back more Neanderthals is important? How do you think we will survive for future generations if there are only six or seven of us to begin with? We'll either die out or all have cousins who are also our uncles!'

'Of course I think it's important,' Ezra responded. 'But your bargain's crap because your terms are unclear. "When the Potiors have been pulled out of power" could mean at any stage. I learnt that in the orphanage. You don't bargain for someone's bread roll that they'll have next week. You bargain for the one sitting right in front of you on their plate.' Ezra drew himself up. 'I'm going back in.'

Turning on his heel, he marched back to Genevieve and Vance with Twenty-Two trailing behind him.

Ezra cleared his throat. 'Genevieve, I want to talk to you about this agreement you've made with Twenty-Two.'

Genevieve stared up at him and slowly rose to her feet. Vance glanced over at her and stood as well. They towered over Ezra, who barely reached Genevieve's chest and whose legs were thinner than Vance's forearms.

'I always believe it's better to stand when entering negotiations,' Genevieve responded.

Ezra's neck was crooked up towards her, his head flung back so he could meet her gaze. 'You probably would feel that way as it lets you look down on people.'

Genevieve ignored his comment. 'You wanted to discuss our terms?'

'We want you to take us to where the genetic information is stored immediately after the planes are destroyed. No detours, no next week, no restocking or regrouping. Immediately.'

'Why are you asking for this?'

'Because if what you say is true and the Neanderthal Project has been abandoned, they could be destroying this information at any moment. It could already be destroyed. It cannot be left for some future date; it needs to be preserved now.'

'And if I refuse?'

Ezra put his hands on his hips, and Twenty-Two appreciated his show of determination. 'Then we're going straight back to Uracil, and we'll tell them everything that you're up to. Going on solo missions that endanger Uracil is pretty frowned upon as I understand it.'

Genevieve laughed. 'They won't believe you.'

Ezra smiled back at her. 'They might not. But with the two of us saying the same thing to everyone who will listen, a seed of doubt will be planted. People will whisper, "No smoke without fire." Once an accusation is raised, it's difficult to extinguish.

It will linger, especially if you're not there to defend yourself. Which will mean you'll have to come back with us and sack off whatever it is you want to do in the old capital.'

Genevieve took a step forwards; Twenty-Two tensed. 'You will not—'

Vance placed his arm in front of Genevieve. His large brown eyes searched her face, and she softened.

'You are right,' she said to Vance. 'Not now, not here.'

Genevieve took a step back. 'I agree to your terms. We'll go directly to fulfil our part of the bargain once we have finished our business in the old capital.'

Twenty-Two stared at Genevieve. What had she pulled Ezra into?

CHAPTER 21

Elise

The group Elise was leading arrived at the outskirts of Adenine in the late afternoon. Max silently stepped to the front, and they fell in behind him as he prepared to crest the highest hill overlooking Adenine. When he reached the top, he dropped to the ground. They all crouched down with him – seven people would be spotted soon enough, and they had to avoid detection.

'The Office of Communications is that building towards the east, the segment two down from the centre,' Max said, pointing towards it for those who hadn't been to Adenine before.

From her vantage point, Elise let her gaze drift over the base. Right in the centre was the Premier's home with its protective moat around it – 'Father's Kitchen Table', as some of the Medius referred to it. Encircling it were the twelve central offices, each one a segment of an orange that pointed inwards towards their base of power.

'Right,' Elise said, retaking the lead. 'We need a couple of us to go into the centre and wait for the Potior who works there, to find out how heavily guarded she is. If we want to get information out to people, we need to know more about her movements. So I'll go, but I'll need someone to come with me.'

'I will,' Samuel said, looking up. Elise tried to hide her surprise that he had volunteered. 'I know Adenine well; I lived there for years. I can spot the Protection Department a mile away. In Adenine, they're a bit more "proactive", shall we say, than in the other bases. So best we avoid them if we can.'

Elise nodded. 'Let's go once I've changed and before the sun goes down. We don't want to miss her.'

As they walked through the woods towards the bridges that linked to the outskirts of Adenine, Elise's body hummed in Samuel's presence. If she reached out with her hand, she could take his. One small movement would let him know that she still cared. She imagined her hand slipping into his. It would be warm and their fingers would interlace in the natural way they always did, finding the places where they belonged, him giving her that half-smile he used to. The one she had last seen before he'd left to find his father. The one she hadn't returned.

Elise knew it was more likely that if she reached for him, he would snatch his hand away. Not because he couldn't bear to be touched, he no longer struggled with that, but because he didn't want *her* touch. Samuel would understand her full meaning in that one gesture. He might not be gifted in reading social situations, but he knew Elise, and she was not one to reach for someone's hand on a whim. Although holding hands was not an outright betrayal of Neve, he would know its implication and where it could lead, and he would not allow himself to be pulled down that pathway by anyone. Samuel was loyal, and Elise didn't want him to do something he found unforgivable. She did not want that characteristic to change. If he could betray Neve so easily, wouldn't that mean he could do the same to her one day?

Elise allowed herself a quick glance in his direction. He was looking straight ahead, his cap pulled low to shield his face from anyone who might recognise him when they entered Adenine. In the four years she had known him, he had grown into his beauty. He had broadened with age, and it suited him.

How had she let him go?

Elise wondered at this but did not mourn it. She knew herself now. If he never looked at her again, she would survive. Because she had learnt that love was a gift but not a necessity. And she already received it from her brother and friends. She did not need it from him too. But, yes, she *wanted* it – she could at least admit that to herself.

'We're nearly there,' Samuel said, still not looking at her. 'You'd better drop behind me.'

It had been Elise's suggestion – mid-end Medius office worker and his servant. It was the most obvious way to justify one who was so clearly Sapien walking with another who had been granted what could only be bestowed upon a Medius. Elise knew Samuel would never have suggested this arrangement, but Elise's pride was not so fragile that she couldn't discard her naturally assumed leadership for a few hours.

She dropped back and dipped her head.

If this works, it might be the last time I have to do this. The last time I have to bend my head in submission and take my place behind a Medius.

These thoughts carried her forwards, into the outskirts of Adenine, where the Sapiens lived. As she crossed yet another wooden bridge arched over the stream below, she heard the thrum of a population returning from work, visiting the Emporium or walking to the various schools to collect their children.

Adenine was the most populated of the four bases. It always amazed her how people traversed past each other on its tightly packed pathways. There was rarely a collision or even eye contact. Still, somehow, they knew each other's locations and could bypass one another without so much as a nod or a glance. She wondered, not for the first time, what these urbanite Sapiens would make of Thymine's Outer Circle with its scattered homes and pathways that you could walk along without meeting another for a mile. She could not imagine it. Maybe they would find it dull or quaint, or perhaps they secretly craved solitude but knew it would never be theirs to have.

She glanced up and saw Samuel striding ahead, the crowds parting for him. Elise tucked behind to benefit from the cleared pathway left in his wake. They passed a group of Sapiens sitting on a veranda, and she overheard snatches of their conversation about new species, traits and more details needed. She realised then that the Potiors had begun seeding the creation of a new species into their minds.

Samuel barely glanced at them, and she admired how he had shifted into his undercover persona. He would never swagger back in Uracil and expect everyone to part for him. He had never even acted like that in Thymine, which was what had first drawn her to him. Remembering her own role, she dipped her head again.

This might be the last time.

When they reached the Medius district, it was now Elise who was the anomaly amongst thousands of Medius making their way home on a summer's evening. Samuel and Elise were largely walking in the opposite direction to the tide. Samuel skilfully manoeuvred his way against the droves of his assumed people, stepping to the side for those he must have instinctively known ranked higher than him and pushing forwards through those below.

As they approached the broad lane intersecting the two office segments, Elise stared up at the two-storey buildings on either side. The Department for Justice and Office of Communications. They were identical, with sandy stone exteriors; the only difference was the metal-plated signs hanging above the doorways with symbols etched into them. One side of the lane had a set of scales above an entrance, and the other the curved lines of sound waves. The crowds had thinned out now. Instead of choosing this lane, Samuel skirted around the outside of the segment until he found the pathway that ran between the Office of Communications and the Office of Provisions. The etched weighing scales were replaced by four stems of corn.

Samuel bent to tie his shoelace, and Elise dutifully paused beside him, her Sapien character never leaving her for a moment. This was about survival, not ego.

'This is the main entranceway and the safer of the two lanes, I believe,' Samuel said quietly, as he finished up with his lace.

They both glanced towards the doorway of the Office of Communications, but it did not open.

'Most definitely,' Elise agreed.

She didn't want to be anywhere near the Department for Justice if she could avoid it.

It was a warm summer evening, and Elise was grateful as the next part of their plan wouldn't work in the winter. Sauntering down the lane, Samuel led the way to the cobbled boulevard surrounding the Premier's residence. As was always the case, crowds of mainly Medius and some Sapiens would spend their evenings here, sitting on blankets or small fold-out chairs, enjoying the last rays of warmth from the sun and admiring the Premier's home. Sometimes, he would make an impromptu appearance on the main balcony, and they were all gently angled towards it in case they were blessed by the words of their wise leader.

Samuel took up his position leaning against a small dry-stone wall. He was carefully placed to see down the wide lane to the main access door to the Office of Communications. Elise stood close by, but not so close as to seem disrespectful. The hum of chatter laced its way around the boulevard as the Medius residents enjoyed the warm evening sun. The Sapiens were pushed to the sides, into the shaded areas. Always second.

An hour later, Samuel straightened.

'She's there, just as my mother used to describe her. Purisian,' he said quietly to Elise. 'She only has two members of the Protection Department with her. Not as many as I feared.'

Elise glanced upwards. A Potior was striding down the lane, away from them – the Communications Department Director. From the back, all that was visible of her was the long curled red hair that reached past her waist and two slim legs enclosed in jet-coloured trousers. Two black-clothed women walked a few steps behind her.

Samuel casually pushed himself away from the wall and checked his screen.

'We must get going,' he said to Elise more loudly, barely looking at her. 'Don't dawdle either.'

Elise dropped her head.

It could change everything.

They followed Purisian through the walkways, keeping far back enough for it not to seem suspicious, until they turned into a small lane. On either side were the exclusive residences of the Potiors, each one individually designed to satisfy its owner's whims and aesthetic tastes. Some were made entirely from shaded glass that shielded the occupant's movements while satisfying their craving for an open view of the outside world. Others looked like squat bunkers, their owner's concern for security clearly winning out against a pleasing exterior.

Purisian stopped outside the door of a pristine white building surrounded by carefully curated gardens. Ignoring the two members of the Protection Department stationed outside her door, she pressed her key card to it and passed through the columns that held up the arch above. The two women who had escorted her through the lanes had already turned to leave, likely returning to the offices for further duties.

Without stopping, Samuel looped off at the end of the lane and walked back through Adenine to the Sapien circle. Neither of them spoke or relaxed from their roles; they were just another Medius and Sapien going about their evening business. It had grown dark and they used it to their advantage, slipping out of Adenine unseen.

Once they were safely back in the forest bordering Adenine, Elise shook her character off, pleased to be back in her own skin.

Samuel dropped back to her side.

'I'm sorry about that,' he said quietly. 'I hate the idea of you having to play that role.'

Elise shrugged. 'It was the one I had to play for the first eighteen years of my life. And it's the whole point of why we're here.'

'But you shouldn't have to any more. It is wrong. And I'm sorry.'

Elise smiled to herself in the dark. 'It's a means to an end. Don't worry about it. By tomorrow evening, we will have finished with this. We know where Purisian lives and how many guards she has with her. All we need to do now is figure out how to enter her home and access her screen. Then it's up to everyone in the bases to decide what to do.'

She could feel Samuel relax by her side. Her hand betrayed her and strayed towards his. She pulled it back.

When Elise and Samuel arrived at the base camp, there was an addition to their group.

'Raynor?' Elise said, unable to stop staring at the woman as she moved to sit by the fire.

'Your approach to Adenine was shite,' Raynor said, between mouthfuls of steaming jacket potato baked over the fire. 'I thought Maya taught you better than that. I noticed you passing a mile off; you left the same tracks as a herd of elephants.'

Elise bristled. 'It's harder when there's so many of us.'

'Tell that to the Potiors when they catch you,' Raynor responded, her mouth full of white potato. 'If I could—'

'Yes, yes. We know,' Luca said. 'If you could have a ticket for every time a new member of the Infiltration Department messed up, you'd be a millionaire. You've already told us a thousand times in the two hours you've been here.'

'So,' Raynor said, ignoring Luca. 'What are you all doing outside Adenine? This lot won't tell me anything.'

'I don't even really know who you are,' Arlo said, leaning back on his hands. 'So, you'll excuse me if I don't tell you a thing about myself.'

'You first,' Elise said to Raynor, accepting the bowl of food Max handed to her. 'What are you doing here?'

'I went to check on the Neanderthals in Adenine for Twenty-Two,' said Raynor, her tone losing all of its previous mirth.

'And?' Kit signed, leaning forwards and gesturing for Samuel to interpret for him.

Raynor turned her head from him.

'How many have died?' Kit signed, his eyes narrowing.

'I don't know,' Raynor responded, still not looking at him and resting her hands on her knees. 'All of the Neanderthal pods were empty. I only just got out of there myself. Something's going on in there; the security is much higher than I expected. Adenine is thrumming with anticipation. It must be the new species project Genevieve was telling us about.'

'And you checked all the other pods?' Kit signed, making sure Samuel was interpreting for him. 'They hadn't just been moved to another one?'

Raynor's gaze flicked up to him. 'No, I didn't check all the other pods; I couldn't get anywhere near them. As I said, I only just got out myself. But there's no Neanderthals in the Neanderthal pods. What's happened to them, I don't know.'

'I'm so sorry, Kit,' Elise signed.

Kit paused for a moment before responding. 'I knew it was likely. But still, there are so few of us left now. We'll die out just as my ancestors did. We are not enough to sustain a healthy, genetically diverse population.'

'That's just a theory,' Samuel said. 'We'll probably never know the real reason they died out. Perhaps it was—'

'This isn't something we have to discuss now,' Georgina interrupted, putting her arm around Kit's slumped shoulders.

Samuel blushed. 'Yes, well, perhaps we should all get some sleep. We have to be ready for tomorrow.'

'And what would tomorrow entail, then?' Raynor asked.

Elise was torn. She glanced at Kit, and he gave a slight nod.

'We could use her help,' Kit signed.

Raynor performed a small bow while still seated. 'That's very kind of you, Mr Kit.'

Kit's eyes widened at the realisation that she could understand sign language.

'Sleep first,' Elise said. 'We'll talk plans tomorrow.'

The old Uracil might have missed the mark on many things, but they'd been wise when they'd set a precedent years ago to only give out mission details in the morning. A plan to break into Purisian's home was already forming in Elise's mind. She would sleep a little easier if she wasn't having to listen out for someone slipping back into Adenine.

CHAPTER 22

Twenty-Two

Twenty-Two had hoped never to return to the city of bone dust. As she stared over the former capital, now deserted and drained of life, she tried to imagine it as it would have been over two hundred years ago when it had bustled with life and smoky land vehicles had clogged up its wide tarmac pathways. She did not believe she would have liked it. At least now it was quiet – not peaceful, but there was a sense of stillness to it that was preferable to how she imagined it would have been.

'We should get going,' Genevieve said, interrupting Twenty-Two's thoughts.

Genevieve led the way, stepping onto the first of the tarmac pathways with grass curling over its edges. Twenty-Two stared at Genevieve's strong form, trying to read her body for any indication of whether she would betray the trust placed in her.

They had walked in pairs for the past two weeks, only speaking to the other set when absolutely necessary. Genevieve had clearly taken the stance that the less said between them the better, and Twenty-Two had been happy to comply. She had watched Faye's parents, heads bent in unison but little passing between them. Did they speak of the daughter they had lost, or did they talk of the weather? She did not know.

'You should stay here,' Twenty-Two signed to Ezra before stepping onto the abrupt beginning of the tarmac pathway.

'Not a chance,' he signed in response.

Twenty-Two frowned. 'But you promised!'

'I'm not leaving you with those two.' Ezra nodded towards Vance and Genevieve's rapidly retreating figures. 'At least if I come with you, I can keep an eye on them.'

'But what if—'

'Then I'll find a suitable bush and hide in it.'

Twenty-Two relented. Perhaps she needed Ezra's help at this moment.

Her feet plodded along the solid walkways that radiated heat after a morning of mid-summer sun. Even though the sky was now clouded and warned of a storm to come, the heat hung around them. Grey above and grey below – Twenty-Two felt certain this was what it was like to have lived in the old capital.

They were soon trudging past the huge block-like buildings. Twenty-Two searched for her favourite one, which had held the smoky land vehicles that weren't deemed important enough to shield with glass. They passed it on her right and she stared up at it, half expecting to see a face peer over one of its barriers, but there was no movement to be seen.

Thunder rippled in the distance, and Genevieve turned her head to the sky. 'Damn it. We have to get inside before there's a full-blown storm. We can't risk the equipment getting soaked.'

She began to run, three sets of feet following her. Twenty-Two almost held out her hand for Ezra, like she had done when they were escaping the airplanes, but she knew he wouldn't appreciate the gesture. He wanted to hold himself up in front of this high-end Medius and Potior.

Genevieve ran towards a looming hangar made from corrugated iron, whose joints had begun to rust. It was the one Twenty-Two had stood outside with Septa and Max when they had been unable to pick its locks. She thought of what might have changed if they had managed to break into it all those weeks back; she certainly wouldn't be here with Genevieve now if they had persisted. She wondered if Septa would ever know how much trouble her stubbornness had caused.

They stopped outside a single door made from the same material as the hangar, only its seam and the chained bolt indicating its irregularity from the sheets of curved iron.

'Your bag, please, Vance,' Genevieve said.

He slipped it off his shoulders. It was twice the size of Twenty-Two's and, not for the first time, she appreciated his strength. Genevieve's hand delved inside the bag and drew out the thickest metal scissors Twenty-Two had ever seen. Vance cocked his head and took them from her. In only a moment, the inch-thick metal was snipped as if it were the stem of a flower. When he was done, Vance placed them inside his backpack and tied it up.

Genevieve drew out a large torch from her own bag, turning it on as she pushed the door of the hangar open. Twenty-Two let Vance go before her, then stepped over the threshold. Ezra followed and pulled the door closed behind him.

The air was musty, heavy with its secrets. The single beam of light danced across the concrete floor, and the squeaks of scattering rats were the only sound. Twenty-Two followed the arc of the single beam and tried not to flinch when two small eyes were reflected back at her from the ground. The torchlight travelled towards the walls, where it methodically drifted up and down, across and around.

'There,' Genevieve said, walking over to where the torch was trained.

She pressed a button.

The strip lights above blinked three times before turning on.

Twenty-Two gasped.

'Stars ...' Ezra whispered.

The vast container held rows of airplanes, their noses all pointing in the same direction. Fat white ones that curved around the belly; small shrewd ones wrapped in grey with noses that jutted out; ones with blades sitting on top of their backs; dark green ones that, although small, looked confident in their worth.

The pattering of the rain on the roof grew louder, and Genevieve glanced upwards. 'We have to get moving.'

She ran towards a large cylinder on wheels tucked into the corner of the hangar. It was larger than some of the airplanes.

'What is that?' shouted Ezra from behind them.

'It's the fuel tanker filled with kerosene,' Genevieve shouted. 'We're going to move it into the centre of the planes and set up a rigging device to explode it when we're far away.'

'Wait, wait, wait!' said Ezra, catching up with the other three. 'A fuel tanker explosion? How big will that be?'

Genevieve stared at him. 'It will probably take out most of the surrounding buildings.'

'You can't do that,' Ezra said, raising his chin to her.

'Why?' Genevieve demanded.

'There might be people living here,' Twenty-Two signed, with Ezra interpreting for her.

'There's no one living here,' Genevieve said.

'I think I saw someone last time I was here,' Twenty-Two insisted.

Genevieve ignored her.

'I won't allow you to do this,' Twenty-Two signed, stepping in front of Ezra. 'You can't take others' lives.'

'It didn't stop you,' Genevieve said quietly.

Twenty-Two met her gaze and signed steadily. 'There is a difference between the two. And you know it.'

Genevieve sighed. 'Fine. We'll do it the less messy way if you insist. We'll cut some of the wires. They won't be able to take off then.'

Three hours later, they were standing at the edge of the old capital, ready to leave.

'That should have done it,' Genevieve said calmly. 'Do you know what those are?'

'They are roads made from tarmac. Max told me all about them.'

'Not quite. They look like roads, so I can understand Max's confusion. But they are actually runways.'

Twenty-Two had not heard this word before. 'Runways?'

'They are what the planes use to take off and land. Some of them need a very long strip of flat ground, and it is less damaging to their wheels than grassland.'

'So that's why the Potiors kept this place as it is. They needed the runways.'

Genevieve nodded. 'It was one of the capital's small airports, although they told everyone it was just another industrial park. I found the original Pre-Pandemic plans for it during my work about ten years ago. I always wondered why they kept it. Why this bit of ugliness? After Uracil ... once I knew they had airplanes, I realised that this was the most likely place to store them.'

Twenty-Two decided to ask the question she had been pondering for the past few hours. 'Why did you need me to come with you? I was no help; you could have done this without me.'

'I needed you for what might come afterwards, not before,' Genevieve said.

'What comes—?'

Genevieve's head whipped around, and Twenty-Two followed her movement. There was nothing she could see or hear that would explain her sudden action.

'Quick,' Genevieve said to Vance. 'We've stayed too long.'

She turned to run.

'Halt!' A woman's voice came from behind one of the brick walls of a building with many chimneys. 'Don't think you can run.'

An ear-splitting bang sounded off in the same direction as the woman's voice.

'You probably don't know what that was, but I'll enlighten you,' the woman shouted. 'It's a Pre-Pandemic gun.'

Genevieve froze.

'No,' Ezra said. 'They don't exist any more.'

'If they've got airplanes, then they could have guns,' Genevieve said quietly, so only their group could hear.

'If you have guns, then why are you hiding?' she shouted back.

The woman stepped out from behind the wall, her hand clasped around a small metal object. Twenty-Two studied what was in her hand. It looked so harmless compared to the weighty bolt cutters Vance was carrying. How could something so small cause all the damage in the Pre-Pandemic years that Ezra had told her about?

The woman was not alone. Behind her, people emerged, dressed entirely in black. Twenty-Two counted ten in total.

She glanced over at Genevieve, who looked unperturbed.

'I am sure there is an amicable way we can resolve this,' Genevieve shouted. 'We can fight, and three or four of you will lose your lives …' She nudged her chin over towards Vance, who now had the bolt cutters in his hand and looked ready to tear the Protection officers limb from limb. 'Or we can resolve this peacefully.'

The woman marched forwards, followed by her colleagues.

One of the officers ran his eyes over the group before directing his question to Genevieve. 'What do you suggest?'

Genevieve smiled around at them.

'That I give you the Neanderthal girl. She must be worth something to you. And I'll throw in a renegade Sapien as well. For good measure.'

CHAPTER 23

Elise

The following night, outside Purisian's white-washed home, there was a curious sight. It was close to midnight, and in the centre of the lane was a woman of middling years who was clutching a bottle and stumbling through a small jig only she knew the steps to. Her wild skirts swirled around her ankles while her languorous top half twisted in the opposite direction. Stopping for a moment, she peered at her feet and rocked on them, before taking a swig from a bottle and beginning again.

She had only just entered the pathway running between the Potiors' homes when she drew the attention of the two members of the Protection Department who guarded the front door of Purisian's house. Round she swirled until she stopped suddenly, and a pained expression crossed her features. She looked up and down the alleyway before deciding to shuffle to the side of the princely house, hitching her skirts up as she went.

The taller member of the Protection Department grimaced. 'You go and arrest her before she urinates in the garden. Bloody Saps. I thought we'd got control of the illegal moonshine production.'

Her colleague wrinkled his nose at the suggestion.

'Quickly,' the first one said, 'I think she's squatting. And when you pass her on, tell them to sling her straight into the containment centre, no warnings for her. Filthy creature.'

The black-clothed man went around the side of the building. As he approached a row of large rhododendron bushes, four strong arms pulled him into the foliage, and a fifth hand clamped over his mouth. Kit and Max pinned his limbs to his sides while Elise covered his lips. Georgina expertly injected a sedation drug into one of his veins.

'That should do the trick for a few hours,' Georgina whispered, after they had waited a few minutes for the drug to take effect. 'I can top him up if he starts coming around.'

'Wouldn't chloroform have been better?' Max whispered, stretching out his arms after battling to hold the man still for so long. 'Just the rag over the mouth, and boom, down he goes?'

Georgina rolled her eyes. 'Chloroform doesn't work like that; it takes at least ten to fifteen minutes to kick in, and there's a higher risk of it killing him. He might be Protection Department scum, but I want to give him a chance.'

Kit made the sign for 'quiet' as Raynor staggered past again, bottle in hand and the other Protection Department officer in tow.

Twenty minutes later, two new Protection Department members stood by the front door with hats pulled low over their foreheads. Max and Arlo made quite the mismatched pair, but Elise had decided to put them there so that Max was occupied and Arlo had a reason to be right next to him.

She waited a further hour to check that there were no reinforcements before signalling to Samuel and Luca to follow her to the front door. Without needing to be asked, Max handed her the key card he had found in the guard's pocket.

'She's likely to keep her screen in her office,' Max said. 'The upcoming releases will be on it, and you just need to attach any files you want to the next release.'

'Thank you,' Elise said. 'Let's hope she doesn't have it locked up somewhere, or we might have to go for Plan B, which is the more confrontational approach. Her bedroom lights went out an hour ago, and I'd prefer it if they stayed that way.'

She held the key card against the door and pushed it open.

The hallway was dark but large enough to hold the entirety of her whole home back in Thymine. The soft rush of water from a small fountain helped to mask their footfall on the marble floor as they crept into Purisian's home. Elise tried not to wonder at the opulence of the place as she signalled to the others to split off into different rooms to search for the office.

She pushed open door after door, unable to take in the sheer size of the place. It was like nothing she had seen before or even had the capability to imagine. The closest thing was Samuel's rooms back in the museum in Thymine, but they were only a mere hint at what could really be done. No expense had been spared in the design; heavy curtains brushed against thick carpet, and each piece of furniture was crafted from the choicest materials. Elise wondered at the logic of it – all this beauty and space just for one person.

The fourth door opened onto a smaller room panelled in carved wood. Majestic scenes of woodland creatures stared back at her from the surface of the oak, wide-eyed at her intrusion, and she tried not to be drawn to them. Instead, she concentrated on her reason for being there: the innocuous-looking screen laid casually on the desk.

She silently pulled the door closed behind her and went to find the other two.

'I've found it,' she signed to Luca and Samuel when she reached them both.

'Good,' Samuel responded. 'Luca, you guard the front door. I'll go and see if I can piggyback our recording onto the next screen release.'

Elise followed him back into the office, straining to hear anyone's approach, ready to fight her way out at a moment's notice if necessary.

'Oh,' Samuel said, as he tapped at the screen. 'They sent a release a few hours ago. An important one, I think.'

Elise stepped away from the door and watched the video play. Aerial shots of Adenine crossed the screen before fading into a close-up of a Sapien-looking man working in a pod in what she presumed was one of the Museums of Evolution. Three new mandatory enhancements flashed up on the screen in bold lettering, enhancements that had never been available before: reliability, steadfastness and tranquillity. The camera swung around, and the most charming pod Elise had ever seen came into full view. There, in the corner, were several Sapien-looking men and women busily working together on building a kitchen table. One held out a length of wood, and another rewarded him with a wide smile. The sound of their laughter rose high above the birdsong and the tinkling of the fountain. But it was not this that held Elise's attention. It was the steel walls in the background of the shots not entirely covered by the ivy growing up them. These people had been raised in a cage.

'The Potiors have done it,' Samuel whispered. 'They're going to convince everyone that a new species is needed and then modify half the Sapiens, so they're more submissive.'

'Submissive?' Elise said. 'But that can't be possible.'

'It is, to some degree. A change in temperament at best,' Samuel responded. 'The real danger is the belief in it, though. If you are repeatedly told that you are programmed to be submissive, you begin to act that way. If an idea is instilled from birth, it is the most difficult of chains to break.'

Elise had been conditioned in the same way for the first eighteen years of her life. She knew the power it held.

Samuel tentatively held out his hand, pausing before gently nudging her chin upwards so she would meet his gaze.

'That's why I followed you here,' he said, his gaze never leaving her. 'Because you broke similar chains, and that makes you worth following. Always.'

Elise smiled back at him and reached out to touch him.

'Am I interrupting?' a woman's voice said from the hallway.

Elise spun around to meet a fist hitting her squarely in the face. The woman's speed was unparalleled. Pain exploded across Elise's cheek and she staggered backwards, unable to steady herself to fight off the four members of the Protection Department who had rushed into the room. The punch was followed up by a jolt of electricity that dropped her to the floor; she narrowly missed hitting her head on the sturdy desk. Her body screamed in protest, but her mouth remained closed. As she tried to recover the use of her limbs, she felt handcuffs placed around her wrists behind her back. She prayed to the stars that the electricity had entered through her legs rather than her chest. She wasn't ready to follow Caitlyn yet.

When her legs had stopped juddering against the floor, she turned her head to find Samuel. She wanted to look at him one more time. He was lying on the floor, curled up on his side, his thick eyelashes fluttering against his cheek. Her heart ached for him, and she tried to shuffle closer.

'Well, that's just beautiful,' the woman's voice said. 'Flat out on the floor, nearly pissed yourself, but you still scrabble towards your love. And that is why you will *always* lose.'

A foot encased in a pointed high heel stepped down inches from Elise's face. Tipped in silver, it looked as if it could slice through flesh.

'Up. Get them up,' the woman said. 'And bring them to the others.'

Elise moaned as she thought of her friends.

'You really have chosen the worst of evenings to commit this unseemly adventure. Things are unfolding in Adenine that you are clearly not aware of. The whole base is on high alert.'

Two Protection officers roughly lifted Elise to her feet, and she stumbled into the hallway to be met by twenty of their colleagues. Luca was slumped on the floor, his lip split. Georgina was standing next to him, her head down, hair dishevelled and face wiped of all emotion. Kit held his head high but was unreadable as ever. Max opened and closed his mouth, still catching up with what had happened. Arlo was cradling his ribs and slowly edging towards the door. Without any ceremony, Elise was stripped of her push knives, throwing knives and sling, which were chucked into a pile with her backpack. All her weapons had been taken from her, and the odds of her escaping reduced even further.

Elise stared at the Potior, who had crossed to the other side of the hallway. Like all Potiors, Purisian was tall and undoubtedly striking, but Elise would not call her beautiful. Her features were perfectly aligned, her thick eyebrows framed her face, her skin glowed and her lips were full. All the perquisites of beauty, but it still evaded her. It was her eyes that marred her. They viewed each of them with utter contempt, and there could be no beauty where cruelty reigned.

When Raynor caught sight of Samuel and Elise, she let out a war cry that shattered the silence. Elbowing the guard next to her in the ribs, she swivelled around as he fell to the floor. Elise had never seen Raynor move so fast – one by one, she took more members of the Protection Department down. Elise spun around to join in.

Ducking a blow from her right, Raynor simultaneously stamped down on a guard's arm. His scream shot upwards.

But she was not fast enough.

Raynor's whole body slammed still as a knife entered her chest. The Protection officer did not pull it out again but instead slowly uncurled his hand from its hilt. Raynor stared down at the knife jutting from her body, and a look of surprise crossed her features as her legs gave way.

'*No!*' Elise screamed, trying to get to her.

Blood began to seep around the blade of the knife. One of the guards moved to pull it out.

'Leave it in,' Purisian ordered. The metal-tipped shoes clicked on the marble floor as she walked past them. 'We need her alive for the execution tomorrow.'

Her clicking shoes carried on down the line.

'What we have here are seven residents of Adenine who have thought to rise against us. A public execution tomorrow morning should show the rest of Adenine that their murmurings of discontent are futile.'

'But we're not from Ad—' Luca stuttered.

He was silenced by the look Kit threw at him.

Purisian stopped in front of him. 'And if you're not from Adenine, where are you from?'

Luca looked away.

Purisian bent down so she was level with him, her cat-like eyes glinting in amusement. 'Who's a brave little soldier? Trying desperately not to tell us he's from Uracil and betray his people? Such a brave boy. Not very bright, though.'

She straightened and carried on down the line, her long red hair swinging in loose waves down her back.

'What we need is to make an example of a few people from Adenine. And you have come along at the ideal time. You are perfect, as you appear to be from Adenine, but no one actually knows you. We can be certain that there will be no father beating his chest in anguish or mother snivelling into a tissue as they bemoan the loss of their precious child, potentially stirring up more discord. Because you don't mean a thing to the people out there, other than as a warning of what could happen to them if they don't toe our line.'

Elise glanced over at Samuel. He shot her a look that told her not to speak.

Purisian coiled a strand of hair around her finger as she paced in front of her captives. 'Sap, Sap, Midder.' She nudged Georgina's chin upwards with one long scarlet nail. 'That's a pity. Such beauty before.' Georgina stiffened, but Purisian carried on down the line. 'Midder.' She stopped in front of Kit and smiled before carrying on to Max and Arlo. 'Potior traitor. And a Sap who is trying to escape through that door.'

One of the Protection officers turned and pulled Arlo back in front of him.

Purisian bent down in front of Raynor, whose unfocused eyes showed that she was swimming in and out of consciousness.

'What do we have here?'

She grabbed Raynor's face and pulled it around. Raynor's eyes rolled back into her head, her plump cheeks dimpled by Purisian's grip.

'If I'm not mistaken, you're one of ours.'

She let go of Raynor and tapped a few times on her screen. 'Yes, there you are.'

Elise's stomach dropped.

'What?' Samuel spluttered. 'Raynor? No!'

Purisian curled her fingers around Raynor's cheek, pulling her face upwards. 'You didn't report this little exercise to us, did you?'

Raynor rolled her eyes to focus on Purisian's arched features. Even if she'd wanted to speak, she couldn't, so tight was Purisian's grip.

'There has to be a mistake!' Samuel shouted. 'Raynor has been with us for *years*. She's no traitor!'

Purisian ignored him and carried on addressing Raynor. 'If you don't report in, then you are no use to us.'

Purisian straightened and smoothed down her tight trousers.

'Take them to the Department for Justice,' she continued. 'You might have to double them up in the cells as we're quite busy. Take them all, apart from those two.'

Elise's head snapped up. Purisian was pointing at Max and Kit.

'Even the stupidest of our residents wouldn't mistake a Potior and a Neanderthal for a Midder and a Sap. Leave them here with me. I want to have some fun with them.'

Elise turned around and head-butted the guard next to her. Pain cracked across her forehead, but she had done more damage to the guard. She silently thanked her dad for showing her how to do it properly years ago. Her hands still behind her back, she shoulder-barged the other guard. Next to her, Samuel swung his leg around to kick his guard away. Luca began to scrabble to his feet but was roughly pushed down.

'Oh, for stars' sake,' Purisian said.

She marched towards the scuffle, sweeping up the wooden ornament of a doe from a side table. In five clicks of her shoes, she had crossed the hallway, and without hesitation, she clubbed first Elise and then Samuel over the head with it.

Stars exploded in Elise's vision, and then darkness took her.

CHAPTER 24

Twenty-Two

Twenty-Two raised her head to the Protection Department officers that surrounded her.

'I cannot believe that you have betrayed me in this way,' she signed to Genevieve.

The officer with the gun looked at her quizzically.

'I'm guessing that she's saying something about me betraying her,' Genevieve said to the puzzled Protection officer. 'I think she might be a bit perturbed by it.'

'And rightly so,' Ezra spluttered. 'You're an absolute trash-lizard!'

Everyone ignored him.

The woman with the gun smiled at Genevieve. 'I don't think you're in a position to be bargaining here, do you?'

Genevieve nudged her gaze over to Vance. 'Have you ever fought a Potior?'

The woman's gaze wavered.

'I've seen him tear the arm off a man. Clean off. As if it were a chicken thigh he was going to eat.' Genevieve's face relaxed. 'Now, I'm no fool. I know we won't be able to take on all of you. But the question you need to ask is, "What are the chances that I am one of the five people that survive?"' Genevieve looked around at them. 'It's fifty-fifty, as far as I can see.'

She paused as the woman with the gun glanced around at her colleagues.

'So,' Genevieve continued, 'in exchange for *all* your lives, I'll give you these two.'

'We just take the girl and the Sapien, and you'll be on your way then?' one of the other officers said before addressing the woman with the gun. 'We'll at least have something to show for why the airplanes have been tampered with.'

'That's the agreement,' Genevieve reiterated. 'One Neanderthal girl, one tiny Sapien. I think you should be able to handle those odds. And you'll never see my Potior friend and me, nor his giant bolt cutters, again. You don't even have to tell your superiors that we were here. Blame it all on these two.'

'It's a deal,' the officer said, eyeing Vance warily.

Vance knelt to put the bolt cutters back into his bag.

The guard stepped forwards to lead Twenty-Two away. As he did so, he visibly relaxed.

It was then that Genevieve pounced.

In a split second, she had knocked the guard nearest her to the ground.

'Run!' Twenty-Two signed to Ezra, before swinging around and punching a guard squarely on the nose.

Her whole force was behind the swing, and the nasal bone cracked when the connection was made.

Vance was already in the air, leaping onto two other guards and throwing them to the ground. He brandished the bolt cutters above his head, and Twenty-Two winced as she heard them strike the guard below.

Genevieve was on to the next guard, his arm snapping as she wrenched it backwards, her blonde hair flying around her face as she turned. She looked full of life, no hint of fear crossing her features. Twenty-Two swung around and punched the next guard to knock him out. Just as Aiden had taught her. She looked down at the officer's unconscious body and felt a sense of satisfaction that it had worked.

The officer with the gun was pulling at the top of it with shaking fingers. Twenty-Two froze.

A shot rang out, and everyone automatically ducked. The officer holding the gun stared down at it, almost in horror.

Without hesitation, Genevieve barged into the officer, the gun flying from her hand. Vance leapt into the air and caught it, smoothly turning it on the group. A Potior with a gun – there was no equal before him.

The other officers turned and fled, their feet sliding beneath them on the gravel. Twenty-Two watched them skitter away, scrunching her eyes at their retreat. Genevieve's plan had worked.

'So, you knew I wasn't telling the truth when I said I'd hand you over?' Genevieve asked, running her fingers through her hair to smooth it.

Twenty-Two simply nodded. If she had not known that Genevieve was lying, she would have been fighting her as well as the Protection Department.

'That's one of the reasons that I needed you,' Genevieve said. 'A valuable bargaining chip. But a valuable bargaining chip that knows when I am lying.' She glanced towards Vance. 'And one that is relatively predictable.'

Vance stared at the gun in his hand before slipping it into his pocket. Genevieve raised her eyebrow but didn't say anything.

Twenty-Two turned around to see where Ezra had hidden. She walked over to a bush to look for him and found him lying on the ground. His eyes were pleading with her to come closer. A small pool of blood lay beneath his body.

She cried out and scooped him up in her arms, pressing his body to her.

'I'm sorry,' Ezra mumbled. 'I didn't hide well enough.'

Twenty-Two scrunched her eyes shut, and Genevieve had to roughly pull her away from him. He had passed out in her arms, and she couldn't wake him.

'I need to check him,' Genevieve snapped. 'There might still be hope. It depends on where the bullet entered.'

Twenty-Two reluctantly let go of her friend and watched Genevieve like a hawk while she inspected Ezra's tiny frame. With the full force of her mind, Twenty-Two stretched up to the stars and to her ancestors. Her body thrummed with the effort.

Genevieve turned to Twenty-Two. 'It entered through his shoulder. As long as we treat the wound properly, he should live.'

Opening her eyes, Twenty-Two gently took Ezra from Genevieve, who rushed over to her bag and started pulling out medical supplies. Twenty-Two cradled Ezra in her arms, inspecting the freckles that lay like a constellation across his cheeks. She prayed to the stars that Genevieve had the right supplies with her to help him.

She only lifted her head when she felt another's presence by her side.

Vance crouched down next to her.

'I know loss too,' Vance said, his voice quiet. 'I lost a daughter once ...'

Twenty-Two froze. They had led her here for revenge.

Twenty-Two stared up at the man who would take her life. Her thoughts turned to the other Neanderthals as she waited for Vance to make his move. The lives of the future Neanderthals would end with hers. She could not let that happen. She had to fight, for their sake.

She gently laid the unconscious Ezra down on the ground and stood. Vance watched her from his crouched position the entire time.

'She wasn't even three years old when they took her from me,' Vance continued, his eyes searching Twenty-Two's face, clearly trying to form a connection.

Twenty-Two stared down at him, not understanding.

Genevieve, blood streaked across her hands, knelt next to him and began cutting open Ezra's shirt.

'He is talking about his first daughter when he lived as a Potior,' she said slowly to Twenty-Two. 'They killed her because her enhancements didn't take. He doesn't remember Faye ...'

Twenty-Two reached out and laid her hand on Vance's shoulder. She thought of that two-year-old girl, younger than Bay. How could they do it? She hoped with every fibre of her being that it had been quick and painless, and the girl had had no idea what was coming.

Something crumbled within Twenty-Two. A final wall that had needed to come down. Vance's child was just a girl, an innocent in this world, too young to make a mark or decide her path and as precious as any other child, whatever label had been placed on her. She did not deserve that end.

She bent down to write in the dirt while Genevieve inspected Ezra's wound before wrapping bandages around it to stem the blood. 'Why didn't you tell him about Faye?'

Genevieve glanced at the words carved into the ground.

'He barely remembers the last fifty years,' Genevieve responded. 'Why give him another daughter, only to take her away?'

Turning her back on the city of grey, Twenty-Two carried Ezra until she found a small stream, where she washed the blood from his skin. He woke briefly to be told that the bullet had to be removed and they had no anaesthetic to help him. All Twenty-Two could offer him was her hand while Genevieve tugged out the small metal ball. His screams rang in her ears for what felt like hours.

It was nearly dusk by the time Genevieve finished the last stitches, and Ezra fell into a fitful sleep. Because it was so late, they decided to stay a further night before travelling to Adenine. Vance had wandered off by himself an hour ago, so it was just Genevieve and Twenty-Two by the fire.

'You do not blame me in some small way for him nearly dying?' Genevieve asked as she approached, holding a small bowl of soup out to Twenty-Two. 'I'm asking you directly as you are so still, it is difficult to guess at your thoughts.'

Twenty-Two studied the older woman before drawing out her screen to write a response. 'Did you hurt my friend?'

'No,' Genevieve said. 'But the circumstances that unfolded were partly by my hand. And for that, I am sorry. I thought he would be safe behind us, that they would concentrate their energies on myself and Vance.'

Twenty-Two took the soup and held it in one hand. Did she blame Genevieve? Did she want to exact her revenge?

No.

She could see where that path would lead, and it was not one she wanted to explore. She had the other Neanderthals to consider. So many lives, both in existence and yet to come, were reliant on her staying focused on her original purpose. She could not bargain with the stars again until she had completed their request.

'A thousand small changes could have prevented him being injured,' Twenty-Two wrote on her screen. 'There is only one group responsible for what happened here, and that is the ones in power. They should never have armed their officers with a thing that can hurt people so brutally or kill them without thought. A split second is not enough time to decide if a life should be taken.'

Genevieve leant over to rest her hand on Twenty-Two's shoulder. As she made the motion, she knocked the soup out of Twenty-Two's hands.

'I'm so sorry,' she said, picking up the bowl. 'I'll get you another one.'

She stood and went over to the campfire. Twenty-Two sat in silence and lightly laid her hand on Ezra.

CHAPTER 25

Elise

Elise's eyes flicked open, and she quickly squeezed them closed again. She did not want to resurface. Pain throbbed across the back of her skull and shot through her eyes like pinpricks.

'You're awake then,' Raynor mumbled from the other side of the cell.

She was slumped on the floor, leaning against the stone wall, her hand pressed against where the dagger's hilt had been.

Raynor.

Elise pulled her legs around and, despite her blurred vision, scrambled across the concrete floor to the woman who had betrayed them.

'It was you,' Elise spat when she was within touching distance. 'You were working for the Potiors all along.'

'It was,' Raynor responded quietly, her face pale.

'You killed my mum,' Elise said, her voice rising. 'And hundreds of others, *children*, innocent every one of them.'

Raynor's eyes widened. 'You found the residents?'

Elise stared at her. How did she not know?

Elise's vision swam, and she rested both hands on the rough floor to steady herself. 'Yes, we did. They had been left to starve on an island by the Potiors. But they were there because of you.'

Raynor let out a low moan and squeezed her eyes shut. 'I didn't know. I promise I didn't know this would happen.'

She turned her face from Elise, who reached out to pull it back around.

'I saw them all,' Elise said. 'Every grave on that island. The losses from the original bombing were a quarter of the real toll.'

'I never meant for Aiden and Sofi to die,' Raynor said. 'You have to believe me.'

'Don't say their names,' Elise said, without looking up. 'You didn't even know them.'

Raynor squeezed her eyes shut. 'In my boot. I keep a smaller screen in there. Pull it out.'

Elise stared at her before reaching her fingers inside the woman's shoe. Her fingertips found a sewn pocket in the sole. Inside was a tiny folded screen. A screen like that, so small, would have cost hundreds of tickets. Elise could guess how Raynor had got them. She dropped it on Raynor's lap in disgust.

Raynor picked it up with her right hand and tried to unfold it. She moved her left hand from her chest and quickly began unclipping the screen. In a matter of seconds, her green shirt was stained dark red – the Protection Department hadn't done a thorough job of stitching her up when they had removed the dagger. Raynor's hands were shaking as she tapped at the screen before trying to hand it back to Elise.

Elise was unmoved.

'Here, take it. Play it from the beginning,' Raynor said, her voice weakening.

Elise stared up at the ceiling of the cell. The whisper of a faint scream came from down the corridor. She didn't know why she was even entertaining this woman's requests, but curiosity won her over.

She pressed the screen, and the unstable image from a tiny winged camera began to play out. It soared above a Museum of Evolution, but Elise was unsure which one. The animals below were grazing, used to its presence. The camera abruptly halted and darted to the main entranceway, where a Medius teacher lined up a row of solemn-looking two-year-olds, their fluttering heartbeats having drawn the camera. Down the row, the camera whirred, assessing each of them in turn. A girl with a short brown fringe turned to the faint buzzing sound and smiled as she tried to reach for the camera. But it was too quick for her. The image lingered for a moment and then cut out.

Another image flickered onto the screen. A cluster of children, farther inside the museum this time, climbing one of the white walkways stretched above the tundra below. The same girl came into view, a touch taller this time, her face thinning, her legs sturdier. Elise thought she recognised her but couldn't believe what she was seeing. In the next shot, the girl's hair was shorter, and she was about to enter the nocturnal display. The screen flickered to a boy for the following clip, taller than most of the others, not much older than two. His face was always turned upwards. The girl again, this time quieter, more contained, not looking around with the same air of openness she had possessed in the previous years.

Elise now recognised the boy and girl. She frowned as she tried to work out what this meant.

On the images went of Elise and Nathan, growing older with each year of their annual mandatory visit to the museum. Elise could not remember what had changed her from a curious child into a less confident one, but she could name several possibilities.

She imagined the woman she would have become if that little girl hadn't been made to bend at such an early age.

'I would break into the museum every year to copy the recordings,' Raynor said, as she studied Elise's face.

Elise dropped the screen and scrambled back to the other side of the cell, as far away from the woman as possible. Her lulled state had been broken. Even the fascination of watching rare footage of herself when she was young was not strong enough to draw her closer.

Raynor gave her familiar half-grin. 'You worried I'm a psychopath? Some sort of creepo who follows little ones around?'

Elise stared at her but did not speak.

'Don't worry. It was only you two that I had an interest in.' Raynor threw the screen across the cell to Elise. 'Carry on watching.'

Raynor moaned as she shifted her body around. A fresh spurt of blood seeped between her fingers.

Elise picked up the screen, her hands shaking, scared of what she might see but unable to stop herself from pressing the button again. She'd rarely seen recordings of herself, as the family screens did not record images, only played them, and the winged cameras were not given to Sapiens. She had never seen images of herself as a child. The Potiors liked to have control over what was recorded, as well as what was viewed.

The images rolled on of Elise up until her sixteenth birthday. Then the last one filled the screen. Elise was standing at the reception desk of the Museum of Evolution in Thymine, a large backpack propped against her feet. Glancing upwards, she touched her short hair and inspected something on her fingers. Nodding at the blonde-haired receptionist, Elise walked over to the lockers and placed her bag inside one of them. Returning to the centre of the foyer, she looked around in awe. The camera cruised closer to her, circling Elise, who resolutely tried to ignore it. Harriet approached from the side, short and bustling, just as Elise remembered her. The feed cut out.

'My first day at the museum,' Elise said, still staring at the screen.

'A proud day indeed,' Raynor responded quietly.

'Why have you been doing this?' Elise asked, as her mind stretched to all the possibilities.

'Because you, Nathan, Aiden and Sofi were what kept me going all these years. You're the reason I agreed to work for the Potiors.'

'I don't understand,' Elise said, staring at her. 'You never even met my parents. You haven't been back to Uracil for the whole time they lived there.'

'And why do you think that was?' Raynor responded. 'Why would I avoid going to Uracil at the precise time that Aiden and Sofi arrived?'

'Because they knew you,' Elise said quietly.

'They didn't just know me,' Raynor said, closing her eyes. 'They grew up with me.'

Elise stared at the woman ... she was beginning to understand. But no. It couldn't be possible. She wouldn't believe it.

Raynor opened her eyes and read Elise's expression. 'What? Am I a disappointment? Not beautiful like Genevieve, or formidable like Maya? Is that what you expected your aunt to be? We can't all be those things, sugarling. My life was a hard one and it took its toll, both inside and out.'

'Lisa?' Elise said, leaning forwards.

Tears began to trickle down Raynor's face. 'I haven't heard that name in so long, nearly twenty-five years now.'

Elise slowly moved towards the aunt she was named after, searching for the similarities between her and Aiden. Perhaps their noses were the same. Not their eyes; they were different shapes.

When she was close enough, she reached for Raynor's wrist and turned it towards herself. 'Raynor Guilder, 23 March 2223, Guanine Base, Sapien.'

'What?' Raynor said, staring down at it. 'You don't think Uracil is the only one in the business of changing tattoos, do you?'

Elise sat up. 'What was the name of your other brother?'

'It was Toby. How could you forget that?' Raynor's eyes narrowed. 'Oh, I see. Want to test me, do you? Check this isn't some Potior scam?'

Elise didn't respond. 'Where did Toby carve his name?'

Raynor smiled. 'Under the kitchen table. I used to run my fingers over it when I was a girl. He was only nine when he did it.'

Elise lowered her head. It was all true.

'What happened to my uncle?' she asked.

Raynor brushed the tears from her face and tried to pull herself up. 'He died a long time ago. Right after they took us both in the middle of the night. They killed him in front of me. He refused to join them, so they slit his throat, right there at my feet.'

Elise squeezed her eyes shut as she remembered running her fingers over his name when she was a girl. He would have been younger than Elise when he died.

'And you? You didn't want to die, so you joined the Potiors?' she said, not meeting Raynor's gaze.

'That would be a simple way of looking at it,' Raynor said. 'That would put me neatly into your "people who have done wrong" box. But it wasn't as straightforward as that. As Toby lay bleeding at my feet, they told me I had a choice. Either I worked for them, or they would bring Aiden in and do the same to him. At my feet again. I couldn't let that happen.

'But, of course, that's what they always used against me from then on. Aiden's safety and Sofi's, and later yours and Nathan's. All in exchange for my continued work. And I paid dearly for it over the years.'

Raynor coughed, and a trickle of blood rolled down her chin. She wiped her finger over it before examining it.

'The first few years, they shifted me around the bases, reporting on the minor slips and grumblings of the Sapiens. I convinced myself I had made the right choice; I could live with a lifetime of getting my hands a bit mucky in exchange for your safety.

'Then they sent me to watch over Uracil. It was nearly twenty years ago. It took me a while to be invited into the Infiltration Department. Once I was, I'd report back to the Potiors, tell them what Uracil was planning whenever I went into Adenine. A few of the Protection Department knew what I looked like, and they'd arrest me for "questioning" if I hung around for long enough. It all looked perfectly normal to the other Sapiens around us when they picked me up. I've had to be very careful these last few months not to be seen by them.' She coughed again, and fresh blood sprayed out in front of her. 'I couldn't give them information on the undercover operatives, as we weren't allowed to know who they were, so I updated them on the inner workings of the Tri-Council. My last report was that Uracil was turning its sights outwards. I tried to keep it from them, but they have ways to get you talking if you hold out on them.'

Raynor couldn't meet Elise's eye.

'And then the Potiors bombed Uracil,' Elise said, unmoved.

Raynor stared up at Elise, her eyes searching her face. 'I swear I didn't know they would do that. When I saw what they had done to Uracil, I never let them pick me up again.'

Elise thought back to those first few days after the bombing. Raynor had spent hours by the graves they had dug, muttering to the dead. Perhaps she'd been asking for forgiveness. Or maybe swearing her revenge. Elise did not want to ask.

'Life got a bit more difficult for me when I heard you'd brought your mum and dad to Uracil. I knew I couldn't return.' Raynor smiled to herself. 'Maya was always cross with me, trying to force me back, but I kept on accepting missions to stay out longer or danced around her orders. And I certainly couldn't tell the Tri-Council about my role now that you had all left Thymine. You and your parents were still not safe, you see. The Potiors could still get to you. They've known of Uracil's location for years.

'I don't have long,' Raynor continued. 'And neither do you. If there's any chance of you getting out of here, you must go and get Nathan. Leave for one of the other Zones. You'll never be safe here.'

'We both know I won't be getting out of here,' Elise responded, staring around at the cell. 'Let's try and stick to the truth in our last few hours.'

Raynor nodded. 'At least Nathan is not in here with us. One of you will survive ...' She indicated the screen on the ground. 'Take that anyway. There's a file on there you might need.' She slumped farther back against the wall. 'He is a lovely boy, Nathan, and will grow into the finest of men ... Those months

I spent with him in the cave over winter were the best of my life. He's so like Toby ...'

Elise tucked the screen into her boot as she listened to Raynor. Slowly she moved over to the older woman. Her aunt. Her imperfect aunt, who had tried to do what was right and had paid such a heavy price for it. She had protected Elise's family all those years, but at what cost? Hundreds had died in their place. It was not a trade that either Elise or her parents would have made. But then, how many people made decisions in a matter of seconds and had to live with the consequences for the rest of their lives?

She leant against the cell wall and took Raynor's hand in hers.

'What were my parents like when they were younger?' she asked, looking across at her.

But Raynor had already gone.

What should you do with your final hours? Rage, scream, try to fight an enemy you cannot reach? Or do you slump in a corner and wish those hours away? Perhaps you bargain with time to slow or halt altogether?

Elise had always imagined she would succumb to one of these options, but when her final hours came, she found that she took another course.

She knew that she would be publicly executed in a few hours, at sunrise, and that no one was coming to rescue her. She was vastly outnumbered, and Uracil did not know where she was. Maya would not be slipping through those doors, nor any other members of the Infiltration Department. Elise had not put her energies into raising an army that could fight the Potiors. Instead, she had tried another way, and it had failed.

Rubbing her face with both hands, she forced herself to stare at Raynor's lifeless body. Her aunt, whom she had spent years trying to find. Who had made a bargain on Elise's behalf that she would have refused if she had known of it. Nathan was everything to her, but she would not trade his life and her own for the lives of a hundred other children. Those weren't odds she could live with.

Elise had always known that her life would be short, but she had hoped it would be longer than twenty-two years. It didn't seem enough. She leant back against the cell wall, tears pricking her eyes. She quickly wiped them away. She had to be strong.

Would it be painful? Would she cry out, begging them to stop? She did not know, and these questions would only lead to her screaming and scratching at the bolted steel door. So, she turned away from them, trying to block them from creeping in and nestling in her chest.

Instead, she thought of Kit. Alone with that woman. Elise sent a promise up to the stars that she would suffer any amount of pain and humiliation if they took it away from him. He had already been dealt enough from that hand in his eighteen years. Her thoughts drifted down the hallway to Georgina curled up in her cell, her heart breaking as she prepared never to see Bay and Twenty-Seven again. Whom would Samuel be thinking of? His mother? Neve ... Elise?

She needed a distraction, something to take her mind away from imagining the method they would choose to end her life and the lives of her friends. It was a public execution, so the Potiors would want a show.

She pulled out Raynor's screen and began to read.

CHAPTER 26

Twenty-Two

Ezra winced with pain as Vance shifted his weight in his arms. Twenty-Two had never walked so far in one day – they had covered thirty miles over a wild landscape with no natural pathways to ease their journey. All of them were possessed, driven forwards, trying to leave what had happened behind and reach Adenine. Vance had been carrying Ezra for the last twenty miles and, for the first time, Genevieve was visibly starting to tire.

The three days it had taken them to walk from the old capital had passed in a blur. Ezra had been able to walk some of the way, until the pain in his shoulder became too much. On the first day, without even asking, Vance had scooped him into his arms in the mid-afternoon and carried him. This pattern had repeated itself over the next few days. Twenty-Two had listened to Ezra jabber away to the taciturn Vance, whom she sometimes caught smiling in response. Ezra talked about their surroundings, his favourite foods, anything that didn't involve the past or their current situation.

'I need to stop,' Genevieve said, as the sun began to set.

Twenty-Two turned around to her and signed, with Ezra interpreting for her. 'But we are nearly there.'

'I know,' Genevieve responded, 'and I'm sorry, but I ... I think I injured myself earlier in the day. My foot is aching and, stars, I'm getting old!'

Twenty-Two studied the woman. Pain was etched across her face.

'Are you sure you couldn't manage a few more miles? We only have ten to go.'

'I could do with some rest, too, and a change of bandages,' Ezra said. 'And it can't be easy for Vance having to lug me around either.'

'Ten miles would take us three hours in these conditions, and it's nearly dark,' Genevieve added. 'I'm sorry, I can't do it.'

Twenty-Two nodded. She believed the woman; this was not one of her tricks.

Vance was staring across the landscape towards Adenine. They couldn't see the base yet as it had been designed entirely with concealment in mind.

'Then we will camp here tonight,' Twenty-Two signed, pointing towards a ledge of rocks that would provide some shelter if it rained overnight.

Genevieve nodded. 'Thank you. I am sure your brothers and sisters will still be there in the morning. If the Potiors had, in an improbable scenario, decided to destroy the Neanderthals' genetic information today, of all days, they would have done it earlier than this hour.' Twenty-Two glared at her, and Genevieve shrugged. 'What? It is logical, and you know it. They would have done it during the working hours, not in the evening, so there is no point in us pushing ahead.'

'There is logic to that,' Ezra said, shrugging apologetically.

'We are so close,' Twenty-Two signed, reluctantly dropping to the ground.

'But not close enough to make the journey tonight,' Genevieve said, already sitting down. 'Do not worry. Nothing will happen overnight, and it's important we're rested.'

Twenty-Two glanced towards Adenine once more before settling down on her sleeping roll.

In the early hours, she dreamt of stars and constellations. When she woke, she watched the sun rise, her first thoughts for her future brothers and sisters.

CHAPTER 27

Elise

When Elise heard the guards approach outside the cell, she tucked Raynor's screen into her boot. No one was coming to rescue her – she had to face her final hour alone. Caitlyn had given her a few extra months. Elise had tried to use them to right the world. And failed. But at least she had tried. Nathan was safe for the moment, and she hoped he could make it to Jerome's cave. As Raynor had said, one of them had to live through this.

She touched her aunt's shoulder, and said her final goodbye.

What would come next?

Elise wiped her eyes before the guard opened her cell door. The stagnant air of the cell rushed out, taking with it the metal tang of the blood that framed Raynor's body.

'You let her die then?' the Protection officer enquired, staring over at the older woman's body curled up on the floor.

Elise shook her head. 'No. You let her die, not me.'

The back-handed slap seemed to come from nowhere. Tears pricked Elise's eyes as the sharp pain slashed across her face.

Before she could even bring her hand to her face, the guard pulled a length of tape across her mouth.

'So you don't start any grandiose speeches,' he said by way of explanation.

Elise's heart raced at the reduction in her ability to breathe. She had never been so aware of her breath and how precious it was to her. Before she knew it, her hands were roughly handcuffed behind her back.

'Shall we go,' he said, as if nothing of note had happened.

It was not a question.

Elise stepped through the door and sized up the three other officers outside. No chance of staging an escape. She would die in a hallway, and right now, she wanted a few extra minutes.

'We have a treat for you,' one of the Protection officers said with a crooked smile.

Elise ignored him and thought of her mum. She would see her soon. Conjuring up her image, she felt her mother's hand on her shoulder, a quick squeeze as she always used to do.

The five of them trudged through the grey corridors, each one the same. Elise couldn't believe these would be the last images her eyes would see. Where were the forests, the lakes and the shores? She had spent the previous years wandering, and it was out there that she wanted to meet her end, the soft moss her resting place, the autumnal leaves her shroud.

A double set of doors was pushed open, and Elise welcomed her first glimpse of the sky. Heading towards the dawn light, she imagined the forest floor beneath her feet.

They walked along a pathway with high walls on either side. Soon, they emerged outside Adenine's courthouse.

The sight in front of her made Elise bend over and retch. Her stomach was thankfully empty, or she might have choked given her sealed mouth.

A guard pulled her up and shoved her towards her friends. They were standing in a line on either side of the courthouse doors. Each was balanced on a high wooden crate, a hastily improvised show. Long lengths of rope hung from the balustrades above. Their heads were inside nooses, but they were still alive. One kick of the crates beneath them was the only thing between life and death.

Samuel looked over at her, fear etched across his features. He never took his eyes from her as she was led up to her own crate, the last to arrive. The one beside her, meant for Raynor, was hastily taken away.

It was quiet in the square, so early that the sun had not cleared the horizon. A few fallen leaves rustled their way across the cobblestones.

In the distance were rows of black-clothed Protection officers surrounding the Premier's home. She had never seen so many – there were hundreds. Why were they all stationed there for a mere execution? It was not as if Elise and her friends had any chance of escape. Lined up in front of the Protection officers were the mismatched uniforms of the Sapien and Medius guards, who must have been drafted in from the public buildings.

Georgina moaned, tears fresh in her eyes, and her body sagged under the burden of her losses. Everything went into slow motion as her foot slipped from beneath her. All of them leant towards her in panic. Georgina righted herself, but as she looked around, her eyes wide with fear, the tears came again.

Arlo was at the end of the line, and Elise knew she was partially responsible for his death. She had asked him here, and he would die because of her. Elise's regrets were deepening.

The distant noise of the residents' morning commute began, and Elise could no longer hear the leaves as they scraped along the boulevard outside the courthouse. She watched them, though, to take her attention away from the rough length of rope placed around her neck.

One of the guards stepped forwards and began reading from his screen.

'You have been charged with Offences Against the People and found guilty of this crime. You will be punished by execution as the Pre-Pandemic Sapiens were, and your bodies will remain here for the next week as an example of the punishment warranted by the seriousness of your crimes.'

Luca began screaming through his taped mouth, his eyes bulging in panic. Elise could not help him. They were each alone now.

'Your exact crimes are ones of Denial, Stirring Discontent, Avoidance of Reparations ...'

Elise glanced down the line of friends and prayed to the stars it would be quick for each of them. Then she focused on Samuel. He would be the last sight she took from this world. His dark brown hair fell over his face as he furtively tried to free himself from the handcuffs. It would not work. Already one of the guards had noticed what he was doing. He took a step forwards and cracked Samuel's hand with his baton.

Elise cried out as Samuel nearly fell, but her scream was muffled.

Samuel regained his balance before glancing over at Elise. Their eyes met. With just one look, she hoped to tell him that she was sorry, that she shouldn't have brought them here, that she had loved him for years but had not been able to admit it to herself, that the containment centre had taken more from her than she'd thought possible and that she wished she could have her memories back of the time they had spent together.

Even in her last moments, she knew that was too much to ask of one look, so instead, she soaked him in. Every detail of his face.

The noises of the morning commute grew louder, but Elise ignored them as the guard droned on, reading out the twenty or so offences, many of which Elise had never heard before.

'... and for these, you have been sentenced to death. Guards, take your positions.'

This was it.

Elise could hear one of the guards step up behind her, ready to kick the crate from under her feet.

In her last moments, she greedily consumed all that her world could offer: Samuel's profile, Georgina's flaming red hair, the bluest of skies above, the scent of the rain soon to come and the soft breeze on her skin.

'On my count of three ...'

The sounds of a swelling crowd turning into the boulevard made the guard falter.

The officer's attention wavered. 'One ...'

Chanting and jeers rang out. The residents jostled against each other, some pushed up against walls, as they bottlenecked down the lane between the Department of Shipping and the Department of Innovation.

'Two ...'

The people at the front began sprinting towards the Premier's residence, their faces flushed and contorted in anger.

'Defensive positions!' the guard shouted.

The twenty other guards shuffled around to face the streams of people emerging into the boulevard.

While the guards were distracted, Elise began frantically trying to work her arms free of the handcuffs. It was no good, they were too tight to slip out of, and she didn't have anything to pick the locks.

'Fall back!' the officer shouted.

The Protection officers turned and ran towards the Premier's residence, past the rows of civilian guards until they merged into the lines of the other officers. Dotted in between them were the statuesque figures of Potiors.

The men and women at the front of the largely Sapien crowds sprinted after the officers, straight past Elise without a second glance. The slower ones began to spread out, trying to release themselves from the dense crowd, some stumbling up the courthouse steps.

'Not our *children*!' a woman hollered at the top of her voice from deep in the middle.

Responding to her rallying cry, the masses echoed her chant as they pushed towards the Premier's residence. They were halfway across the boulevard, banging the pots and pans they had brought, the only items that could be construed as weapons. They sounded these as they ran towards the centre, the drumming noise seeming to keep their spirits high and all possibilities within reach. There were thirty of them to every Potior, ten to every Protection officer and guard. And the ratio was rising in their favour – some of the Medius and Sapien civilian guards edged away from the sheer numbers that could overwhelm them.

But just as Elise thought the two groups would collide, the sea of Sapiens halted in front of the civilian guards. They banged their pots and chanted, 'Not our children!' but did not push forwards any farther.

Around Elise, the shouting soared upwards as she tried to free her hands again.

As some civilian guards began to melt away, the Medius Protection officers stood their ground. Armed with tasers, which they discharged liberally, they shouted commands for the residents to return to their homes. No one listened to them. Adenine's fallen men and women were pulled to the side, brushed down and propped against walls until they recovered.

Elise felt light-headed as people began surging up the courthouse steps. The noise was overwhelming, while the crowds moved as one. A swirl of individuals spilt over the pathways with one destination in sight. She tried to catch their attention, but the few who glanced her way looked at her in confusion, clearly not sure whether she was on their side or not. They were so distracted that Elise was terrified one of them would accidentally barge into her crate and knock it from underneath her. The tide of people washed closer to her, and she began screaming behind her taped mouth, trying to get them to stop, to help her. But as their numbers swelled and the space tightened, their looks of alarm showed that they were solely focused on their survival. They had lost control of their creation.

The smell of sweat and dirt filled the air. A man directly in front of Elise tripped on one of the steps in his urgency to overtake the person in front of him. Elise's eyes widened as he fell forwards into a woman who lurched towards Elise. The first man disappeared beneath the maelstrom, his cries drowned beneath an ocean of boots and stumbling steps. Elise's thoughts flicked to Michael's mother, Etta, who had died on another courthouse step.

She braced as the crowds streamed up around her, behind her, all eyes turned from the Premier's residence as they jostled to keep upright and not be dragged under by the ungovernable tide.

An elbow slammed into Elise's side and she managed to balance herself, her strong right leg countering the knock.

It was the second blow to the back of her knee that forced her leg from underneath her.

The crate slipped, and she fell with it. Everything went into slow motion as she felt herself drop, the rope ready to snap around her neck.

And then an anchor – strong arms that grabbed her from behind. Her weight taken, her feet inches from the ground.

In only a few seconds, the rope was loosened and hastily pulled from her neck. A hand came around and ripped the tape from her mouth.

Elise gasped in the air as she was gently placed on her feet.

She turned around to face Samuel, braced against the people surrounding them, trying to protect them both from their shoves. She remembered the first time he had saved her, the day they had met when he had kept her from the attention of Fintorian. Since then, she had learnt that he always watched over her. Quietly, with little fuss, and never expecting anything in return. What more could she wish for? What more could she want?

For a moment, it was just the two of them, circled around each other, protecting each other from the crashing waves that were trying to pull them under.

She reached for his hand, and his touch was just as she had imagined it would be. She pulled him towards the others, and, one by one, they released them from the ropes.

More hollers came from the crowd and the chanting started again, but no one approached the guards. Instead, the first lines of people linked arms, swaying as they chanted. A calm began to come over them.

Some of the Protection officers and Potiors had run onto the bridge, the only entrance point to the Premier's residence. From there, short, sharp cracks began sounding out that reminded Elise of the airplanes that had flown overhead and felled Max. They had brought out guns.

The atmosphere changed instantly. People screamed, unlinking themselves and scattering as the bullets flew outwards.

Elise worked frantically to loosen the noose around Arlo's neck as the cries around the Premier's residence grew louder. The crowds were pushing backwards now, desperate to get away. Elise realised they probably didn't even know what was being used against them. None of them had ever seen or heard a gun before.

An explosion rang out, and Elise automatically ducked, her hands pressed to her ears. Screams laced over the top as the rumbling noise died out. When she straightened, the bridge was gone, and plumes of smoke rose from where it had once been.

'We've got to get out of here!' Samuel shouted above the noise. 'The Potiors have blown the bridge!'

Grabbing Elise's hand, he began tugging her towards one of the pathways leading out of the central square. Elise turned around to check that the others were following. Luca grabbed hold of Georgina as she stumbled after him, her eyes wildly scanning the area. Arlo took her other arm and the two of them pulled her through the crowds.

Samuel was pushing forwards, using all his strength to barge against the people and make them part for him. Elise charged forwards with him, checking all the time that the others were following. When they entered the pathway alongside the Department of Education, the crowds began to thin. Samuel steered them towards a doorway so the others could catch up. Elise pressed her back against the stone wall, grateful for something solid behind her.

Samuel stepped around the doorway, and they came face to face. The noise of the crowds receded as Elise stared up at him. His eyes searched her face, trying to read her, and he reached out to brush her cheek.

'There you are,' Arlo said, pulling Georgina and Luca behind him.

Samuel's body stiffened, and the moment was gone.

They all stared at each other, unable to express how close they had come to dying, before Elise pulled Georgina into her arms.

'I'm so sorry I got you into this mess,' Elise said. 'You must have been thinking about Bay and Twenty-Seven all night.'

Georgina pulled away and smiled at her, tears forming in her eyes. 'I thought that was the end. I spent the whole night praying to the stars that Tilla would have the strength to look after them both by herself.'

Georgina wiped her face, and the movement caused Elise to focus on her scar. She rarely noticed it now; it was just another layer of her beauty.

'Who did you share a cell with?' Luca asked.

'I was with Arlo,' Georgina said, glancing over at him.

Arlo smiled. 'I'm not ashamed to admit that I also cried last night. Georgina sat quietly with me and held my hand.'

'We were both crying,' Georgina said. 'But we got through it.'

'Were you two together then?' Elise asked Luca and Samuel.

'We were,' Luca responded. 'But we didn't sit holding each other's hands. Samuel refused to because he doesn't like touching people. I had to soldier through the dark hours by myself, hand bereft of company.'

'I would have held your hand if you had asked,' Samuel said dejectedly. 'I've got over that now.'

Luca rolled his eyes. 'I'm just teasing you, you incredibly bright moron. I know you would have done it if I'd asked.' He ran his hand over the back of his shaved head. 'We just talked a lot. About anything and everything.'

He gave Elise a pointed look.

'Where's Raynor?' Georgina asked, glancing between Luca and Elise.

'She died in the same cell as me,' Elise said, already hoping she could wait until later to explain everything.

'Good riddance, bloody traitor,' Luca said.

'No, no,' Elise responded. 'It wasn't like that.'

'So she wasn't the traitor?' Samuel asked, relief crossing his face.

'Well, yes, she was,' Elise admitted. 'But she made a decision a long time ago, back when she was barely twenty, that she had to live with for the rest of her life. The decision—'

'Was whether to become a traitor?' Luca interjected, raising an eyebrow.

'Let her speak,' Arlo snapped.

'She was my aunt,' Elise blurted out. 'I only found out last night.'

They all stared at her.

'The Potiors took my dad's brother and sister in the last Rising in Thymine. They killed my uncle at Raynor's feet. They told her that if she didn't work for them, they would kill my dad and mum in the same way. My mum was pregnant with me; she was Raynor's best friend ...' Elise shrugged. 'And she made her choice.'

'Fu—' Luca began, staring around at them.

'It's not important now,' Elise said quickly. 'We've got other things to consider.' She glanced up at Samuel, trying to read his reaction to her new family member.

'What about all of this lot?' Luca said, nodding towards the swell of people on the pathways.

'We should keep away from them,' Samuel said. 'They're too unpredictable. We nearly died back there because the numbers were too large to be contained. If one of the women in the crowd hadn't taken pity on me and helped me out of my noose, I'd never have been able to break my handcuffs.'

Luca looked at him disbelievingly. 'You can snap metal handcuffs?'

Samuel grinned. 'No. But I am strong enough to snap the tiny screws that hold them together.'

Luca rolled his eyes.

'So, where do we go now?' Georgina asked, staring around her.

'We have to get Kit and Max,' Elise said firmly. 'Stars know what that woman has done to them.'

CHAPTER 28

Twenty-Two

They knew they were close to Adenine when they saw the smoke plume up into the sky from two miles away.

'I believe it has started,' Genevieve said, before quickening her pace.

'What has started?' Twenty-Two signed, hurrying to catch up with her alongside Ezra.

From this far away, it looked like the smoke of one of their campfires, but she knew it had to be much larger than that to be visible from such a distance.

'Another Rising,' Genevieve responded.

'Like the one in Thymine?' Ezra asked, wincing in pain at their increased pace.

Genevieve nodded. Twenty-Two knew what this meant; she had spoken to Elise's mum about it in Uracil. She began to jog towards the base as she thought of the precious information about her ancestors that might be destroyed at any moment.

'Elise's mother, Sofi, told me about the one in Thymine,' Twenty-Two signed, with Ezra speaking her words. 'People took to the pathways.'

Genevieve fell silent for a moment as she matched Twenty-Two's pace. Vance looped around, took both of their bags, and scooped up Ezra. He ran by their side, his gaze fixed on Adenine.

'She was one of the people who died on the island, wasn't she?' Genevieve said quietly.

Twenty-Two nodded. 'And Elise's father died in the bombing.'

Genevieve was silent for so long that Twenty-Two allowed her thoughts to drift elsewhere.

'I noticed in the new Uracil that Samuel displayed some feelings for Elise,' Genevieve said eventually.

Twenty-Two nodded. 'Elise loved him once, perhaps still does.'

'She still does,' Ezra said, his head bumping along with Vance's strides. 'She would always wear his jumper when we were in the cave over winter.'

Genevieve glanced at them both. 'Tell me, is Elise one for revenge?'

Twenty-Two considered the question. 'No, I believe not. She is always very controlled. But I suppose that depends on what it is in relation to. Exceptional circumstances can create the most unpredictable of responses.'

Genevieve rubbed her forehead before changing the subject. 'In our Post-Pandemic history, people have taken to the pathways several times in different bases. It's what comes from it that matters.'

'Has anything come of it before?' Ezra asked.

'No. Trivialities. Tokens. Appeasements. That is all. Perhaps it needs to be conducted differently.'

Twenty-Two studied Genevieve's profile as they ran side-by-side. 'Why do you feel guilty about Elise's mum dying? It had nothing to do with you.'

'I don't feel guilty; I feel sad that she has lost both of her parents.'

'I don't believe you.'

'I don't need you to.'

Twenty-Two picked up her pace. 'We have no time for this. We have to get to the museum.'

Twenty-Two brushed her fringe over her eyes and pulled her hood up. They had waited until the sun had gone down before entering Adenine. Twenty-Two had protested at the further delay but had to admit that what was happening in Adenine was not something she wanted to try and traverse in the daylight. The Museum of Evolution contained the remaining Neanderthal DNA and that was what she focused on; all of the other required equipment could be replaced.

For once, it was not Twenty-Two who was the most conspicuous one. Instead, it was Vance they had to hide. He walked next to Twenty-Two, with Ezra beside Genevieve. They hoped that his Sapien height would lessen her Medius threat.

Vance was bent low as they walked briskly through the Sapien region. Groups of people sat on doorsteps, keeping watch, their lively chatter slowing when they noticed the four strangers crossing a bridge in the distance. Twenty-Two silently observed the people sitting outside their homes for any signs that they were likely to apprehend them before ducking her head and walking quickly down the pathway that linked up the Sapien homes in the Inner Circle.

'Did they take the water treatment facility yet?' an old woman sitting on a porch asked her equally ancient friend.

'Not from what I've heard,' the other woman responded.

'They need to be quick about it,' the first woman mused. 'The Potiors have cut off our water supplies. We've only got a day or two if we're careful.'

'It's the main place they're concentrating on. That, and the Premier's home. Split between the two.'

A woman of middling years came out onto the porch carrying two plates of food. She frowned as she listened to them.

'You two hush now; you don't know who's listening,' she chided, placing the plates on the small table between them.

Twenty-Two and the others hurried by.

The crowds had thinned overnight, and many had returned home to sleep. Whether they would return to the centre in the morning was not known.

The Medius districts were far quieter. Windows and doors were boarded up on some of the higher-end Medius homes. All the lights were out, although Twenty-Two sensed that people were inside and not sleeping. She thought she saw a curtain twitch out the corner of her eye, but when she turned to it, the material stilled.

They stayed away from the central boulevard, where the Premier's home was. In the distance, there was chanting from those surrounding the water treatment facility, trying to persuade the Medius guards to abandon their posts. Twenty-Two's small band of four avoided all the places where others might congregate.

When they passed through the last Medius district, Genevieve pulled them into a darkened alleyway. The streetlights had been cut off, and Twenty-Two found herself groping for a wall to steady herself.

'We will skirt outside the boulevard and cut down to the museum,' Genevieve whispered. 'We must keep our heads down as we can't afford to get involved in any sort of confrontation.'

Pressed against the buildings' walls, they crept towards the glass dome of Adenine's museum, just like the one in Cytosine. Twenty-Two kept her eyes trained on this one landmark.

The sound of smashing glass from the adjacent alleyway made her jump. They passed an intersection, and she glanced down the pathway that crossed the one they were on. In the distance, she could see a bonfire and some darkened figures surrounding it. The wind changed direction and pushed the smoke down the narrow alleyway towards her. She began to blink, her eyes stinging. She rubbed them and then covered her mouth.

'Not our *children*!' one of the faceless figures cried out.

The other three repeated his call.

Twenty-Two put her head down and caught up with Vance, who was now striding ahead.

Not my brothers and sisters either, she thought.

The sound of distant gunshots popped into the air, and Twenty-Two turned towards it. The gunfire was coming from the direction of the water treatment facility. The Potiors had clearly brought their guns to Adenine too. Distant screams filtered across from the other side of the base, and Twenty-Two glanced over at Ezra. That he had nearly died because of such a small object still seemed incomprehensible.

Twenty-Two put her head down and carried on walking.

*

Never had she been so pleased to see a Museum of Evolution, its stone entranceway a prelude to the glass dome behind it. They slipped around the building until they came across a single guard patrolling the area. In only a few minutes, he was tied up and relieved of his key card.

Genevieve pressed it against the side door. Twenty-Two quickly followed and overtook Genevieve, leading the way to the double doors that opened up to the main museum. She had to see it one more time.

Letting the doors swing shut behind her, she breathed deeply and closed her eyes. Far away, she could hear the call of a sea lion to her pup and the quieter response of one so young and new to this world. A toucan's sharp cry pierced the background thrum of hundreds of species of birds. Twenty-Two breathed out slowly and let the sounds of those brought back to life soothe the discord of the outside human world.

She slowly opened her eyes and let her gaze roam over the individual water pods in front of her. On a rocky ledge, overlooking a grey-coloured pond, were several great auks, similar to a penguin, except their flightless wings were tucked up into their sides. Without a glance in her direction, one of them dived into the deep waters below. In the next pod, a pink Amazon river dolphin leapt up into the air from its small freshwater lake, its body twisting in the air. Across from it, a giant beaver, the size of a bear, momentarily surfaced to see if there was any danger he should be aware of.

'It's just like when we wandered around Cytosine's museum,' Ezra said from her side.

She scrunched her eyes at him, grateful as always that he had happened to open her pod door.

Farther back from the individual streams and ponds were some of the larger animals who preferred terra firma. A Zone 5 diprotodon, a giant furry wombat-looking creature, lumbered across its pod, sniffing the air as it went. Its attention was caught by a black-flanked rock wallaby waking up in its pod of dusty stone. A snow leopard prowled in the pod next to it before scaling a steep rock slope.

In the distance, an aiolornis, which looked like a colossal condor, glided down from a cliffside, its wingspan of sixteen feet impressive even at a distance. Passenger pigeons, once abundant in Zone 2, but driven into extinction by the Pre-Pandemic humans only a few hundred years ago, soared directly above, almost touching the glass roof ... but no farther.

Twenty-Two held herself there for a moment before reluctantly turning from them. First, she had to find the ones who had not yet been brought back.

CHAPTER 29

Elise

They ran along the sides of the streets towards Purisian's home, avoiding as best they could the streams of people making their way to the Premier's residence. Elise's only thoughts were with Kit.

Distant explosions made them all duck and cover their heads. Elise thought they were coming from the water treatment facility on the other side of the base. She wondered whether these reverberations would be normal in a day or two, and they would not try to guess which direction they were coming from. She was already beginning to acclimatise in other ways. She did not jump at the clamour of the other residents now – the cries of discontent would pierce the air on an adjacent pathway, and her group would simply pick up their pace, not wanting to be dragged in whatever direction the crowds were taking. Smoke clogged the air in places, and they wrapped T-shirts around their noses and mouths to try and prevent it from seeping into their lungs. The weak midday sunshine failed to filter down to the pathways through the thick, clogging air. A shrill cry from behind threatened to pull them off track, but they pushed on south, hoping that whoever it was would be helped by someone else. They had to get to their friends.

The pathway that bordered some of the Potior residences had remained largely untouched, the crowds focusing their attention on the water treatment facility and the Premier's residence.

'How can we get inside?' Georgina asked, eyeing the unguarded entranceway of Purisian's stark white home. 'We don't have the key cards any more.'

'I think the old-fashioned way,' Elise responded, glancing towards a stone statue of a helix that was the focal point of the lawn.

Within a few seconds, Samuel had picked it up and launched it at one of the side windows. It shattered beneath the force, and they all froze as they waited to see if there would be any response from inside. Elise moved silently to the side of the window and pressed herself against the wall. She waited to see if anyone would come running to it, but all was quiet from within.

After a few minutes, Elise covered her arm in her coat and knocked out the remaining shards of glass. She pulled herself through the small opening while Samuel helped Georgina. Landing almost silently on the other side, she stretched her senses out, trying to anticipate whether the Protection Department was still there.

The home was silent and already had a feeling of abandonment. Drawers had been pulled out and rummaged through without anyone bothering to push them in again. Elise walked silently through the hallway, uncomfortably aware that she had none of her weapons. Without telling the others, she made her way to the office, hoping that Purisian had left her screen behind. She had not. Closing the door behind her, Elise made her way to the kitchen while the others searched for Kit and Max.

Scattered across a table that could easily seat twenty, she saw the belongings that she had been stripped of, along with everyone else's. Rummaging through her bag, she found the most precious item, the small camera she took everywhere. Pulling out her screen, she directed the camera out of the door and filmed some hovering shots over Adenine and the uproar below.

She then directed the camera to the water treatment facility to see what was happening there. Crowds surrounded its doorless walls, the Medius workers already having pulled up the metal ladders used to scale its sides. Elise had to smile to herself. It was intentionally built like a fortress. Not because what was inside was actually precious, but to convince the residents of its worth and occupy them in a fruitless mission. They did not need the Potiors' treated water to survive, but they did not know that.

She began to record the circling crowds seated on the ground below. Without warning, a Medius Protection officer stood up behind the balustrade at the top and, without looking down, sprayed bullets into the people below. Elise jumped at the noise and quickly directed the camera to film what was going on. The crowd scattered in response, leaving behind the ones caught by the bullets. A few bodies were lying in the grass. Elise watched as people returned to retrieve the injured and the dead. But they did not flee the area. Instead, they remained outside the water treatment facility, just farther back, out of the gun's range. They were not so easily deterred.

While she waited for the camera to return, Elise strapped the push knives to her legs and the throwing knives across her chest, placing the sling in her back pocket. She was ready to go out again.

'It's no good,' Georgina said, as she entered the kitchen. 'We've looked everywhere, and they're not here.'

Elise nodded. 'Then we have to work out where they've been taken. Let's go and get the others.'

As she passed through the wide arch separating the kitchen from the hallway, she noticed a seam in the wood underneath the staircase. She touched the panel and watched as a small door opened towards her. Darkness stretched down a set of worn wooden steps. Fumbling for the light switch, she blinked when it snapped on.

'You stay up here,' she whispered to Georgina. 'Go and find the others and bring them.'

Silently, she made her way down the steps. Keeping her gaze fixed on the compacted earth floor, she tried to ignore the spider webs that brushed up against her skin. The ceiling was low, and she had to bend to enter the basement. She hesitated outside the second door for a moment, unsure whether she should wait for the others. She knew that only a fool would enter an enclosed basement by themselves unless it was absolutely necessary.

A moaning noise from inside decided for her. She pushed open the door at the bottom of the steps with the tip of her boot, knives in hand, but did not enter. Standing in the doorway, she swung her torchlight into the low-ceilinged room, and her shoulders slumped in relief.

In the corner of the storage room were Kit and Max, tied up, a rope between their arms and legs, their bodies pulled uncomfortably backwards on themselves. In a few steps, she was by their side.

Elise ripped the tape off Max's mouth.

'They all went to the Premier's residence hours ago,' he said between deep breaths. 'Most of the Potiors and high-end Medius have taken refuge there.'

Elise began fumbling with the knots around Kit's hands.

'Come down and help me. I've found them!' she called out, hoping her voice would stretch far enough for at least one person to hear her.

Moments later, Georgina, and Samuel clattered down the wooden steps and began to help untie their friends.

As Elise helped Kit to the steps, she signed, 'Did she hurt you?' It was just the two of them now.

'No,' he responded, his features as still as always. 'But she would have done if she had not been summoned to the Premier's home. She said she wanted to collect her reward for capturing a Potior and a Neanderthal. She is missing something. She has no humanity.'

Elise nodded as she climbed the steps, trying not to think about what Purisian would have done if she'd had the option.

They all met in the hallway, each careful to avoid looking at Max and Kit's stained trousers.

'Where's Raynor?' Kit signed, after looking around.

Elise blinked as she thought of her aunt. 'She died in the cell with me.'

'You killed her?' Max spluttered. 'I know she betrayed us but—'

'I didn't kill her. She died from her injuries. And she didn't betray us in the way you think she did.' Elise stared at each of them. 'She was my aunt.'

'Your what?' Max said in stunned confusion.

Elise didn't bother repeating it as she knew he had heard. 'Over twenty years ago, the Potiors threatened her with killing my family. That's why she did those things. To keep us safe.' Elise shrugged. 'Others might have made a different choice.'

She kept her face still, hoping they would realise that she didn't want to talk about it any more.

'So, what now?' Luca signed. 'Do we go back to Uracil? Or go after the Premier?'

Elise shook her head. 'We pick up where we left off. And if that means that we have to break into the Office of Communications, then so be it.' She looked around at them all. 'And we're certainly not going after the Premier. If we go to his palace, then we are at a disadvantage. Stars know what's going on in that place right now.'

Max nodded. 'Just give me a couple of hours before we head out again.'

'Yes,' Kit signed. 'I need to shower and find some clean clothes.'

Elise was already making her way back to the kitchen. 'Take three or four. We all need to rest before leaving, and there's something else I have to do.'

A few hours later, Elise found herself sitting on the most sumptuous sofa in Purisian's home. Squidgy cushions were strewn across its length, and she sank into their depths. Elise had done what she needed to and felt her eyes droop. For once, she let them. She was entering her second day without sleep as she curled up on her side and drifted off.

She woke to the light pressure of someone sitting down next to her. Blinking open her eyes, she stared up at Arlo, whose broad frame only took up a quarter of the sofa's expanse.

'I'm sorry I got you into this mess,' Elise mumbled, her eyes half open.

'We got out of it, and that's the most important part,' he responded, allowing himself to lean back.

'Are you going to stay with us?' Elise asked, her eyes beginning to focus.

'I'm sorry,' Arlo said, reaching his hand towards her but not close enough to touch. 'I have to get back to Synthium and warn my people about what is happening on the mainland. If the Potiors are not defeated, they might turn their sights on us. We must prepare.' He looked towards the doorway, focusing on Max, who was bustling around Purisian's home. 'And I don't think you need me any more.'

'I understand. And thank you for coming with us. I am in your debt.'

Arlo smiled at her. 'You are indeed. And I'll be calling in that favour one day.'

Elise raised her head onto her elbow and smiled back at him, watching him through her half-closed eyes.

'I don't suppose you want to come with me?' Arlo asked, raising an eyebrow.

A fork in the pathway presented itself and she hesitated, imagining the quieter, simpler life that could stretch before her.

'I can't,' she said finally. 'I haven't finished what I am meant to do.'

He leant over and laid his hand on hers; she knew he would not hold the decision against her.

'If you change your mind, you know where to find me.'

Elise nodded. It was not an offer she wanted to refuse outright.

She watched as Arlo stood and picked up his belongings, then swung his bag onto his shoulders. Without looking behind, he gave a wave from the doorway. Elise continued to stare at the place he had been long after she heard the front door close.

'He's gone then,' Samuel said a few minutes later, entering the room.

He wouldn't meet her gaze, and it felt as though there were a chasm between them.

'Yes, he has to get back to Synthium. I don't know when I'll see him next.'

'Time will heal you,' Samuel said quietly. 'It won't feel so raw in a few months.'

Elise lifted her head; she was exhausted and knew her mind wasn't functioning as it should. 'What? I don't understand.'

Samuel dipped his gaze. 'I'm sorry, I shouldn't intrude. It's none of my business.'

Elise stared at him. 'You think I'm heartbroken about Arlo leaving?'

Samuel folded his arms in front of his chest. 'I thought—'

'I wasn't with Arlo,' Elise said, more forcefully than she'd expected. 'He's just a friend I needed help from. And what does it matter anyway if I was? You're with Neve!'

She sat up and glared at Samuel.

'Neve?' Samuel took a step into the room. 'You think I'm with Neve?'

Elise faltered.

'Well, aren't you?' she said quietly, not daring to look at him in case he saw the effect his next words would have on her.

She felt a light pressure on the couch as he came to sit down next to her.

'I don't feel like that about Neve,' Samuel said. 'I've spent a lot of time with her because of what we went through in Zone 5, and then because of what happened to her parents. Perhaps she wanted more, but I think it was because she'd had her world pulled from under her, not because of some deep desire for me.'

Elise snorted. 'So, you did want to be with her, but you were being too chivalrous to let it happen?'

The warmth of Samuel's hand enveloped hers, and she stared at it.

'No. Not while I was thinking of you every day. It wouldn't have been fair to either of us. I'd rather be alone than in a half-life.'

Elise turned to him. 'Every day?'

'Every. Single. Day.' He smiled at her. 'There was barely an hour when you wouldn't enter my thoughts. I knew you didn't want me any more. You made that perfectly clear when I went to Zone 5. So, I set about doing everything I could to remove you from my thoughts. But you stayed. Even though you weren't physically present, you were always with me. Always by my side, never leaving me, even though I knew it was impossible. My constant shadow.'

Elise leant forwards, brushed the brown lock from his forehead and kissed him. Through that kiss, she tried to convey everything she felt for him, every apology she should have made and every hope she had for their future. Time slipped by as they lost themselves in each other, wrapping themselves around one another as a protection against the world outside and what was to come.

'I've found it!' Max cried out from the hallway. 'I've bloody well found it!'

Elise started and sat up. Samuel stared up at her, a look of amusement crossing his features.

'Do we have to?' he said quietly.

Elise nodded before pulling her T-shirt back over her head. 'You know we do. There will be time enough for this later.'

Samuel pulled his shirt on and held his hand out to her. She took it, her heart full of love for this strange, awkward, beautiful man.

She paused as they entered a room she hadn't been in before. Shelves lined the walls, crammed full of Pre-Pandemic books. She ran her fingers along their clothbound spines, soaking in titles she had never seen before. She crouched down and pulled out a tome from the bottom shelf that had caught her eye. A book of maps. So much of the world that she did not know about. She pushed the atlas back in its place and resolved to return to it later if she had the time.

Dotted around the room were large armchairs with lamps craning above them. In the centre of the room was a lush fern on a plinth, its fonds spraying over the carved sides. She glanced over at Samuel on the other side of the room; he was watching her every move. She blushed at the attention.

'There, there! Over there!' Max said, turning to face them.

He was pointing towards the corner of the room where an ornate desk was facing the wall. One of its drawers had been pulled open.

Elise crossed the room, swept up in his enthusiasm.

She didn't know what she was looking at. Inside the drawer was a black box about the same size as her grandfather's Pre-Pandemic encyclopaedia.

'It's a box,' she said, raising an eyebrow.

'Pfff...' Max said, rolling his eyes. 'It's not a box. I wouldn't have called you all here to stare at a mere box. I'm not so devoid of visual stimulation after my time in the cellar that I would shout about a *box*.'

'Then what is it?'

'I believe it's one of the few access points to the entirety of the screens in the four bases of Zone 3. I knew as Director of Communications it was a possibility that Purisian would have one.'

Elise's smile lit up her face. 'We can still send a screen release.'

'And we don't have to piggyback it on another one,' Samuel added, matching her grin.

Elise pulled out her screen and, over a few minutes, organised what she wanted to send.

'Here,' she said, handing it over to Max. 'Let them make up their own minds.'

Max plugged in the screen, and they all drifted off to various parts of Purisian's home. An hour later, he had managed to make it past the security systems.

They gathered in the room Max had informed them was called a 'library'. A room that only a Potior could have, since all Pre-Pandemic books were deemed Infactualities and, therefore, illegal.

Max looked over at them. 'Shall I do it? I think a unanimous decision is required.'

One by one, they each nodded their agreement, their eyes wide with the momentous decision.

Max pressed the button. Elise leant forwards so she could watch what he had sent.

The black screen snapped into a shot of Purisian's kitchen with Elise standing in the centre – the recording she had reluctantly made a couple of hours ago. Elise studied herself as she leant over Max's arm. She was surprised to see that she looked like a warrior with her two push knives strapped to her legs and the sharp throwing knives laced across her chest. Elise did not think of herself that way. The only other time she had seen herself on camera was in the images that Raynor had kept. She could see the difference four years had made. Gone was the girl who bent her head and feared being noticed. She knew she was still not beautiful, or even that pretty, but in its place, a sense of power and warmth circled her that she had not been aware of before. The woman on the screen appeared calm and confident, all the things she had always wanted to be. The Medius could keep their beauty – Elise wanted more.

The small mobile camera held steady as it focused on her face.

'I was hoping I would have more time to prepare,' Elise said directly to the camera, 'but I've had to make this in a hurry. Adenine is in the middle of a Rising and there are a few things everyone in the bases needs to know.'

The footage cut to a panned shot of Adenine that Elise had taken outside. Crowds surrounded the Premier's home, spilling out onto the pathways. Even the most cynical viewers couldn't doubt the authenticity of the footage.

'I am from Thymine, where, twenty years ago, there was a Rising that failed,' Elise continued from the kitchen. 'It failed because the residents thought the water processing plant was essential. I'm here to tell you that it's not.' Adenine's water treatment facility with the crowds below flashed onto the screen. Elise's voice continued over the top. 'We have been taught that we need the treated water so we don't get ill again. But that's not true. The Potiors have made us reliant on their treated water and they ration it, so we think we can't survive without it. You can actually drink water from any stream or river if you boil it first.'

The screen cut to an article Dahlia had given her just after Caitlyn died. 'That's one of the original documents the Potiors created over a hundred years ago when they were first organising the bases. I took it from the university in Guanine. It shows the process the Potiors put into place to treat the water and confirms that it has a similar effect as boiling it. At the bottom, you'll see the Premier's signature. There are hundreds of these documents locked away in the university in Guanine. The Potiors have kept a record of all their "achievements".

'I left Thymine four years ago and went to a hidden base called Uracil. It was a peaceful place up in the northeast of Zone 3. Some of you may have heard rumours of it. A few months ago, the Potiors decided to bomb Uracil with the Pre-Pandemic airplanes they have kept.'

On the screen, three planes soared overhead in the footage Elise had taken at the time. The engines drowned out Max's cries as Elise tended to his leg.

'This is what is left of Uracil now.'

The feed cut to footage Elise had taken the previous year with her small camera on Uracil's island when they had buried the dead. A ravaged landscape took up the screen, bodies lying scattered and torn on the ground.

'They haven't just kept airplanes; they've also kept guns. The people of Adenine know this now, but they remain firm in their simple demand: their future children and grandchildren should not be raised believing they are submissive.'

The crowds at the water treatment facility scattered as bullets sprayed down on them from above. A few were left wounded, and two people were clearly dead.

'The Potiors have been feeding us lies since we were born. We are told that we are a separate species to them when we are not. Tweaking a few genes doesn't make a different species of human. But if we are taught this from birth and prevented from learning about ourselves, is it any wonder that we have believed them for so many years? Think about who decides what you are taught. Some of the Medius who studied at the university in Guanine know the truth. And I've also sent you documents with this screen release to prove it. If you're one of those Medius, now is the time to be open about what you know. This isn't about Sapien versus Medius because that distinction doesn't really exist. Instead, it's about one simple thing. The truth. And how it has been kept from us for generations.'

Lab 412 in Cytosine flashed up on the screen with the furry tapping leg on one side and blinking eye on the other.

'They have been mixing and splicing animal DNA for years without telling us. What if it got out of control? What if some of their creations escaped? What would happen to our precious ecosystems?

'Two days ago, you were sent a screen release and told that half the Sapien pregnancies were being altered. This won't create a new species, but it will create another group of people who are told that their genetics define their future choices and expectations from life. The people of Adenine have responded to this. What will the other bases do?'

The image cut out.

'They've been shown the truth. We've done everything we can,' Georgina said. 'It's in their hands now.'

'As it always should be,' Elise said quietly.

The sound of breaking glass made Elise pause. It was an hour later, and they had separated into different rooms to gather supplies from Purisian's home. Georgina was working her way through the medicine cabinets, Luca was in the kitchen and Elise was on weapons duty. Max and Kit were conducting a general sweep of the upstairs rooms, and Samuel was back in the office trying to find any other information they could send out in a screen release.

Muffled noises were coming from the other end of the house. Sprinting towards them, Elise dropped the paper knife she had been inspecting and, as she ran, replaced it with one of her throwing knives.

By the time she reached the hallway, all had gone quiet.

She opened door after door, trying to locate the source of the disturbance. She hadn't imagined it; she was sure of it. But then she hadn't slept properly for two days. Was she so sleep-deprived that she had begun to hallucinate?

She pushed open the door to the library. Something wasn't right. The corner of the rug was flipped upwards, and she sensed something had happened there. She crossed to the window and pulled back the curtains. The glass had been carefully cut out of a large pane. A smaller horizontal section, no larger than her hand, had been smashed, and the shards hastily kicked under the rug.

Someone had broken in. Elise felt a tingling sensation travel down the length of her spine.

She crossed to the hallway, knives in both hands. Now was not the time for stealth or subtlety.

'Everyone, come to the hallway! Someone has broken in!'

She waited.

Kit was the first to skid along the marble floor in his haste to find out what had happened.

'Was it the residents?' he signed.

She shook her head. 'Too well executed.'

Max flew into the hallway, closely followed by Luca.

'What did they take?' Max said.

Before waiting for a response, he raced off to the library.

'*No!*' came his cry from several rooms away. 'They've taken the broadcaster!'

Elise didn't respond. It must have been the Protection Department.

'I'm here!' Georgina shouted over the wooden bannisters on the first-floor landing.

Elise began to relax at the sight of Georgina. She was the one Elise worried about the most as she didn't have the same defensive skills as the others.

Elise counted to sixty in her head, giving him a chance to appear. Her hands were clammy as she tried to calm herself. She walked to the library and inspected the window again, the others following. There had to have been a struggle. Why bother cutting the glass pane away to enter the building only to smash a much smaller pane? The smaller pane couldn't be deliberate – it had resulted from a scuffle. Samuel must have tried to stop them, and they'd taken him to try and cover their tracks.

She turned to the others. 'Get your bags. We're leaving in five minutes.'

'But ... ?' Georgina said.

'The broadcaster isn't the only thing they took – they've captured Samuel as well.'

CHAPTER 30

Twenty-Two

The rumbling noises of a discontented crowd increased and soaked through the museum's walls. Twenty-Two imagined a surge of people could enter the museum at any minute, destroying everything in their path.

'Where do they keep the Neanderthal records?' Twenty-Two signed quickly as the doors to the main museum closed behind her.

She should never have become distracted.

'Down here, I think,' Genevieve said, hurriedly leading the way through the low-ceilinged hallways to the laboratories and pods at the back of the museum.

When they reached the Neanderthal pods, Twenty-Two stared around her. Only three years ago, she had taken her first steps into a similar hallway, back when she had been fixated on the ceiling falling down or the grey concrete seeping upwards and turning her to stone. She had come far since then, although she still preferred the sky above her head and that which the stars had made surrounding her.

Twenty-Two indicated for Genevieve to stop. 'We need to check all the barred pods. There might be others like me.'

'We should check,' Ezra agreed.

The noise of the crowd outside seeped away; perhaps they had moved on. The museum became eerily quiet, stripped of most of its personnel. Twenty-Two hoped they would return soon as the animals needed feeding. She did not want them to be forgotten as she once had been.

Genevieve nodded and called for Vance, who was up ahead. 'I also need to check on whether the first of the new so-called "species" of humans is still here. I owe them that much.'

They split off into the separate hallways, sliding back the steel bars and checking for any occupants. Twenty-Two found none. When she came to the last pod, she drew back the final set of bars and stepped inside. It was deserted, just as the others had been. She walked through the meadow, the uncut grass brushing against her bare ankles. The overnight sprinklers had been on, and a light dew made everything shine in the early dawn light. She remembered sitting in an identical pod back in Cytosine with Dara, sprawled out on the grass with her face to the sun.

Pushing through the ferns and brambles that bordered the meadow, she emerged onto the riverbank, its treated water swirling into a rippling pool. She bent down and stared at her reflection. Her hair was thick now and no longer fell out in clumps as she ran her fingers through it.

She hopped over the stepping stones. Her sturdy legs pushed her up the steep bank when she reached the other side. Sniffing the crisp air, she found comfort in the familiar scent of the pine trees. She made her way to the sleeping area, her heart thumping a little louder as she imagined five or so of her brothers and sisters turning to welcome her. Could they still be here? As she weaved around the trunks, she scrunched her eyes in anticipation.

Twenty-Two stared at the blanket of pine needles. There wasn't even a sleeping roll laid out on the ground.

Where had her brothers and sisters in Adenine gone? She knew she would probably never find out. The Potiors had treated them like dispensable exhibits, and it was likely they had simply been disposed of.

Turning, she made her way back to the steel door. She did not admire the setting any longer; any lingering sentimentality for her formative years had gone. It had just been an elaborate cage where she had spent the first fourteen years of her life. There were more important things to consider now. She had to find the genetic information of her other brothers and sisters if there was to be any hope of her kind surviving.

'Did you find them?' Genevieve asked from the end of the hallway.

Twenty-Two caught up with her and Ezra. 'No. They were probably removed months ago, maybe even a year or two. There weren't even any sleeping rolls laid out. The sprinkler systems are still working, perhaps in anticipation of a new occupant, whoever that may be.'

Genevieve sighed. 'I had guessed they were gone, but I hoped otherwise. For what it is worth, I am sorry.'

'I am as well,' Ezra said, rubbing his face with the sleeve of his jumper.

Twenty-Two turned away.

'Did you find what you were looking for?' she eventually asked Genevieve.

The older woman shook her head. 'The best-case scenario is that the Potiors took Ben and the others like him to the Premier's home. I don't want to think about the alternatives.'

Together they walked down featureless grey hallways, lost in their thoughts. As they proceeded farther, Vance's tall frame straightened, and a slight spring formed in his step, similar to Samuel's when he felt optimistic about life.

'I can read him,' Twenty-Two signed to Genevieve, with Ezra speaking her words. 'He is coming alive here.'

Genevieve turned and smiled at her. 'I was hoping this would happen. There was another reason I wanted to come here besides fulfilling my part of our bargain. I wanted to see if I could help Vance.'

'The museum is important to him?'

'It was once everything to him.' Genevieve glanced towards Vance, who was walking ahead and had almost disappeared out of sight down the corridor. 'Long ago, before Vance founded Uracil and before he lost his daughter, he went by a different name. He was the Potior responsible for creating the museums. I think it is why Samuel took such an interest in them; he wanted that connection to the father he so rarely saw. Vance used to be the Chief Director of all the museums and designed them down to the smallest detail. It was his passion.

'But when he lost his daughter, he turned his back on them and took what was deemed a menial role outside the museums as a tracker. The museums reminded him of his daughter too much; he used to take her around Adenine's when she was a baby and toddler. He would spend hours with her wandering through the exhibits. In his mind, the two became inextricably linked. He had spent years studying the animals in the museums and how they interacted and moved through their environments. Fortunately for him, he was able to use that skill elsewhere.'

Vance turned and gestured at them to hurry up and follow him.

When they reached the lab, he pushed open the door and went straight to a large screen in the corner.

'Vance will download all the information about the Neanderthals onto your screen,' Genevieve said, as she walked over to a set of steel drawers. 'The samples you need are in here. There are around two hundred. More than enough to start a small population with the right equipment and scientific knowledge.'

'The equipment is here as well?' Ezra asked.

'Yes, and the people you need are in Adenine too.'

Twenty-Two nodded. The samples were safe, and that was her main priority. She would work out a way to find the people she needed to bring them back to life once the turmoil in the bases had settled.

She looked over at Vance and asked Ezra to interpret for her.

'Am I on there?' she asked.

'Yes, you will be,' Genevieve responded. 'All the Neanderthal genomes are based on a previous Neanderthal.'

'Please find me.'

Vance nodded and tapped in a few commands. Up on the screen flashed a single bone, delicate-looking and splintered at the end.

'That is the sample you were based upon,' Genevieve said, as her eyes skimmed across the information on the screen. 'It's one of the metacarpal bones in the hand. It was found in a cave in the part of Zone 3 that the Potiors don't rule over, over the sea and east of here. Vance has been there several times.'

Genevieve stared upwards as she continued scanning the screen. 'It says it was dated to around 49,000 years ago, and the girl was around five to seven years old when she died.'

Ezra bounced up and down on the balls of his feet. 'You know who you are now! See, they didn't mess around with you. You're pure Neanderthal.'

Twenty-Two stared up at the bone. She had not lived long the last time – she really had been given a second chance at life.

'Thank you,' she signed. 'I have always wanted to know more about where I came from.'

Genevieve began pulling small vials out of the drawer and placing them in a bag for Twenty-Two while Vance continued downloading information from the screen above them.

'I am leaving now,' Genevieve said, when the last container had been carefully placed inside the bag.

'What?' Ezra said. 'Why?'

Vance looked away from his screen towards her.

'No. You have to stay with Twenty-Two,' Genevieve said gently. 'Help her get back to Uracil safely. For me.'

Twenty-Two stopped pulling the bag closed. 'Where are you going?'

'There is something I have to do. The details of which do not matter.' Genevieve turned and took a seat while Twenty-Two remained standing. For once, she was the taller one. 'But there is something else ... someone needs to know the truth in case I don't come back.' She gestured for Twenty-Two and Ezra to come closer. 'They need to know how far ahead of us the Premier is and that the Potiors have known of Uracil for decades.'

Twenty-Two observed Genevieve closely. 'What is it you want to tell me?'

'It is more of a confession, really. I realise now that I should have made it a long time ago. No more secrets for me. I'm tired of them. I cannot honour their deaths if I continue with this deception.' Genevieve paused. 'It concerns my bargain with the Potiors. When you return to Uracil, you must tell them that the Potiors know their new location, as the Potiors chose it. Uracil must move to a place that no one has considered before. Its safety is more important than my reputation.'

Twenty-Two nodded. She had suspected that there was something important that Genevieve had been holding back for a long time.

Ezra glared at Genevieve.

'When the Potiors arrested me in Adenine, I met with the Premier. He told me that the Potiors had known of Uracil for years, decades even.'

Twenty-Two listened quietly while Genevieve related the impossible choice she had faced.

'So, I agreed to steer Uracil to the new site the Potiors had selected and turn their attention inwards again.' Genevieve's voice caught in her throat. 'They told me that if I didn't comply, they would find someone else who would. And if I betrayed them, they would bomb Uracil again. I thought I was being clever, that I could outwit them. But I was wrong. They were one step ahead. I didn't know the Potiors would starve the people on the island. I promise on Samuel's life that I knew nothing of it. If I had …'

Twenty-Two thought of the people in power and what they had forced onto others. With fraught times came impossible decisions. Culpability rippled outwards, and few avoided its coating. She leant over and patted Genevieve on the arm with one hand.

'It is right that you have told me. Uracil can prepare now. No more lies,' Twenty-Two signed.

Genevieve embraced Vance, and a silent message passed between them. Genevieve shook her head before picking up her bag. At the doorway, she turned and smiled at him, his gaze never leaving her. Twenty-Two watched as the older woman closed the door behind her. She did not know if she would ever see her again.

Twenty-Two stared down at the bag she held in her hands and began transferring the vials back into the steel drawers. Her brothers and sisters were safe here for the time being; if the Potiors remained in power, she would pack them up again and make her way to Uracil. She had fulfilled her promise to the stars.

'What are you doing?' Ezra asked, hovering by her side.

'I'm staying here for a short while. The museum and everything inside needs looking after during this unrest. You've seen yourself that nearly everyone who worked here has left.'

Ezra gave a wide grin. 'Then I'm staying with you.'

Twenty-Two scrunched her eyes in return, her gaze shifting to Vance. 'Will you stay with us? Help us look after the animals until things have settled here, one way or another?'

Vance's voice was quiet, hesitant. 'I shall also stay. I cannot stand back and idly watch the animals' demise. I've been gone too long from them, nearly five years now.'

Twenty-Two and Ezra exchanged a glance but didn't say anything.

Twenty-Two turned towards Vance, who tentatively smiled at her. In response, she scrunched her eyes.

Placing the now-empty bag on the ground, she signed, 'Where do we start?'

Vance looked around. 'With the ones who are hungry or thirsty. We will visit every pod and make sure they have everything they need. We'll then start making a decision about which ones we can release. I never wanted the ones native to this island to be kept in the museums. It's about time we started doing the work properly, as I always intended.'

Twenty-Two stared up at him and scrunched her eyes. She thought this partnership was going to work very well.

She tied back her hair and clipped her fringe to the side so that it didn't fall in her eyes, her heavy brow ridge clear for the world to see. She was ready to begin and gestured for Vance to lead the way, Ezra by her side.

For the first time in her life, she did not let her mind wander to the past, back to her childhood with Fintorian or her closeted time with Dara. Instead, she focused on the future. Her mind pushed forwards, five, ten, twenty years away, where she saw hundreds of her brothers and sisters who had returned to her. And, if things went well, perhaps thousands in the future.

Their time would come again, just as hers had done.

CHAPTER 31

Genevieve

Genevieve held her head up to the pale morning sun as she exited the Museum of Evolution. It had been over twenty-five years since she had lived without a secret that affected every choice she made, and she felt a new lightness. She had told the truth of what had happened with the Premier and felt worthy of having a story again.

The displaced parts inside of her had begun to slide into position, and she hoped this meant they would start to unite. As she pulled her hood over her head to shield her face, she remembered the girl she had once been when she had lived in Uracil. Beth would never have made a deal with the Potiors. She would have been indignant at the mere idea of it.

At what point had she lost herself? It was not with a change of name from Beth to Genevieve – that did not carry her essence. No, it was with the slow slip into the role of the high-end Medius that she had assumed. There had been too many compromises and justifications that her seemingly benign actions were for the 'greater good'. And with each one, her new identity had begun to calcify into this hardened sculpture of a human being.

There was only one thing to do to absolve herself and earn back that young woman's trust – she had to return to being Beth, not in name but in action.

Genevieve glanced back at the museum before quickly turning down the lane that would take her to the Premier's residence. She hoped that Vance and Twenty-Two would remain safe. She smiled to herself at her newfound concern for Twenty-Two's wellbeing when at one point she had been seconds from taking her life. Only a few days ago, she had handed Twenty-Two a bowl of soup laced with one of Mortimer's pills as she waited to hear if the girl would blame Genevieve for Ezra nearly dying. She could not have a lifelong enemy at such a crucial time, but Twenty-Two had made the right decision, and Genevieve had knocked the bowl from her hands.

Her shoulders hunched and eyes down, Genevieve tried not to draw any attention to herself as she joined one of the busier pathways. She hadn't been certain of the outcome of their journey to the old capital. She had decided to assess the girl and consider whether Twenty-Two really was the virtuous champion she claimed to be. Over the weeks, Genevieve's attitude had come to change towards her – never so far as liking her, but it had softened somewhat.

Genevieve had always known that life was far more complex than 'wrong' and 'right'. A decision had a lifetime of influencing factors behind it. Twenty-Two had done what she had thought was right at the time, even though in the eyes of many, it was not. Genevieve's own daughter, Faye, had also strayed far from the line but for different reasons. She had become corrupted by power, and it pained Genevieve to admit it. She wished more than anything that she had been in Uracil in the months preceding Faye's death, not just to prevent it but also to halt Faye's course and provide counsel. Genevieve squeezed her eyes shut. Would Faye even have listened to the mother who had been absent from her life for years? Likely not, but at least Genevieve could have tried.

She pulled her travelling coat tighter around herself as she pushed through the crowds. The residents of Adenine seemed to have more purpose than the evening before. Something had clearly changed, and they were united in the direction they were moving. It was the same one as Genevieve, towards the Premier's home. They had an outstanding matter to settle. With her head bent, she tried not to catch the notice of those around her. Their shouts and cries made her wince, her sensitive hearing resulting in an overload that threatened to make her clamp her hands to her ears. She had never witnessed such uproar, and it unsettled her. Disorder always did.

A Sapien bashed into her, and instead of him turning to apologise, he glared at her. Genevieve shrugged; it was as much his fault as her own, and she wasn't going to apologise if he wasn't. As someone so clearly 'Medius', she might be viewed as the enemy now, but she wasn't going to pander to any of the Sapiens' misconstrued beliefs about her. Genevieve knew the advantages she had lived with and was grateful to have been born in Uracil, but she did not believe in self-flagellation by way of apology for her gifts. Instead, she had devoted her life to a cause that rebelled against the people who were responsible. She would not shoulder the blame for the Potiors' actions; the responsibility for this crooked, corrupt society lay firmly at their door.

The Sapien man was still staring at her, weathering the jostling around him. Emboldened by the surrounding chaos, he stepped towards her. He was large for a Sapien, and the muscles in his neck strained as though he was ready for a fight. Without hesitation, Genevieve took a step forwards. She snarled at him – animalistic and raw – so only he could see. If that didn't knock him off course for a moment, she would have to try other methods. He faltered at the sight of this half-wild Medius with her teeth bared and glanced around him. But there was no one to confirm what he had seen. When he turned around again, she was gone.

Revenge. It was a word often misconstrued in Genevieve's opinion. It was sometimes cast as a trait of the petty and weak-minded, but she disagreed with this interpretation. She believed the critical question was not *who* was wielding revenge but *whom* they were exacting it upon. If it was against a lost Neanderthal girl who had spent most of her life in a cage, treated as an exhibit and abandoned like a runt that didn't deserve to be cared for, Genevieve would accept the traditional connotations of the word. However, if the revenge that was sought was against a force far more powerful than the seeker, the odds very much against them, she believed there should be a heroic element to the word. For it was the enemy that lent it meaning, not the action itself.

The one whom she was seeking was the most powerful individual in Zone 3. That did not deter Genevieve, who was filled with visions of her people starving on an inconsequential island to the southwest. It was her sheer outrage at the callousness of the act that burnt brightly inside of her. Such a small effort on the Potiors' part could have saved hundreds of lives, yet they had decided not to. It made the lack of action intentional.

If Genevieve were entirely honest with herself, she also did not like being taken advantage of. She was now guilty by association and wanted to scrub her name clean. She had been forced into a position where she was stripped of all reasonable choices, and this grated on her. She'd tasted weakness, and it was bitter, unpalatable. So, like a moth to a flame, she too was drawn to the Premier's residence. She hoped that Beth would approve.

'Huh,' she said to herself, as she emerged into the boulevard.

She had not been expecting what met her.

Many lower-end Medius guards had abandoned their posts around the Premier's residence and joined the Sapiens. Together they stood in the square, their faces turned to the seat of the Potiors' power.

The crowds grew denser as Genevieve pushed forwards. In amongst them, she thought she caught the eye of another Medius she recognised. Elijah. The man who had tried to confide in her at a dinner party she had held a year ago. They pointedly ignored each other, clearly unsure if they were both there for the same reason.

Genevieve bent in on herself, trying to lessen the height that had helped carry her through life. She picked her way through the circling people towards the rear of the Premier's residence. Hardly anyone turned to her, and she thanked the stars she was wearing her travelling clothes rather than the high-end Medius ones she used to wear.

She had already seen that the bridge had been blown. All that remained was its two curves on either side of the moat, ending abruptly in jagged stone, the rest of it presumably below the surface. This was what had stopped the Sapiens crossing before, but now they clearly had new information. A few of them had rolled up their trousers and begun to tentatively wade through its waters. Someone must have explained to them that it was not virus-laden as they had previously been taught all their lives. More importantly, that person had been believed. In only a few minutes, the Premier's first line of defence had been transposed into nothing more than an inconvenient water feature.

The creak of the main doors being pulled open by a few guards caught Genevieve's attention – a kind of symbiosis was emerging between the Sapiens and some of the Medius. The twelve-foot-high wooden doors swung open. Turning around to face the sound, Genevieve knew she had to act quickly, or her prize would be taken from her. She began to unlace her boots.

Holding her backpack, socks and boots high above her head, she slid down the grassy bank to the moat, hoping it wasn't too deep. It had barely rained for the past month, so the water only reached her waist. In the winter, it probably would have been so deep that the only way to cross would be to swim. She tried to ignore her mild fears of what might be living in the water. With each step, she imagined a crocodile swimming towards her silently under the surface. Even though she knew that the water wouldn't harm her, fear lay in what other precautions the Potiors might have set.

Her toes curled with each footstep into the soft mud, hesitating in case there was sharp glass or silt so thick that it wouldn't release her. She tried to remind herself that if a carnivorous animal were below the surface, it would have tried its luck with another before her. It would not be holding out for the taller lady at the back. Repeating this logical thought, she concentrated on the bank on the other side. Fifteen steps to go.

When she began to rise out of the water, she scrambled up the grass. Quickly stripping off her soaking trousers and socks, she tried to dry her legs with an old T-shirt. She then changed into clean underwear, trousers and socks and put her dry boots on, all thoughts of modesty leaving her. She did not pack the wet clothing – this was a one-way journey.

She walked towards the doors, ignoring the guards who had opened them. They stood in huddled groups, speaking in whispers. They did not appear to know what to do next. Several days of being ordered to attack the people they had recently shared pathways with had clearly led them to question those orders. But what to do now? They had never been trained or encouraged to think independently. Instead, they were following their gut instincts to stop taking orders from people who couldn't even be bothered to remember their names. The gatekeepers had opened the doors but did not yet dare go inside.

Genevieve walked past them as if she had every right to be there. She nodded to the few who caught her eye before quietly slipping through the first set of doors to her left.

She closed them behind her. Instinct kicked in. She immediately ducked when she heard a mechanism release on the other side of the room. An arrow was lodged in the door panel where her head had recently been.

Everywhere was rigged. She would expect no less of the Potiors.

'It will take more than a few bolts and cogs,' she whispered, heading directly to a window that faced an inner courtyard.

On the way, she snatched up a heavy metal globe and placed it in her backpack. As she re-tied the drawstrings, she caught a glimpse of herself in a gilded mirror, the first sight of her reflection in months. Fine lines had settled around her mouth and splayed out from the corners of her eyes, and her forehead was now permanently creased. Line by line, time was clawing back what belonged to it – she looked to be in her early forties now. She had aged a decade in a matter of months. She smiled at her altered reflection. There was still a decade of grace that time hadn't caught up with yet.

Sliding open the sash window, she automatically ducked again, but this one was not rigged. *Still, better to be safe than dead.*

Climbing outside, Genevieve shimmied over to a drainpipe. Using her innate strength, she pulled herself up the inside of the courtyard. She had an idea of where the Premier's quarters were, but she didn't want to travel through forty rooms laden with bear traps to get there.

Up above were the glass panes that sealed the courtyard from uninvited guests. Her arms and legs still wrapped around the drainpipe, she studied it and her gaze alighted on a small latch near the drain that could only be accessed from below. She pulled on it, and a panel of glass swung inwards. Holding its weight with one arm, she gently lowered it until it was hanging by its hinges. Another architectural detail to protect the Premier, this one allowing the occupants to escape but inaccessible to someone trying to break in.

Once she was on the roof, she surveyed her surroundings. The gently pitched roof was covered in clay tiles, and she dropped to her hands and knees and crawled along their surface in an easterly direction. It wasn't a particularly graceful method of traversing the roof. Still, it would safely get her where she needed to be.

A scream punctured the air below. Genevieve flattened her body against the tiles, straining to hear anyone climbing up towards her. After a few minutes of silence, she peeked over the edge and into the quadrangle below. A young Medius guard, a boy really in Genevieve's eyes, stared back at her. His eyes were wide with shock, and his hand rested against the slash across his throat, unable to make anything more than a gurgling noise. Her gaze flicked to the retreating figure of a Potior slipping through a set of doors back into the house. Genevieve crouched down and held her breath. When she dared peep over the side again, the guard stared back at her, but all life had gone.

Across the terracotta tiles she crawled, ignoring the occasional cry from below, until she reached the domed glass roof in the centre. The dome was a vanity, a show of superiority; she knew this was where the Premier would be. Naturally, he would also want as many rooms as possible between himself and the outside world.

Peering through the glass, she saw a line of Protection officers circling the Premier. Hands clasped behind his back, he steadily paced in front of some steps leading up to an ornate chair. 'Throne' would have been the Pre-Pandemic word for it. A delusional high-end Medius would probably refer to it as 'Father's Kitchen Stool', despite its back reaching ten feet in height and its positioning nowhere near any type of table. *Fools,* Genevieve thought dismissively.

Her attention was drawn to a curled figure in the corner, tied up and lying limply on his side. She stared at him. The surprise of recognition was quickly replaced as her worst fears aligned in her mind.

The Premier glanced up at the dome roof, and a small smile crossed his features. He crooked his finger at her before pointing at the body by his feet. It was her only living child, Samuel.

CHAPTER 32

Elise

They had taken Samuel. Elise could think of nothing else as she swung into action.

'There's a tunnel system,' she shouted as she threw her backpack onto her shoulders and began marching towards Purisian's front door. 'We have to get to its entranceway by the recycling centre. I've got it marked on Raynor's screen.'

The others hastily shoved belongings into their bags before following Elise out of the Potior's home. She sent a quick thanks up to Raynor for the screen that she had insisted Elise should take. Raynor had been painstakingly collecting information about the Premier's residence for nearly twenty years and had kept it all hidden in case she needed it.

As Elise hurried outside, she tried not to think of what was being done to Samuel at this very moment. The idea of anything happening to him was unbearable. A sensation crept through her, one she had only ever experienced when it came to her family. She knew that if anyone harmed him, she would tear them to shreds. He was not to be toyed with; he was too precious for that. He was hers to protect, just as she expected that same protection from him.

The sound of her friends' feet running after her brought some relief. She was leading them into danger again. She didn't know how many of them would survive, but they were still following, which meant they still trusted her decisions. It was their choice. They all knew the risks by now. Turning, she saw Georgina's red hair bobbing behind, and she slowed for her to catch up. She was desperate to get to Samuel, but she wasn't going to be dismissive of Georgina's life in the process. A few steps taken more slowly wouldn't alter the outcome.

The streets felt emptier than before, and Elise wondered where the residents had gone. Perhaps they had dared to cross the water surrounding the Premier's residence now that they knew it wasn't dangerous. If that was the case, the Premier would soon be fenced in, and a caged animal could panic and lash out. The thought made her speed up, and she took Georgina's hand in hers, tugging her along.

An explosion from the adjacent pathway made her duck, pulling Georgina down with her. The sound of masonry tumbling to the ground was deafening, and a cloud of dust rose and spread over them. Still crouched, they all fought to cover their noses and mouths with T-shirts to keep the worst of the dust from entering their lungs. Elise rubbed her eyes, and they began to water. She glanced at Max, who had a fine layer of light-coloured powder over his hair and skin, giving him a ghostly appearance. She realised that she must look the same. After the earth-shattering noise melted away, the pathways were suddenly quiet, any nearby onlookers having fled for their lives.

Just as they were standing, a second explosion rang out that shook the very ground beneath them. Elise looked up, and her eyes widened as one of the buildings at the end of their pathway collapsed, followed by another.

'*Run!*' Elise grabbed Georgina's hand and began tugging her away from the falling buildings.

The sound behind them was deafening as they pelted down the pathway and turned the corner into the adjacent lane. Her ears ringing, Elise skidded to a stop and turned to check that the others had made it out.

'What the stars is going on?' Luca signed with one hand, clutching a T-shirt to his mouth with the other.

'The Potiors have begun their revenge,' Max responded, hardly out of breath but fear etched across his features.

'We need to check if there are any survivors,' Kit signed, white dust coating his hair.

Elise nodded. 'Let's wait a few minutes more to see if that was the last of the buildings to fall.'

They were a few of the longest minutes of Elise's life. Every second she imagined what was happening to Samuel. She thought of Raynor and how she had put her family above everything else. Elise knew her help was needed elsewhere.

'I can't wait any longer,' Georgina eventually snapped. 'There could be people dying underneath all that, and I need to help them.'

Without waiting for the others, she marched around the corner.

The scene that met them was one of utter destruction. Building after building was reduced to rubble, the damage escalating the farther down the lane it went towards the explosion site.

A yawning crack had shot up through the frontage of the building nearest them, but it had held firm. Elise imagined that the Potiors must have blown up one of the buildings farther down but had misjudged the effects of the explosion on the nearby buildings. Or maybe they had just decided to start laying waste to Adenine. Who knew with the Potiors?

All was quiet, as if there were no space for sound in such a visually altered world.

A distant noise caught Elise's attention and had her running down the lane. In amongst the rubble, she had heard the smallest of cries. She ran over to the plaintive sound and gestured for the others to follow. The building was only half collapsed, its two side walls holding firm.

All five of them began frantically digging through the debris that had been the front wall, launching bricks behind them. Soon Max and Kit could move a large table aside that had shielded whatever was buried below from the worst of the damage.

A small hand surfaced through the gravel, and Elise held on to it as she cleared rubble with her other hand. The fingers clasped hers, and she felt their grip weakening. As they cleared more rocks, a small head emerged, and a boy, no more than six years old and entirely covered in grey dust, wriggled his way out of the last of it. Elise pulled a shirt from her bag and splashed water onto it before wiping his face so that he could see. His skin shone through as she cleared the dirt from it. A Potior child. No Sapien or even Medius had violet eyes.

'Are there others?' Elise gently asked as he stared at her, clearly in shock.

He nodded before gesturing behind him.

'How many?'

'Two,' he said, raising his chin to her. He tried to assert himself, but it was only momentary; he began to cry. 'We wanted to see what was happening, so we snuck out. It was my idea.'

They carried on digging until an unconscious boy and a dazed girl were also pulled free. Georgina set to work.

'What do we do with them?' Luca said quietly, watching Georgina check them over.

'Get them somewhere safe,' Elise responded.

She tried to take in the destruction that had reduced this small pathway to rubble. She had already run down to the end of the street and stood quietly for five minutes. There were no noises from the pyramid of debris that was the initial site of the explosion. If anyone had been inside those buildings, they were now with the stars. No one could have survived a blast of that size.

'But they're Potiors,' Luca whispered, glancing over at the three huddled figures. 'Shouldn't we—'

'Lock them up?' Elise said sharply. 'Maybe execute them? That would ensure they didn't turn on us in the future.'

'No, I didn't—'

'Yes, you did,' Elise said, still staring at him. 'But we can't go down that path. They're only children. Being a Potior is a choice, and they are not yet old enough to make it. Imagine if one of them were your child and the situation were reversed. Wouldn't you want someone to help them no matter their supposed species?'

A look of resolve settled on Luca's features, and she knew she had managed to get through to him.

'I'll take them somewhere safe, maybe one of the schools,' he said.

'Thank you.' Elise wiped the dirt from her face and turned to Georgina. 'Are they all safe to be moved?'

Georgina nodded. 'The boy is conscious, but I don't like the look of the knock he had to his head. He needs medical attention.'

Elise nodded. 'Luca, go with Georgina to find somewhere safe to take the children. Maybe one of the medical facilities is still open. There must be somewhere the casualties are being taken. Max and Kit can come with me.' She halted for a second, hearing herself. 'That is, if you want to ...'

'I will come with you and help find Samuel,' Kit signed. 'He is family.'

Max nodded his agreement. 'You might need my help too, and I've always liked Samuel.'

Elise took a step towards Georgina and Luca. 'Stay with them until we know they're safe. Some people will be looking for revenge, and a few will want an easy target.'

Georgina grabbed Elise's hand. 'I can agree to that as long as you don't do anything stupid.' She had put on her best big sister voice, and Elise suddenly felt twelve years younger than her. 'Just get Samuel and get out of there.' Georgina jutted her chin out. 'You've done enough. And Nathan needs you alive. So don't do anything foolish.'

Elise smiled at her before giving her a quick hug. 'I'll be back before you even know I'm gone.'

She looked towards Kit, and he nodded to show he was ready.

Elise's anxiety had begun to ebb once they entered the residential Sapien districts. She was with the people she knew and understood now. Not the Potiors and high-end Medius who would blow up the whole base if they felt their power slipping. As she ran along the pathways, she admired the efforts of her people. Something akin to pride took over as she watched them at work. The Potiors had misjudged the Sapiens. They had assumed they would be distracted by the inaccessible water treatment centre and had counted on them making another weak bargain like Thymine had. But it was different this time.

The Sapiens returning to the centre of Adenine had filled their bottles with boiled water at stations outside people's homes. Nearly every pathway had an older woman sitting outside on a stool, keeping pots bubbling while their grandchildren or young neighbours carried buckets back and forth to the streams. These older women, who'd thought they had seen it all, shouted words of encouragement to those returning to Adenine's centre, along with a swift glare at any dawdling child. They had lived all their lives in the small sphere of their pathways, and when it came to organising them into action, there was no one better.

For the first time, Elise believed that this Rising would succeed. Now the residents were freed of the belief that they needed the Potiors to provide their basic provisions, they had begun to organise amongst themselves a steady stream of food and water with which to furnish the people down in Adenine. They did not need a single hero. They had shown that they were perfectly capable of saving themselves.

Elise's smile faded as she thought of the other group whom she also considered her people. The ones she had spent the last three years checking on but had not been able to help.

'Max,' she said, halting abruptly. 'Would you go and check on the people in the containment centre? There's no one there to protect them.'

Max stared at her. 'Won't you need me to help with Samuel?'

Elise shook her head. 'They need our help too.'

'How will you get inside the containment centre?' Kit signed.

Max gave him a half-smile. 'I'll start with charming the guards outside, and if that doesn't work, I'll order them to let me in.' He shrugged. 'One thing I learnt as a Potior is that most of the mystical element of power is simply a lesson in self-belief. Act as if you should be in charge, and you will be.'

Elise gave him a quick hug and turned to watch his retreating figure. She hoped that she had made the right decision.

'It's just the two of us then,' she signed to Kit.

He scrunched his eyes at her. 'Let us go and save Samuel.'

CHAPTER 33

Genevieve

The dramatic entrance Genevieve had planned – of smashing the domed glass roof with the ornament she had picked up earlier and jumping down into their midst – seemed a little moot now that everyone in the room below was staring up at her. She'd had visions of landing in front of the Premier and finally exacting her revenge by ending his life.

All that had changed once she'd realised he had Samuel. There were too many variables. She couldn't attack the Premier and protect her son. She had to choose between the two and would pick Samuel every time.

Instead, she shuffled backwards from the dome to the roof's edge and dropped down into the courtyard below as gracefully as she could muster. Four members of the Protection Department waited for her, one of them having already opened the glass hatch for her. Without a word, they stripped her of the two knives that hung from her belt and escorted her into the Premier's quarters.

Familiar steel shutters snapped down inside Genevieve's mind. Samuel's life depended on her retaining control; now was not the time for an emotional response. She was vastly outnumbered and would have to rely solely on her best and only resource in a time like this – her mind.

The Protection officers who had escorted her inside joined their colleagues lined up against the walls.

'Let him go, and you can take me instead,' she said with complete authority when she was halfway across the midnight-blue room that contained the Premier's throne. There was no other furniture as everyone who approached the Premier for an audience was expected to stand. 'If it is a hostage you want, then I am more valuable.'

'That is where you are wrong,' the Premier said from his seat, his bright green eyes entirely focused on her. 'For it is you who are best placed to help me in my current predicament.'

Without another word, the Premier stood and began to pace. He wore military clothing like the Protection Department. A borrowed uniform to lessen the chance of him being singled out. Genevieve eyed him. *That is his first mistake,* she thought. Everyone knew him by sight; he had made sure of that. If he wanted to blend in as just another Potior, he would have to change more than simply his clothing.

A Potior with scarlet-coloured hair that hung down her back approached the Premier and spoke quietly to him. Genevieve recognised her as the Director of Communications.

'Sir, we have to leave now. It is not safe. They have breached the walls of your residence. We should go to the tunnels.'

'Quiet!' the Premier snapped. 'I have to deal with this first.'

The Potior dipped her head and retreated to the corner of the room. As if on cue, a distant explosion reached their ears, and the red-haired Potior glanced nervously at the set of doors.

Genevieve stared at Samuel. He was curled on his side close to the Premier's throne, tape over his mouth. He had begun to strain against the cuffs around his ankles and wrists. At least he was conscious now.

The Premier followed her gaze.

'He is an insurance policy,' the Premier said. 'And now you will have to capitulate.'

'What do you want?' Genevieve said, trying to ignore the Protection officers who were also staring directly at her.

'It seems that my advisers have underestimated the Sapiens.' The Premier threw a look around him that managed to capture everyone in the room. 'Half my Potior brothers and sisters in Adenine have disappeared. Abandoned me for the coastlines at the first sniff of trouble. A few have managed to get themselves blown up. The others are in the process of returning Adenine to how we found it. And the Protection Department ... well, let us just say this hasn't been their finest hour.'

Genevieve nodded and tried to look as if this were the most normal of conversations to be having.

'The sheer number of Sapiens always had the potential to overrun you,' she said carefully. 'What caused this uprising?'

'It is a response to the screen release we sent. They seem to disagree with our proposition of mandatory enhancements to half of their progeny.' The Premier curled his lip. 'A project I believe you once worked on.'

Genevieve nodded in response. She hoped that they had included footage of where the new 'species' of human had been raised. Genevieve had flattered Constalian and told her the Sapiens would want to see the serenity of the place, but Genevieve had known they would only see the steel walls. It seemed she had been right. She did not mention this to the Premier, though, as it would only be point scoring when her son's life was at stake.

'The initial uprising would have been containable,' the Premier continued. 'The Sapiens should have begun to panic about their lack of treated water and accepted a treaty. But then your son and his friends sent out a further screen release with classified information never meant for the masses.'

The Premier glared at Samuel's curled form. 'We were alerted to the box's location and a unit was dispatched to retrieve it. Your son resisted our attempts, so he was arrested. At the time, they did not know his connection with you. When he was later scanned, I was notified of his identity, and it brought you to the forefront of my mind. I began to think of how you could help me.'

'What do you want me to do?' Genevieve asked.

'I am going to leave Adenine shortly and go to Thymine. And I want you to come with me. Help me contain any uprising in Thymine. They were turned before. They can be turned again. Without the manufacturing base, the other bases will soon have to bend to me once again. There was a reason we made Thymine separate from the others.'

Genevieve nodded. It was what she would do if she were the Premier.

'You seem to understand them better than most,' the Premier continued, 'having lived on the outside of our conventions for so long. All the rest of them ...' his gaze swept around the room, 'they do not understand how they think. Become one of my advisers, and I will let your son go.'

'And if I don't?'

The Premier shrugged. 'Then you will both die.'

Muffled shouts came from Samuel's taped mouth.

The Premier glanced down at him. 'What's that, Samuel? You don't want your mother to die?' He crouched down next to Samuel. 'What if I told you something about your mother that you do not know? I think it might alter your opinion on the matter.'

The Premier glanced up at Genevieve, and she saw he was enjoying himself.

'Let us ensure you do not come running after your mother and try to rescue her.' Samuel stilled and the Premier smiled. 'Now, did you know that Genevieve made an agreement with me back when she was arrested in Adenine? At my urging, she promised to go to Uracil, assume her leadership in my name, take the survivors to a destination pre-determined by the Potiors and turn your attention inwards again instead of towards us.'

Genevieve kept her face still, but inside her newly united pieces began to sever. To have her son know her greatest shame ...

'I made a bargain with you before,' Genevieve said, 'and I thought at the time it was the right thing to do.' Even though she spoke directly to the Premier, her words were for Samuel. 'I was wrong. I didn't know those people were starving on that island, but I still hold myself partially responsible. Not a day goes by when I don't think of them and what else I could have done.'

Samuel blinked rapidly, clearly processing what had been said, before thrashing against his restraints, trying to release himself. Genevieve took a step towards him but stopped midway. She had to let him go if she wanted him to survive.

The Premier stood up and smiled to himself. 'Like a fish in a net, yet still he struggles.'

'You didn't have to do that,' Genevieve said quietly.

'And yet, I still did.'

Another distant explosion sounded.

The red-haired Potior approached the Premier and whispered, 'Sir, I really must insist—'

'I don't know why you are whispering, Purisian. One of her genetic enhancements has given her remarkable hearing.' Purisian frowned, and the Premier seemed to soften towards her. 'But, yes, you are right. It is time for us to leave. So, Genevieve, have you made up your mind? Will you and your son live to see another day, or will this be your last?'

'Yes,' Genevieve said. 'I will go with you and help you take back control of Thymine. But you have to let Samuel go.'

The Premier smiled. 'Excellent. But know this, I am one who likes insurance policies. If you turn on me in the future, I will send my spies after Samuel and ensure he is killed. If you step out of line, we finish what we started here today.'

Genevieve nodded. It would seem she had made another bad bargain with the Premier.

Genevieve silently watched as the Protection officer kicked aside the intricately patterned rug spread across the Premier's chamber. Underneath was a trapdoor with a looped iron handle. He tugged at it and the panel lifted, revealing only darkness below. Everyone shuffled into a line before being swallowed into the shadowed hole. Genevieve threw one last glance towards her son, still tied up and alone in the room. Her heart ached for him; she saw him as a newborn baby with ropes tied around him. She shuddered. Someone would stumble across him and free him. They had to, or all of this would be for nothing.

Down she went on the rickety ladder, another's boots only inches from her head. She was doing this for Samuel, her last living child. The passageway was narrow, but as they walked farther along, its compacted earth walls began to broaden. Several of their party had torches, and she could pick out the Premier ahead, taller than most. Forwards she pushed, slowly catching up with him, not enough to draw attention to herself.

A muffled explosion from above shook the passageway's walls; they all felt its nearness through the vibrations it sent through the ground. Earth crumbled away from the ceiling, onto their hair and into their eyes. Without stopping, they all quickened their pace, terrified that another explosion would cause the passageway to cave in.

Eyes straight ahead, Genevieve palmed the hidden blade she always kept in the sleeve of her jacket and concealed it within her hand. It was small, only a few inches long, but as sharp as a razor blade. She had one shot at this before being killed. All their attention was focused upwards, fearful of another explosion that would bury them alive. She might not get another opportunity like this for days, weeks even.

The measure of a man is what he does with power.

The quote from a Pre-Pandemic philosopher Genevieve had admired when she lived in Uracil circled her mind. She knew that if history ever had a chance to be objectively written, the Potiors would not fare well in any reasonable assessment. That was what she had to do: provide history with an opening.

A small thought entered Genevieve's mind. What did this blade in her hand say about her own use of power? Whom was she doing this for? Was it her shattered reputation or all those who had suffered and died at his hands? Or was it to protect future generations? She did not know. All she could do was hope it was for the right reason, if there was one.

Was she ready to die? No, of course not. She felt no older than she had when she was twenty-five. It was as if time had played a cruel trick and encased her in the body of a woman of middling years. But this was no longer about her survival. There were far more important things at stake.

As they hurried through the underground passages, Genevieve stared at the Premier's back, analysing every movement. She was directly behind him now, within touching distance. Everyone else was fixated on what was above them, eyes scanning the crumbling earth for signs of its collapse. Her hands began to feel clammy, and she worried the knife would slip. Anticipation of the act was often worse than the thing itself. Water dripped from the earth above, and all she could hear was the sound of twenty sets of feet echoing around her. They would be out of the tunnel soon; they must be nearing the recycling centre.

It had to be now.

Genevieve sprang into the air towards the Premier, the knife turning in her hand simultaneously. With all her weight, she pushed the blade deep into his back, hoping to have pierced his heart. He staggered forwards under her weight, and she used that extra second to twist the knife, once, twice.

The noise of twenty officers leaping into action exploded around her. Her body slammed into the ground, and with her last glance upwards, Genevieve saw her daughter, bathed in golden light, waiting for her. It was time to return home.

CHAPTER 34

Elise

Elise pulled a torch from her backpack and began jogging through the tunnel, her light trained on the ground, so she did not trip. Kit did the same, his beam straying in front of her feet.

Please still be alive, Samuel. Please still be alive ...

The thought circled her mind in time with her quickening steps.

Midway, she tentatively stopped. The light had skimmed over a form on the ground. A body. She held her arm up to Kit so he would wait as she carefully walked towards the sprawled figure. It was a Potior lying on his front. Kit took a step forwards and trained his beam on the figure while Elise knelt and brushed the black hair aside so she could feel their neck for a pulse. Nothing. She turned the Potior's head to the side, skin pale and eyes devoid of life. The Premier was dead.

She felt no remorse. A life had been lost but countless others had already been snuffed out or left to a lingering demise. It was better this way. Perhaps he should have been tried, incarcerated for the rest of his life – however long that might have lasted – but it was done now. Others deserved her pity, but not him. She stood up and didn't think of him again.

There was another figure farther up, curled around on itself protectively, long blonde hair strewn out as if still in flight. Elise walked over to it and bent down.

Please don't let it be ...

It was. Genevieve. Elise closed the woman's eyes and said a prayer to the stars for her.

Elise and Kit froze at a noise up ahead. Elise crouched down, her thighs already aching, and her thoughts darted back to when she had hidden behind the reeds in the forest – it felt like a lifetime ago.

This time darkness was on her side. Silently she straightened and backed up against the wall, both of them clicking off their torches. Someone was running towards them, their feet pounding against the ground, their torchlight a mere pinprick coming around the bend. Elise remained pressed up against the wall. Only one person was approaching, but a Potior could easily kill them if they faced them head-on. Too many lives had already been lost that way.

Each of Elise's muscles tensed as she prepared to spring into action and she peered into the distance, trying to pick out anything that would let her know who she was dealing with. The figure skidded to a stop only a few feet away. A flash of torchlight crossed his face.

'Samuel?' Elise asked.

His head snapped up. 'Elise!'

He was by her side in a second.

'Are you okay? Are you hurt? The others?' Samuel gabbled.

Elise turned and pulled him close to her and breathed him in. He was safe.

Kit clicked on his torchlight and signed, 'We are all well, apart from one.'

Samuel froze. 'Who?'

'I'm so sorry,' Elise said, pulling him gently to the figure curled up on the ground. 'It's your mum. I think she died killing the Premier; his body is over there.'

Samuel bent down and touched the blonde hair. He gently pulled the face around, all the confirmation he needed. He laid his hand on her cheek.

'She did it for the people who died on that island,' he said quietly.

When Elise gently pressed him, he wouldn't say any more. Instead, he took off his light jacket and laid it over Genevieve's body, some warmth that she no longer required.

'I'll come back for her,' he said, straightening. 'And give her the proper burial she deserves.'

'We could try and carry her out together,' Kit signed.

Samuel faltered for a moment.

He took Elise's hand, his grip firm. 'No. We have to go. The guards who untied me said that the Potiors are blowing up Adenine on their way out. We have to find the others.'

They emerged into an altered world. The smoke was thick and impenetrable in places. Buildings were alight, the flames providing the only colour in a blackened world where ash rained down from the sky. In a matter of hours, the centre of Adenine had been destroyed.

'Where are the others?' Samuel asked, his eyes watering from the fumes.

'I don't know,' Elise responded. 'Maybe the hospital? Let's try there. If it's even still standing.'

Samuel led the way, trying to navigate the ruined city, picking his way around the rubble that blocked their path. A journey that would normally take ten minutes took nearly an hour.

'*Elise*!' a voice rang out from the end of the lane.

She peered into the distance, unable to see whom it belonged to.

They picked up their pace, coughing at the dense smoke. Elise tried to ignore the bodies lying next to the buildings and kept her gaze straight ahead.

'*Elise!*'

She looked up; in a high window of the hospital were Luca and Georgina's faces. Her friends were safe.

The three of them waited at the bottom of the building, gazes darting up and down the pathway for signs of more disturbances until Georgina's red hair bobbed out of the doorway, sprinting towards her with Luca close behind.

'You made it!' Georgina exclaimed, throwing herself into Elise's arms. 'I thought ...'

'We're all fine. Max is back at the containment centre. And the Premier's dead!' Elise halted as she stared at Luca and Samuel embracing. 'Genevieve is as well.'

'I'm sorry,' Georgina said, reaching for Samuel. 'Rumours are swirling that the Potiors have left Adenine. Is it true?'

'Yes, I think so,' Elise said, hardly believing what she was saying.

It was over.

Luca turned to Elise and pulled her into a giant bear hug. 'We did it. We bloody well did it. What do we do now?'

Elise shrugged. 'Help everyone defend Adenine and then send messages to the other bases to show them what is possible? I don't know!' She grinned at him. 'It's not as if I'm an expert in this, is it?'

Luca spun Elise around in a circle and did a little dance of his own. 'We did it!'

Dizzy, she watched him celebrate in the best way he knew how. She felt Samuel by her side and allowed herself to lean into him. She stared around at her friends, the four she had left Thymine with all those years ago.

Luca's voice interrupted her thoughts. 'What's *she* doing here?' He glanced down the alleyway. 'She's got a bloody cheek thinking it's safe for her to go walking around here.'

Before Elise could stop him, Luca stormed off down the pathway.

Elise spun around after her friend.

'Luca! No!' Elise screamed, her lungs bursting as the adrenaline surged through her. 'She's got a *gun*!'

Everything went into slow motion. Luca flinched as he saw Purisian raise her arm, a blank look in her eyes. Samuel let go of Elise and flipped around to run after Luca.

In a split second, Elise had launched two throwing knives at Purisian. No hesitation this time. Their silver blades spun through the air before they both buried themselves in the Potior's chest. Purisian stared down at them, confusion crossing her features.

Luca dropped to the ground in shock as Samuel kicked the gun from Purisian's hand.

Elise was sprinting towards Luca, with Georgina and Kit close behind.

'I thought ...' Luca mumbled as he stared up at her face. 'I thought that was it. That my time was done.'

Elise crouched down beside him and took his hand.

'It'll take more than a rampaging Potior to finish you off,' Georgina said, her smile not quite reaching her eyes.

None of them spoke as the alternative scenes played out in their minds. They'd been so close to losing him.

Georgina's hand was on Elise's shoulder, and she took comfort from it.

'Is she dead?' Elise asked Samuel when he walked back to them.

'Yes,' was Samuel's quiet response. 'Your knives met their mark.'

The living stood in a loose line to watch those they had loved – those they still loved – finally meet the stars. It had been three days since the Potiors had left Adenine and the fires in the crematorium had remained lit every hour since.

On the edge of Adenine, standing on the hill closest to the crematorium, Elise looked down as black smoke pumped out of a distant flue. Raynor and Genevieve had been cremated that day, and Elise and her friends had held an informal service for them. Later she would collect their ashes and travel back to Uracil to deliver them home. She had witnessed so much death and destruction in the past few years that the smallest thought could send her mind spinning away from her, bringing the past back with it and overwhelming all her senses. She knew it would be years until she would heal and find some semblance of peace again.

The sun shone high in the sky, oblivious to the human destruction below. The natural world carried on. The planet turned, the tides still rose and fell, day followed night, and the summer showers came and went. She thought of everyone who had roamed this planet, their fleeting time no more than a single leaf on one of the many trees that had pushed their way through the soil.

'Let's go down and collect Raynor's ashes,' Georgina said. 'I need to get back to Uracil, back to Tilla and the children.'

Elise nodded. 'We should set off before dark. I need to know that Nathan is safe.'

Georgina took Elise's hand and squeezed it. 'He will be. Uracil is safe now. Any remaining Potiors will have turned their attention elsewhere.'

'I need to get back to Septa too,' Luca added.

He had been unusually reserved these past few days. There was a change in him that Elise recognised. She knew what it felt like to come so close to death that you were split in two – the part that continued, and the one left behind.

'Have we heard from the other bases?' Kit signed.

Max nodded. 'We've received messages from Thymine, Cytosine and Guanine. All three have been overthrown. I'm leaving for Guanine tonight as they are having the most trouble. Some of the Medius and Potiors have barricaded themselves inside the university.' He glanced over at Elise. 'You promise when you get back to Uracil, you'll tell Maya to send more people?'

They had already been over this several times, but Elise confirmed it as if it were the first time he had asked. None of them had slept properly in days, waking themselves up from fitful dreams, crying out in the night. How did you suffer such losses, see such things and then expect them not to haunt you? It was not possible. The toll had been greater than any of them could have imagined. They were starting a new life with a scarred population. It would take years until the devastation they had all suffered simmered into something bearable.

'Are you sure you don't want me to come with you to Uracil?' Samuel asked Elise. 'Is this one of those times when you say "no" and really mean "yes"?'

Elise smiled up at him, and they stared at each other for just a moment too long. The colour reached her cheeks, and she looked away. Kit watched them, scrunching his eyes.

'No, I really did mean it when I said we'd be fine travelling to Uracil by ourselves,' Elise finally answered. 'And I know you're itching to help your dad and Twenty-Two at the museum.'

Samuel gave a broad grin. 'Kit is going to help me too. Keeping the museums going while we sort through the displays will take all our time. And there are the other bases to think about. I will need to travel to them as soon as possible. Tomorrow maybe ...' He squeezed her hand. 'Thank you.'

Elise frowned. 'For what?'

It was Samuel's turn to look away, but he held her gaze. 'Oh, I don't know. For everything, really. For showing me how to be brave. For letting me have my own life as we also build one together.' He pushed back his hair. 'For just being—'

Elise stood up on her tiptoes and kissed him lightly to hush his words and momentarily silence the world around them.

EPILOGUE

Five years later

Elise

Elise turned over and snuggled farther down into the soft mattress.

Her dream tugged her gently back, but she resisted. The day held more enticing promises. Her eyes fluttered open, and she ran her hand across Samuel's broad shoulder. Leaning forwards, she kissed it lightly, as she did every morning. He rolled over onto his back and pulled the covers across his smooth stomach as he succumbed to sleep again. She studied his features in the early dawn. He looked at peace.

Slipping out of their shared bed, Elise stretched her arms above her head. She had woken early, but the dawn light was already streaming through the windows of their home. It was one of those summer days when the early-morning warmth always drew her outside. She quietly slipped into some shorts and a T-shirt before padding into the kitchen to make coffee. Pulling down the battered tin, she thought of her mum and dad and how they could only afford to use it on the most special occasions. A lot had changed since then. Things were not perfect, but they were infinitely better.

She blinked at the bright light as she emerged outside, carrying the cup of black coffee in her hands. She paused in the sunlight, just for a moment, before sitting at her favourite spot on the wooden bench that ran its way around the porch. Adenine was still, hardly stirring, and she stretched out her bare legs in front of her. Scars dotted their surface from the years of travelling and fighting to survive. She did not mind them, cherished them even – they had led her here.

Her gaze ran over Adenine. Years ago, she had chosen their home at the edge of the base, simple and unadorned. She did not want to live in the centre like Georgina and Tilla, who craved the excitement and bustle. Instead, she wanted to be close to the forest so she could slip out into the wilderness whenever the inclination took her. She smiled to herself – she had started life in the Outer Circle in Thymine and now lived in the Outer Circle in Adenine, although it now went by another name.

As she sipped her coffee, she glanced at her wrist. A new tattoo covered the old one. No mention of her name, age or supposed species. Instead, an elaborate design of the compass points covered the inside of her wrist, reminding her that the world was larger than a pathway, a base or even a Zone.

She glanced over at the doorway as she heard the familiar sounds of Samuel clattering around the kitchen and pouring himself a coffee. He came and sat next to her on their bench and put his arm around her shoulder.

'Is he not back yet?' Samuel asked, after he had taken his first sip.

'No, but he will be shortly,' Elise responded. 'What are your plans for the day?'

'Well, I thought as you are about to head off to Uracil for a few weeks, I would spend the day with you. I've asked a few people to eat with us tonight.' He kissed her brow. 'Quite a few, actually. And then I shall throw myself into my work at the museum, probably not get enough sleep and annoy my father until he sends me off to Guanine.'

Elise smiled to herself. Samuel was still absorbed in his work at the museum, and it was one of the things she loved most about him.

'Who will go with you this time?' she asked, after she had re-filled both of their coffee cups.

'Probably Kit as Twenty-Two is spending less time at the museum now.'

Elise raised an eyebrow. 'I didn't know that. She hasn't said anything about it to me.'

Samuel pulled Elise onto his knee, and she enjoyed the warmth of his touch. 'She wants to set up a school, or nursery really, for the newest Neanderthals.'

Elise thought about this. Around fifty had been born in the past three years or so.

'Will it just be for Neanderthals?' she asked.

'No, I don't think so. She and Kit haven't decided yet, but I think they will have Sapiens in the classes as well. It's their decision, though. Only they can make it.'

Elise's attention was caught by a figure striding towards them along the end of their pathway. Hopping off Samuel's knee, she stood up to get a better look. Satisfied it was the person she had been waiting for, she placed her mug on the veranda's wooden boards and began to jog down the pathway.

'Elise!' Nathan signed when they met in the middle. 'I can't believe it's been nearly six months!'

Elise pulled her big little brother into her arms. At eighteen, he towered over her, just like their dad had. She pulled away to get a better look at him. He'd broadened out again.

'Your room's all ready for you,' Elise signed. 'I didn't know if you wanted to sleep now before we set off tomorrow?'

Nathan gave her his widest grin. 'No, I slept last night with the others, a few miles outside of Adenine. Made the rest of the journey as the sun was rising.'

'How was your time across the sea?'

'Good ... really good,' Nathan signed. 'It's not until you see a bit of the world that you realise how tiny our little island really is!'

'And you're sure you want to set off for Uracil tomorrow?'

Nathan looped his arm across her shoulder as they walked back to the house they both shared with Samuel.

'Of course,' he signed with one hand. 'I haven't been back there for a few years, not with all the times they've sent me abroad.'

Nathan grinned. Elise knew he loved his new job as one of the trainee ambassadors to the other Zones. A small group of delegates travelled around the world making contacts, forging alliances and trade networks. It suited him as he was someone that everyone warmed to. He was also clever about it, did his research and put in the time to learn about the local customs and cultures. He had been the right choice.

As they walked back to their home, Elise thought of the limited opportunities he would have had if their world hadn't changed. If he'd been lucky, he might have worked with her in the museum as a Companion. But to what end? If he had been Bay's Companion, he would have been put on display, just as Elise would have been with Kit. A slightly larger cage.

Before long, Nathan was sitting at the kitchen table, tucking into a large plate of eggs and ham fresh from the market the previous day. Elise watched him as he ate and decided she would need to buy twice as much next time. His appetite hadn't lessened in the past few years and showed no signs of abating.

'How's your work been?' Nathan signed to Elise when he took a short break from his plate.

Elise smiled and leant back. 'It's going well. The aurochs were released in the northern regions, and their numbers seem stable. As are the lynx; they are thriving in the forests. We've been monitoring them for a while, and we think it's time for the elks to be released next month. I'll be gone for a while once we return from Uracil.'

Samuel glanced over and smiled. It was the perfect pairing in many respects. He, alongside his father and Kit, looked after the remaining animals inside the museums. They were the ones that couldn't be released onto their island as they weren't native to it and would upset the delicate balance of the natural ecosystems. One of their first tasks had been to halt all the Potiors' experiments in splicing animal DNA. The blinking eye and long-legged creature had been moved into the main museum of Cytosine to live out their days in adjacent pods so they could still see each other. The first and last of their kind.

To complement Samuel and Kit's efforts, Elise and her team had set about reintroducing whichever species they could to their small island to repopulate it naturally. When she'd been eighteen, she had accepted the job at the museum in the hope that one day she could be a keeper there. But she had found that this newly created role suited her better as it allowed her to wander the expanse of Zone 3. She was not meant for a museum; her world lay outside, in the moors, lakes, forests and grassy plains.

In the early days, she had been offered alternative work. Something akin to a people's army had sprung up, and she had been told she would be perfect for a leadership role. But she'd wanted no part in it. She had fought and spied for Uracil because she couldn't have lived with herself if she hadn't. Things had changed now, and she had seen enough death in the first years of her twenties to settle the matter.

She had then been offered roles to help reorganise their society, and again she'd turned them down. She had no interest in politics or bureaucratic affairs. Michael had told her this aversion would make her the perfect candidate, but she'd declined his urgings anyway. She had not the stomach for it. She craved something else. When peace had finally settled in the region, the army of civilians had been disbanded, much to Elise's secret approval.

She returned Samuel's smile across the table and took his hand, grateful for his understanding that she could not remain in one place for too long. She had learnt that when she had something at home that was precious to her, she did not feel the need to wander as far. Samuel tethered her to this place, and she always returned to his side.

'Right,' Samuel signed, standing up and clearing their plates. 'I must get to the market before all the fresh fish is gone. I have planned quite the feast for us tonight to celebrate your return.'

Nathan grinned at him. 'I'm always grateful when it's you doing the cooking.'

Elise kicked him under the table.

Nathan shrugged, but there was a glint in his eye. 'What? You know us Thantons were never known for our culinary skills!'

'Just as long as you're including yourself in that.'

'Of course!'

Elise didn't mind Nathan's teasing one bit. She was just grateful to have her brother back for what little time he could spare.

By 7 p.m. the house was crammed with guests, and they decided to move to the veranda and sprawl around the edges of the house and onto the grass below. Elise had laced fairy lights and lanterns outside their home, and their neighbours had been drawn to the prospect of a semi-impromptu party. Samuel had loaded the table with salads, breads and desserts. In pride of place was the plate of bream he had spent the afternoon gently baking over a log fire outdoors.

'Elise!' Georgina shouted as she neared the steps.

Elise stood and ran over to help her friend, who was laden with the plates of food she had brought from her home in the centre of Adenine. Georgina's bright red hair was usually halfway down her back, but tonight she had piled it high up in a coil at the top of her head to accentuate the elegant neckline of her dress. Her scar was still there; she refused all offers of Dermadew to fade its presence.

'It's always the same, isn't it?' Georgina said, trying to balance the plates. 'The younger ones will help carry it up here, and then as soon as we arrive, they tear off to spend time with their friends, leaving you with eight plates and only two hands.'

Elise glanced around and noticed the retreating figures of Bay and Twenty-Seven disappearing around the back of the house, heading for where they had spotted Nathan. Some of their other friends were crowding around him already, wanting to hear the tales of the other Zones.

Elise smiled to herself. Bay was now nine, and Twenty-Seven was fourteen. He had chosen not to change his name, just like Twenty-Two, with whom he spent most of his free time.

'Is Tilla not coming?' Elise asked, taking some of the plates from her friend.

'She's working late but will be along later. They have a new exhibition opening tomorrow, so she's probably standing in front of a white wall and nudging canvases slightly upwards by only a few millimetres.' Georgina shrugged. 'It makes her happy.'

The people sitting on the steps leading up to the veranda shuffled to the sides so the two women could pick their way into the house. Elise heard a slight lull in the conversation as they put the plates out on the table. She could guess who had arrived. Wiping her hands on a tea towel, she hurried outside.

'Max!' she exclaimed. 'You made it! I didn't know if you would get back from Thymine in time!'

The cluster of people on the steps relaxed at her greeting and returned to their conversations.

Max pulled her in for a hug, and she felt her feet lift from the ground. She looked over his shoulder to the three people behind him.

'Who have you brought with you?' she asked, smiling at the three statuesque people standing there, their perfect skin indicating they would once have been referred to as 'Potiors'.

'This is Fen, Grace and Lyle,' Max said, pointing them out in turn.

Elise gave each one a small wave and introduced herself before ushering them inside to get some food. It had become fashionable amongst those who had cast off the title of 'Potior' and their four-syllable names to choose a one- or two-syllable name for themselves. Not many had stayed, around a quarter, and they were primarily the younger Potiors with less to lose. The oldest had mostly left for the other Zones or been tried for their war crimes. Adenine, in particular, had suffered at their hands. They were in their own containment centre now, but one where they had access to sunlight, books, healthcare and, for a few, the chance of release. A vast improvement compared to what others had suffered through before.

Samuel came over to the table and leisurely traced his hand down Elise's back as she stood talking to the newcomers.

'Grace Summers, if I'm not mistaken!' Samuel exclaimed, recognising one of them. 'You authored that study on the extinction of wolves from Zone 3 and whether they should be reintroduced. It was quite brilliant!'

Grace blushed at the attention and dipped her head. 'Co-authored. My colleagues Alice Gunnel and Tiro Guan wrote it with me. They'll be pleased to hear you've read it.'

'I've read it too,' Elise said. 'Samuel is right. The argument you put forward was compelling. I was the one who passed it to Samuel; it was so well researched. Because of your paper, we are seriously considering their reintroduction.'

Grace smiled down at her, and Elise remembered what it was like to be momentarily overwhelmed by someone's beauty. The remaining Potiors had not had the easiest of times. People were naturally wary of them, and outside of their workplaces, they tended to socialise together, compounding the unease others felt about them. Elise knew it would be another generation or two before the tensions abated.

She spotted a man climbing the veranda stairs outside who was greeted by every single person he passed. He was somewhat of a celebrity. He had been known as 'Ben' inside the museum, but once he had escaped the Premier's residence along with his brothers and sisters, he'd promptly taken another name that he had chosen for himself. He stopped to warmly greet everyone as he climbed the steps. Given some freedom and time to heal, he had taken on a leadership role in Adenine. By all accounts he excelled at it.

Excusing herself, Elise made her way to the side of the house. The late-summer sun was too much for her, and she wanted a moment in the shade. She sat on the bench next to three more friends and rested her head against the wooden cladding. She closed her eyes for a moment, only opening them when Kit tapped her knee.

She smiled over at him. 'Have you seen Nathan? Hasn't he grown again?'

'He is like a bear,' Kit signed, scrunching his eyes. 'A very friendly bear, but still a bear.'

'I think he will be bigger than your father,' Twenty-Two added, also scrunching her eyes.

Ezra, her ever-faithful companion, nodded his head vigorously in agreement.

Elise smiled over at her friends, who were also suffering in the heat.

'Is Ali not coming?' Elise asked Kit.

'No,' Kit signed, a blush forming from his neck upwards. 'It is early days, but we will see each other tomorrow.'

Elise grinned at her friend's recent attachment.

'I'll be back in a moment,' Kit signed, as he stood up.

'I'm going to find Georgina,' said Ezra, jumping up with him.

While he was gone, the two women caught up on the last few days' events before the conversation turned back to Nathan.

'Well, me and the bear are off to Uracil tomorrow,' Elise signed to Twenty-Two before sitting up. 'Why don't you come with me?'

Twenty-Two shook her head, her long hair swirling around her face. 'I have important work to do. I can't leave Adenine at the moment.'

'Yes,' Elise said with a smile as she accepted the cup of mead that Kit handed to her. 'Samuel told me something about you setting up a nursery or school for the Neanderthals.'

Twenty-Two took a sip of her drink before placing the cup down. She had changed over the past five years, grown into herself, no longer possessing that awkward edge that had sometimes isolated her from those around her.

'They need somewhere to learn,' Twenty-Two signed. 'There are fifty-three of them now. The oldest will be four next winter and will need more structure to his day. He cannot play forever.'

'We have to think of their future,' Kit signed with one hand. 'They need to learn as much about this world as any other children their age.'

Elise nodded, pleased that the mistakes of the past would never be repeated.

*

Three weeks later, as Elise and Nathan crested the final hill to the original site of the once-hidden base, they stopped for a moment to stare down at it.

Uracil did not have to hide itself any more.

The island had been left as it was, the craters healing with every seedling that found its home there. In the centre was the vast white monument waiting to be unveiled, too far away for them to pick out any detail.

The people of Uracil went about their business on the banks of the lake, their tree houses now built into the surrounding forests. Reflections were not needed to mask their homes. In amongst the trees were bright flashes of colour where someone had decided to paint their home the colour of the sky or sunshine yellow. Elise smiled to herself, grateful that they were still allowed to express their personalities through their homes.

Crossing the bridge that stood proudly above the water and led to the island, Elise looked down into the lake's grey depths. There were still some residents unaccounted for. No one knew whether they had fled to a more remote area or even crossed the seas to another Zone.

As they headed to the island's centre, Nathan disappeared to inspect the statue. Elise smiled when she recognised her old mentor and friend.

'Elise!' Maya said, at her approach. 'I didn't know when you would arrive. How was your journey?'

Maya seemed not to have aged a day since they first met.

'The journey was good,' Elise said. 'Samuel sends his love.'

A tap on her shoulder had her turning.

'Luca!' she exclaimed, taking in the child on his shoulders, another in a sling strapped to his front and a shy little one clutching his hand. 'You look—'

'Exhausted? Ten years older? Like week-old canteen food that has been served up?'

'I was going to be diplomatic and say, "busy",' Elise responded, trying to wave at the child still clutching Luca's hand.

'Three under five,' Luca continued. 'Complete madness, but beautiful all the same. You're going to eat with us tonight, aren't you? Nathan too?'

'Of course,' Elise responded, pleased to have been invited.

As she spoke, her gaze drifted upwards to the curve of the monument that shot up into the sky.

Maya glanced up at it. 'It's bigger than we expected, but I think it is perfect.'

'I cannot believe it has been five years,' Elise responded.

The memorial was not what Elise had expected, but then she was not a sculptor and had never had the opportunity to learn about art. She was a blank slate regarding these matters, so she trusted her emotional response rather than a finely tuned artistic eye.

On a plinth stretching up forty feet into the air stood the curved figures of men, women and children balancing on each other's shoulders until the highest one at the top held up a globe above his head.

Tentatively, Elise approached it. The names of those who had died in the bombing at Uracil and later on the island were carved into the surface of the figures. She traced her finger over the lines etched in stone, each one acknowledging a life lost. Nathan stood on the other side of the sculpture, and it was not long until he beckoned her over. There, running up the arm of a woman, were two names, so close together that it was difficult to tell where one started and the other finished:

Sofi Thanton Aiden Thanton

They slid their fingers over their parents' names, Nathan's hand almost twice the size of Elise's, but both strong and capable. Her gaze scaled the curved limbs of the figures, each balancing on another while, in turn, lifting those above. Hundreds of names, immortalised in stone, who had chosen another way to live.

She thanked the stars that they had dared to try. For where would she, and the rest who lived, be without them?

ACKNOWLEDGEMENTS

I want to thank my friends and family for supporting me in writing the final book in the Tomorrow's Ancestors series. In particular Lee, Jo, Darryl, Julie, Lindsay, Mike and Lorraine. Your feedback and enthusiasm have been invaluable, and I appreciate all your help and advice.

I'd also like to thank Bev James for supporting the series throughout. Many thanks to Sam Bradbury at Del Rey for always making the book better, and Sara Litchfield for her expert eye. Thanks also to Del Rey UK for publishing my books about Neanderthals, genetic engineering and a found family.

Thank you to all the readers who have supported the series. It has been five years since I took a chance and self-published the first book, and some readers have waited patiently for the first two to be re-released before the third and fourth could come out. I've loved writing these books and they are like family now. Thank you to everyone who has championed my books, left reviews, or dropped me a note to tell me that you enjoyed them. I hope the fourth book has finished as you wanted for Elise and her friends.